UTTER CHAOS

JEWISH LITERATURE AND CULTURE
Alvin H. Rosenfeld, *editor*

A HELEN B. SCHWARTZ BOOK

Published with the support of the Helen B. Schwartz Fund for New Scholarship in Jewish Studies of The Robert A. and Sandra B. Borns Jewish Studies Program, Indiana University

UTTER CHAOS

SAMMY GRONEMANN

TRANSLATED BY PENNY MILBOUER

Foreword by Joachim Schlör

Indiana University Press
BLOOMINGTON & INDIANAPOLIS

This book is a publication of

INDIANA UNIVERSITY PRESS
Office of Scholarly Publishing
Herman B Wells Library 350
1320 East 10th Street
Bloomington, Indiana 47405 USA

iupress.indiana.edu

The paper used in this publication meets the minimum requirements of the
American National Standard for Information Sciences—Permanence of Paper
for Printed Library Materials, ANSI Z39.48–1992.

Manufactured in the United States of America

Library of Congress Cataloging-in-Publication Data

Names: Gronemann, Samuel, 1875-1952, author. | Milbouer, Penny,
translator. | Schlör, Joachim, 1960- writer of foreword.
Title: Utter chaos / Sammy Gronemann ; Translated by
Penny Milbouer ; Foreword by Joachim Schlör.
Other titles: Tohuwobahu. English
Description: Bloomington : Indiana University Press, [2016] | Series: Jewish
literature and culture | Includes bibliographical references and index.
Identifiers: LCCN 2015034850| ISBN 9780253019608 (pbk. : alk. paper) | ISBN
9780253019578 (cloth : alk. paper) | ISBN 9780253019639 (ebook)
Subjects: LCSH: Jews—Germany—Fiction.
Classification: LCC PT2613.R6 T613 2016 | DDC 833/.912—dc23 LC
record available at http://lccn.loc.gov/2015034850

1 2 3 4 5   21 20 19 18 17 16

For Shep, who knows how to laugh.

Warnung! In diesen Blättern wird viel von Juden und jüdischen Dingen die Rede sein. Ich mache aber ausdrücklich darauf merksam, dass niemand irgend etwas daraus lernen oder etwas Neues erfahren wird, und wüsste er von Juden und Judentum so wenig, wie ein australisches Kaninchen oder ein Ordinarius für Völkerkunde oder ein Synagogenvorsteher des Westens.

(Warning! In these pages there is a lot about Jews and Jewish things. I expressly call your attention to the fact that no one will learn anything here or find anything new, even if he knew as little about Jews and Judaism as an Australian rabbit or a professor of ethnology or a leader from a synagogue in Berlin-West.)

—SAMMY GRONEMANN, *Hawdoloh und Zapfenstreich*
(Havdoloh and Military tattoo), 1924

Contents

FOREWORD

Samuel (Sammy) Gronemann was born on March 21, 1875, in the West Prussian town of Strasburg (today Brodnica, Poland) to Rabbi Selig Gronemann and his wife, Helene Breslau. Selig Gronemann (December 7, 1843–March 6, 1918) had been a student of Zacharias Frankel and Heinrich Graetz at the Breslau Theological Seminary. Selig held office in Danzig (Gdańsk) before going to Hannover, where he took the position of a *Landrabbiner* (a rabbinical official appointed by the government to oversee Jewish institutions), responsible for the smaller Jewish communities outside the city. From early on, Sammy's life was shaped by three interrelated allegiances: adherence to orthopractical Judaism, which was concerned with right belief and right behavior ("I really cannot change my diet every three thousand years"), combined with *ahavat Israel,* a love for the Jewish people; a deep interest in justice and the workings of both Jewish and general law; and a profound admiration for literature, especially the theater.

At first, Sammy Gronemann followed in his father's footsteps. He studied for a year at the Halberstadt Klaus, the only German-Jewish Talmudic school that came close to an Eastern European *yeshiva.* He even enrolled at Esriel Hildesheimer's Rabbinical Seminary, which, according to his memoirs, was located not in Berlin but "in der Gipsstrasse." Located in close proximity to the Scheunenviertel, the area of settlement of Eastern European Jewish immigrants, the street was a separate world, a part of German-Jewish orthodoxy that opposed the predominant Reform movement. This was a milieu too narrow for him. He left it, he remarked, in order not to lose it completely. He studied law at Berlin's Friedrich-Wilhelm University, graduating in 1898. During this period around the turn of the century, Berlin was home to Germany's largest Jewish community and the capital of Jewish fantasies—between complete assimilation into German culture and the dream of a Jewish national revival. It was also home to a wide variety of movements and intellectual, cultural, political, and religious opportunities.

Like many young Jews of his generation, Gronemann was searching for a direction that would help him integrate his Jewish and his German identities; he found it in Zionism. His father was among the very few German rabbis who did not want to be counted among the *Protest-Rabbiner,* that is, those who opposed Theodor Herzl's plan to hold the first congress of the Zionist movement in Munich in 1897. The congress would finally be held in Basel. Gronemann participated in his first Zionist meeting in 1900, and soon thereafter he founded the local Zionist group in Hannover. In 1901 he represented Hannover as a delegate to the Fifth Zionist Congress, and he would participate in all the following Zionist Congresses between 1911 and 1947, first as a delegate and then as the chief judge of the Zionist Congress Court and until 1933 as the president of the Zionist Court of Honor.

In 1902 Sammy married his cousin Sonja Gottesmann, who came from the Ukrainian city of Zhitomir. In his memoirs he describes a trip to the region, the very hospitable family, the peace and quiet of the surrounding forests—and his immediate need to flee this pastoral scene and return to the bustle of life that was Berlin.

During his legal clerkship both in Berlin and in different cities in the German provinces, Gronemann often witnessed the confrontation between the Jewish and the secular Prussian law systems. He realized not only that there was a need to act as a translator between these two worlds but also that the confrontations provided humorous and satirical insights for him as a writer—court debates about dietary laws or the rules of the Sabbath and of holidays. He mined his observations and experiences for such miscommunications in *Schalet: Beiträge zur Philosophie des "Wenn schon"* (Cholent: Essays on the philosophy of the "so what"), a collection of stories and anecdotes from that period published in 1927.[1]

Already thirty-nine when World War I broke out, Gronemann was drafted in 1915, wounded and hospitalized, and then sent back to the front, but this time to a special unit that provided even more material for anecdotes, stories, and the novel we have in our hands right now. The Pressestelle beim Stab Ober–Ost (Military Staff Press Office for the Supreme Commander–Eastern Front) of the German occupation army in Eastern Europe—Poland and Lithuania between Bialystok, Wilna (now Vilnius), and Kovno (now Kaunas)—consisted of a group of "former intellectuals," as they called themselves: writers such as Arnold Zweig and Herbert Eulenberg and artists such as Magnus Zeller and Hermann Struck, who all served in functions that were rather irrelevant to the overall war effort. Gronemann and Struck were responsible for the censorship of the Yiddish press (albeit after publication), and Gronemann, together with a group of others, worked on one of the most fascinating and most useless books ever written: The

Sieben Sprachen Wörterbuch (Seven languages dictionary), a lexicon that translated German military and administrative expressions into the languages of the occupied countries and their main minority groups: Polish, Russian, White Ruthenian, Lithuanian, Latvian, and Yiddish. The occupying German army was having difficulty communicating with the population. One order, to greet German military officers with respect, had been translated into the local White Ruthenian dialect as an order to greet the officers by shaking hands, with undesirable results. The need for a dictionary of useful terms was obvious. Gronemann was responsible for the Yiddish part, although he didn't really speak the language. His translations were often philologically original. *Burgfrieden* (truce), a frequent military tactic in World War I, was translated with the Hebrew phrase *shalom bayit,* which is in Jewish law the harmony of domestic relations. The supreme commander of the Eastern forces decreed that *shalom bayit* (peace in the home) was to be used in all official communications. The book was finally published shortly before the occupation and the war were over.[2]

More importantly, during his two years on the Eastern front, Gronemann and other German-Jewish soldiers discovered what they saw as the authentic world of Eastern European Judaism. They went to synagogues and restaurants, to libraries and private family homes, and they showed their non-Jewish comrades around the Jewish sections of the cities. Contrary to what most German Jews of the time thought about their Eastern European brethren, they felt there was nothing they could teach these poor but confident Jews of Vilnius; instead, Gronemann, Zweig, and Struck wanted to learn from these Ostjuden (Eastern European Jews), from their deep knowledge of religion and Talmudic learning, their strong sense of community, their inner independence.[3] For the Zionists among Gronemann and his comrades, this experience strengthened their feelings of belonging to a nation apart. Despite the fact that even if their non-Jewish German comrades-in-arms respected them during battle, they realized, as Gronemann would later put it, that they were different. The Eastern European Jews taught them that one could be proud of being different and did not need assimilation into a society that was anything but welcoming. Zweig and Struck produced their book *Das ostjüdische Antlitz* (much later translated as *The Face of East European Jewry*) in 1920, with portrait etchings by Struck and Expressionist prose by Zweig; and Gronemann wrote his war memoirs, published in 1924, under the title *Hawdoloh und Zapfenstreich: Erinnerungen an die ostjüdische Etappe 1916–1918* (Havdoloh and military tattoo: Memoirs of the Eastern Jewish campaign 1916–1918), with drawings by Magnus Zeller.[4]

The first book that Gronemann published after the war, as early as 1920, was *Tohuwabohu (Utter Chaos).*[5] The novel is based on stories of life in Eastern Europe that he collected from the Gottesmann family; his own experiences on the Eastern front; his perception of contemporary Jewish life in Berlin; and, of course, his Zionist convictions. Thankfully, his intellectual curiosity and his love of storytelling were at least as considerable as his political persuasions, and we are not required to read the book as a political novel in the narrow sense of the word. Instead, we read an *Entwicklungsroman* (a novel of an individual's development) whose two main protagonists follow paths arising from the same "Jewish Question," yet each arrives at a very different place. Yossel Schlenker, the young *yeshiva bocher* (yeshiva student), begins his evolution when he encounters the girl Chana violating the rules of the Sabbath by sitting on a bench outside the *eruv*, the Sabbath border, to read Goethe's *Faust*, the book emblematic of German high culture. A very different and yet parallel development concerns Heinz Lehnsen, the distant relative in Berlin who not only has assimilated to Germanness but also has converted to Christianity. Yossel and Chana travel westward from the fictional Russian shtetl of Borytshev to Berlin, where German-Jewish life, Westernized and acculturated, can be contrasted to the Eastern European traditional Jewish life and culture through the confused and at times uncomprehending eyes of the strangers from the East. Heinz makes a trip to Borytshev and survives an anti-Jewish pogrom there. Questions of perception and (mis)conception, which are quite modern questions, are thus at the core of the novel and form the basis for the many discussions, understandings, and misunderstandings in *Utter Chaos*. These continue to be serious and contentious questions today. They touch on personal identities, challenge concepts and convictions on all sides, evoke both a longing for the past and a belief that the future demands different opportunities. And these important and intractable questions are presented to us in a humorous, even playful way.

Nobody could do that today. When Israeli writer Yoram Kaniuk published a collection of stories in Germany that all relate in a very funny way to his long years of trying to understand postwar and post-Holocaust Germany and to find an adequate partner for a real dialogue between Germany and Israel, both the public and the professional critics were embarrassed and preferred to ignore the provocation.[6] But in 1920, shortly after World War I, it was possible to imagine such a dialogue. It was the dawn of the new democratic society that was Weimar. Many ardently hoped the fresh winds of democracy would abolish the remaining barriers and integrate the Jewish minority into German society. Despite increasingly virulent anti-Semitism, Hitler's rise to power was far distant, and his success was beyond imagination for a majority of the German-Jewish population. One way or another, Jews were an integral part of this country, this culture, so much so that the overassimilation of some and the remaining strangeness of others could even be the target of satire. Maybe not by any writer, but certainly by Sammy Gronemann, who was respected across the religious and cultural spectrum within German Jewry, whose stories everybody had read in the short-lived satirical paper *Schlemihl*, and whose background gave him a high degree of credibility.

During the 1920s, Gronemann worked as a lawyer. He was the cofounder and for many years the head of the Rechtsschutz-Kommission (Legal Protection Committee) of the Schutzverband deutscher Schriftsteller (Association for the Protection of German Authors), the representative organization of Germany's writers. He supported both the Yiddish theater group Die Wilner Truppe and the Hebrew-language theater Habima, which had been founded in Bialystok in 1912 and moved to Tel Aviv in 1924. Gronemann toured Europe as a speaker for the Zionist cause. Like many leading Zionists, he did not really consider life in Palestine as an option for himself and Sonja. In 1929 the couple made a trip to Palestine, documented by their friends Selma and Georg Kareski in a photograph album that shows they visited archaeological and monumental sites from Port Said to Baalbek, the cities of Jerusalem and Tel Aviv, and Sammy's old friend Hermann Struck, who had immigrated to Haifa in 1922. Only four years later the unimaginable did happen. Hitler became chancellor of the Reich, and anti-Semitism in the form of vicious propaganda and as violent reality forced German Jews into emigration. Sammy and Sonja Gronemann left Berlin in the spring of 1933 for Paris, where they spent two years working for different refugee aid organizations. In 1936 they finally moved to Tel Aviv.

Then tragedy struck again. On the very day they arrived in Palestine, Sonja was killed in a car accident in front of Tel Aviv's central bus station. Sammy moved in with his sister, Elfriede Bergel-Gronemann, who, like Sonja, had been very active in the Zionist women's movement and had published essays in Martin Buber's *Der Jude* (The Jew) and other journals. Like many of the German-speaking Jews, Gronemann had immigrated to Palestine without a working knowledge of modern Hebrew and without a profession that was regarded as useful. Gronemann, already sixty-one years old, resigned himself to his fate and joined with several fellow immigrants in private practice as consultants with an office on Nahalat Binyamin Street. He rediscovered his old love for the theater and started writing plays, most of which were staged, if not too successfully, by the Habima.[7] The one big success came long after his death, when the play *Der Weise und der Narr* (English version, *The King and the Cobbler*) was set to music by Sasha Argov, with songs by Nathan Alterman. Under the new title of *Shlomo ha-Melekh v'Shalmei ha-Sandlar* (King Solomon and Shalmei the cobbler), it became Israel's first musical. In the 1940s he also wrote, or, rather, dictated to his secretary, Eva Sänger, his memoirs, which were published in Hebrew in 1947 as *Zikhronot shel Yekke* (Memoirs of a *Yekke*), and only in 2002 and 2004 did they appear in their original German.[8] Sammy Gronemann died in Tel Aviv on March 6, 1952.

He has not been completely forgotten. There is a street named after him in Ramat Aviv, not far from Tel Aviv University; the English transliteration of the Hebrew name renders the name as "Gruniman." A memorial plaque has been planned for summer 2016 to be placed on the front of a new building on Tauent-zienstrasse 13 in Berlin-Charlottenburg where his law office was situated.

Until their emigration, Sammy and Sonja Gronemann lived in a house on Monbijouplatz 10, very close to the original area of Jewish settlement after 1671. This area in Berlin's Mitte district today would have been of interest to Grone-mann. In 1995, fifty-seven years after the destructions of Kristallnacht and fifty-four years after the beginning of the deportation of Berlin's remaining Jews to the death camps, the golden cupola was returned to the roof of the New Syna-gogue on the Oranienburger Strasse. The synagogue opened in 1866, and it is the building that Yossel Schlenker takes for a Christian church. Today it houses the Stiftung Neue Synagoge–Centrum Judaicum (Foundation New Synagogue–Centrum Judaicum) and is one of the two main centers of Berlin's growing Jew-ish community. Since 1991 the emigration of Jews from the former Soviet Union has completely changed the demographic composition of this community. Since about 2005, Jewish life in Berlin has also been marked by a steady stream of young and creative Israeli immigrants, quite a new and of course very different sort of utter chaos that has not yet found its author.

Joachim Schlör
Southampton, March 2015

NOTES

1. Sammy Gronemann, *Schalet: Beiträge zur Philosophie des "Wenn schon"* (Berlin: Jü-discher Verlag, 1927; new edition, with an afterword by Joachim Schlör, Leipzig: Reclam, 1998).
2. *Sieben Sprachen Wörterbuch, deutsch, polnisch, russisch, weissruthenisch, litauisch, lett-isch, jiddisch*, herausgegeben im Auftrage des Oberbefehlshabers Ost [Seven-language diction-ary: German, Polish, Russian, White Ruthenian, Lithuanian, Latvian, Yiddish, compiled by order of the supreme commander Eastern Front] (Presseabteilung des Oberbefehlshabers Ost für den Buchhandel, Verlag Otto Spamer in Leipzig, 1918).
3. Steven E. Aschheim, *Brothers and Strangers: The East European Jew in German and Ger-man Jewish Consciousness, 1800–1923* (Madison: University of Wisconsin Press, 1982).
4. Hermann Struck and Arnold Zweig, *Das ostjüdische Antlitz: Mit 50 Steinzeichnungen* (Welt Verlag, 1920); Arnold Zweig, *The Face of East European Jewry*, with drawings by Her-mann Struck, ed., trans., and with an introduction by Noah Isenberg (Berkeley: University of California Press, 2004); Sammy Gronemann, *Hawdoloh und Zapfenstreich: Erinnerungen an die ostjüdische Etappe 1916–1918. Mit Zeichnungen von Magnus Zeller* (Berlin: Jüdischer Verlag, 1924; new edition, Frankfurt am Main: Jüdischer Verlag / Athenäum, 1984). This new edition lacks an introduction and an afterword and for this reason has been heavily criticized by Scha-lom Ben-Chorin, the Munich-born journalist, poet, and theologian who had as an émigré been close to Sammy Gronemann, Max Brod, Else Lasker-Schüler, and others.
5. Sammy Gronemann, *Tohuwabohu* (Berlin: Jüdischer Verlag, 1920; new edition, with an afterword by Joachim Schlör, Leipzig: Reclam, 2000).

6. Yoram Kaniuk, *Der letzte Berliner* [The last Berliner] (Munich: List Verlag, 2002).

7. For Gronemann's theatrical work, see Jan Kühne, "'Das schönste Theater bleibt doch das Gericht': Todesstrafe und Talion im Drama Sammy Gronemanns" ["The best theater is always the courtroom": Capital punishment and the law of Talion in the dramatic works of Sammy Gronemann], *Aschkenas* 24, no. 2 (2014): 305–323.

8. Sammy Gronemann, *Erinnerungen* [Memoirs] (Berlin: Philo, 2002); *Erinnerungen an meine Jahre in Berlin* [Memoirs of my years in Berlin] (Berlin: Philo, 2004). Both versions are edited by Joachim Schlör.

TRANSLATOR'S PREFACE

I stumbled across Sammy Gronemann's novel in a brief but enthusiastic reference on the Internet. Although *Tohuwabohu* has been reprinted a few times since it first appeared in 1920, the novel remains unfamiliar to readers today. The story takes place in 1903 at the time of the Sixth Zionist Congress. I found it to be a page-turner, even though it reflects a world long gone. Nevertheless, it is certainly more than an historical artifact, and I heard in Gronemann's buoyant and sly prose an eerily current conversation about living as a Jew in the secular world.

The title of *Utter Chaos* in German is *Tohuwabohu*, which means "confusion" or "extreme disorder." The German word is taken from the Hebrew phrase in the second verse of Genesis meaning "unformed and void." The German word is well chosen as the title of a story about Jewish assimilation, Jewish identity, and anti-Semitism in a society proud of its culture and trustful of the rule of law. *Utter Chaos* captures the moment in nineteenth- and early twentieth-century German history when yet another movement arose to claim "Jewish identity": Zionism. Without explicitly mentioning the Dreyfus affair, the novel reflects the aftershocks among Jews and their response. *Utter Chaos* is a funny story written with a satirical but not cynical view of human delusions and illusions. It is a haunting story not only because the author did not shy away from the history and consequences of corrosive anti-Semitism but because we, the readers, know how history played out.

In his memoirs, Gronemann wrote with his typical wink to the reader that he was astonished that the book was considered humorous; he meant it *bitter ernst* (dead seriously).[1] A contemporary review of *Utter Chaos* praises the book for its humor and characters that aim to reflect the entire range of Jewish life but calls it a *Tendenzroman* (tendentious novel) that becomes more and more doctrinaire and stilted toward the end.[2] As a reader in the twenty-first century, I found these conversations remarkably familiar: What is my response to increasing anti-Semitism?

The discussions today are the same, only different, and perhaps they are even more intense now than they were in Sammy Gronemann's day. The question of Zionism is different now, but Sammy Gronemann's response is instructive. To form his own opinion he attended many Zionist and anti-Zionist meetings, such as the Zionist rally described in the novel, and decided, according to his memoirs, *blitzartig* (like a bolt of lightning) that it was impossible *not* to be a Zionist.[3]

In the course of preparing the manuscript, I discovered a family connection of sorts. Sammy's father, Selig Gronemann, studied at the Breslau Jewish Theological Seminary under the preeminent scholar of Jewish history, Heinrich Graetz. My great-grandfather, who was ordained there in the late 1850s and was an enthusiastic proponent of the historical study of Judaism (known as *Wissenschaft des Judentums*), must have studied under Graetz. On my shelves of books from the family library is the 1894 English edition of Graetz's monumental *History of the Jews*, which my great-grandfather's oldest daughter, my great-aunt, edited at the Jewish Publication Society in Philadelphia.

Once I read *Tohuwabohu*, I went on to discover Gronemann's essays and memoirs. His German is still fresh, conversational and witty in Berlin fashion, using irony, self-deprecation, and wordplay. To describe himself once he immigrated to Palestine he often used the slightly disparaging Israeli term for a German-speaking Jew, *Yekke* (a German Jew identifiable by the suit jacket worn even in the stifling heat of the Mediterranean country who always knew better than anyone else).

The verve of German literature, theater, and art in the first decades of the twentieth century owes much to a long roster of Germans who were Jewish, including Sammy Gronemann. He embodied the success of the German-Jewish symbiosis. But because he refused to compromise his Jewish identity, he was among the few acculturated, Westernized Jews who questioned this marriage of cultures.

A note on my word choice in the text: I use "yarmulke," not "kippah," "esrog," not "etrog," and "Sukkos," not "Sukkoth," because the story takes place in 1903, before the conventions of modern Hebrew replaced the Ashkenazi ones used in northern Europe. I use "Strasse" (street), "Herr" (Mr.), "Frau" (Mrs.), and "Fräulein" (Miss) throughout.

Penny Milbouer, translator
Houston, March 2015

NOTES

1. Gronemann, *Erinnerungen an meine Jahre in Berlin*, 275.

2. Felix Goldmann, "Einheitsfront" [United front], *Im deutschen Reich: Zeitschrift des Centralvereins deutscher Staatsbürger jüdischen Glaubens* [In the German Reich: Journal of the Central Association of German Citizens of Jewish Faith] 26, no. 11 (November 1920).

3. Hanni Mittelmann, *Sammy Gronemann: Ein Leben im Dienste des Zionismus* [Sammy Gronemann: A life in the service of Zionism] (Berlin: Heinrich & Heinrich Verlag, 2013), 14.

ACKNOWLEDGMENTS

I would like to acknowledge and thank all those who directly and indirectly helped me translate Gronemann's *Tohuwabohu* into *Utter Chaos*. With this help, I found the better word, the historically more accurate phrase, and the image to illustrate the world Gronemann was fictionalizing. Copyeditors, and editors in general, never receive enough praise for their patience and devotion to accuracy; the editors at the Indiana University Press questioned my choices, smoothed my language, and proposed alternatives to enable me to bring Sammy Gronemann's extraordinary little masterpiece to the English-language reader.

UTTER CHAOS

ONE

Goethe in Borytshev

I

Berl Weinstein had himself baptized again, and this time with great success. All in all, he probably made about eight hundred marks. His expenses this time were relatively minor. He had made a detour from Amsterdam, which had been on his itinerary to London; he had spent almost three weeks taking care of payments accruing to charity in all the Jewish quarters and only then showing up at the mission society's large meeting in Whitechapel: he had long been making a number of workers in the vineyards of the Lord happy in their hearts—he had managed to give a hot-headed young man of the cloth, handing out strong tea and very watery speeches, the triumph of his first success in conversion—presenting the image of deep emotions and pensive contemplation, he had allowed the baptismal act to flow over him in the tiny mission chapel—he had pressed the hands of his patrons and godparents, humbly but with a suggestion of inner resolve, apparently unable to put into words what he was feeling, arousing in them the happy sentiment that his future life, dedicated to heaven, would be filled with an awareness of eternal gratitude and marked by the knowledge of an unpayable debt—he had a splendid tract from the mission, generously decorated with Bible quotations, written in classical Hebrew by the Reverend Hickler, who hoped for everlasting fame as the author and for great success in the Lord's work—in short: he had made a lot of people happy, exuded an atmosphere of trust and bonhomie, and thereby had earned approximately eight hundred marks; he could congratulate himself in every way, and he decided to pledge in the temple next Sabbath a stately sum for the poor in Palestine.

Berl Weinstein always had himself baptized whenever he needed a dowry for a daughter. This time it was Chana's turn, the fourth and youngest daughter. An excellent candidate had turned up: Yossel Schlenker, the son of Moische Schlenker, the scribe, was considered an especially fine light of Talmudic scholarship—a pious, "fine" young man whose reputation stretched far beyond the borders of his synagogue throughout all of Borytshev; in spite of his somewhat clouded ancestry he could have easily found an affluent father-in-law who would have agreed to board him to allow him to study without having to worry about the cost of feeding himself, in honor of the House of Israel in general and the house of the father-in-law in particular. There was some vague talk that Kleinmann himself—the wealthy Kleinmann of the Kleinmanns in Kiev—had sent Rosenfeld, the *shadchan* (matchmaker), to Moische Schlenker—but Yossel had refused all candidates. He did want to marry, what pious Jewish young man does not want to fulfill this important commandment of the Torah?—But for him it wasn't just a question of fulfilling the commandment in general; in an especially peculiar way he put great importance on stepping under the chuppah with one particular young woman—namely, Chana, the fourth daughter of Berl Weinstein.—It was strange, but there was nothing to be done. Moische Schlenker ran around in despair—he pleaded and threatened, he prayed and he swore—but nothing helped; Yossel grew older and older, it was an embarrassment; he was already nearing the age of twenty-two and still single. Moische Schlenker finally gave in—Rosenfeld went to Weinstein—the engagement contract was signed, and Berl Weinstein took off on his journey to get ahold of the dowry.

Everything is connected in life: if Yossel Schlenker hadn't met Chana by chance back then, sitting on the last bench on the last boulevard on that Sabbath afternoon as she was deep in a book, and if he hadn't struggled to overcome his shyness for the sake of a sacred purpose, namely, to make the young lady aware that she was, possibly from negligence, breaking the holy commandment by holding a book on this bench on the Sabbath even though the Sabbath border, the *eruv,* ended a few steps in front of that bench such that up to the bench and therefore at that bench, where she was sitting, carrying anything at all was not permitted, not even a book—then Yossel most likely would never have made her acquaintance—Moische Schlenker would never have been forced to plead and curse—all for naught anyway—the letter offering the engagement would never have been written—Berl Weinstein most likely would never have had to take off on the dowry trip—and Reverend Hickler most likely would never have gained a reputation as a missionary and Hebrew author, which later earned him the offer of a position in America. One cannot calculate at all what sorts of changes might have resulted in the development of human society in general and of the Borytshev community in particular if Chana's reading matter violating the commandments on the bench beyond the Sabbath border had not thwarted the house of Schlenker joining with the house of Kleinmann—and Regional Court Director Lehnsen in Berlin would later have been spared a great deal of annoyance.

Thus it was that for some reason Yossel Schlenker felt compelled to defend the commandment under attack—maybe also out of a vague fear that a less kindly intentioned protector of the commandment might see Chana's unseemly behavior and create difficulties for her—to pull himself together to speak to her. With a slightly mocking smile, Chana calmly glanced at Yossel, who was blushing and rather confused, and she admitted that she was guilty of breaking the commandment—thanked him nicely for his attentive comments, and after a moment of silence, just as Yossel was awkwardly trying to reverse his steps, she asked what she was supposed to do now that the damage was done. She didn't know the commandments, she added innocently, he was so well versed and surely knew what had to be done in this particular situation. Should she step over the boundary with the book, or should she put the book on the bench and leave it there? Or what?

Yossel went from one cause of embarrassment to another: all the subtle arguments about the commandments of carrying on the Sabbath went through his mind. The dense casuistry from the house of study overwhelmed his ability to think and blocked a quick, decisive answer. The actual transgression lay just in *transporting* the burden—in this case, the small volume—the border here was an almost invisible wire stretched high above: reversing the transport would mean repeating the transgression—thus committing a new one. That wouldn't do. Leaving the book on the bench—that also wouldn't do. To put down a burden, no matter what size, out there, would really be a violation of the commandment—as long as one was carrying the burden without laying it down and as long as one didn't step beyond the Sabbath border, only one of which was designated as the forbidden sin to start with but not actually a transgression, assuming of course that the person who carried the burden did not go more than four steps with the burden from his seat.—So, what should be done? Chana was quietly following Yossel without interruption as he dissected the problems somewhat laboriously for her; he had never found any lecture, even one on the most difficult Talmudic question, so difficult. The fact that he had never even had a conversation with a young female nonrelative—the necessity of finding generally understood terms for technical terms customarily used in the house of study—the painful anxiety that a fellow student could surprise him in this odd scholarly discussion—everything combined to make him sweat profusely. And as he finally finished explicating the entire extent of the relevant arguments, Chana calmly asked if she then had to stay seated on the bench until the Sabbath was over, a question that showed she had understood his lecture, for nothing else seemed feasible under these conditions. When Yossel remained awkwardly silent, thinking about this case, a noisy group of people approached—the book disappeared into her pocket as she stood up, and to Yossel's horror, she called out a cheerful Sabbath greeting apparently without a single pang of conscience as she strode farther into the fields.—Yossel stared after her quite upset for a long time until her bright blouse disappeared behind a bush, and, confused, he turned to make his slow way home, sweating more than usual in his thick caftan and heavy hat.—

Actually, Yossel should have been outraged by Chana's violating the strict Sabbath commandment against work in this way—that she was apparently fully aware of performing the work of transporting a burden beyond the Sabbath border—but instead he buried himself in studying the texts for this question over the next week, and so it happened that the following Sabbath he was well armed with knowledge as he walked toward Chana, who was sitting once again on the forbidden bench with her book. But the closer he came, the more it dawned on him that he was confronted with an intentional assassination attempt on the commandment. Now she certainly knew, having had her attention drawn to the matter, that the bench was outside the Sabbath border; which of course made all the arguments he had researched during the week moot.—And now he stood in front of Chana in even greater confusion than during his first meeting, but when she was looking at him with a mocking smile, anger welled up, and he stormed off to demonstrate to her what sort of sin her flippant attitude had caused and how she was bringing calamity upon herself and all Israel.—Annoyed, she listened, looking somewhat bored—then she said something and then asked a question, and from that there developed a lively debate in which, as he later had to admit to himself, he did not come off well; for the first time in his life he suddenly had to defend things that he had always taken as self-evident, as natural laws that needed no explanations at all.—

Chana suddenly asked out of nowhere if he was familiar with the book she was reading and held it under his nose. He carefully bent his head to look—after all, he couldn't pick up the burden himself—and read *Faust* and "Reclams-Universal-Bibliothek."—He said he wasn't familiar with it, and she asked him if he wanted to borrow the book for a week. He hesitated—of course he couldn't take it in hand today, at least not outside the Sabbath border—then she laughed, grabbed his sleeve, and pulled him across the border formed by the wire, stuffed the book into his pocket, and hurried away with a gay "See you in eight days!"— and she called from a distance that he would find things that pertained to their earlier discussion.

II

Yossel "learned" Goethe's *Faust*.

What did Goethe mean to him?!—He had certainly often heard the name before, and he remembered in an anthology that he had come across that he had read a poem by Goethe that he hadn't liked at all. It was the story of a man who was riding for some crazy reason through a damp, foggy area: there wasn't any clue for this peculiar behavior. And the child seemed just as crazy as the father; the child seemed filled with phantasmagoric ideas and babbled, probably feverish, absolutely stupid nonsense.—The matter was of no further interest to him, and he had no further interest in Goethe.

Thus, it was significant that on Chana's recommendation he was willing to try Goethe again. He had carefully put the little book in his pocket, and as he hurried home, he kept gently checking with his hand to see if it was still there. The book was precious to him—he didn't quite know why—and he smoothed it carefully and fondly as he opened the book in his room. Herr von Goethe profited little from this: Yossel was incorruptible, and as he began to read he was totally and completely the critical and skeptical Talmudist. In any case, there was a hidden desire to pick the poet to pieces—to prove his acumen to Chana, using something she knew more about than the Talmudic tractate about the Sabbath border, to prove to her that he was smarter than this book scribbler whom she had carried across the border of the commandment. He already knew he would ask questions that neither Goethe nor Chana could answer, questions that would occur to neither of them. He would . . .

And with furrowed brow Yossel read the Dedication—plain verses, apparently concerned with personal matters that were of no interest to him. This Goethe fellow certainly wasn't modest. If he wants to write and publish this book, that's his affair after all. If it doesn't suit him—or if his audience doesn't suit him—he should just forget about it. But why was he saying these things at all?!—Is the book not good enough for the world—then neither is the Dedication for sure. Yossel decided that it's to make the book seem really important, merely affectation, like a singer who makes all sorts of excuses and gives all sorts of reasons when someone asks him to sing—and then sings very happily and then won't shut up. Yossel noted with concern that the last page had a large number.

"Prologue in the Theater." Another introduction!!—What's with this "Jester" who doesn't say anything funny at all? And this "Poet" speaks more scornfully of the audience than the Dedication. The "Director"—finally a practical fellow: he really just says what he wants. He wants money! And it's just fine that he has the last word.—But really: "Enough words have been exchanged.—Let me see at last—"

Another prologue!—Oh Chana, Chana!!

Yossel leaned back to reconsider the scene on the boulevard.—He burned with embarrassment at the thought that he had on the whole behaved quite awkwardly; at the end, Chana acted as if it weren't worth the effort to debate anything further with him. And by pressing this book, this *Faust,* on him it looked as if she thought he would be defeated once and for all after he read this book. With this book?—He shook his head in confusion.—But she had said, "In eight days."—So, that was good! In eight days he would show her who he was.—But first of all read the book. Everything else would take care of itself!

And once again he began to rock back and forth, a movement that seems to be inseparable from serious study such as prayer, indeed from every act of mental concentration among Jews in Eastern Europe.

And immediately the "Prologue in Heaven" grabbed his attention. This was the story of Job—the bet between the Lord and Satan over the soul of a humble man. The humble man—Job or Faust—was to be tested. But there was a huge difference between the two: Job had lived grandly and happily until then—and Faust, on the other hand: "The fool's food and drink is not of this world." So therefore Job is to be tested by trials—but Faust is to get just the opposite by being allowed to savor every earthly joy to test his steadfastness.—

This really raised a lot of questions: and Yossel became warm. Now *Faust* no longer intrigued him for Chana's sake: now he wanted to understand it—not just to show off.

Yossel "learned" *Faust*.

He "learned" him—what's called "learning"—the way one "learns" the Talmud—questioning every word, every sentence, and questioning it again—always mistrusting the meaning discovered and checking oneself—rereading each page and doing it again—groping for a new, still more hidden meaning—nowhere more wary than when a passage seems to be obvious—easy to understand means to misunderstand—always going back to passages that had seemed to be understood—catching contradictions and resolving them—Yossel "learned" *Faust*.

In this way he made slow progress, and it was possible that he wouldn't see the grand whole while poring over and meticulously puzzling out every detail—he wouldn't have been much better off than a German high school student for whom the classics were ruined by a dedicated philologist as a literature teacher. But Chana saved Yossel and Goethe from such a fate; soon Chana and Yossel were no longer reading and debating about their *Faust* only on Sabbath afternoons, but they met almost every day on the boulevard.—They were almost safer from interruptions by friends during the week than on the Sabbath, as it would not occur to any Borytshev Jew to walk out that far—almost a quarter hour's walk from town, while on the Sabbath young people would indeed now and then extend their walk that far. The two Goethe scholars sat there deep in their discussion, and it was often so late that the two had to press their heads close together in the deepening twilight to make out the small print. And whenever Chana's hair happened to brush against Yossel's cheek it didn't exactly cause him to gather his thoughts more sharply or express himself with more clarity.—He truly had to pull himself together when he was, say, ardently explaining the scene in the witch's kitchen to Chana: he had found this scene especially fascinating. Number puzzles similar to the witch's number spell were familiar to him from the Talmud and other old texts; he quickly came up with not only one explanation but just as quickly another for the uncanny witch's spells, both shrewd and convincing.

One explanation held that the ten numbers of the spell referred to the Ten Commandments—and another held that they referred to a cabalistic legend about the ten things created before the rest of the world was created.—Chana wasn't particularly interested in either of the explanations; she wasn't even particularly interested in the witch's number spell itself. She pressed on—to Gretchen's room, to the garden, to the cathedral—and she loved to discuss the meaning of the whole rather than individual words—she even managed to get Yossel to first read the whole work through in one go to the eternal feminine in the final scene before he dug too deep into each line.

That was not easy for Yossel; there was still the garden scene right after the "Witch's Kitchen" ("How do you stand on religion?"), at which he broke out in a sweat for a moment; he involuntarily, it seemed, thought of the discussion about the meaning of the Sabbath border. Wasn't that about the same thing?—Then there was the "evil spirit" and so many other obstacles to proceeding quickly. Especially the Walpurgis Night, with the golden wedding of Oberon and Titania. Who is Oberon—who is Titania? Who is Mieding?—His enthusiasm only really picked up in Part II until Helena approached with her Trojan women—and the whole classical baggage train of a second Walpurgis Night. Here he was marooned by his knowledge—and pater Marianus and pater Seraphicus provided the rest—*una Poenitentium* and the whole Catholic Olympus. Confused, he shut the book and had to admit in all modesty that was otherwise quite out of character for him that he hadn't understood the book! He hadn't understood *Faust,* even though he had read it without annotations.

He crawled to the next meeting rather discouraged; it was only weak comfort to him that Chana also didn't know much more than he did. They agreed that the difficulty was merely that they simply didn't have knowledge of many things the poet assumed the reader knew. This Herr Goethe just hadn't imagined their sort of reader; they must belong to the unknown crowd in the Dedication.—For now there was just no likelihood of plugging the gaps in their knowledge, but they bravely began anew to thoroughly study the work. And many would have been quite astonished if they could have sat in unseen on these *Faust* lessons.

Pastor Bode was at least a little surprised. Doctor Strösser, on the other hand, wasn't at all surprised; but he compensated for that by being all the angrier.

III

Pastor Bode and Doctor Strösser, the senior high school teacher, were coming up the muddy path leading from the riverbank to the boulevard. The Pastor glanced down with a melancholy sigh at his trousers, from which his wife, Marie, had so lovingly just removed every speck of dirt and which now looked so pitiful. The teacher chuckled in comfortable satisfaction that only a pair of high boots can provide and suggested, as he filled his pipe anew, "Yes, Pastor! This is different from Pasewalk! You'll have to break your habit of wearing those low shoes."

He held a burning match over the bowl of the pipe, adding as he continued to puff, "And a whole lot more!"

Pastor Bode stopped and removed his hat.

"We'll talk about all that another time!" he said, somewhat annoyed. "I know that I'm in a world here entirely new to me and have a lot to learn. But I certainly want to get a pair of high boots. That was a miserable progress through the mud.—Is there any place here we can rest a bit?"

"There's a bench," Strösser said, walking ahead. He sprawled on the bench next to some bushes.

"Yes," he said. "I've just shown you a Russian specialty. Up here a smooth road that suddenly stops and leads directly to a wasteland of mud. And that's the way it was when I landed in this spot thirty years ago.—Russia is a country of beautiful beginnings with no sequels. Everywhere! Every beginning is easy!—But why don't you sit down, Herr Pastor?"

The Pastor stood there indecisively, and, adjusting his glasses, he peered into the bushes, looking embarrassed.

"It's just that behind the bushes," he said self-consciously, lowering his voice, "there's a couple sitting on a bench, and I wouldn't like to—perhaps we should seek another place to rest."

"What are you afraid of?" Strösser laughed. "Disturbing them or being embarrassed yourself?—Human, all too human!—"

He glanced behind him with an exasperated gesture.

"Just come and sit down, Herr Pastor! I'll take the responsibility!—Those are Jews, you know!"

"That makes no difference to me," Bode said, hesitantly taking a seat. "I mean of course—in this respect."

"And it's something different in every respect," Strösser said. "You'll soon see! Be very quiet now!"

The Pastor felt uncomfortable, but he froze when he heard the name "Goethe," and then fragments of Goethe's verses chimed in his ear.—Otherwise the couple was talking in Yiddish, and the Pastor was unable to understand more than a few words.

He grabbed Strösser briskly by the arm.

"Just listen! The two of them are reading *Faust*."

Strösser puffed serenely.

"Quite right," the Pastor said excitedly. "They're reading *Faust*!—Just think! *Faust*!"

Strösser cleared his throat and spat in a mighty arc.

"It's nauseating!!" he said sternly and calmly.

Bode looked at him aghast.—

"What are you saying?"

"I'm saying that it's perverse!—Perverse people!"

"Who? Perverse? These young people are certainly not that if they are reading *Faust* almost in the dark.—Our great Goethe?"

Strösser emitted a sharp burst of laughter.

"Do you know, Herr Pastor!—You're a good deal younger than I—not an old bachelor! Surely you can still remember how it was when you were a student and sitting with some young maiden in the twilight somewhere in a garden!"

"I don't recall any such situation with 'some young maiden,'" the Pastor said emphatically.

"Fine!—So not with just anyone—but with Fräulein Maria Lodemann, now Frau Pastor Bode!—Did you also read *Faust* and discuss it?"

"Let's just leave personal examples out of the debate, my dear Doctor! I don't understand you. If you are trying to say something.—"

"Why the devil doesn't the rascal back there throw his arms around her neck to canoodle like any other European?—Sitting there and ruining their eyes by reading the wretched small print, dissecting Goethe—until they've quite cleverly squeezed out all that's beautiful, by the way.—"

"What are you saying! What are you saying!—How can you say that? From the few words you managed to pick up!—and that business with—with canoodling.—"

"Herr Pastor! I understand a bit more Yiddish than you do by now—as to the rest, by the way I am so much older than you are."—

"You're in a joking mood today!"

"Me? Not at all!—The sort of company like that back there quite spoils the lovely evening for me!—Do you think that these sorts like those people back there even conceive how beautiful this evening is—that they waste even a glance at the view over the river, at the entire vista!? They only see the world in books."—

"If that were true, you would have to admit that they did choose *Faust*.—"

"I do not admit to anything! Nothing at all! Do you know that this Jewish boy just—it seems that we've startled them! They're leaving!—You see how he gestures with his hands: now he is lecturing peripatetically and seems apparently to still be trying to persuade his Donna how immoral and dissolute the entire Gretchen story is.—He remarked earlier that if Goethe were a Jew.—Such impudence! The very thought!—If he had been a Jew, then he would have been ashamed of writing such a story!"

"What are you saying!—He should read Heine—whom I recommend anyway without hesitation!"

"Now just think!—on this splendid and lovely evening he's reading the Gretchen scene with *her*, and that's the result!—Wouldn't a German boy have succeeded if he weren't a total idiot?! He would've known how to take advantage of things properly—even if he were a student of theology himself!"

"Perhaps she's really ugly," the Pastor said meekly.

"A German boy wouldn't have sat down with her in the first place," Strösser decided.—

"Joking aside!" Bode said after a short silence. "This case interests me!—There's a lot here—for example—say, where has a Jewish young man here learned so much German he can even read Goethe at all?"

"Where?—It's just natural for these young men!—These Talmud students!— They learn nothing but their Koran! They claim it contains everything that's worth learning. They snap up everything else without effort whenever they encounter it without even paying attention!—Maybe he learned German from reading *Faust*."

"Remarkable! You know, I'm quite interested in Jewish things. These people have been scattered among the nations of the earth for a reason after all. That gives us certain responsibilities—responsibilities that, I fear, have often been underestimated."

"Oh, good heavens!" Strösser said, involuntarily shifting slightly away from Bode, staring him in the face. "Responsibilities?—Quite interested?—What are you getting at?—Please—excuse me! Keep talking!"

For a moment, Bode looked embarrassed, like a man who realizes he's said more than he intended to.

"Listen, my dear Dr. Strösser!" he said in a firm voice. "I hope you will assist me in my new pastoral sphere here with your experience and knowledge of how things are. You should then get to know me and my aims. When I left my native Pomeranian soil and my quite pleasant and familiar pastoral sphere to follow the call to come to the tiny Lutheran congregation here, it was from the certain feeling that I was following a greater divine providence. I saw and see the veritable divine hand in this opportunity offered to me.—I attended, as you may know, the seminar for the Jewish Missionary Society when it was held at the University of Berlin and—"

"Oh, good heavens!" Strösser groaned. "You are—my God! You want to here—? —Well, one certainly doesn't learn anything from someone else's experiences. Good luck with fishing for souls here!"

"Just listen a moment, Herr Doctor!" Bode said, and his face went red with anger. "The joke ends here!—I am no fisher for souls, but I don't want the Jewish Missionary Society to be considered a joke!—"

Strösser puffed away and didn't utter a word.

After a while Bode stood up and said, "I think I'll go home now."

They walked in silence beside each other for a while. Bode was the first to speak again.

"I'm truly sorry if a misunderstanding should arise between us.—I am slightly disturbed about the multitude of hostilities that we pastors are subject to when we step outside the well-worn tracks expected of us.—See, I spoke earlier of Christian responsibilities toward the Jews that people have often ignored. Whenever I just think of the pigheadedness of our anti-Semites—"

"Stop!" Strösser began to laugh. "We're even now!—Now I understand that when it comes down to it. Not a joke!"

"Are you an anti-Semite?" the Pastor asked slowly.

"Aren't you?" Strösser merrily answered.

"Anti-Semite? No—absolutely not. I do not deny a certain instinctive aversion to these people, especially in my younger years, was not unthinkable; but now I am a priest of the religion of love—only of love. And I bring this to those who need it most.—"

"There are all sorts of anti-Semites. They want to remove being Jewish from the Jew—if that were only possible!—They want to kill the Semitic itself, so to speak, in the Semites. Isn't that the real anti-Semitism?"

"Let's not get lost in splitting hairs!—I want to preach the doctrine of salvation—to all people—even to the Jews!"

"Well, you'll learn from your own experience!"

"I know I still have much to learn. And I even think that we all have a thing or two to learn from the Jews. That they cling tenaciously to their teachings and their commandments has always struck me as exemplary—their devotion and reverence always seemed to me—"

"Reverence?—Jews and reverence! A real Jew has no reverence for anything—not even for his own God!"

"Yes—the liberal Jews from Berlin or the like—"

"Oh, who was talking about such groups!" Strösser waved his arm dismissively. "No, just take the old Jews here, the pious old Jews—by the way, the word 'pious' is awkward! They aren't pious in our sense of the word.—"

"Who isn't pious?—I would think that the deep religiosity of old Jews could still be an edifying example for everyone. Just look at the little boys reading their holy books: I was once in one of their Jewish boys' schools—a cheder they called it. Naturally I couldn't understand much, and my impression reminded me of a Negro school such as I've seen on occasion at an exhibit in Berlin, but still—this holy fervor—"

"And do you know what these little Jewish boys study with such holy fervor?—It could be the commandments on marital intercourse—which they say is fixed in every detail—or—"

"Really! Boys of eight, nine!"

"See, there you have it! You apply European standards! That's all wrong! The content of the texts is completely irrelevant; they scarcely note it in their verbal fiddling with details and playing with words. And the boys' 'prayers'!—No, there are no young Jews! They are all born old! And they are the most disrespectful lot of people there is, completely hostile to all authority. There's only skepticism and doubt and questions and opposition; they take no word on trust, and the youngest little Talmud student impudently challenges the oldest rabbi who's been dead and in Abraham's bosom for a thousand years. They want to know everything and believe nothing! They certainly do believe in themselves! That's their one belief."

"Come on, that goes way too far," Bode exclaimed. "No belief—Israel, people of belief—the people who were the first to preach the belief in one God—from whom we ourselves—"

"Let's not discuss this topic any further, Herr Pastor," Strösser said cautiously. "Perhaps another time!—The question remains whether we have our faith or lack of faith from the Jews. And in the end the late Ramses was more religious than the dean of the theology faculty at the University of Greifswald. At any rate, he believed *more*!—But what's more important for our discussion: What do you think is the relationship of these people to God?"

"How should I put it?—In any case just like any believer to whatever his faith is—just as any of us strive and endeavor to do!"

"Ah—you should get to know these people better! It makes your hair stand on end to hear what stories your old Jews with the beards of patriarchs tell—what a human role their beloved Lord God plays in them—how He even is led by the nose.—"

"I just can't even imagine that! That would of course be incompatible with the veneration that—"

"I know! In Prussia it's considered sacrilege to cite a Bible verse in a profane way."

"Not without a reason, Herr Doctor! Holy Scripture is Holy Scripture."

"Tell me, Herr Pastor! Did you consider the ancient Greeks pious—I mean, did they have reverence for that which was holy?"

"For that which they considered holy! Without a doubt—in the earlier periods!"

"Good! And how do you reconcile that with Greek mythology, in which Papa Zeus and some of his relatives often played a quite delicate and often entertaining role?"

"Indeed!—and you are saying that's like what the Jews—"

"I am saying nothing about the Jews! And if I ever do believe something like that, it will be denied in the very next moment.—I am only ascertaining certain facts.—And I know that one should avoid constructing an image of Jews according to one's fantasies and that one shouldn't slip into false sentimentality about them either, which path you most certainly are on, Herr Pastor!—Things are truly miserable for the Jews in Holy Russia. No? We Germans have to protect ourselves now by seeing that they don't flee to us, as they did back then when they fled from us to Poland.—They are capable of upending all of our little bit of culture and have already managed to do so to some extent!"

"You don't consider Jews to be a people of culture?"

"What is a 'people of culture'? All people are people of culture! Every people has developed its own culture more or less! There is no accepted standard of what culture is! Jews might have a better culture—or their culture might be older and more developed! All the worse—because it's all the more dangerous! You have to squeeze their throats shut before it's too late! It's self-defense! The Russians are justified!"

"That's not Christianity!"

"That's practical Christianity! The church treated them differently when it held power.—That isn't hatred, that is love showered upon the right object, upon one's nearest neighbor!—That is self-preservation!—Just look at the Jews—endowed with uncanny intelligence—unshackled from a belief in authority and from dogma—with no respect for any sort of mummified caution—sober in every respect—in every respect most industrious—they acquire appalling power through their close family connections and intense focus on their tribal purity, and through their exclusionary commandments they not only preserve all their attributes but cultivate them and make them stronger.—We have to kill them before they become aware of this power and use it!"

"You've actually listed a number of good qualities there, Herr Doctor," the Pastor suggested with a smile. "If we delete the conclusion, one might readily think you are the panegyrist of Judas. Consider Balaam in the Bible, who came to curse the children of Israel but blessed them when he saw their tents."

"Quite right—who recognized and counted their merits!—Of course! Good King Balak, who had called on Balaam, must have cursed a blue streak. He had after all paid for some cursing!—But the Jews are smarter, and they count Balaam to this day as one of the worst anti-Semites—just because he saw their *strengths*!—Don't think, Herr Pastor, that I'm meddling in your trade—if you are considering Balak and Balaam—Balak tried mercy and love according to the Bible; he tried to defeat the Israelites with love instead of with the sword like Amalek, trying to persuade them to ally with him and convert them. The result proved that Moab was more hated by the Jews than Amalek. You won't earn great thanks from Jews."

"I'm not concerned with their thanks, Herr Doctor!" the Pastor said, standing at his door.

"There's still a lot in what you say that doesn't make sense to me. There are inconsistencies I believe.—"

"Of course! I make no claim whatsoever to have developed an entire system! I myself see the matter as being different at different times.—But my *ceterum censeo* is—"

"*Hierosolymam esse delendam,*" the Pastor laughed, shaking hands with Strösser. "So shall we part. Grant me this and—I shall return your advice. With your speeches *against* the Jews that look like praise for Jews, you will not find approval from any side.—It's probably better to keep these views to yourself or at least not voice them in wider circles."

"That's what Balaam's mount thought too. Adieu!" Strösser said and stumped off crossly.

IV

"You've been out a long time today, Johannes!" Frau Marie called from the kitchen and sailed into the room with a warm face and in her hands a bowl of steaming potatoes in their jackets. "Now serve yourself quickly!—Enjoy your meal!—The potatoes are very overcooked. And I was really quite afraid too; it's still rather spooky here. Those women with their head scarves and especially the Jewish wives with their wigs—and the men with their huge beards. As if they all wanted to conceal their faces!—Papa had a shave every day, and you know just how smooth Mama's hair was always brushed back: I'm just not making sense of things!—and you should just be able to tell from afar if someone is simple and simple-minded—that's what Papa always said. Naturally he was talking about the simplicity of the heart. Blessed are—if you stare at your plate so long, Johannes, your potatoes will get all cold.—I also think it's not going to work out with Liese permanently; she's too stupid, and then she always misunderstands me; I just can't stand listening to her ghastly German. She's certainly become half Russian, and I think she has her scraps of German only from Jews. And that came later!—It's no wonder after all; her parents have been living here for twenty years or more, and she's never seen Germany. Where was she supposed to learn any German?—and the fact that I can't make myself understood at the market! I swear to God I have to go to the Jewish market women—and even then it only halfway works. But they do speak a funny German, and I don't like being around them. They are, after all, marked by the Lord, as Papa always said—and what you've been telling me, Johannes, that the Jews here were expelled from Germany hundreds of years ago, coming here—that's all fine and good—but I think—they shouldn't have been allowed to forget their German so quickly. What they do to our lovely good German!—You can just tell what bad Germans they must have been! And you know why they were expelled.—Although they are an uplifting example for Christians, and I think we ought to keep some of them.—Dr. Lilienfeld often came to visit us at home: Mama would not have any other physician, and Papa is always so indulgent.—The other doctor, Dr. Wendel, actually was always drunk, and then people told such wicked stories about him. Otherwise no Jew would have come to our town—but Wendel of course became the district doctor because we do live in a Christian state after all. And just think—Lilienfeld moved away right after that—to Stettin. These people just have no sense of loyalty, and he's said to have done very well. Mama has been quite angry with Jews altogether ever since, and Papa's used clothes weren't offered for sale anymore to old Lewin. The sins of the fathers are visited on their children!—Actually Lewin was far older than Lilienfeld, and after all he wasn't related to him either.—But that's all neither here nor there! What's right is right, Papa always said. Enjoy your meal!"

How Frau Marie actually managed to do justice to her appetite during her unceasing fountain of conversation at dinner always had been a mystery to her husband and her guests. But her round plumpness, her satisfied expression, and her good-natured, pretty face allowed no serious concerns arise about her bodily well-being.—Because the Pastor preferred to take his meals with calm composure and tranquility, both parties had what they wanted.—After dinner he could speak: Frau Marie silently laid the gilt-bound volume of *The Hours of Domestic Edification* before her husband and sat down in the corner of the sofa with her crochet work. Bode read a chapter, adding a few remarks—all sorts of fruitful thoughts occurred to him, so he made notes for future sermons now and then. Frau Marie scarcely added a word, the married couple always speaking mainly in monologues. Bode read, meditated, and made notes usually for a while after his wife had fallen asleep in her corner until he squeakily wound his watch at ten— never later, sometimes a bit earlier—whereupon Frau Marie awoke, and both retired to their bedroom.—It was a comfortable and wholesome domestic regime from which they seldom departed.

Today, however, the Pastor browsed indecisively in the book for so long that Frau Marie looked up surprised and said with a wisp of impatience, "Read something, Johannes! Anywhere in the book is lovely, and it's edifying everywhere. You can start anywhere.—I'm already a little bit sleepy."

Bode snapped the book closed, asking somewhat hesitantly, "How would you like it if we read *Faust*? Do you want to?"

Frau Marie stared at him, her eyes wide with wonder.

"*Faust?*"

"Yes. *Faust!* Goethe's *Faust!*—I think it would do me good to read him again, and you probably have forgotten a lot."

"Yes," Frau Marie said slowly, "I played the waltz once: Mama really didn't want me to play dances—but Papa said, 'Goethe!'—Papa was always so indulgent."

"But, dear child!" Bode said and began to browse in the *Edification Hours* again. "I'm not talking about the opera!—When did you read Goethe's *Faust*— have you even read it—the actual *Faust*—the *Faust* by Goethe—have you actually read it?"

"I really don't know," Marie said innocently. "Wait! We read *Maria Stuart* by Schiller in school and *The Bride of Messina* and Goethe's *Torquato Tasso*—

oh, that was heavenly! How we all had a crush on Dr. Rütenbusch!—But wait a moment—I know more plays by these poets. In our little circle we read *Iphigenia* by Goethe, each taking a role, and *In the House of the Commerce Councillor* by Mrs. Heimberg or by Mrs. Marlitt—I don't remember anymore because we read books by the other two; I can't recall the names exactly. Papa thought we ought to read some modern works to learn how the world works.—No—I didn't read *Faust*. But I know of it of course: Dr. Rütenbusch gave me a history of literature for my confirmation—in a single silver-gray volume—and because it came from him I really studied it.—That was of course the result of being in love; I don't think it was good for me.—Papa always said that such things aren't for young ladies; and later, I think, when you're married you have more important things to do of course—ah, yes—then the duties begin. And whether you've read *Faust* or not, your dumplings aren't any better. Quite the opposite! If I think of Hilde Lilienfeld—she buried herself in books the whole day, but I doubt if she can make a decent pancake—at all!"

Bode had fetched the volume of Goethe from the bookshelf and skimmed the pages forlornly.

"If you'd like, dear Johannes," Marie said, "go ahead and read a bit of *Faust* out loud. It's already late, and I'm about to fall asleep. It would be a pity to miss our edification hour."

Thereupon Bode put the book aside, hastily took up the gilt-edged volume, and began to read, loudly rushing the words; his grim tone contrasted strangely with the gentle, sugar-coated words he was reading.—But soon his voice became milder and burbled monotonously along; and when Frau Marie, just as she predicted, had fallen asleep he picked up the Goethe volume again and lost himself in the literary historical introduction of the scholarly editor.

Pastor Bode had decided on a plan!

V

Once Pastor Bode had decided on a plan, he was also the man to carry it out. He had come to Borytshev for the purpose of bringing the Jews the gospel of salvation or at least studying at the source the souls of those whom he hoped to save.— He hadn't had any opportunity to come into contact with Jews until now. He was looking for a point of contact and was convinced that only the initial steps would be difficult.—He thought that the encounter with the young Jewish *Faust* reader had been a sign from heaven; he was determined to take advantage of this opening. Thereupon he girded his loins, so to speak, with spiritual arms.

Over the next few days he took frequent evening walks along the boulevard, regularly encountering the couple always deep in their study of *Faust*. He contemplated them carefully, but they paid him absolutely no attention.

One evening as he was following them at a distance until they parted, he hurried to catch up with Yossel, who was slowly walking along, the book dangling from his hand.

"You have there a good book in your hand, my young friend!" Bode said, pointing to the Reclam volume; he pretended to have read the title as he was passing by. "Don't be startled!" he added pleasantly when Yossel swirled around as if startled from a deep dream. Yossel stared at him uncomprehendingly. "Don't be so startled! I only said, 'You have a good book there!'"

"Huh?" Yossel managed to utter, apparently totally addled. His mouth hung open and awry, his eyes squinted half closed, and his head was cocked to the side. "Huh?"

"I said, 'You have a good book there!'"

"The book?" he gasped.

"Yes—the *Faust* by Goethe. That's a very good book—certainly not for everyone!"

Yossel had pulled himself together by now.

"You know this book?" he asked suspiciously.

"Certainly," the Pastor smiled. "It's a German book, of course, and one of our best works.—Now tell me, do you understand the book?"

"If I understand it?—The book?—Why ever not?—You don't understand it?—"

Bode furrowed his brow: he didn't feel that his friendly condescension had been sufficiently recognized, and he hadn't counted on being catechized himself.—He wasn't so sure anymore that what he planned to offer, explaining *Faust* to this fellow, would be greeted with overflowing gratitude.

"Would you like to visit me?" he decided to say. "I'm willing to discuss *Faust* with you."

"Good!" Yossel said indifferently. "You probably have questions.—I'll be happy to explain things to you."

Bode hadn't anticipated this turn of events at all; he had to smile. The main thing, though, was that he was taking up closer contact with Jews and that there was now a topic of common interest.—Everything else would take care of itself.

And so it came to pass to Frau Marie's great astonishment that half an hour later Yossel was sitting next to the Pastor at his enormous desk and was talking with him as if it were all self-evident.

The initial language difficulties were quickly resolved: if the Pastor didn't understand a word, Yossel could offer hundreds of circumlocutions; aided by lively and impressive gestures, he could almost always make himself understood: he guessed practically by instinct whatever the Pastor was saying.

Bode, who saw *Faust* as the means to an end, energetically steered toward his goal. He hadn't studied the literary historical essay of his Goethe edition for nothing.

"The things you touch on here, dear friend," he said, cutting off a long-winded discussion about the Earth Spirit, "these things are all just minutiae and details. Look at the concept of the whole: What is the basic idea of *Faust* that underlies everything?—I'll tell you: it is the blissful love that encompasses everything, unites everything! Love—as has been preached for centuries. But the doctrine of love is often not heard by those whom it most concerns, and their heralds are nailed to the cross.—

"Here at the beginning, in the 'Prologue in Heaven'—there is the mighty, strong, inflexible Old Testament—the bet between the Lord and Satan—the contract—the law!—But here at the end, here we have transfiguring love—which is united with belief and hope. Faust has lost the bet—he is 'content.' And according to his bet his soul belongs to Satan. Satan insists on the certificate, on the bet—on what is, one might say, his legal right, according to the strict legal wording. But love triumphs over the law, and the 'damned!' of Part I becomes 'saved!' through divine mercy. Faust does not go to Hell, but his immortal soul is carried to eternal salvation—while the disappointed Satan is crushed, defrauded of his hope.—That is the concept of *Faust*—and therein lies its great moral power!"

Yossel gaped at the Pastor; he finally comprehended what the Pastor was trying to say by asking a few questions. Thereupon he began to page wildly through *Faust,* rocking back and forth excitedly for a long time and speaking to himself in an incomprehensible singsong.

Bode watched this gymnastic-musical method of *Faust* research with astonishment, waiting patiently until Yossel finally came to a conclusion.—He didn't have to wait too long—until Yossel turned to him and said, "I'll explain everything to you: you are completely wrong.—It's entirely just that Satan doesn't get Faust—because Satan simply lost the bet.—It's even there, no love is necessary."

Then he explained in a long speech that according to the Pastor's interpretation Goethe had swindled the reader and the Lord had swindled Satan. The reader pays close attention at first to the way the bet is carried out, and later at the end it doesn't matter at all.—and Satan is still more honorable than the Lord, on whose promise he relied.—It's really offensive the way He agrees to the bet with Satan at first, and then afterward, when He sees the deal isn't going well and He loses, thanks to His superior powers to grab the prize for Himself and on top of that to mock Satan, who made all that effort and had all those expenses.

And what's what with love here?—Everything just completely comes to a stop! Then there wouldn't be justice anymore at all!—Then the sinner is treated the same as the good man!—If love forgives everything—What does Goethe understand Satan to be? What does he live on? How does he carry out his business?—Which souls can he then ever catch?—

No! The matter is quite simple, and the Pastor just got confused because he combined the conversation between Faust and Mephistopheles with the bet between the Lord and Satan.—Faust didn't enter into any bet, but he concluded a contract under which Mephistopheles is supposed to serve him on earth—and the other way around—he would serve Mephistopheles in the event that he went to Hell. "*If* we find ourselves there."—He cannot contract about anything as to whether he actually goes to Hell. The conditions under which he would go to Hell are set in the "Prologue" after all.—and when Faust says, "If I should ever say," etc., just pinpoints the moment of death.

But the Lord won His bet because Faust never succumbed to any temptations, never sank into debauchery, never is diverted from his wellspring.

The bet is legally completely fulfilled, and nowhere is there any mention of the triumph of love over justice!—

Bode was completely taken aback!—He definitely suspected that Yossel's arguments were vulnerable. But he could only defend his dogma of love as the highest ideal over the principle of justice in general terms. He didn't feel capable of proving his interpretation of *Faust,* and so right from the start he lost the support of his second, Goethe, on whom he had depended. Yossel could not be budged from *Faust* and proved to be totally disinclined to consider any philosophical speculation in general.

The Pastor soon took heart, taking down his Petiscus from the shelf and introducing Yossel to the mysteries of Greek mythology, which included the mysteries of the classic Walpurgis Night. And thus it was that the Gospels met the Talmud on Olympus.

Having peeked into that world of knowledge, closed to him until now, Yossel's desire to learn more grew greater by the day. Little by little he now found more and more gaps in his knowledge, and ever since he had dared to leave his familiar field, the study of the Talmud, he felt himself to be on shaky ground.

Chana, in whom Yossel had confided all his new joys and sorrows, encouraged him in his great plans—which coincided totally with her own burning desires of long standing—to escape the narrow world she knew in order to study, to learn— to breathe freedom. She wanted to cross beyond the boundary of the ghetto, as she had crossed the Sabbath boundary.

And her Yossel also followed her across this boundary. They discovered they both were driven to be free and to acquire knowledge; when the engagement contracts were drawn up, it was guaranteed that right after the wedding they would go to Germany to study.

No one knew of these plans—Pastor Bode did not know that some of his hopes were about to steal away—nor did Berl Weinstein as he started out on his accustomed journey. But Pastor Bode in Borytshev was indeed indirectly responsible that Reverend Hickler could successfully perform Berl Weinstein's baptism in London. Only it was a pity that the Pastor knew nothing of this success, because Berl Weinstein was very careful to never breathe a word in Borytshev of this lucrative line of business he had discovered.—

What tipped the balance for Yossel was a letter from his former teacher Wolf Klatzke, from whom he had learned to read German years ago and who had recently emigrated to Germany. Klatzke had written to Yossel how much he liked Berlin and how splendid the country was. All the world's wisdom could be found there, he wrote, and a man who worked hard could easily establish a decent living enabling him to dedicate himself to the study of wisdom.—He, the letter writer himself, had a fine position—he was very successfully engaged with literature and would be happy to offer help to him, Yossel, to get ahead. He advised him urgently to also move to Berlin.

Even before Klatzke had become Yossel's teacher, this former teacher of Yossel had had a series of jobs, sometimes several at once, as fruit dealer, speculator, vagabond, schnorrer, and choir singer, and he had been active in still other lines of business. He had been all of ten years old when he had met Yossel.

TWO

A Literary Enterprise

I

To some degree it is doubtful whether a Goethe or a Lessing, certainly men who understood their métier after their own fashion, wouldn't have been hard-pressed to succeed in the branch of literature practiced by Wolf Klatzke. Although these men had picked areas that were relatively easily achievable, Wolf Klatzke had chosen a thoroughly difficult specialty as the showcase for his talents, having founded an office for the manufacture of begging letters.

Imagination, linguistic and stylistic flair, and good penmanship alone did not guarantee success; a schnorrer letter supplier has to do a lot more—he must be a shrewd psychologist, he must understand how to play with virtuosity on all instruments of the psyche, including reason—he must possess a broad knowledge of many, many things and of circumstances—he must—and what all must he have!—and what's the most important characteristic of this type of literary production, which is different from every other kind of literary genre and which makes it so much more difficult and problematic: every product of the pen of the begging letter writer is as a rule only for one reader, or at most for one small circle of readers; the letter must affect this one reader, and the effect must spontaneously convert into cash.—Thus the tone and contents must perfectly match the recipient, and he must be a miserable bungler indeed who thought to affect several people in the same way with one and the same letter. The very circles that represented Wolf Klatzke's clientele comprised only distinct individuals, who had to be carefully studied.

Now Wolf Klatzke was still a neophyte in this art, making serious mistakes on occasion. He had definitely underestimated the difficulties in his chosen profession when he took up this work in the dark back room of Bornstein's pub on the Dragonerstrasse in competition with the red-nosed Brandler, who had been doing the same work for years in the front room. Brandler wrote his schnorring letters with a speed derived from many years of practice for ten pfennigs apiece, at the same time running a brisk business with addresses of suitable schnorring targets.—Klatzke took it upon himself to deliver a letter for eight pfennigs and—as an unheard-of innovation in the industry—established a bundled price of five pfennigs per name for the addresses, whose price otherwise, as is well known, fluctuates between one pfennig and a mark per donor adjusted for his generosity and credit.—

It goes without saying that the names and addresses alone are not what are being purchased, but the actual object of value is the familiarity with the nature and essence of the characteristics of the person in question: this knowledge is expressed in the form and contents of the applicable letter, the particular composition of which is the subject of frequent and detailed conferences between the writer and purchaser.—No credit agency in the world has such delicate questions to resolve as do the agent and the secretary of the schnorrer guild. He has to know precisely how the letter could appeal to the purse of the person receiving the letter, how to hold his interest—he has to know whether he is pious and observant or lax in his views—he has to know whether he loves hearing that the petitioner is desperate or if he is overflowing with devout trust. For some, the threats of suicide are effective—for others, it is necessary to explain how it is possible to live for weeks on a few crusts of bread. For some, the story of the merciless landlord is enough.—Others prefer only widows with helpless children—and still others only give money for a child who has lost both parents; quite popular is the impoverished workman, less so is the merchant pressed by creditors or whom a dishonest associate pushed into misfortune. Some love to give money for a bride's trousseau—others have an outspoken preference for cripples.—Romantically inclined souls are gratified by helping victims of Russian pogroms and political prisoners escaped from Siberia—certain circles like very much to give to the poor in Palestine—while others again wouldn't give one single pfennig for this cause, who on the other hand then have an open hand for emigrants returning from America.—Then there are still particularly abundant sources to be found for publishing Hebrew works or for rebuilding burned prayer houses.—In short, one must have a command of a rich assortment of templates considering the variety of tastes and must always be able to select just the right one for the particular case.—and as in every business presentation is everything: the style of the letter is of the utmost importance. One must write only in Hebrew to quite a few—others demand that the text is generously sprinkled with Bible quotations: now and then flawless German is required, but in general a particularly bad, naive, and farcical quasi German is the most effective. People read that out of sheer curiosity—they are both touched and amused, and they take note.

The real agent in many cases will naturally write no letter at all but will advise his client to make personal contact. In which case he tells him all the required information about the necessary and suitable manner of behavior, what story to tell, and of course the best hours to pay a visit, how to deal with the servants, the methods of getting into the office, and a hundred other details.

A schnorrer who takes his profession seriously must have a dependable list of clients and always keep it current. The credit agencies and scriptoria for schnorrers thus meet a pressing need, and thus in every metropolis where a large number of Jews live there are countless such establishments that enjoy a hefty volume if they keep business costs to a minimum.

It's not exactly easy for someone new to enter the business: the old firms warily protect their secrets, their ploys, and their knowledge of people. And they possess the loyalty of their clients: the whole business depends entirely on this loyalty, on the clients' conviction that they are actually being provided a service delivered with care. If such an agent were to foolishly give addresses away, and if it were to come out that postage and fees had been wasted, he would completely lose all goodwill.—The schnorrer knows exactly what his agent is worth; whenever the agent comes to make his rounds in Berlin, the first thing he does is go to the schnorrer; he takes out his old list, compares, deletes, corrects—and buys new names, places new letter orders, and then, well armed with information, he visits the associations and private individuals who have been noted.—He is careful not to provide anyone else with the addresses and notes, thereby creating competition, as well as the enmity of his agent. And above all he is careful not to let any of the donors know the name of the person who had given him the address. Even the promise of higher pay will not loosen his tongue; his own profit forces him to be discreet about the honor of his own name to the same extent that he is about the source.

II

After a checkered career in his youth, Wolf Klatzke had landed in this difficult profession for the time being; he had no intention of staying in this sort of work forever. This was only a transitional stage for him; nevertheless, he burned with ambition to accomplish something extraordinary and more than anything else to earn as much as possible.—Dedicated aspiration to reach the top had animated him since childhood; as a young schoolboy he had shown initiative and sharp cunning. Scarcely eight years old, having already long run through odd jobs of every description, he had managed to earn a few kopecks at the train station and taxi stands here and there, which he faithfully handed over to his mother, a very poor widow rich in children. He started to look around for opportunities with better returns: in front of the Jewish school, the cheder, where he was enrolled, a fruit seller had her stand; she briskly sold to the boys who had some money. Little Wolf figured out that the fruit vendor in front of the German school, which was about fifteen minutes away, sold his apples for a little less.—Wolf pondered what advantage he could make of this fact and soon had a plan, which he energetically implemented. Every morning he left the house a half hour earlier no matter how difficult it was to get up earlier, bought fruit from the cheaper seller, and quickly succeeded in pocketing a significant profit, thanks to his schoolmates, by underbidding the fruit seller at her stand.—Soon he was forced to madly dash to his supplier during the morning break, where he arrived dripping with sweat, back at his school barely in time, carrying a new supply of apples. The second half of his morning's business took place during and after the rest of the lessons.—His meager initial investment of capital of a few kopecks increased considerably: he gave his mother only a portion of his profits—he had learned instead to continuously enlarge his capital through a series of similarly lucrative opportunities and speculation. A risky speculation in candle stubs would have been nearly fatal for him when the Feast of Lights provided the youth of Borytshev with a superfluity of wax for months; but he surmounted the slump and vowed to be more careful in the future.—One day he was no longer there; instead of going to the cheder he had set out for the train station and gone off into the world—always following the tracks, to seek his fortune and to return one day a wealthy man, making his mother and brothers and sisters wealthy—and to punish the schoolmaster with the violent temper and to be the top man in Borytshev.—He returned after only a few weeks—somewhat bedraggled and more withdrawn than usual. He had by no means used up his entire capital, but he had realized in time that to succeed in the world he had to be better equipped with money and, most importantly, with knowledge. So he turned around without any misgivings and with no hesitation and struggled to reach home without spending another kopeck. His mother showered him with reproaches alternating with cries of joy, all of which he bore patiently—along with the blows that rained down on him at the cheder; he accepted them as a fitting punishment for his impertinence, thinking constantly of how he could realize his plans. One day he went to the son of the caretaker at the German school to begin learning German from him—three kopecks an hour. He only needed a few weeks of such instruction; then he could continue on his own, and he figured out how to turn discarded newspapers into cheap exercise books. In the summer he cut classes at his Jewish school, where only Hebrew was taught, to crouch under the open window of the German school for hours on end, where he learned the words and the contents of the lectures.—After a while he began to give German lessons himself, giving him the double advantage of earning money while advancing his own studies. During this time he came to know Yossel Schlenker, who was several years older, and the two diligently studied the German language together for a long time.—In order to find the opportunity to continue his education without having to worry about earning a living and to not burden his mother, he took a position as a tutor out in the country—with a tavern owner who was looking for a tutor for his two daughters and his only son; Wolf didn't have it all too easy in this home: the adults and his charges treated him with contempt, he slept in an unheated room, he had little to eat, but he did have time for his own studies. He ordered all sorts of books that looked useful and studied by candlelight until deep into the night while starving and freezing in the snow.—Finally he felt the time had come to seriously begin to put his plans into effect. He had been with the family nearly three years when he gave notice; there was no objection to his leaving because he and the family had remained strangers to each other the whole time. Wolf returned to Borytshev for a few days, bid his mother and siblings farewell and an especially fond farewell to Yossel, whom he had come to feel close to. He began his journey to Germany on foot, to the land of his dreams. Giving his mother half his savings, he now slogged on from town to town, finding a cheap ride now and then. Arriving at the Vistula River, he performed all sorts of little services for the raftsmen, who took him along, and after an interminable journey and all sorts of difficulties, he finally arrived at the border, at Thorn on German territory. From here on he took meandering back roads through to Berlin—always seeking out the Jewish community offices to get tickets and provisions for a short distance of the journey. On his way from Thorn to Berlin, he passed through, among other places, Schneidemühl, Dirschau, Danzig, Königsberg, Stettin, Eberswalde, Frankfurt an der Oder, Posen, Breslau, Kattowitz, Dresden, Leipzig, Halle, Halberstadt, Magdeburg, Braunschweig, and Hannover; only here was he fortunate enough to get off the insane merry-go-round trajectory that the Jewish communities prescribed to anyone who turned to them for support; forced against his will onto the circuitous route, he finally liberated himself to make his way to Berlin at his own expense.—The weeks he spent on this carousel weren't lost, however; he had seen and heard many things, had won some insight in his lodgings into the secrets of the schnorrer guild. When he arrived in Berlin, he knew he wanted to became an agent and secretary of this guild.—He found meager lodgings on the Dragonerstrasse at Bornstein's for five pfennigs, and a few days later he set up in his special new role in the back room, much to the annoyance of fat Brandler, who watched many of his old clients disappear into the back room. Brandler just continued mechanically to work his routine, lacking any new ideas. Many guests whom he had met on his travels or in the lodgings on his journey considered Klatzke to be an ingenious thinker; his knowledge of many things was also highly praised. Above all, he was sponsored by one of the most esteemed and skilled clients, a smart man particularly highly esteemed in all schnorrer circles—a compatriot of Wolf Klatzke's—Herr Berl Weinstein from Borytshev.

III

"How do you spell this word?" Berl Weinstein asked, leaning over Klatzke, who was assiduously writing, bent low over the table, his head cocked to one side. "You spell 'philanthropical' with one 'f' at the beginning? Is that right?"

"Yes!" Klatzke said. "It's spelled with a 'ph.'" And he opened the Duden. "Here it is: *Ph*ilanthropic—with 'ph.'—I've spelled it correctly."

"So?" Berl Weinstein said. "I really thought it was spelled with an 'f.'"—

"No! It's wrong with an 'f.'"

"Then it's right!"

And the "f" stayed put.

"Yes," Klatzke said. "That's a little detail, and I have to really watch out that I don't misspell such a word right out of sheer carelessness. People don't like that; it upsets them. A schnorrer letter has to have misspellings—from beginning to end. With the common words I know how they aren't spelled, but there are just so many difficult words."

"Whom are you writing to now?"

"Quite elegant people who aren't on any list yet. Listen: to Privy Medical Councillor Bamberg, to Justice Councillor Krotoschin, to Professor Mandelbrot, to Regional Court Councillor Levysohn, to Theater Director Loewe—"

"Really elegant people!" Berl Weinstein said, amazed. "And they give money for *Jewish* causes?—How do people build churches then?"

"People also contribute to Jewish causes—these are all pious and involved Jews!"

"Remarkable! Privy councillor! Professor! Theater director!—Where did you get the addresses? You're still so new here!"

Klatzke smiled mysteriously.

"What name are you signing there?" Berl Weinstein asked, shaking his head.

"Ephraim Lifschitz."

"You could just as well have signed Yossel Schlenker. Not a soul in Berlin knows my son-in-law."

"Why should I use the real name when there are so many false names?" Klatzke replied. "And I think something can be done with Yossel—a doctor or a professor. Then it's better if his name isn't attached to such a letter."

"I suppose you're right," Berl Weinstein said. "He's a capable man. And my Chana isn't stupid either. Only—you know how children are! Old man Schlenker wasn't a little taken aback when the two told him that they wanted to move here after the wedding! To Berlin!—to study!—What an idea!"

"I advised Yossel myself to come here. I thought he could truly get ahead here. But I had no idea that he married: now everything is different!"

"How so?—I'm quite pleased.—I would have been forced to have them both in my house for a year. They are remarkable people—children nowadays!"

"And old man Schlenker agreed?"

"What could he do?—and that's a story too! An old story!—Moische Schlenker had a brother—he went to Germany as a young man: Moische Schlenker was only a child at the time. But he told me how sad everyone was at home when one day his brother disappeared. He left only a letter behind. Later, he wrote a few times, but the letters never arrived; and then there was no word of him.— Moische Schlenker thought it was better his Yossel left *with* his permission than run away without a word."

"He was right!—But I don't know—with the letters here—I'm a bit afraid of Yossel. He has such extravagant ideas.—"

"Just let me do it!" Berl Weinstein said soothingly and approached the young couple that had just entered. "Did you sleep well? Now sit down and have some coffee!"

"We've noted what we need from the address book," Yossel said merrily. "We want to leave at once."

"Where to?" Berl asked, bewildered. "What addresses did you select?"

Yossel wanted to answer, but Chana was curt. "The various addresses we need! —Hurry up, Yossel! We've got to leave soon."

There was silence around the table for a moment; Berl Weinstein glanced carefully at Chana and then Yossel, his eyes filled with concern. Then he began speaking with a touch of solemnity—causing Yossel to look up startled; Chana put her cup down and looked directly at her father.

"My dear children," Berl Weinstein said, "I would have preferred that you lived at home with me for a year or at least for a few months.—You, Yossel, would have continued to study, and Chana would have taken care of you. You would have had no worries. Those would have been mine—and that would have been good according to our ancient holy custom.—Now—you wanted to do otherwise; you wanted to go abroad—to Berlin. Just as well! I did not say no—and your father also didn't say no, Yossel.—It is a different time, and you may understand that better.—But—you shouldn't come to harm, and I want no benefit on that account. I want to help you as you start out even here; life in Berlin is expensive.—"

Berl paused; Yossel peered unsuspectingly with astonishment at his father-in-law; he started to say something, but Chana waved him to stop.

"Stop, Yossel!" she said very seriously. "What are you thinking of?"

"Certainly nothing bad!" Berl Weinstein said, hiding a little bit of embarrassment behind a smile. He stood up to take a place behind Klatzke's chair. "Wolf, tell them what I have done for the children."

"Me?" Klatzke said, aghast. "What do I have to do with it?"

"Well, what is it?" Chana said, pressing her lips together.

Yossel stared uncomprehending from one person to another.

"Oh, very well!" Klatzke said, peeved. "Your father instructed me to write letters at his expense: whatever we get is yours.—The money will be directed to the landlord, to Bornstein for Lifschitz, and the money will be paid to you, Yossel."

There was silence for a long time.

Yossel still didn't understand.

"What kind of letters?" he asked unsuspectingly. "Who is Lifschitz?"

"Let me speak!" Chana said, slamming her hand on the table. "You still don't understand what kind of letters your friend Wolf is writing all day long? Schnorrer letters! Letters begging for money, full of lies and deceit!—and my father is paying him for these letters for us to collect money that these poor people send who have reprehensibly been swindled out of money and whose generosity has been terribly abused."

"God forbid!" Yossel cried, horrified.

"Let me speak!" Chana exclaimed. "I know you wouldn't take such money, and if you did take it, we'd be quits.—All of you should know once and for all: Yossel and I—we don't want to have anything to do with this sort of business! Nothing! Nothing! And we don't even want to hear about it!—We are now, praise God, on our own and are no longer children; we want to be independent.—We want to leave this—all this filth. And we will find us a place to live where we can work and study. We want to work, not beg.—We don't want to accept anything from anyone anymore, not from relatives and not from strangers!—It's high time we Jews work. That's why we went abroad, because Russia won't let us work and because it bars our entry to schools.—I understand that if many, many people don't have work, then they have to beg. And still many there work hard enough. Certainly the young people!—But we are now here in Germany—in a free country. Here we are certainly able to work! Here everyone can work!—So it's a disgrace to go begging and schnorring—even if there's no deceit.—A disgrace to us and a disgrace to others! And a disgrace to German Jews!—Yossel and I, we will find our way—even without help; but I think every German Jew will be glad to show us how we can achieve something.—No more the disgraceful schnorring and the swindle racket!—Come, Yossel! We're going!"

She stood up briskly, taking the entirely bewildered Yossel by the shoulder.

"Stay seated, children!" Berl Weinstein said pleasantly. "Stay seated!—I wanted to do something bad to you?—Perhaps I'm wrong! Perhaps I'm old and don't understand how things are nowadays anymore!—But one can at least finish what one has to say!"

Chana shrugged her shoulders.

"You've hurt me, Chana," Berl said wistfully. "My own child tells me I am a con man! My own child thinks I could deceive someone!—and I have never as long as I've lived—and I'm not a young man anymore—I have not cheated a single person in my whole life of even a single pfennig!—Before I would set up a fraud to trap a single person, I would rather die."

Chana gestured toward the letters and murmured under her breath, "Lifschitz."

"You say 'Lifschitz' and think you've got me because the person who is getting this letter is going to send money to an Ephraim Lifschitz—who doesn't exist—and a Yossel Schlenker will get it.—"

"I won't take a pfennig!" shouted Yossel, now wakening from his stupor. "Thank heavens I don't need it. We have enough to live on for now—and if not—I still wouldn't take the money!"

"Take it or not," Berl said. "Wait and see what comes in—if anything comes in. Then it's up to you what you do with the money.—The letters are going to be mailed, and with that I've done my duty.—I have to ask: Does it make a difference to the man who sends the money whether a Lifschitz or a Schlenker or a Klatzke gets it? He doesn't know one from the other, and he doesn't want to know any of them at all. What he wants is this: to fulfill the holy commandment to give to charity. He gives and thereby feels good that he's fulfilled a commandment and that he's done a good deed.—and I tell you that it is better, much better, to give than to receive.—He should be grateful to me that I have afforded him the opportunity—that I make it so easy for him."

"But," Chana exclaimed, enraged, "there are others who might need it more!"

"Then let them write letters!" Berl said. "Write them or go themselves in person. And if they don't write and don't go, then he has no opportunity at all to help them. He certainly isn't going to run after them.—He has to have someone come to him if he's going to give.—If I write and he sends, at least I know who's getting the money. Otherwise any old swindler or a nobody will get it and just spend it. In my case I know for sure how it is being spent—maybe," he concluded meekly, "even for work."

"Are you trying to say that these letters contain only the pure truth?" Yossel asked. "There's nothing but pure deception in these letters!"

"Look, Yossel!" Berl said triumphantly. "You haven't read any of the letters, but you know even so that it's impossible that they contain a word of truth. How do you know that? Because simple reason says that one can't do otherwise. Truth! What's truth?—Take the newspaper here and look at the advertisements; every one claims that its wares are the best. Is that the truth? Is that fraud maybe? No! One understands when one reads them: the merchant wants to sell his wares and exaggerates. One understands that it isn't all meant exactly as it is written there!—and if one did write the precise truth that his wares were only mediocre, everyone would say to himself he had only terrible goods, and no one would buy from him.—The man would be lying—to his own disadvantage. Truth is a kind of deception—it *can* be a sort of deception. It's all just words.—It just depends whether an injustice is done to someone or if someone was harmed.—Who is harmed here? Who is being swindled here?"

"The man who receives such a letter," Yossel said, upset. "He might be moved by the sorrow he is hearing of, and—"

"So?—That's harm? And I tell you: that alone is a good deed! If such a wealthy man is even moved once—he should just feel it in his own heart! He becomes a little bit better and nobler!—Just imagine: there is a man, a real pious Jew—he's in desperate need of help.—There is another, a wealthy man with a very good heart: he would like to help the poor man if only he knew of him. But he doesn't know him at all, and he gets a request for help, and so many poor people come to him that he doesn't know who would be better to give to—who's worthy and who isn't.—The poor man of whom we were speaking knows very well that he is worthy, and he knows that the rich man would prefer to give to him if he only knew him. What should he do?—He has no choice but to preempt the others. He has *one* child—he writes that he has *seven* children; he has a weak eye—he writes that he is about to go blind. So now the wealthy man takes note of him, and the poor man gets just as much as he would have been given had the wealthy man known him really well. So he hasn't been swindled at all! Not in the least!—On the contrary—the wealthy man, the donor, even has a great benefit. He has the joy that he has helped *seven* children when he's only helped the one.—So his reward is greater—in his mind—than he actually deserves.—So where's the fraud?"

Chana was about to jump up; Berl signaled her to calm down.

"Let it go!" he said mildly. "My child! You have sorely offended me; but I forgive you. You don't know the world, and you don't know German Jews at all.—You've upset yourself about schnorrers!—They need us more than we need them!—Isn't that right, Klatzke?"

"That's right!" Klatzke said, nodding solemnly. "Do you all think that I like doing this? I didn't come to Germany to schnorr or to assist in schnorring.—This business makes me sick enough!"

"Why are you doing it then?" Yossel said, annoyed.

"Why?—I got into it without really wanting to.—This business is essential; I can do it as well as anyone else. They need schnorrers in Germany like daily bread. Without schnorrers there is no Judaism in Germany! Without them they wouldn't begin to know what to do. And therefore even in Germany very special institutions have been established to turn every Russian Jew who arrives here without much money into a schnorrer and to ensure that as many communities and people as possible rejoice in every schnorrer. Back then when I arrived in

Thorn I went right to the Jewish community office and said straight out openly and honestly what I needed—that I wanted to go to Berlin and see what I could do there to earn something.—They said they couldn't send me to Berlin—that's too far—and they put me on the train to go a few stops down the line to another town. I thought—I didn't know my way around back then—they were sending me on my way to Berlin. But no! It turned out that they had recently been sending all too many people in that direction—they now wanted to send people to another community. And in the next place it was the same: they took care of me for a day—very well—and then sent me off again somewhere. And so it went, from one place to the next; I arrived in towns whose name I'd never heard of and of which I had never even dreamed. They hauled me all over Germany—back and forth. I had no idea what was happening to me. They played with me as if I were a ball; one community would toss me to the next.—Finally I caught on: I was really dizzy from traveling in circles. In Hannover they gave me a ticket to Lüneburg; what was I supposed to do in Lüneburg? There was a stop on the way—Lehrte was the name of the place, I think. I got out there and traveled to Berlin—at my own expense.—Of course I registered with the station that I had gotten out at Lehrte and hadn't used my whole ticket. I was able to get some money back from the railway. There's order here in Germany!—But the joke lasted for months until I got from Thorn to Berlin!—"

"But who paid for all of that?" Yossel asked, dumbfounded. "The train—lodging —food?"

"Who paid?—The communities of course!—If they had sent me directly from Thorn to Berlin, I would have been there in a day—that would have been cheaper and easier. But then all the other communities wouldn't have benefited from me! They preferred to send me touring around the country.—I've seen how people need schnorrers. They don't have nearly enough!—Where would all the money they waste go otherwise? And what would all those presidents of the community associations and financial directors for the pauper funds do and the commissioners for travelers and the caretakers! One has to help people: it's an act of charity!—I tell you, a schnorrer has a holy mission in Germany!"

"That's true!" Berl said emphatically. "The unvarnished golden truth!—*Mission.*—That's the word. I recently heard a sermon—by a famous German rabbi. I tell you, I was moved to the depths of my soul when he spoke of the *Jewish mission.* As he put it, the entire Jewish people have the mission to be schnorrers— and I thought that the schnorrer is the real Jew. He proved that it is the mission of Jews to go, without a home, from place to place to make it possible for everyone else to fulfill their moral purpose—to be the object of charity—to accept charity and to be grateful. Thus, that's the whole life of a schnorrer—the schnorrer is the right representative of this mission!"

"Lovely morals!" Chana said. "But the rabbi doesn't go schnorring."

"But sometimes he does!" Klatzke said. "But am I schnorring then? The rabbi and the community president and the Jewish newspaper editors in Germany are all doing what I do, only on a large scale. I write letters, and they write articles and hold speeches; they say the same things I do in my letters. What do I write? I write perhaps that the petitioner is poor and is unable to work; he was once an industrious workman who has met with misfortune and has had to permanently relinquish his independence and so forth! And I name him Schimon instead of Ruben, which is his real name, or instead of Schlenker I call him Lifschitz. And what do they do? Strictly speaking, the same thing—only they write to all the Jewish people! Earlier they said the Jewish people achieved a lot—earlier! Today they say that they aren't capable of that anymore—today, Jews have lost forever their independence, they've ceased to be a people. They only want handouts!—They only want to sit at the table of strangers.—I just want to show how people, the rabbi and the others, do the very same thing I do, the same fraud—if it is fraud.—They don't speak out and don't want to know what the Jewish people can do—and say they are more abject than they are.—and even the false names express it exactly: a Jew in Germany doesn't say he's a 'Jew' but that he's an Israelite or 'of the Mosaic confession,' and the Jew doesn't belong to the Jewish people, but he says he's a Teuton or a Slav or something.—Is that not a fraud?"

"I just thought of something," Berl Weinstein said. "You have to write a letter for me—to old man Karger."

"In Garz?"

"Yes—he's a very decent person. I spent a few days as his guest again.—So a letter must be sent—but not to schnorr—but it has to be a letter from the community presidents and the rabbi from some sort of small Jewish community in Galicia or Hungary. It can say that the synagogue burned down or during the fire someone—a poor but worthy man, a great scholar who happened to be there—appeared. He rushed into the fire, he wrapped himself first in his prayer shawl, and he calmly rescued one Torah scroll after another from the Holy Ark. And the name of the man who did that is Berl Weinstein. And the community wants to tell of this miracle to all benevolent people in Israel."

"But that's a shameless lie!" Yossel shouted, beside himself; Chana had turned her back on everyone and was standing at the window.

"Lie? Always a lie?" Berl said sadly. "You don't understand that I only do this to make an old man happy. How can I show my gratitude in any other way?—I am going to travel to Hungary—I can mail the letter there!—I may never go to Karger again, and I don't want anything of him. But the man has been so friendly toward me."

"And that's your thanks!" shouted Yossel, incensed.

"That certainly is my thanks!" Berl said firmly. "There isn't any better! When the man gets the letter he's happy! He is reminded now of these things and wants to experience a miracle.—Do you have any idea what old Karger is? He lives only for the poor! Who is going to travel to that dot on the map, to Garz on the Oder?! No one! But he has certainly promoted the place."

"Promoted? Why?" Yossel asked in astonishment.

"His inn for schnorrers.—But it's a hostel where no one pays but still receives money. And the guests are clothed anew. They stay there three or four days, relax. They are genuine guests.—Honored guests.—and he's proud that sometimes there are as many as ten guests living there; he built a special house for them. That's why he's known all over the world wherever there's a schnorrer!—Why shouldn't I give joy to an old man?—and maybe I'll visit him again sometime!"

"And this man believes such a stupid story?" Yossel asked uneasily. "Can a Jew be superstitious enough to believe something like this?"

"Shows what you know!" Klatzke said, laughing. "What German Jews don't believe!—They even believe in the Jewish mission I told you about."

"There are Jews in Germany," Berl said, "who believe in everything, whatever you want, except in the Torah. Only the people who have to believe in that, who are paid to do so! The rabbis, of course! If the rabbi isn't pious, he falls out with everyone; even those who don't obey all the commandments in the Torah themselves scold him.—and the schnorrers! They say there was once a schnorrer who traveled by train on the Sabbath!—or ate a piece of pork!—But it is true that the schnorrer is still the one who salvages a shred of Jewishness in Germany!"

"No!" Yossel said as he stood up. "I cannot believe this—Jewish mission— schnorrers who go for a drive—false names—I want to see for myself—with my own eyes!"

"With his own eyes!" Chana said and stood in the doorway. "Come along, Yossel! We don't have anything to do with this!—It's not possible! And if it is, it will change!—I believe the worst is that the Jews in Germany only know us Russian Jews as schnorrers—and that until now we in turn only know certain types of German Jews.—The schnorrer is not the Russian Jew—and the preacher is not the German Jew; there must be other kinds of Jews! But if all the Jews were like that"—her voice failed her for a moment in her agitation—"then it would be better if we disappeared with our shame from the earth!"

And they both left.

"Children nowadays!" Berl Weinstein said indulgently. "They'll see.—Now— I'm going to the exchange."

"What do you want there?" Klatzke asked as he dipped his pen in the ink.

"I want to buy a coat," Berl said. "The coat I have from Karger fits me too well. I can't make my visits in that! I need to find one that doesn't fit me."

With that he went to the old clothes exchange on the Kaiser-Wilhelm-Strasse.

Once more Klatzke earnestly set about his work, which had been interrupted for so long. He jabbed his pen in the sleeve of his woolen jacket until finally a thread stuck, and writing with the primed pen, he smeared the envelope lying before him with crooked, awkward-looking letters to write the address:

> to misser reegionl court judg
> Levysohn
> Berlin
> Mattäikirchstrasse 8

IV

Vrry honored Sir Highborn. That You arre nowne as a great filantropist by jewish pore people i am turrning to You from great sorro i have no bredd to eet for the wif and children Verry honored Sir! Highborn i haf read your call to the liberals from last yeer. I am always for the liberals so i haff written fine books about our holy torah-moshe skool to keep schabbes and eet kosher and i am a famous jewish learned rabbi, from Russia only anger in great sorrow and Your Highborn in Your nowne liberality and nobility and jewish piety will support with great heart Efraim Lifschitz, Dragunerstrasse 44 to send to Bornstein for Lifschitz.

In this letter directed to Regional Court Councillor Levysohn, Wolf Klatzke had heaped blunder upon blunder; he proved that he was still quite a long way from understanding how things are in Berlin. Otherwise he would have known better than to take the addresses simply from the long list of signatures on that pamphlet he had found among the old newspapers at Bornstein's for the letters he sent on behalf of Yossel's interests at the behest of Berl Weinstein. What had impressed him was the run of impressive-sounding titles he found listed there, and he had carefully selected the most promising after skimming through the pamphlet, which seemed to confirm that he was working here with just the sort of suitable human material he needed.

The pamphlet was titled:

> To the liberal-thinking members
> Of the Berlin Jewish Community

and in urgent phrases advocated voting only for the liberal candidates to the chamber of representatives of the Jewish community in the coming election. Above all, the undersigned notables of the community warned everyone with concerned gravity against the temptations and ploys of that certain recent loud and inflammatory movement calling itself "Jewish national" that was unfortunately now showing up in Berlin. "For the sake of our holy religion," the pamphlet said, "we protest against any falsification of the beliefs of our ancestors. Only the deepest comprehension of our creed as the ethical basis of our moral community of all citizens' desire and action, unalterably bound with our dear Fatherland, fully and completely guarantees us the religious meaning of our true

Jewish being and finally, despite everything written about it, is still misunderstood by those who wish us ill or are poorly informed. If even our own religious nest is befouled by those from the ranks of those confessing the Mosaic belief of the Israelite faith through a failure to recognize all Jewish contributions in literature, this deserves to be more prominent, and our religion must be protected to a greater extent to oppose those demagogic elements, and it expects as surety the support of all true liberals."

So it was, of course, quite reasonable that Klatzke, who wasn't yet familiar with Berlin politics and the jargon of the German-Jewish party organizations, understood the pamphlet as saying that here pious, observant Jews of Berlin were defending themselves against innovators and reformers of any kind. He rejoiced to find so easily a list of people able to cough up money who apparently were the support of old synagogues, upright, engaged, pious Jews, and were certainly inclined to help a pious Jewish scholar who had gotten into difficulty. But he had taken the word "liberal" as meaning the same as "pious."

He then composed the letter accordingly.

How could he know that among all the names appearing under the exhortation there was scarcely a single one who cared about the Sabbath or the dietary commandments, scarcely one who cared about Jewish erudition—and only a few who even had more serious Jewish interests at all—that most of them year in and year out did not bother with Jewish matters at all and that they had signed the pamphlet in part simply to do a personal favor, but also in part out of irritation about the new Jewish party, whose strident appearance on the scene was threatening the discretion with which Jewish affairs had been handled until now.

And, most significantly, how could Wolf Klatzke know that Regional Court Councillor Levysohn on the Matthäikirchstrasse, who had made such an earnest effort a few months ago by signing this pamphlet to protect the Jewish faith—that this very guardian of that which is sacred, if he even was still inclined to accept the role of protector of religion, would be obliged now to transfer his protection to the Protestant Church if need be. Just after the pamphlet had been distributed he had withdrawn his membership from the Jewish faith and converted, along with his family, to the state church; he was no longer the regional court councillor, he was the regional court director—his name was no longer Levysohn; his name was now, with sovereign permission, Lehnsen.

But he still was living at Matthäikirchstrasse 8 because his lease ran for two more years, and it wasn't as easy to cancel as the contract that tradition had handed down a long time ago on Mount Sinai. So it was that his Old Testament past was still known among the staff in the house and in the neighborhood, and so it was that Wolf Klatzke's letter arrived at the right address, the postman showing the envelope around the neighborhood with a smirk, brightening briefly the existence of the porter's family, as well as a number of both male and female servants.

THREE

A Pious Fund

I

The Lehnsen family was drinking its morning coffee.

The Regional Court Director was reading the daily newspaper, the *Deutsche Tageszeitung,* with a furrowed brow—his wife was dedicating herself with devotion to her meal—Elsa was amusing herself by fabricating funny little figures out of bread crumbs, toothpicks, and tissue paper—Heinz had already left the table to sit in a rocking chair off to the side and was smoking one cigarette after another.

"Don't forget, Heinz!" his mother said. "Check to see if there's anything in the *Tageblatt!*"

"Ghastly!" Elsa said. "Now we only hear if there's anything new when Heinz comes back from court!—This *Tageszeitung* Papa is reading!—Don't you think, Mama, that our intellects are atrophying?"

"I have to do this for my position!" the Director said, listening only with half an ear.

Elsa laughed.

"And people speak of the unworldliness of judges!" said Heinz. "We have sworn off reading Theodor Wolff and converted to Oertel, who single-handedly makes us happy. We have to make sacrifices for our beliefs."

"—and now gets his solid, well-founded views from Oertel instead of Wolff!" Elsa laughed.

"What kind of nonsense is that, Elsa!" her mother asked reprovingly. "Who are these people: Oertel and Wolff?"

"You know Loeser & Wolff!" Heinz said gravely. "They are the cornerstones of Berlin: Oertel and Wolff are the pillars of public opinion.—I draw my supplies from neither of these firms! I find their products are alike as coals."

"This drivel is impossible to listen to!" said the Regional Court Director churlishly. "Just stop this silly joking. That only reminds us of our—of times past.—That's probably still the influence of your beloved *Tageblatt:* just read this editorial here—"

"Oh good heavens!" said Elsa. "Mother and I, we get our intellectual sustenance strictly from the personal notices. And now we must depend on Heinz to know whether someone interesting has died and who is counted as one of the lost by becoming engaged.—That's why we both always grabbed directly for the financial daily, the *Handelsblatt.*—It's not at all a bad joke of the *Tageblatt* to have the engagements right after the other business news.—Joseph and I, we absolutely have to be in the *Handelsblatt* too when it's time.—Hey, Heinz! What does one actually call civil assistant attorneys now?"

"Child! How you do talk!" said Frau Lehnsen. "If you would just leave that be when we have guests. Recently, Leah had—"

"Oh! Leah!—Joseph is only happy when I'm showing off!"

There was a moment of silence.

"Mama!" Heinz suddenly said. "Mama! Would you have any objection if I set up a flea circus in my room?"

Elsa burst out laughing.

The Director rattled the paper violently but did not emerge from behind the pages.

Frau Lehnsen was so frightened that a piece of cake stuck in her mouth. When she caught her breath again she said angrily, "You can scare a body to death with your crazy ideas!—Whatever is that supposed to achieve?"

"One has to do something," Heinz said negligently but seriously. "I feel the need to do something in one sort of field or another. That's why I want to train fleas; this makes more sense than a so-called professional occupation.—Sport is fashionable right now: but I don't care much for horses—I require something more subtle! I certainly can't train dogs; so I prefer to just get some fleas.—I want to create new ways in general for animal trainers to follow! What sort of cultural value is there in keeping animals in cages after they have completed their academic training? One must continue to trap new individuals and then train them—those that have been trained must be set free so that they can spread education and enlightenment among their tribal colleagues."

"Meshuga!" Frau Lehnsen exclaimed.

"Splendid!" Elsa laughed. "That must be very nice when you catch a flea and it suddenly begins to do clever tricks—dancing or marching—"

"Tell me, Heinz! Are you serious?" Frau Lehnsen asked hesitantly.

Brother and sister laughed.

"I never know with you!" Frau Lehnsen said, reassured. "I cannot comprehend how either of you can even let such words out of your mouth."

"Oh, that's an unfounded prejudice." Heinz said. "Yesterday I saw the little beasts for the first time in large numbers, and they were very well behaved.—I was at a flea circus at the amusement park in Grünau—"

"Why didn't you take me, Heinz?" Elsa asked.

"That would have been difficult. I already had someone with me—"

"Tilli?" Elsa asked, perking up.

"Elsa!" the mother cried out, scandalized.

Elsa shrugged her shoulders.

At that moment, Sophie, the parlor maid, brought in the mail; she put the letters in front of the master of the house and began slowly to clear the table.

"Joseph must of course show me that too, Heinz," Elsa said. "You have to tell me where this establishment is! That is something special for Joseph! So he can shock Leah afterward!"

"You can clear things later," Frau Lehnsen said, and Sophie withdrew slowly. "Elsa, I think you don't always need to talk about Leah and Joseph in front of the maid. She's probably imagining—"

Sophie entered again, supposedly to retrieve a forgotten tray.

"Heinz," Elsa said and nudged him in the ribs, "remind me when Sandersleben is coming—"

"What impertinence!" the Director said angrily and crumpled the letter in his hand, looking around for the maid.

She disappeared quickly from the room.

"Sandersleben!" Frau Lehnsen said. "What that sounds like! The girl certainly thinks—"

"Yes, how should I put it then?" Elsa asked innocently. "I can't do anything about Herr Baron von Stülp-Sandersleben having the biblical name of Joseph and that his sister is named Leah."

"These people can get away with having such names," Frau Lehnsen said.

"What that sounds like!" Elsa said. "Joseph—comma—Freiherr von Stülp—hyphen—Sandersleben! Two punctuation marks in a name! I'll have him on the basis of the comma alone! Joseph—comma!"

"Just read this letter!" said the Director as he stood up to begin a promenade around the room. "And just look at the address! Such an impertinent familiarity!"

Elsa snatched the envelope to see for herself. She read "to misser reegionl court judg" and laughed easily. "That's why Sophie didn't want to leave the room. She wanted to see the effect!"

"Impertinent person!" the Director growled.

"And I thought she was flirting with me!" Heinz complained.

Frau Lehnsen had quickly skimmed the letter and tossed it on the table, her face bright red.

"I hope, Adolf," she said, "you aren't going to let this go! The man must be punished as an example.—and then you must file a complaint with the post office! How could the mailman bring you that letter. Our name is *Lehnsen*! He's making a fool of himself!"

"I'll take good care," the Director exclaimed, "not to make a big issue of the matter!—But of course downstairs everyone is amusing himself royally!—This pushy rabble—schnorrer riffraff—never lets go!—Whoever accepts such a letter from now on will be dismissed!"

"Would you prefer," asked Heinz, who had in the meantime read the letter, "if Herr Ephraim Lifschitz would show you the personal honor of a visit?"

"That's just what I need!" the Director exploded, standing still. "I will hand the first Jewish schnorrer who shows up here over to the police. I'm sure I'll have peace and quiet once and for all from that gangster!"

"But the letter is just charming!" cried Elsa with a burst of laughter. "The spelling! Priceless! I have to show this to Joseph—and Leah—"

"Don't you dare!" Frau Lehnsen said angrily.

"The poor devil must have gone to a great deal of effort with such a style of writing," Heinz said. "And maybe he really is a poor man!—I would like to send him something."

"I'll give something too!" Elsa said.

"You're crazy!" the Director said.—Before he could say another word, Sophie stepped into the room and announced with careful emphasis, "Herr Rabbi Dr. Magnus! Herr Professor Dr. Hirsch!"

Delighted, Elsa sprang to her feet. "Magnus? Darling Magnus?!"

"Show the gentlemen into my study," said the Director. "And ask them to have a seat for the time being."

Sophie disappeared.

Elsa bounced toward her father.

"What does Magnus want with you?—You don't want to convert back to Judaism, do you?"

"You are really crazy!" Lehnsen said, flying off the handle.

"No, Papa!" Heinz said gravely. "If you want to change your faith again, I would advise waiting until after the regional court president is named. If you were to change again, you would be sure of being the only Jewish president of the highest distinction that Israel has to offer."

Lehnsen gave an annoyed chuckle.

"The thought isn't so stupid!—"

"Don't you want to tend to your guests?" Frau Lehnsen asked. "You just can't leave the gentlemen waiting so long; they should keep their good mood."

"Let them wait a bit!" Lehnsen said. "Hirsch and Magnus are probably exchanging blows by now. That suits my purpose just fine!"

"Hirsch! Magnus!" Heinz said in bewilderment. "Your list of visitors today seems rather on the denominational side."

"Yes—today's the meeting of the board of trustees of your grandfather's foundation.—Besides me, his last will and testament named as members of the board a rabbi from the Jewish community and a scholar from the rabbinical seminary.—I had wanted to resign when I—when we completed our conversion, but Mama was of the opinion that was what her father would have wanted—"

"Most certainly not!" Frau Lehnsen said. "My late father wanted you to be involved with these charitable sorts of things, and charity is interdenominational—"

"Oh, that's the foundation—the stipend for a pious Jewish rabbinical candidate?" Heinz asked. "And you are still a trustee?"

"Nonsense!" Frau Lehnsen said briskly. "There's nothing in the will about Jewish and nothing about a rabbi. I made sure of that when the will was being written.—"

"Yes," said the Director uncomfortably. "As an attorney, I crafted the language as my father-in-law wanted, and then I just added the words 'for a pious student who wants to devote himself to a spiritual profession.'—Father trusted me completely, and I wasn't thinking of anything bad! I only didn't want the whole thing to look so specifically Jewish—especially on account of the people at court!"

"In effect, nothing is actually changed!" Heinz said carefully.

"Yes—things have changed a bit, as you all know!" Lehnsen said as he paced up and down. "For example, there's the candidate Ostermann, in whom Frau von Stülp-Sandersleben takes an interest. It seems that he is a very deserving young man, strictest church inclination—"

"Frau Sandersleben emphatically wants him to get the stipend," Frau Lehnsen said. "And she can demand this in a way. Leah is no longer all that young—they don't have money; later he can count on a parish once he has his studies behind him. And since Joseph and our Elsa will be united—the stipend stays in the family, so to speak."

"Yes, but whether that's what Father intended," the Director wondered, "is a question. Indeed, times have changed!—But this young man, Kaiser—from the rabbinical seminary—his recommendations are excellent. His father is the rabbi in a small community in southern Germany; his people don't have much extra for him—"

"But Adolf," Frau Lehnsen was outraged, "you absolutely promised me—and even Frau Sandersleben herself yesterday. She will probably come by afterward to hear the news."

"When I promise something, I keep my word," Lehnsen said sulkily. "But I am in a difficult position: I'm one person against two!"

And with that he went to his meeting.

"Say hello to darling Magnus for me!" cried Elsa after him.—"Should I wait for him in the hallway afterward?—We were all in love with him in our confirmation class."

"I still recall his dinner conversations in the evenings quite well," said Heinz. "From the home that knows how to happily join the old and honorable tradition of Israel with the modern spirit—from loyalty to the parents and steadfastness to faith."

"It was a delicate matter having him," Frau Lehnsen said. "He ate no meat, and I had to invite the Pinkus family and the Gersons just for him so that he could sit between them and no one would really notice."

"He wrote a maxim in my prayer book that I was honored to receive from him—that he gave me 'as your guiding star, my dear child!' What was that he wrote again? Yes! 'Children are their parents' pride—but the children's happiness is the glory of the parents!'—I think Joseph appreciates this too—the parents' reward!"

II

Dr. Magnus and Professor Hirsch had met on the Potsdam Bridge.—The Professor was standing on the streetcar platform when he saw the Rabbi, who was trying to attract attention by vigorously waving his shiny top hat. He crossed the street from the tram stop—the hat in his left hand, armed with an umbrella, and stretching out his right from afar to greet the Professor; his red cheeks beamed from his coal-black, well-trimmed beard, his face shining with amiability and joy.

"My dear honored Herr Professor!" he cried and heartily shook the hand offered to him. "My honored Herr Professor!—How nice that we meet here!— I'm happy to see how well you look!—You are becoming younger every day as your energy takes on more and more duties. Your new article in the *Annual Review* is phenomenal; it throws a whole new light on the history of suffixes of praenomina—"

"You've read my article?" the Professor asked suspiciously. "I'm surprised that you have time to read scholarly articles with all your different responsibilities."

"Yes, unfortunately—unfortunately! It had always been my ideal to devote myself entirely to my studies! But it's still my ideal!—Impossible, like all ideals!— One has so many calls on one's time—from everyone!—What can you do! One is simply a slave! The General Command just called on me, for example—about the preparation of recruits for defense; that took up some time.—and so many meetings and lectures—and the lodge: I absolutely must take over the presidency for the Association for the Improvement of—of—now I've forgotten what the Association is: but something is supposed to be improved!—There's the house over there, Herr Professor!"

"You know your way around here, Rabbi?"

"Do I know my way around here! I used to come here frequently! Earlier!—Yes, it makes me quite sad when I go up these steps I know so well!—Bad, bad times for our Jewish community!"

"I find it repugnant!" said the Professor, stopping on the landing and thumping his walking stick. "Just repugnant that circumstances compel me to enter the house of this *baptized* person."

"Perhaps it's even harder for me, my dear Herr Professor!" Magnus said with a sigh. "I have memories of this house. I attended all the special ceremonies held at home! Really, our best people are abandoning us!—But today here we are, Herr Professor!—We cannot leave the Regional Court Director waiting!"

"Ten horses couldn't drag me here if it weren't a question of rescuing the stipend for our good Kaiser!" grumbled Hirsch, going up the rest of the steps.

The parlor maid opened the door to let the gentlemen in; Dr. Magnus gave their names with a soulful look and went into the Regional Court Director's study, bright with the sun shining through the three windows.—

Magnus glanced nervously at the Professor.

"Honored Herr Professor!" he said, somewhat embarrassed, smiling affably. "Excuse me for pointing it out to you: You must be distracted and have forgotten to put out your cigar. Apart from the fact that the gentleman of the house has an excellent brand of cigar on hand—I assume he's more loyal to this estimable custom than to our faith.—Could you possibly be so good as to—"

"I'll just continue to smoke my cigar," Hirsch said briskly. "I'm not on any social call to a *baptized* Jew; I view this meeting purely as a business matter; I am attending a board of trustees meeting. Duty demands this of me, and I cannot do anything about the fact that Herr Regional Court Director considers it polite as the presiding officer of the board to compel me to enter his home. There's no such thing as social ties between him and me, and I won't let any sort of constraint be put on what I usually do in my relations with him."

The short, white-bearded professor was puffing away angrily; as each tiny cloud of smoke that was propelled into the air slowly expired with a wobble against the ceiling, each puff seemed an act of protest.

"And I think it outrageous that you presume to let this Levysohn—as he was named at birth—offer me cigars!" he added in a rage. "But of course don't be upset by this!"

"But my dear Herr Professor!" Dr. Magnus said, abashed. "How can you distress yourself so over such a harmless remark. Nothing is further from my mind than any inappropriate tolerance for those who betray our faith. I too plan to behave strictly on the basis of cool politeness!"

"I think the Herr Director has been letting us cool our heels long enough in the antechamber," said Hirsch, outraged as he glanced at the clock. "I have taken sufficient notice of the Madonna and *The Casting Out of the Moneychangers* that he's put in front of our noses to display his conversion!"

"The pictures have been here for years," Magnus said. "These are just works put up here for their artistic value—without regard for the subject."

"So! Artworks!—Without regard for the subject!—Right, and there's now supposed to be artistically executed pictures of the new Jewish apostle—who made our entire Jewish youth rebellious. I'd like to know what the head of your Jewish community would say if you were to hang a picture of Dr. Herzl above your desk for the sake of its artistic value!"

"But my dear Herr Professor! What are we saying!—A picture of the Zionist leader in the home of a rabbi would be absurd.—But in our case only simple tolerance is called for—"

"Nonsense! Your sort of tolerance or whatever you want to call it annoys me.— You are willing to go into those homes and sit down at the table under pictures of saints where you cannot partake of a meal, smoke good cigars, and give speeches in praise of the Jewish host; you just let it go!—Just make Judaism nice and easy for people—so it can't upset anyone in any way or draw any sort of unpleasant attention. Until the good people forget what it is and they take the final step!—Then of course—then you are flabbergasted, wring your hands, are stricken with grief, and scream bloody murder!—You beat your own breast! You alone are to blame— You and all those lukewarm people with their famous so-called tolerance."

"Pardon, Herr Professor!" Dr. Magnus said, annoyed. "You are upset and quite unfair about the increasing frequency of baptism. I understand and share your grief, and so I don't take what you've just said amiss."

"Nonsense—'Take amiss'!—I speak my mind!—How could such a family sink so low so quickly!—I knew the father of the lady of the family quite well when he was still a teacher in the province of Posen; he was a competent man, he worked hard, and he became exceedingly wealthy. He had something to do with the emigrants and was first a border agent for an emigration agency—he had opportunities there for all sorts of business—well, he became rich, but he didn't forget his Judaism.—The proof: the foundation that is bringing us together here!— and the man paid the expenses for the son-in-law, this Levysohn, to complete his studies—the young man was very poor, an orphan;—then he married the daughter.—How did these people come to slide into Christianity?—Because they were caught in your wake!—The old man was an Orthodox Jew who was strictly observant!"

"And just how are these people caught in this 'wake'? How did they slip away from you and your faction and land in mine, which you consider to be so pernicious.—You are just putting into words what you are convinced of, that those of us who represent a more conciliatory and milder approach are responsible for conversions. Permit me now to make a comment, and please don't misunderstand!—In my opinion it's your faction, strictly speaking—it's the Orthodox that are primarily responsible for the terrible increase in conversions.—"

"Just stop!" shouted the Professor.

"Pardon, Herr Professor! I don't mean you personally, of course. The honor and respect I have for one of the pillars of our Jewish scholarship—that's you! Without a doubt!—My feelings of honor and respect are way too deep for me to permit myself to criticize you personally. I was speaking in general! And I must say: sharp edges can wound! Many people are pushed away by the cold rigidity of an Orthodoxy that rejects any concession to the spirit of the day!—They make it very difficult for people—they make life almost impossible. The Sabbath commandments! The dietary commandments! Commandments everywhere, whose great historical value I personally highly value and to which I am glad to submit. But we must have sympathy for what is modern—we must bridge the abyss—and seek the middle way between law and life—so that everything doesn't get lost all at once—the important along with the unimportant—the important thing with the unimportant things—"

"Nothing is unimportant!" Hirsch exclaimed.

"There is certainly a difference whether I fail to observe the Day of Atonement or whether I carry a pocket handkerchief on the Sabbath!"

"But you carry an umbrella on the Sabbath!" Hirsch shouted.

"Permit me, Herr Professor! What I personally do doesn't depend on—"

"But it depends on exactly that!—There is nothing that is unimportant!—It is the deed, not the word, that is of value, not what people say. All your nice sermons are not worth a farthing without the deed that underlies the word!"

"I sincerely regret your derogatory criticism of what I do as a speaker; I can only say as far as I am concerned that my point of view, which differs from yours, never would mislead me to subjectively evaluate your scholarly work.—"

"But you don't understand my work!" the Professor exclaimed passionately. "You can't even understand it! No one can understand it who hasn't immersed himself in the study of the grammar of Oriental languages and the special area of suffixes!"

"Please, your brilliant account of the origin of suffixes—"

"Can only be appreciated by specialists!—But not by someone who has to bury three Jews a day and mourn twice that number and at best can only devote time to satisfy his scholarly needs that he has on the journey from one to the other. This is the superficiality that you are all accustomed to when you judge things."

"Herr Professor, you are in a mood that makes a discussion not exactly pleasant."

"I do not see why we should continue! I'm leaving now. I'm not the house fool for this baptized convert!"

But at that moment the Regional Court Director entered.

III

"Excuse me, gentlemen," said the Regional Court Director courteously, "for un-avoidably keeping you waiting.—How are you, Herr Doctor?"

He held out his hand to the Rabbi; the Professor crossed his hands behind his back, and the Director extended his half-offered hand toward the cigar box.

"Will the gentlemen help themselves?"

"Thanks. I smoke my own cigar," the Professor said in an irritated tone of voice. "But the good Rabbi has praised your excellent tobacco. Allow me."

He took the cigar box with a jerk, opened it, and offered it to the Rabbi, his eyes flashing angrily through his spectacles. "Please."

"I've already mentioned to the worthy Professor Hirsch," Magnus said, blush-ing, "that a cold compels me to deny myself the pleasure of smoking for a while—as much as I have always esteemed your choice of tobacco!"

"Yes," Lehnsen said, who was glad to postpone a conversation about the topic of the meeting for a bit. "You were always, when you visited, a much-honored guest; I almost said a dear one," he continued with a friendly smile, "because you usually robbed me for some sort of pious purpose. I ask you not to pass by my house in the future. In the matter of charity nothing of course has changed with me.—Charity must be done on equal terms!"

Magnus bowed without saying a word.

"Yes," the Director went on. "We happily think of you. Just this morning my daughter mentioned your name with special pleasure."

Magnus bowed again, visibly flattered.

"Very gracious of the young lady!" he said. "I can also only say that the lessons back then gave me deep satisfaction. The unusual talents of your daughter—her serious, steady nature—her deep piety—"

He paused and turned beet red.

The Director cleared his throat. The Professor sat there smiling grimly. "Gen-tlemen!" he said. "I sincerely regret that I must interrupt your exchange of pleas-antries. I do assume that you'll find the opportunity to continue. My time, how-ever, is limited, and we are going to begin already later than I planned.—If you please, shall we get down to work?"

Embarrassed, Dr. Magnus slid back and forth and stared out the window.

"Excuse me!" Lehnsen said coldly. "Let's go directly in medias res. I hope the matter won't take all too long—assuming that you agree with my suggestions, which I trust you will.—I had the files circulated: there are, as you know, two applications for the approved stipend—one is the philosophy student Jacob Kai-ser and the other is the theology student Gustav Ostermann. Both candidates have equally good recommendations and seem to perform well in their field. Their chances by themselves would logically be equal, since both competitors appear to be equally in need of financial support.—I am of the opinion," he bent over the files and continued in a raised, almost rumbling voice, "that Ostermann should be awarded the stipend under these circumstances. After all, there is only one to award! Now Ostermann is a Christian—a theologian in training. I do not need to emphasize that this circumstance is not decisive for me. I know I am not only free of anti-Semitic attitudes—that is of course self-evident!—but I am even proud in a way that—that I myself—you get the picture, gentlemen!— But—for that very reason! Matters of charity must be handled with fairness, as I mentioned before—definitely! Up until now, as you can see for yourself, only Israelites have been awarded the stipend since the foundation was established; certainly for the sake of appearances, it seems to me to be called for that when a Christian young man applies for the first time as far as I know, we consider him with special care.—Moreover, there's to be taken into consideration that there is such a large number of exclusively Jewish foundations that the young man Kaiser will certainly find a chance to win a stipend there.—Are the gentlemen agreed?"

The Professor stood up and started to leave.

Dr. Magnus leaped between them nervously. "Just a moment, Herr Professor! —It would perhaps be useful to look at the foundation's charter to see who may be an applicant.—As far as I know, the stipend is strictly for rabbinical students, and quite frankly I have been wondering about this application from Herr Ostermann."

"The foundation's charter," Lehnsen said with ill humor, "speaks only of a 'pious student who wishes to dedicate his life to a spiritual vocation.'—This generally worded provision just proves that it is not restricted to a follower of the Mosaic faith. Finally, as the son-in-law of the founder and as the actual executor of his testament, I am also the first one called and duty-bound to interpret it!"

"You are duty-bound to resign your position at once," the Professor spluttered. "You should have done that long ago—right after you converted. Your own sense of tact alone should have told you!"

"You will allow, Herr Professor," Lehnsen said coldly, "that I am the judge of that, and above all I do not permit anyone to make the rules in questions of social tact—not even you. Please do not forget that you are my guest—"

"The devil if I'm your guest!—I protest most vigorously against calling me a guest!—We are at a board meeting of the foundation, and this is its meeting room!—and I will not permit my statutory right to be abridged!—You know as well as I that the late founder never in his whole life would have even thought of supporting Christian theology. How this more than remarkable language came to be in the charter is something perhaps you as the son-in-law and legal advisor are in the best position to explain."

"That goes too far, Herr Professor!" the Rabbi said, trying to smooth things over. "We certainly don't want to insinuate that the Regional Court Director has subverted the intention of his father-in-law."

"So you take his side?!" Hirsch exclaimed. "Better and better! It had to come to this!—Just what I never expected!—I'm certainly not needed here, then!"

And abruptly he turned to go. Magnus restrained him.

"You are too hot-tempered, dear Herr Professor!" he said, upset. "You don't want to listen.—I am absolutely of the same opinion as you that we are a completely Jewish foundation—at least for now, until I am shown evidence to the contrary. I certainly even hope to persuade our dear Herr President of the error of his opinion."

"In that case, Herr Regional Court Director Levysohn—pardon me! Lehnsen —won't be changing his opinion so quickly," Hirsch said grimly, but he turned around. "I move that we take a vote."

"Herr Professor!" Lehnsen now protested. "Your manner of conduct does not exactly contribute to reconciling differences.—You are pleased to make precipitate remarks and biting comments. I have neither the inclination nor the vocation to teach you tolerance and understanding for a point of view that differs from your own.—But I will say one thing to you in this matter: you and your sort are the ones increasing the numbers of those turning away from your religion. Your fanaticism repels, even if its source is honorable and, as far as I'm concerned, noble. You seek artificially to create isolation—you want to lock your coreligionists away from the existing world—you seek to build a wall around your community; but life is stronger than anything you construct. And success tells us this is so! You and the men of your type are just unteachable!"

Dr. Magnus cleared his throat softly and smiled triumphantly at the Professor.

"I don't believe," he said, "that a discussion with you on this topic has any practical value. My time for theoretical discussions is at a premium.—Let's stay with the agenda, please."

"I too consider that to be the correct thing to do," Lehnsen said, "and I invite you gentlemen to take your seats again.—I have explained my own views to you. Herr Professor Hirsch has certainly stated his opinion with all possible clarity. The decision depends on you, Rabbi. I put it to you again to consider all elements with complete objectivity—"

"I'm in a painful position, then," Dr. Magnus said. "I believe that my objectivity and my tolerance are unquestionable; I have never been a—fanatic—or a party lackey.—"

"I know that, Herr Doctor!" Lehnsen said warmly. "I've always admired you on that point. And that's why you enjoy the greatest affection everywhere.—I hope my appeal to you succeeds for just that reason! How often have you sat at my table speaking of the brotherhood of all humankind—you praised the quotidian love of humankind that embraces everything in splendid and truly edifying words that didn't stop at any barrier of religious confession. I recall your remarks on the theme: Are we not all the children of one Father?—I tell you, I was so proud then in front of my Christian guests that a clergyman of my religion spoke in that way.—You cannot wish to repudiate those words now and score a notch for fanaticism and intolerance.—I know that for certain, Herr Rabbi. You surely don't wish to rob me of my trust in the truth of the opinion you held at that time!—I have remained the same person I have been; I agree with what you indicated at the time as the essence of all religions—still one thing.—Where I've changed is that the name for the thing is different, not the thing itself!"

"Aha!" the Professor exulted. "I congratulate the Rabbi! Here you see what has come of your famous tolerance!"

Dr. Magnus went into a rage. "Herr Professor! I must object to this treatment—gentlemen!—Herr Regional Court Director!—You are entirely mistaken about me!—You cannot assume that I excuse such a step, much less approve of it. And you will be so good as to not refer to me. I assume of course that you do not intend to destroy my reputation.—If someone can be that misunderstood—indeed, every possibility of successful activity becomes impossible for the likes of us!—"

"Herr Rabbi!" Lehnsen said. "I didn't want to start a debate about this topic. I—"

"Yes, please forgive me, Herr Regional Court Director. But it has now become a matter of honor for me to prevent any possible distortions.—I must ask you to swear in the presence of Herr Professor Hirsch that I have never betrayed the flag of my belief in your house—"

"But Herr Rabbi! Of course not! I even said—"

"You hinted after a fashion that your conversion had not changed your spiritual relationship to religion and that your views conformed to mine. It is inexplicable to me how you could say such a thing!—I can only say to you when I heard of your conversion that it was a stab in my heart.—I most categorically condemn the step you took—at least as much as the Professor; giving up one's ancestral religion is under any circumstance—"

"Just what have I given up? Explain that!" Lehnsen exclaimed, drawing himself up. "Don't beat around the bush! Since the day I was baptized I haven't changed one iota who I am. I am the same person I always was and whom you have known for years. I've never played hide-and-seek.—There's absolutely no difference at all in any aspect of ethics or morals between an enlightened Jew and an enlightened Christian. I haven't observed the commandments for rituals for a long time, and you've seen that directly for yourselves. Since there's no longer any difference at all between me and my non-Jewish fellow citizens—or do you believe that Judaism is something other than a religious matter?—Have you so fundamentally changed your views, Dr. Magnus, that you are acknowledging a Jewish *nation*?"

"Heaven forbid!" the Rabbi said, horrified.

"There you are! I have just drawn the rational conclusion from which you and many Jews shrink out of a sort of piety—for reasons I respect even if I am unable to make them my own.—I didn't subscribe to any dogmas when I converted. I believe no more and no less than hundreds of thousands of Christians and Jews here in Berlin.—The state in which we live is, after all, a Christian state; with no pressure on my conscience, I could have my name assigned from one enrollment register to another.—It is perhaps even a sort of sacrifice on my part—do not underestimate that, gentlemen! A sacrifice I willingly undertook in the interest of the whole. I subordinated myself to certain humiliations—I tore myself from many a dearly held memory—I slashed the tie between me and many of my cherished friends, and I know just how much I have exposed myself to misconstrued opinions of all sorts that are, alas, fashionable; so many people consider my act to be social climbing without a conscience—a renegade—a traitor—and who knows what else. But whoever, as you do, Herr Rabbi, wishes that the boundaries would disappear among the citizens of our German folk, he must, if he is honest, approve and support anyone who feels himself to be entirely one with all the folk, which is externally validated by confessing the state religion.—I have fulfilled my duty to myself, my family, and the state, and in my opinion I have not breached any duty to my former coreligionists. Whoever truly and devoutly holds fast to the Jewish faith has my respect; however, whoever has long since lost his inner faith and holds fast to it out of inertia or of fear of being misunderstood is incomprehensible to me. I had especially expected that you, Herr Rabbi, would understand. I was wrong! Unfortunately!—Perhaps you are really infected by the Zionists and are a Jewish nationalist!—"

"Me?" the Rabbi exclaimed, outraged. "I protest against such an insinuation most emphatically!"

"There you go. You've gotten rid of your sermon, Herr Rabbi!" the Professor said, quite satisfied. "That's what comes of your tolerance!"

"No—your fanaticism!" Magnus exclaimed, incensed.

"Only the strictest observance of God's commandments of our Torah—" the Professor exclaimed.

"Above all there is belief!" the Rabbi exclaimed. "Tell me yourself, Herr Regional Court Director, can ritual alone satisfy someone who lacks faith?"

"And Herr Director," thundered Hirsch, "was belief without ritual able to sustain belief in your house? Was there anything recognizably Jewish?"

"Gentlemen!" Lehnsen said quietly. "I don't think that I'm the competent authority to decide Jewish differences between you.—Let's return to our agenda and vote!"

"I've been trying to do that for some time!" the Professor said.

"Well, gentlemen, we conclude! I vote for Ostermann!"

"I vote for Kaiser!" the Professor said.

"And you, Herr Rabbi?" Lehnsen asked, bending over the files.

"I too vote for Kaiser!" the Rabbi said and stood up to tug at his collar.

"Good!" Lehnsen said. "Two votes for and one against! Kaiser will be awarded the stipend.—Done!—I might ask you, Herr Rabbi, to make the appropriate announcement to the young man. I would like to have as little to do with the matter as possible and reserve the opportunity to truly resign the chairmanship in the near future.—That should be welcome to you too!—Good morning, gentlemen!"

He made a formal bow without offering his hand to the Rabbi.

The Professor left with heavy steps—apparently quite pleased with himself and the results of the meeting. The Rabbi followed in confusion that increased as he crossed paths with a very elegant young lady in the entry hall.

The lady stopped and looked at him with a gay expression. "Don't you recognize your former pupil any longer, Herr Rabbi?"

"Oh—Fräulein Levysohn—"

"Close enough, Herr Doctor!—No matter!—Yes, we have all changed a bit. But you look just the same as when we all fancied you."

"Oh—Fräulein!"

"But you certainly knew that.—All the girls in the confirmation class were in love with you, and that's still true. Something of the confirmation lessons still sticks!—So I'm very happy to see you again—very! Adieu, Herr Doctor!"

And then Dr. Magnus went down the stairs too, consoled and satisfied with himself.

IV

Soon after the Director had gone into the board meeting, Baroness von Stülp-Sandersleben along with Joseph and Leah were seated in the salon. They were waiting for the results of the meeting. Heinz had to slip out to go to court.

Elsa and Joseph were sitting in the bay window; Joseph was recounting all sorts of racy stories from the club—Elsa added droll comments, and they were amusing themselves royally.

It was less jolly in the opposite corner, where the two older ladies and Leah were sitting.—The conversation was tedious and dragged, and all three listened in the direction of the door to the study, where the murmur of voices reached them from time to time.

"The gentlemen are rather loud," the Baroness said. "It seems as if they aren't all that much in agreement as you believe, Frau Lehnsen."

"Oh, please!" said the lady addressed, herself somewhat disquieted. "Dr. Magnus has eaten so often at our house—it's all so obvious—"

"Dr. Magnus—that's the rabbi—no?" asked the Baroness. "I would have liked so much to have seen him once.—I once knew a rabbi; he came every now and then to my father's at the castle; Jews on the border often got into all sorts of difficulties—smuggling and such. My father would put in a good word with the Russian border officials; they all were visitors in our home. We children had fun with the old man—but he was a little bit peculiar to us children, with his long, unkempt full beard, his huge fur hat, the long caftan, and his bushy eyebrows. The peasants said he could do witchcraft.—Does Dr. Magnus also look like that?"

"Oh my, not in the least," Frau Lehnsen said, embarrassed.

"Tell me, dear Frau Lehnsen," Fräulein Leah said, "is it true that Jewish clergy are all vegetarians?"

"Certainly not!"

"Why would you ever think that?" the Baroness said. "The old rabbi sometimes even brought us a sausage; it was such a treat for us children. And here in Berlin there are so many butcher shops with the Hebrew letters—three letters! What's the word?"

"You must know, Frau Lehnsen!" Fräulein Leah said amiably.

"I—I think, yes—kosher or something like that."

"That's it—kosher," the Baroness said. "I knew that: kosher—and in German that means 'meat grocery.'—Do you still buy your meat there?"

"But we never did such a thing," Frau Lehnsen answered in a strained voice.

"My!—what you don't say! That is quite fascinating!—Yes, that is a matter of conviction; the sausage always tasted so good to me!"

"The gentlemen seem to be going!" Frau Lehnsen exclaimed with a sigh of relief.

"So—we'll now hear how things are with dear Ostermann!" the Baroness said as she trained her lorgnette toward the door.

"Just a moment!" Elsa said, jumping up. "Don't forget that story, Joseph; you were telling about Count Renknitz trying to cadge money from Gaby. I have to say hello to my dear Magnus."

"Oh, dear Frau Lehnsen!" Joseph said, walking to the table quickly. "I want to take this opportunity to talk to you. Mama has bought something for Elsa's birthday the day after tomorrow—I don't know if it's just the right thing for Elsa.—See for yourself."

He laid on the table a large plain cross on a thin silver chain.

Frau Lehnsen felt a little stab of fear.

"Very nice," she managed to say with an effort.

"Yes, isn't it?" the Baroness said. "I can't imagine what Joseph thinks could be wrong with it. I think it's simple and appropriate.—Elsa already has so many expensive pieces of jewelry—the likes of us can't keep up.—"

"Yes—it is really quite superfluous," Frau Lehnsen said quickly. "Elsa inherited so much jewelry from my late mother.—"

"But she certainly didn't inherit that," Leah said.

"That's just why we chose a cross," said the Baroness. "If you have no objections—"

"Me? What sort of objections would I—? A very pretty piece!—It will certainly be a great surprise!"

"You see, Joseph!" the Baroness said happily. "Frau Lehnsen doesn't think it tactless at all!—What ideas you have!—Just think, Joseph thought that the cross here would be a symbol of submission—"

"But, Mother! How can you—?"

"What?—It is certainly a symbol of humility!—and dear Elsa can now wear it with justified pride.—There they are! Put it away!"

Joseph pocketed the package in a surly mood as the Regional Court Director and Elsa came into the room.—

After having met the Rabbi, Elsa entered the room laughing.

"The sweet man Magnus is as sweet as ever," she exclaimed, "the perfect gingerbread man—and I wrapped him in glances and sighs until he became quite gentle.—I really didn't waste my time in confirmation class; it was just the right school for coquetry!"

"You should be ashamed of yourself, Elsa!" Lehnsen said, laughing irritably. "But who knows? If I'd only had your help, perhaps I could have persuaded him."

"What's the matter?" Elsa asked, becoming serious. "Did the matter with Ostermann go badly?"

"Yes, it did! Unfortunately!—Now I'll suffer the consequences for what happened in there!—It's annoying enough for me that I had to play this role!—You can just imagine that the matter made me uncomfortable. At the least it is disrespectful of your grandfather.—"

"Yes—after all, we're Christians now! One must make sacrifices for one's religion!"

"Well, really!" grumbled Lehnsen. "I didn't convert to play the martyr!—I could have done that with less effort."

With that he led the way into the salon.

"Dear Baroness!" he said as he strode toward her. "I deeply regret that I was unable to accomplish anything for your protégé. I did my utmost, but I was just outvoted!"

There followed an embarrassed silence.

"Well, damn!" Joseph said barely audibly and pulled Elsa back into the bay window.

"That's outrageous!" Frau Lehnsen exclaimed. "This organization!—They dispose of my father's money with no regard for anything!—It's no wonder that people are anti-Semitic!"

She bit her lip.

"But not at all, dearest Frau Lehnsen," the Baroness said. "We are, after all, Christians and withhold judgment. These people are trapped in their worldview, and we cannot begrudge them at all. Where should they have learned tact!—Nonetheless, I am very grateful to you, dear Lehnsen! I am sure you did all you could!—I am, of course, most sorry for Ostermann!—He will now have to find a Christian sponsor.—"

"Ostermann just doesn't have any luck!" Leah said in a tight voice. "He would have to have been born Jewish to get ahead as a Christian."

"There's something else that greatly bothers me!" the Baroness said with concern. "I've been able to restrain him from revealing his anti-Semitism until now. I'm afraid that this will give him the impetus to publish his articles criticizing Jewish immorality.—"

"But why didn't you say so earlier!" Frau Lehnsen cried. "I'm sure if he had known this, Dr. Magnus would have certainly voted for him—if only to prevent him from taking this step!—After all, he's on the board of the society whose sole mission it is to fight anti-Semitism."

"Well, there's nothing that can be done now," the Baroness said as she extended her hand with a gracious smile to take her leave. "It appears that we poor Germans don't understand which side our bread is buttered on!"

V

A few hours later Heinz entered his father's office in the regional court building and shoved a rather thick file under his nose. "Just look at this mess!"

"What's wrong?" the Director said and read the case name, *Pfeffer v. Boruch.*

"Your perfidious colleague Bandmann just gave me this file to report on. 'Dear colleague,' he said as he handed it to me, 'your department is probably the one to take over this appeal; I am unfamiliar with this subject; you are probably more familiar with it.' I immediately suspected something of what sort of topic was coming!"

"What's it about, then?"

"About a shipment of a type of fruit called esrogs or 'apples of paradise,' which seem to be used during the Jewish Feast of Tabernacles, where the congregants shake them in the synagogue—there seems to be a sort of dervish dance performed—and a number of stems seem to have fallen off with this shipment. The defendant refuses to pay, because he claims that the fruit cannot be used for this ritual if the stems are missing. He's called in experts. At trial level the complaint was denied on the basis of a number of reports from rabbinical experts. And Bandmann's given me the file because I'm supposed to be familiar with the subject!"

"Intolerable impertinence!—You must tell him that you are equally unfamiliar with the subject!"

"I'll do nothing of the kind! He knows that as well as I do! And he also knows of our baptism!—That's probably what even made him notice I was Jewish.—"

"But you know as little as he does about the subject of esrogs."

"Unfortunately. I'm really sorry!—I think if you're born a Jew, then you should certainly take a little bit of interest in your culture and history. I've read more about Indians and the Incas than about my own people."

"Your interest comes a bit late."

"That's the peculiar thing! I think I've become aware of my Jewishness only since I converted. It's the very act of leaving Judaism that was the first act of my life in which I took a position about the Jewish religion.—I actually acknowledged I was Jewish for the first time when I left Judaism."

"And now you want to study esrogs?"

"Well—in any case I'd like to know what the explanation for all this is. What are these strange holiday rituals? What's their origin?—I'd like to know something about Jewish history.—I even want to go into a synagogue and see what goes on there."

"Just be careful that you aren't seen as a backslider.—It could end badly for you!—I was almost insulted in my own house this morning!"

"Ah yes—the board meeting!—How did that go?"

"Ostermann didn't get it, and Judah won!"

"Oh Lord! Poor Leah!—But I can't really blame either of the Jews!"

"I can't either!—I would have probably done the same thing. If one goes strictly by the law, one had to vote as they did.—Your late grandfather was only thinking specifically of Jewish theologians!—But we were just forced to make concessions to maintain our position and to earn our emancipation.—"

"Our?—Us?"

"Naturally I'm talking from the point of view of Jews!—But that's true even for us!—We, who have happily taken the ultimate step and have renounced what hasn't made any sense to us for a long time, we have to fight all the more now for our position. For Bandmann you have now become *a Jew;* I must now prove that I have really left the Jewish community.—Today I almost envied Hirsch and Magnus, who can freely defend what they consider right without a care or thought of what others think."

"Did they do that?"

"Well—you know Magnus! But still—they voted for Kaiser of course!—and of course they locked horns quite nicely!"

"Who? Hirsch and Magnus?"

"Of course! Each naturally laid claim to the one true and uncorrupted Judaism. And each was in possession of the only effective panaceas for all the ills and sufferings of Judaism."

"That must have been something like the quarrel of Molière's doctors.—The only thing to do is to take the radical cure of the baptismal waters."

"They're all charlatans.—They demand faith! They require faith!—Which is sort of nonsense in itself! You can't just compel someone to believe.—That's the path to hypocrisy!—These are, after all, reflective people. Heaven knows what these people have in the back of their minds!—"

"Yes—it certainly must be something specific!"

"But they completely lose themselves in theories.—I'm supposed to have faith, and I don't.—I'm supposed to run around with this esrog, and it doesn't mean a thing to me!—What sort of right do these people have to hold a grudge against anyone for whom these things mean nothing anymore—through no fault of his own—that he leaves?"

"If there's nothing Jewish besides religion and ritual commandments—but that may be just the question!"

"Even Hirsch and Magnus seem to agree about that.—Judaism is a religion and nothing else!"

"What people see in the end would then be a religious institution under the protection of the state!"

"Well—then we would happily end up according to the logic of Zionist gentlemen and finally could take them seriously!—Nope—I'm just happy that we are finally finished with all that!"

"Are we really?—Doesn't it strike you that we never had conversations before about Jews and Judaism, and now we often do?—and I think that once we would've ignored such a letter like the one today!"

"That schnorrer letter!—What's happened with that?"

"I put it in my pocket.—It makes you think, doesn't it, that I felt compelled to see that ten marks were sent to the person who wrote it."

"You have?—Are you out of your mind?"

"I don't know.—For a moment I had a sort of feeling as if I owed something to the man or rather to Jews.—So I made a kind of installment payment."

"Well, I must forbid such sentimental stupidity once and for all!" the Director scolded. "You must stop this! Every bond has been torn asunder!—That's just what we need! That you set the Polacks on our neck!—I have had enough of the dear Magnus and the raving Professor.—I will set the police at once on the first schnorrer who dares to come to our door.—I will try by every means to make my home Jew-free and see that it remains so.—and I would like to hear no more discussion of anything Jewish; not one Jewish thing is to ever cross my threshold!"

"Yes—but I'll probably be bringing the esrog file home with me!" Heinz said, shoving the file into his briefcase as he took his leave.

FOUR

Pastoral Care

I

"Yes—my dear Herr Kaiser!" Dr. Magnus said, looking benevolently at his visitor across his desk, which was piled impressively high with serious books. "I asked you to come here to give you the good news. I have been authorized by the foundation's board to tell you that the stipend your dear father, my honored colleague, applied for has been approved—just for one year at first. If you continue to get good recommendations from your teachers, which I have no doubt you will, and will prove yourself worthy of the trust placed in you through industry, piety, and a virtuous way of life, the stipend should be secure for the entire course of your study.—Please accept my heartfelt congratulations."

"I am very grateful, Herr Rabbi," the young man said slowly, looking as if he felt somewhat uncomfortable in his black coat and yellow gloves.

"Yes—I quite put myself out for you," Dr. Magnus said with a deprecating gesture. "I must tell you that I had no easy time of it.—But I thought of your dear father and said to myself: You *have* to succeed! And then I *did* succeed.—Professor Hirsch voted for you too, of course, but—confidentially—it was I who carried the day. I can say that with confidence, and I'm proud of that.—I ruthlessly ignored old, valued personal connections, and I sacrificed several hours of my time.—But that is our fate!—One is a slave to one's calling!"

"I'm terribly sorry, Herr Rabbi, if on my account you—"

"One is a slave!—Especially here in Berlin!—Yes, your dear father, who was well off in his idyllic little community in dear, cozy southern Germany. But here, in the raw north—in the cold metropolis! There one knows his community—knows every single person—has joy in his work. But here—here is Consul Michelsberg, for example; I had to bury him this morning. Yes—I didn't know the man—and what I heard about him now sort of in private is not exactly laudable.

But what good does that do?! The point is to find the right words; I hear that a nephew will be there—a lieutenant—baptized, of course. One must be tactful!—and in the afternoon a wedding at the Four Seasons. The people are from out of town—from Bremen, I think. In any case—they must be wealthy. I can't just give a garden-variety speech.—And everything lands on my lap! One is a slave!—"

"Herr Rabbi!" Kaiser said with a start. "I—I can't accept the stipend!"

"What?" Magnus exclaimed, his eyes bulging. "I'm not hearing right.—You are refusing the stipend?"

"Yes.—I think—as a decent person—I must do so," Kaiser said, blushing.

"And that's why I've sacrificed my time and my energy?" Magnus exclaimed, upset. "What's the matter?—What is the matter with you?—Have you won the lottery?—Did your dear father bequeath you a fortune?"

"Oh no!" Kaiser said uneasily. "It will hit my parents hard; but I have to see if I can get by—without their help."

"Yes—but please just explain to me—"

"I have—second thoughts.—The foundation is intended just for *pious* Jews. And—" Kaiser managed to get out.

"Ah!" Magnus said more calmly. "That's all?—That's why? You have second thoughts?—You can get over that.—You can take the money in good conscience!"

"But I don't know," Kaiser said, looking at the Rabbi doubtfully. "I don't think you have rightly understood me. When my father submitted the application half a year ago, I wasn't that far along yet. And I was at home and saw how difficult it was for my father—so I agreed.—But meanwhile so much has changed—for me—and altered—"

"That is a spiritual fermentation process!—A Sturm und Drang period!—You are in a period of doubt!—You are perhaps doubting everything—even the basic premises of religion—the fundaments of belief!—But my dear young friend—who has not gone through such periods?—Even I!—Yes! I too!" said Dr. Magnus emphatically and beat his hand on his breast. "I too was once young like you and pondered and ruminated about things!—But what does that matter?—Do I fulfill my obligations today any worse?—That's the important thing! Everything else settles down with time. Doing one's duty—active effort, that's what is true! That brings satisfaction, and recognition by others follows. I tell you that a captain in the service recently thanked me with tears in his eyes after the funeral of his mother-in-law.—That meant something to me!—That's how one comes to love his profession!—I just forced myself! And you will force yourself too!—Don't let these doubts discourage you—courage—my dear young friend! Courage!"

He stood up and patted Kaiser on the shoulder.

"I don't know, Herr Rabbi," the student said hesitantly. "I don't know but that I should go into a different profession—as bad as it would be to lose a few semesters."

"You want to change horses?—Yes, but think of your family at home! You need to begin to support them as soon as possible.—Your feelings are honorable—but you have a duty after all!"

"I—I think I am doing my duty.—I don't want to take on obligations by accepting the stipend."

"What kind of obligations?"

"Moral ones in a way.—Some might hold it against me in the future as ingratitude—if I don't—"

"What you do later is neither here nor there.—For the time being you can accept the money with a good conscience! I can assure you! Take it, for God's sake!—What is it?"

He opened the door to answer someone's knocking and looked out.

"A schnorrer!" he said with contempt and shut the door. "These people overwhelm you. Of course—a rabbi is available to everyone. One is a slave!—and gratitude? Recently I gave fifty pfennigs to one—fif-ty pfennigs!—Later I saw him walking about with his peddler's box on the Sabbath!—Wait a moment. I need to take care of the man; meanwhile, you can think over the matter—and you can also study for your future job on how one gets rid of these people quickly and painlessly."

He opened the door again.

"So—please just come in!" he called and remained standing in the door.

Yossel Schlenker entered the room; he didn't look bad in the nice suit he had bought new for his wedding; but the over-long jacket and the curly beard that no pair of scissors had ever touched framing his expressive face betrayed his Eastern origins.

"Good day!" he said politely and bowed to the two gentlemen.

"Where are you from?" Dr. Magnus asked.

"From Russia—"

"I can imagine!—and where to?"

Yossel didn't understand the question.

"Answer, if you please!" Magnus cried impatiently. "I don't have time for this! —Where are you going?"

"I want to stay in Berlin."

"Sooo?—Of course! Stay in Berlin! Well, fortunately, that's not as easy as you think, my dear friend!—Were you already at the Jewish community office?— What did they give you?"

Yossel stared at the Rabbi without comprehension.

"Oh yes—my God! If you don't want to talk!—There!—and now go with God!"

Whereupon he pressed a coin in Yossel's hand and gently shoved him to the door.

"Please—excuse me!" Yossel said, getting excited as he extricated himself. "I don't want the money!"

As he spoke he held out the coin to the Rabbi.

"Sooo?—Then what do you want?" the Rabbi asked ironically, putting both hands into his pockets.

"I need advice."

"Sooo?—Advice?—Fine!—So what should I advise?"

He took a step toward Kaiser and said with a chuckle: "These are the worst!—Cost time *and* money!"

"Herr Rabbi!" Yossel said, taking a step closer and putting the coin on the table. "Excuse me—I came to Berlin to study.—I thought Herr Rabbi could show me where I should begin.—I wanted to consult with Herr Rabbi."

"Sooo?" Dr. Magnus said and looked at the clock. "Are you finished?—I advise you therefore to disappear as quickly as possible from Berlin—but most quickly! In the community hall you can get a train ticket and some support—"

"But I don't want any support!"

"Listen, my dear friend!" Dr. Magnus said impatiently and deliberately. "I'm not fooled by such turns of phrase!—I know my Russian Jews!—Here, take your money that's on the table and go!"

Yossel looked at the Rabbi a moment, not saying a word; then he turned on his heel and went to the door.

"Good-bye!" he said.

"You are forgetting your money!" Magnus shouted—he grabbed the coin and followed Yossel. "Here!—Now don't make a face, and just take it!"

Yossel left.

"But take the money!" Magnus cried almost pleadingly. "Don't be an ass!"

But Yossel had already closed the door.

"Have you ever seen anything like that?" the Rabbi said, absolutely outraged. "He is certainly a very dangerous man!—This schnorrer—now they don't even take money anymore—these Polacks!"

Kaiser stood up and indicated that he was leaving.

"Do you want to go already?" Magnus asked. "Have you considered the matter? Or do you want to think everything through in the quiet of your room?"

"No, Herr Rabbi!" Kaiser said meekly but firmly. "I am sure: I cannot do otherwise. Many thanks for your kindness!"

"Now—if you cannot do otherwise and don't want any advice—I wash my hands of all blame!—Say hello to your father when you write."

Kaiser left, and the Rabbi grabbed for the telephone.

He soon had the desired connection.

"Herr Regional Court Director himself?—This is Rabbi Dr. Magnus!—At your convenience?—Oh—I won't take long—only good news.—You will be happy in any case.—In the scholarship matter something's happened that changes everything. Candidate Kaiser has just been to see me; he refuses to accept the stipend—yes, re-fus-es!!—For personal reasons.—It's too complicated to explain on the telephone. I don't want to take up your precious time.—Yes, I did talk with him for a long time.—What? Of course! That's why I thought—now nothing stands in the way—of course, Ostermann now gets the scholarship!—Oh, please, please! I scarcely deserve thanks! Yes—isn't it? I'm not so bad as I—what? Ha—ha—ha—very good!—Oh, I'm very grateful! Many thanks on behalf of my poor!—Thanks, you too—Give my regards to the lovely ladies!—Good-bye!"

II

Jacob Kaiser ran down the steps and hurried out the door. Yossel was standing on the other side of the Oranienburger Strasse in front of the synagogue, where a crowd of curiosity seekers watched elegant couples dismount from carriages pulling up in front to hurry into the building. When the ladies tugged at their trains or in some other unobtrusive way halted for a moment to give the public a fleeting glimpse of the costliness of their toilette and jewels, each time there was an extended "Aah!" of admiration to be heard. The gentlemen all looked very important and the ladies a bit distracted, and the whole thing was an attempt to imitate the ceremony of arrival at the royal court.

"Excuse me!" Kaiser said as he approached Yossel. "I saw you up at the Rabbi's. My name is Kaiser, and I'm a student. Perhaps I can be of help somehow."

"You're a student?" Yossel asked with interest. "Are you Jewish?"

"Certainly!" Kaiser said with a smile. "Doesn't one see that by just looking at me?"

"I don't know," Yossel said. "Recently I asked a man who I assumed was Jewish. I wanted to know where the Rabbi lived, and as I uttered the word 'rabbi' he began to yell and said I was an impertinent man and I shouldn't insult him."

"That was definitely a Jew!"

"I don't know! And I certainly don't know whom I can ask. I certainly thought I could speak with the Rabbi. But you can't speak with him—and he doesn't hear what you say!"

"Herr Dr. Magnus is very busy; he doesn't have much time to talk. So many people come to see him."

"Is he that way with everyone?—It seems to me that *you* were sitting there well enough.—Perhaps I'm not dressed like the people here. Beautiful clothes!—What's the occasion?"

"It's a wedding!—Do you have time?"

"Yes, I have time.—I didn't think the visit to the Rabbi would be so short."

"Let's go inside, then, and watch.—Come on!"

They entered a sumptuous room; Kaiser checked with an attendant and said, "I happen to know the family of the bride by name.—It's a first-class wedding!"

The mighty sounds of an organ engulfed them as they entered. The clergyman, with a comfortably round shape, a beard flecked with gray, and curls cascading to his shoulders, stood with his head canted to the side in front of the young couple. He was looking at them with a sweet, wistful smile showing that he was deeply moved; his hands lay folded tranquilly on the robe over his tummy.

Kaiser and Yossel stayed quietly in one of the back rows.

Yossel looked nervously at Kaiser.

"Don't you have to take your hat off?" he asked.

Kaiser indicated he didn't understand; then as the final chord of the organ died down, he laid his finger on his lips and cupped his ear so as not to miss a word of the clergyman's speech.

Even so, they couldn't catch everything, especially Yossel, who was still not used to the German language, particularly as the rabbi enjoyed either speaking almost in a whisper or suddenly switching from a murmur to thundering pathos. It was still all more an aria than a speech: He stretched out vowels interminably, sibilated the *s* sound with a terrifying hiss through clenched teeth, emitted howling, sobbing, quavering sounds that died away, and executed dramatic gestures. Sometimes he jerked up both arms violently in the direction of heaven, sometimes he appeared to want to embrace the whole world, and now and then only his hands came together to rest again quietly on his stomach.—At the conclusion he spread his hands for the blessing over the couple and whispered unintelligible words to some people at the back of the room.

Suddenly Yossel grabbed the arm of the man standing next to him.

"He just said something in Hebrew!"

Kaiser looked at him astonished.

"Yes, of course.—He spoke the wedding blessing!"

"In Hebrew?"

"What do you mean?"

"How does the pope know Hebrew?"

"Pope?—What pope?"

"There is only one there; is there even Hebrew in the church in Berlin?"

"In the church?—Where do you think we are?"

"So where else but in a church?—I'm in a church for the first time. We don't go to a church at home. I'm very interested in this!"

Kaiser looked at Yossel suspiciously; he was certain that Yossel wasn't making a joke.

"Come on outside!" he said and made an effort to appear serious. Outside in the vestibule he burst out laughing.—Hurt, Yossel stared at him.

"Why are you laughing?" he said angrily. "Did I say something stupid? I'm a foreigner here, and I've never been inside a church. All this is absolutely completely new to me."

"Don't be angry," Kaiser said, trying to suppress his laughter. "But why ever do you think you're in a church?—This is a temple, and the rabbi just married a Jewish couple."

"This is a temple—with music? And the pope—the fat man with the black shirt and the tall hat, that's a rabbi? That's what popes look like at home.—And why did the man howl and scream so?—These customs are different from ours.—Perhaps you're joking with me?"

"No, no!" Kaiser assured him and pulled Yossel out onto the street to show him the Hebrew inscription over the portal.

"So?" Yossel said slowly. "This is a Jewish wedding?—It's quite different at home! I really thought—but really, there are really fine Jews here. What jewels and what clothing!—It must be a really wealthy family! It was really nice how he spoke of the late father of the bride—everyone cried! What kind of man was he?—The way the rabbi was talking he must have been a great scholar and a very noble person."

"The old Hendelsohn?—The worst sort of usurer in Berlin!—and the household is completely not Jewish!"

"Wha-at?—"

Yossel sank into deep thought.

"But then it's still nice," he said, "that the daughter got such a pious husband!"

"What?—A pious husband?"

"But I heard how the—rabbi said that he knows that they will be a 'refuge for the piety of the heart.'"

"The bridal couple is leaving!—The wedding dinner is at Dressel's."

"Is that a Jewish restaurant?"

"What do you think?—Of course they don't keep kosher!"

"So?—and the rabbi knows that directly after the wedding they are—?"

"Certainly! What can he do?—He does everything he can! He gives speeches!"

III

Yossel and Kaiser started walking in the direction of Hacke's Market.
Yossel seemed upset.

"Excuse me!" he said. "Does this rabbi give speeches at every wedding?"

"Either he does or another rabbi.—There are very gifted speakers. Some are more popular for funerals—some for confirmations—others—"

"There are always speeches?"

"Yes—that's what they do here now. The first speech happens to a little Jewish boy when he is circumcised, and the last one is given at the grave. He holds still, especially during the last one."

"So from birth to death, one's entire life, the rabbi is standing there, holding speeches?—German Jews seem to like speeches!"

"And the rabbi also gives speeches almost every Sabbath in the synagogue and then at all holiday meals and in all the associations and clubs—"

"When does he have time to attend to his business?"

"His business?—But that *is* his business!"

"Speaking?"

"Yes—that takes up most of his time. He has to prepare for the speech, after all."

Yossel was thinking.

"You told me earlier," he said slowly, "that Dr. Magnus didn't have much time to talk. It seems that by holding too many speeches he doesn't have any time to speak with people who need him."

"You mustn't hold that against him; first of all he's responsible for the members of the community; so many foreigners come to Berlin—"

"Aren't all Jews brothers?"

"All people are brothers!—Dr. Magnus recently gave a sermon about that."

"A sermon?—That's the same as giving a speech?"

"Yes—in the temple on the Sabbath.—Don't they give sermons in the temple where you're from?"

"At home?—No!—Why?—You read from the Torah—"

"Here too, of course."

"Can a preacher do better than Moses?"

"Yes, what does a rabbi do, then, where you're from?"

"He doesn't have any time for such things!—He studies and teaches—he settles disputes—he offers advice—he takes care of the poor—a thousand things!—But maybe it's good to preach, and I just don't yet understand.—What does he preach?"

"He tries to make listeners better people—and more pious."

"They become better and more pious from the speeches?"

"He does what he can! He gives speeches!—and sometimes he really scolds too!"

"He scolds?"

"Well—he rebukes what he doesn't like in them!"

"And people put up with that?"

"What difference does it make to them?—That's why he's the rabbi! He's allowed to scold. They even like it!"

"And they do everything he says?"

"Well—not exactly!—But it's still a good thing that they finally hear the truth."

"Yes—Bode told me that—in the second part of *Faust*—that in the past the kaisers had their own man who was permitted to tell them the truth, and he wouldn't be punished," Yossel said pensively.

Kaiser wanted to ask a question, but Yossel wasn't finished with his questions yet.

"So, for example—what does he say in his sermon? You said that Dr. Magnus preached about all people being brothers. What exactly did he say?"

"Well, that all people, Jews and Christians, should be tolerant of each other— that one shouldn't reject the other and shouldn't disdain the other. Everyone should have equal rights."

"Do Jews want to take rights away from others here?"

"Jews—from others?"

"Yes—do Jews not want to live in peace with others?"

"Jews?—Of course they want to live in peace! But the others don't!"

"The others!—Do they come to the temple?"

"Of course not!—They go to church!"

"Then Dr. Magnus should also go to church and preach there!"

Kaiser laughed.

"Maybe that's not a completely silly idea," he said. "Many in the congregation do go to church a few years later instead of going to temple.—Perhaps then they would take the rabbi's sermon to heart."

"I don't understand that!" said Yossel.

"You'll soon understand when you've been in Berlin longer."

"What else does he say in his speeches?"

"All sorts of things: he often exhorts people to go to synagogue!"

"If they don't go, they certainly aren't going to hear that speech; if they're there and hear that—what's the point of his speech?"

"Of course, if you take it that way! Most of the speeches are held for people who don't need them—not only the sermons. Everyone likes to go to the speaker with whom he knows he'll most agree—who will say exactly what he's thinking himself.—Yes, how is one supposed to speak otherwise?"

"One shouldn't hold any speeches at all!"

"Hmm—somewhat drastic!"

"What are you saying?"

"According to that logic, almost all the editorials in the newspapers are superfluous.—No! The point is this: The rabbi holds a speech so that the listener enjoys an aesthetic pleasure—so, to help you understand: to hear a good speech—that's like looking at a beautiful picture or reading a poem or hearing beautiful music.—"

"Ah!" Yossel said. "Now I understand.—We have something like that at our weddings too. We have a *badchen*—a jester.—Now I also understand what's in *Faust*: a comedian could instruct a pastor."

"You know *Faust*?" Kaiser asked in astonishment.

"Certainly!" Yossel said placidly. "I read it with Chana, and I explained it to the Pastor."

"Which pastor?"

"The one at home—the German pastor—Bode. But he's not too bright—he didn't understand it!—Chana got it at once!"

"Who is Chana?"

"My wife."

"You have a wife?"

"What sort of Jew has no wife?—I'm already twenty-two years old."

Kaiser had to laugh.

"It's somewhat unusual here if students are married."

"My wife wants to study too."

"What sort of education do you have, then?"

"I have to begin at the beginning. I think when I get to know what's required to enter the university everything will go quickly. A month or two!"

"What?—Oh my! You are certainly miscalculating what the difficulties are!— What do you want to study?"

"Everything!"

"Everything!—and what do you want to become?"

Yossel looked at Kaiser with astonishment.

"Become?—I don't want to become anything—I want knowledge!"

"Yes, but you must have some sort of practical aim in mind!—How are you going to earn a living?"

"Oh, that's what you mean!—I'll earn a living somehow! What does it matter!"

They had slowly walked in the direction of the city train, the S-Bahn, and had now reached the Kaiser-Wilhelm-Strasse.

"I think—here's where I turn," Yossel said. "You said you can help me?"

"I'm happy to help you enroll as a student," Kaiser said. "I'll be glad to give you a hand in any way I can.—Where do you live?"

"Chana's gone to look for an apartment.—We need everything!—"

"And food?"

"What does it matter!—A little spirit stove—I can make tea myself.—One can certainly buy a little bit of sausage!—But maybe you know where I could find a place to teach—Hebrew or Jewish things.—and my wife would like to find something in an office—she can write Russian letters very well."

"And when is she going to study?"

"She'll find some free time somewhere."

"Hmm—you know, you should go to Rabbi Doctor Rosenbacher.—"

"Another rabbi!—"

"He's different from Magnus. He's from the Orthodox community; he will certainly listen to you.—I'll write the address for you.—"

"He doesn't give talks?"

"In fact, he talks three times longer than the others. But at least he doesn't prepare his talks. He has time for everyone. You'll see.—Above all, he'll know where your wife can find a job. It has to be one that's free on the Sabbath?"

"Of course! What else?"

"Then Dr. Rosenbacher is just the right person for you.—Here's the address, and here's mine too. Come to my place maybe in two or three hours, then we can discuss everything about your studies."

"Thanks; I'll be there!—You don't have any more time right now?"

"No; you'll have to excuse me now.—I have to hold a talk myself now—I'm a budding rabbi myself!"

"You are studying to be a rabbi?—What kind of talk are you going to give?"

"A eulogy!—A man had a fatal accident on the train; he leaves behind a widow and seven little children. The wife just lost her parents last month."

"Terrible! Terrible!—and you're laughing?"

"Yes—I'm only giving the talk in the Homiletical Society."

"What's that?—A burial society?"

"Not at all!—It's a society where future young rabbis can practice their talks.— The case is invented to give you practice in touching speeches. Good-bye!"

Kaiser ran after the streetcar, and Yossel stood there in bewilderment.

IV

Wolf Klatzke, who was in a bad mood, was staring at the cigarette packets heaped up before him on the wobbly table. Every now and then he extracted a cigarette, sniffed at it suspiciously, and then peevishly put it back.

Chana was diligently reading a book, her elbows on the table and her hands covering both of her ears.

In came Yossel.

"You got some money," Klatzke said. "Here's the check. It's ten marks.—From Levysohn—from my letter. You already know!"

Chana looked up.

"From the schnorrer letter?" she asked. "We have to return it at once."

Klatzke shrugged his shoulders.

"You can't even read the name," Yossel said, shaking his head as he examined the check. "It *could* be Levysohn."

"Here's the address," Klatzke said. "I checked my list. Matthäikirchstrasse 8— that's Levysohn.—The only one who sent anything!"

"I'll send the money right back! Do you have a remittance?"

"Wait a moment!" Chana said. "What name are you going to use as the payer? Schlenker or Lifschitz?"

Yossel was disconcerted.

"That won't do!" she said. "You will go there yourself and take the money back."

"They'll ask me questions."

"They don't ask questions of someone *bringing* money," Klatzke said.

"If they ask you anything, you'll find an excuse," Chana said. "You'll say it was a mistake, or Lifschitz left town. You'll think of something!"

"Good! I'll go!"

"Maybe you can give Levysohn cigarettes instead of the ten marks?" Klatzke asked sheepishly.

"Cigarettes?"

"I have cigarettes just lying here; I don't smoke and don't understand anything about cigarettes, but somehow I've come into them: Gurland was here—he still owes me for twelve letters, and I lent him another six marks—I'm a fool!—All of a sudden he's deported and has to take off—he's gone to Dresden; he took off with Chana's father.—He didn't have any money to give me—so I had to take the cigarettes!—"

"So tell me, Yossel," Chana said. "What have you been up to?"

Yossel reported what he had done and seen—his visit with Dr. Magnus that had ended badly, meeting Kaiser, the wedding ceremony they had witnessed, and his last conversation with the rabbinical candidate.

"That must be a very decent young man!" Chana said. "It seems he will really be able to give us advice."

"Maybe he smokes?" Klatzke asked, showing interest.

"I'll go to Dr. Rosenbacher at once!" Chana said. "I'll do that while you're off to see the young man."

"That's a fine idea to go to Dr. Rosenbacher!" Klatzke said too. "He's a capable person—and a good man. You can talk to him!—Maybe he'll take a few hundred cigarettes off my hands?"

"You know Rosenbacher?" Yossel asked.

"Yes—I sort of know him!—and I've been there a few times when he's preached. I go anywhere where I can hear the right accent. You should do that too—meetings, theater, and sermons. The sermons are free. And you learn quite a lot when you listen to Rosenbacher!"

"Are his speeches particularly good?" Chana asked.

"I don't know what he says at all! I am listening only for the accent. But he talks so well for a long time, so you can learn a lot!"

"Does he dress like the pope? Does he imitate everything?"

"Yes—of course! But I've been going only for a few years. Because rabbis from other communities do as Christian clergy do and wear a gown—he's doing what his colleagues do. Every German Jew imitates someone!"

"There's more than one community here?"

"Of course!—and each community has its own rabbi and own butcher and their own schools and their own dairy shops and their own butcher shops and their own restaurants. And God forbid that someone from one community goes to the business of another or goes to eat in the restaurant of another rabbi."

"The rabbi owns a restaurant?"

"He doesn't own a restaurant, and he doesn't have a dairy shop. But people rely on him to make sure that a business under his oversight is kosher and that one can eat or buy there."

"Does it ever happen that a Jew sells something that isn't kosher?—or that he says it's kosher when it isn't?"

"That happens!—That's why the rabbi puts someone there to supervise things."

"I wouldn't like to eat in that kind of restaurant where a supervisor is necessary," Chana said. "If the owner is a decent man, a supervisor isn't necessary. If he's a swindler, a supervisor doesn't do any good. And how can a decent man accept a supervisor? I'd throw him out!"

"That's what's been done in Germany! No Jew trusts a Jew!—Here, for example, a decent pious Jew—he opens a restaurant and says, like Chana, he doesn't want a supervisor—then the rabbi won't allow people to eat there.—Then there's someone else—who has no idea if one has to slaughter fish according to kashrut or if you can cook meat with milk—and moreover a dishonest man; the rabbi puts a supervisor there—there you are allowed to eat!"

"Strange people, these German Jews!" Yossel said, amazed.

"Dr. Rosenbacher is especially interested in this—in this and food in general.—He's written a thick book about this and many articles in Jewish publications; he proved that you couldn't eat a particular kind of chocolate—I can't recall what kind—at all because there was something—I can't recall what, but something Jews are forbidden to eat—used in its manufacture. And he put supervisors in dairies and in candy factories and in pharmacies; he sees that kosher bouillon cubes and kosher malt extract and kosher margarine are manufactured, and I think even kosher laxatives! He supervises milking cows and distillation of wine; he's very busy with thousands of such things!"

"It seems to me," Chana said, astonished, "that a German rabbi is mainly concerned with matters of the stomach!"

"That's it exactly!" Klatzke said. "They even have a special word for it here—a remarkable word!—What is it now?—Right! I remember: they call it *pastoral care*!"

V

Pesach was approaching—the Jewish Easter—and as usual this festival, which retold the story of the exodus of the children of Israel from Egypt, brought about a small revolution in every Jewish household.—The commandment to remove all "leavened foods" from the house requires a thorough spring cleaning of the most fearsome sort: no piece of furniture that didn't have its drawers emptied— no coat pocket that wasn't turned inside out—no carpet that wasn't beaten—no inkwell that wasn't washed—no book that wasn't dusted!—When the chairs were put upside down on the tables and their legs stretched pitifully toward the heavens—when the crockery that had loyally served throughout the year disappeared into giant baskets—when a large supply of matzah, that unleavened travel bread of the ancestors, is lying piled up in chests carefully protected from contamination from not-kosher-for-Passover things—then it really looks as if a new exodus from the land of slavery is imminent and as if a call to return to the land of the ancestors is expected soon. Until the festival evening finally arrives and everyone gathers solemnly around the family table to take the consoling words of the family patriarch as the longed-for call to return home:

> *In this year we are still in exile—*
> *But next year in Jerusalem!*

And so the children of Israel console themselves year after year; for almost two thousand years they have prepared every year for the exodus and patiently comforted themselves with undiminished hope.

But it wasn't so far along this year yet; utter chaos still reigned in the house of Dr. Rosenbacher as it did in every Jewish home throughout the entire world; only those in the know were able to detect the spirit of the holiday that hovered over the waters, which were spilling out of buckets onto the floors of rooms, disgorged over forecourts and stairwells.

Up until now, the Rabbi had managed to fend off the attack on his study by the feminine troops armed with scrub rags and wielding brooms. All the other rooms had already fallen to the spring cleaning and were therefore off-limits and not to be used before the holiday. His study, therefore, now served simultaneously as reception room, waiting room, dining room, and living room. And anyone who wanted to lay claim to the much-beleaguered Rabbi for help squeezed into the room; it couldn't be helped that everyone heard the troubles of anyone else seeking advice.

Chana observed in astonishment the bustle in the modest room filled to overflowing. She had plenty of opportunity to let her eyes wander over the room. The Rabbi had listened to her kindly and carefully, had asked her to take a seat and wait—and then had begun to pace around the room again.—He dictated as he strode back and forth with his hands clasped beneath his coattails and a cigar in the corner of his mouth, a small round yarmulke on his still-youthful white-blond hair and a short goatee on his narrow face.

"Paragraph 18.—The joint party August Ferdinand Kluck expressly forgoes every right to which the law may entitle him to review the business records and documents to examine the balance or other statements—specifically any future communications concerning the operation of the joint business."

The narrow-chested little man with spectacles sitting at the desk was scribbling everything down.—Whenever the Rabbi paused to say something to someone waiting, he quickly pulled out one of the many forms in front of him and hurriedly filled it out.

A smartly dressed gentleman with a graying goatee was relaxing comfortably in the club chair next to the desk; his top hat brushed to a high shine was lying next to him there.—He was listening carefully while browsing distractedly in a book of commercial law that he had taken from one of the massive bookshelves lining almost the entire room.

Next to him was standing a woman wrapped in a cloak, hatless but with a large wig, holding an open basket filled with a freshly slaughtered goose.

Then there was a lady on the divan who was wearing an expensive fur collar and large diamond stud earrings. She was visibly nervous, her anxious eyes following the Rabbi's wanderings.

At the window stood a gaunt man who had arranged a collection of tubes and tins on the little smoking table in front of him.

Next to him waited a short asthmatic man who was carrying several large keys in his hand. A number of strangely formed belts dangled from his arm.

Several Russian Jews stood next to the door, books and papers in their hands.

Chana herself sat next to a charming little cabinet that had been cleverly built into the bookshelf with a magnificently embroidered curtain indicating that a sefer Torah, a Torah scroll, was kept there.

Several men and women opposite the desk whose clothing suggested the most diverse ranks of society formed the last group; each person was leading what seemed to be a child of six by the hand.

In a dark corner next to the desk, barely visible at first glance, stood a plump man in plain dress with bristly red-brown hair and moustache. He showed no interest in what was happening in the room, nodding as he dozed, apparently asleep on his feet. From time to time the man at the desk gestured toward him to come near; he then shoved closer, took a pen already dipped in ink from the hand of the man sitting at the desk, bent his glowing red face over the surface, and signed in large, awkward strokes the one word "Kluck" as he raised his fierce eyebrows without taking the least notice of the content of the papers put before him.

"Paragraph 19," dictated the Rabbi as he continued. "With regard to the dissolution of the general partnership of Germersheim & Co., it is set forth—ach, Herr Germersheim!" he turned to the gentleman in the club chair. "Look up for me the provisions in the law code! I can finish off a few other things while you're doing that!"

He went to the desk and picked up a pack of completed forms.

"Heilbrunn-Kluck contract. Purchase of apothecary shop is in order!—Meyenberg contract—Kluck—also a grocery store!—Lindenberg—Kluck—prussic acid —good!—Stop! Here—you forgot to fill out the amounts for the ethyl alcohol factory, Herr Bluth!—All right, the distillery goes for a purchase price of seven million five hundred thousand marks to become the property of Herr August Ferdinand Kluck!—Do you approve of the price demanded, Kluck?"

"Yes, indeed, Herr Doctor," the man in the corner said indifferently.

Chana stared in astonishment at the nondescript man who was so calmly spending millions.

"As down payment," the Rabbi continued, "the purchaser Kluck pays fifty pfennigs.—Agreed, Kluck?"

"Yes indeed, Herr Doctor!"

"Good! Add that, Herr Bluth!—Frau Bergmann!" the Rabbi turned to the lady with the fur collar at the same time he flipped open a knife and began to cut around in the goose that the woman in the cloak was eagerly holding out to him. "Unfortunately I have to give you bad news about the crockery. Your maid has made a pretty mess with the milk here! If the milk had only been cold!—But the crockery is now completely unusable. You must toss out the whole set.—The knives can be saved.—Stick them in the ground for three days—maybe in flowerpots. Then they are perfectly all right to use!—The goose is fine. Hope it will taste good!"

The woman with the goose went out beaming with joy.—Frau Bergmann bid good-bye with a sigh.—

"Now come here!" the Rabbi said to the Russian Jews at the door. "What is it?—"

He took care of them quickly but pleasantly; they were messengers from Talmud academies in Lida and Brest-Litovsk who were collecting funds for maintaining the institutes—and also authors of scholarly Hebrew books that they were trying themselves to sell—and common schnorrers.—Everyone left satisfied.

"Herr Bluth!" the Rabbi said. "You can register the applications for religious classes in the meantime!—Please, gentlemen!" He gestured to the group with the children. "Hand all the papers to the gentleman!—So! And what do you want?" He turned to the man with the tubes and cans. "Ah! The new shaving gear— Kluck! Come here a moment!—"

The man who was so comfortable with things worth millions of marks approached.

"Very nice! You obviously haven't shaved for a few days!—Sit down on the chair! And now, dear Krause, show your art! Shave the good Kluck!—Ah, understood! As a non-Jew you perhaps don't know what's important! According to our law no cutting blade may touch the beard!"

"It's also not necessary in the manufacture!" Krause reassured him. "The salves burn the hair off down to the skin and are removed with a spoon. It is better than the best razor!"

"We'll see! Just begin!"

And Chana watched with growing astonishment as the ritual procedure of shaving began to be implemented upon the incognito millionaire at the window of the rabbinical study.

"Have you found the paragraphs, Herr Germersheim?" the Rabbi asked. "But just a moment! I want to show you something nice—a new, unbelievably practical invention!" He gestured to the man with the belts and the keys. "Take off your coat and put on a belt! See! Up until now it was a calamity that you couldn't take your house keys or apartment keys with you on the Sabbath on account of the prohibition against carrying anything. Now I had a special belt made that has hooks but no eyes on both sides.—Now the key is hooked on both sides with its ring—like this! The key now really holds the trouser waistband closed. And thus it becomes a necessary part of your clothing and can be carried!—What do you say to that?"

"Splendid!" Germersheim said, taking a belt in hand to look more closely. "I sincerely congratulate you! Once again you have solved a problem of immense importance! And how simple it is! Truly of striking simplicity!"

Bluth as well as the people who had wanted to enroll their children at Easter time were also curious and had drawn closer, exhausting themselves in exclamations of joy and admiration over this new achievement of Orthodox technology.

"Of course, a patent must be filed with the Patent Office as soon as possible!" Dr. Rosenbacher said. "Perhaps we should set up a company to manufacture these sorts of objects; Kluck will of course be a shareholder!—Yes—now what do you want, miss?" he said, turning to Chana. "Could you give the young Fräulein a job, Herr Germersheim? She would like to have off on the Sabbath!"

"Pardon me, Rabbi!" Chana said. "I'm married.—"

"So?" the Rabbi said slowly and glanced sharply first at her gloved hands and then at her hairdo. "You're married? Is your husband here too?"

"Yes!—He wants to study!"

"Sooo?—and it's important for you to be free on the Sabbath?"

"Certainly!"

"Well, Herr Germersheim?"

"Sorry!" Germersheim said coldly. "I require a pious Jewish woman to fulfill *all* religious commandments, even those that command a woman to not show her own hair. The lady seems to prefer, I see, to not wear a sheitel. Therefore—!"

He shrugged his shoulders.

The Rabbi fretfully adjusted his yarmulke.

"Nevertheless!" he said. "Maybe the lady would choose—"

"To put on a wig?" Chana said as she stood up. "Pardon me, Rabbi, that I bothered you."

"Wait a moment!" Dr. Rosenbacher said. "Herr Germersheim! Perhaps some arrangement—"

"But Herr Doctor!" Germersheim said. "I've now accepted Kluck as a partner in my factory on your advice.—We really need to conclude the contract! I have to get to the board meeting of the Association of the Friends of the Sabbath!—I can now keep my factory operating even on the Sabbath. That's why I'm forced to let go all my Jewish employees."

"All your Jewish employees?" the Rabbi asked uneasily.

"Of course!—If the business operates on the Sabbath, I have to require all my employees to show up for work on the Sabbath.—Of course, there are still quite a few people among my sixty employees who would work on the Sabbath—but naturally I shall never allow a desecration of the Sabbath by Jews in my factory. I am not allowed to do that at all!"

The Rabbi looked disgruntled.

"Still, most unfortunate!" he said. "It will hit many people hard.—Yes, dear lady," he said, turning to Chana, "for now I can't help you, as you can see. I'll keep an eye out for you! If you would come again—Ah, are you finished, Krause?—Perhaps you will be so kind, Herr Germersheim, to verify that Kluck has been shaved well!—Oh, Herr Bluth—don't forget that all the purchase agreements must be stamped!—Yes, right, dear lady! Perhaps something can be arranged; Herr Germersheim has excellent contacts. If only he wants to use them!!—Do make a small compromise! It wouldn't hurt you if you would wear an artificial braid; he would be satisfied with that.—That way at least form would be observed—we can confirm that, if necessary, as sufficient—"

"Herr Rabbi!" Chana said, blushing. "Don't try so hard! What sort of nonsense are you trying to tell *me*—I'm not the dear Lord!" and left.

VI

It had been agreed that Chana would meet her husband at Kaiser's; so she climbed the narrow stairs in the gloomy, musty building on the Auguststrasse. She was barely able to make out in the semidarkness the names on the many business cards tacked to the doors. The whole building was filled with students.—Finally on the fourth floor she found the card of *Jacob Kaiser, cand. phil.,* under the porcelain name plate with the name of Deneke. Next to Kaiser's card was another: *Fritz Hamburger, cand. med.—*

She pressed the bell, which yielded reluctantly, and a short double bell sound-ed.—Behind the door a piano playing a waltz stopped—a door creaked, and shuf-fling steps approached. Then the door opened a crack. Then the crack opened against a chain, and a flushed female face peeped through the opening.—The door finally opened all the way, and the broad figure of a portly woman appeared. She held out her hand to Chana in a friendly gesture and vigorously shook Chana's hand.

"Do come in, little Fräulein!" she said and laughed for no reason. "All right, children! It's going to be nice now!" she shouted to the rear of the apartment. "Here Herr Germersheim also gets his wife! Nope—isn't this a world!—So come on in! The later the evening, the better the guests!—We want to get a look at you under the light!"

She had pulled the bewildered Chana into the dark entry hall; bright light fell through an open door to the next room; there Chana saw a blond young man in shirtsleeves at the piano and another young man sitting between two girls on the sofa. The one with black hair had a cigarette in her mouth and was busy trying to put up her hair, which had come loose; the one with blond hair jumped up and ran into the entry hall. The silhouette of a gangling young man dressed in slov-enly elegance in a frock coat appeared behind her in the doorway.

"Just go in to the good parlor!" the blonde exclaimed. "Whom else have you got there for us?" She stepped in front of Chana. "I'm Amanda—born and con-firmed dumb and learned nuttin' since!—" She latched onto Chana's arm and squealed with laughter. "And you, miss?—Where are you dancing in from?"

"Please—I think I've made a mistake here," stammered Chana, now com-pletely confused. "I am—I wanted—Doesn't Herr Kaiser live here?"

"Oh yeah!" Amanda screeched, letting her go and grabbing the tall man in the frock coat by both arms, rocking him as well as herself back and forth with laughter. "And I thought—about you too, Herr Germersheim!"

"Well, really!" said Frau Deneke. "I thought—oh well, the quadrille is now complete.—Well, you are something, Herr Germersheim!"

"Oh don't be so stupid!" the black-haired girl called from the sofa. "Who knows what the young miss must be thinking!—Just show her where to go!"

The tall man had approached Chana, sniffing her like a puppy, and said as he bowed: "My name is Germersheim!—Please—dear lady—here's the door!—May I? My friend Kaiser is at home—there are more people here.—We are namely right in the middle of studying, dear lady—we're studying a Talmud tractate—"

He opened a door.

"Herr Kaiser—you have a visit from a lady!" Amanda screeched and burst out laughing again.

"Excuse me, people!" Frau Deneke exclaimed.—

Chana stepped into Kaiser's room, followed by Germersheim.—It was a long room lit only by a window in a niche at an oblique angle to the room, looking out onto the courtyard.—

In this niche was a table on which were a few folios Chana easily recognized as Talmud volumes. Four people were bent over these books; Yossel and an even younger man—the person she immediately recognized from his description as Kaiser—and finally a man of barely medium build who was about forty with a dirty yellow goatee and a man about the same age with a face that definitely resembled that of a sheep.

In the next room there was giggling and whispering; then the interrupted waltz began again, and one could hear the shuffling of the dancing pairs.

Kaiser jumped up to greet Chana and stepped toward her.

"Surely this must be Frau Schlenker!" he said, greeting her cordially. "Welcome! You bring a rare glamor to my student's room!—Germersheim introduced himself of course?—Here's my old friend and teacher Joelsohn—who is kind enough to study Talmud with us and who is in mortal combat with your husband over a difficult passage.—This here is Löwenberg!"

"I've discussed everything with Herr Kaiser," Yossel said happily. "He will help me!—I now know how one gets books and where we should begin.—He even wants to study with us!—and he thinks there's even a room for us here."

"And tell us about your visit to Dr. Rosenbacher!" Kaiser said. "I'll go fix some tea."

He opened the door to the next room; the blond girl squeezed through the opened crack and stared in with curiosity.

"Could we have some hot water perhaps, Fräulein Amanda?" Kaiser said, blocking the door.

"W.d.!—Will do!" Amanda said and slowly pulled back.

"Listen, Kaiser!" a voice called from the next room. "I still don't get the story with the Prince of Homburg!—The scene in the cathedral supports my view—not yours! The Great Elector doesn't really want to have the prince shot at all."

"We'll talk about it!" said Kaiser and came back into the room. "Right—what happened at Rosenbacher's?"

"Not much!" Chana said and reported in detail.

"The whole thing," she concluded, "seemed to me to be more a large business operation than a rabbi's study.—The most important person seemed to be this Kluck; what kind of strange man was he?—It seemed as if he was buying everything—apothecary shops, distilleries, grocery stores, and everything else; he was tossing around millions in promises and was only paying a few pennies down. He is the partner of giant companies and dressed like a worker.—He had a shave at the Rabbi's and answered everything with just 'Yes, indeed, Herr Doctor!'"

Kaiser laughed heartily.

"Yes—even if you don't know Kluck!—Kluck is the pillar of the Orthodox Jewish community in Berlin. He isn't Jewish, and that's why he has his job. He has lived for many years among the Orthodox and is comfortable there.—But woe—if he should convert to Judaism. His means of earning a living would be destroyed, and he would become penniless on the spot."

"Why?" Chana asked. "Is it one of the principles of German Orthodox Jews to not have any Jewish employees—as I saw in the case of Herr Germersheim?"

"My father?" the young Germersheim asked. "That's completely different!— But I would certainly be more gallant!"

"Kluck's life task," Kaiser said, "is to do all those things that the Orthodox Jew is not permitted to do himself but cannot do without—and moreover Kluck does make all sorts of things easier by doing these things."

"I understand exactly!" Yossel said. "He has to turn on and off the lights on the Sabbath.—and he can make a living with this?"

"That's only the least of what he does. He goes from house to house on the Sabbath, opens letters, stokes the ovens, and does that sort of thing, which isn't very strenuous!—You got quite a glimpse today of his versatility.—The main thing is that he always is available to sign his name for a few marks; the magic word is *Kluck* on the correctly drawn-up document, removing all pangs of conscience as certainly or even more certainly than the absolution of a priest.—There is, for example, the question of the Sabbath peace! The sharp competition and of course the obligatory Sunday rest force even pious Jews to open their businesses on the Sabbath to stay alive.—In order not to break the strict commandment in the Torah and the Talmud, many seize upon an expedient alternative of having a non-Jewish partner. Then the business isn't strictly Jewish and can stay open on the Sabbath; the Jewish co-owner stays away from the place of business, of course, on that day.—If he can't really use a partner, he hires a straw man for a little money—and that's Kluck, of course."

"And this is common?" Chana asked.

"Well, rather frequent!—The worthy Kluck has come to be a co-owner of a considerable number of businesses in this way.—"

"Funny!" Yossel said. "But that's quite proper!—What should people do otherwise?"

"And the main thing!" Kaiser said. "Now—Kluck's really busy season is beginning as the Easter season begins. You know the strict commandment to get rid of all 'leavened' food for the holiday week is difficult enough for a private household and impossible for many businesses. Fortunately, the good Lord invented Kluck just for this. Whatever you can't keep during the holiday, you sell to him beforehand. Before Pesach Kluck buys everything: kitchen equipment—wine cellars— barrels of vinegar—distilleries and sugar mills, real estate and apothecary shops, coffeehouses and offices and everything else!—It goes according to plan, and there are even printed forms to use. There's always a large purchase price filled in—otherwise a third party could eventually interfere and make things serious; Kluck, of course, only pays a few pennies down and reserves the right to withdraw. And the day after the holiday he punctually shows up and most solemnly declares that he regrets the purchase and insists on his right to withdraw. He gets a tip—the contract is shredded, and everything goes on as before!"

"Odd!" Yossel said. "At home the same sort of thing goes on now and again; but here everything is like a factory. Forms!—It's no joke when they talk about German efficiency!"

"I find the whole thing outrageous!" Chana exclaimed. "Whom do you plan to cheat there?—The good Lord? Or oneself?—That's really swindling the holiest of holy!"

Kaiser shrugged.

"You shouldn't take it like that!" he said. "I admit I don't like all these things either. These are the unavoidable consequences of the peculiar situation we Jews happen to find ourselves in."

"Then the situation should be changed!" Chana exclaimed.

"Well said!—But for the time being we're stuck in the situation, and we have to just stay where we are!—What are people supposed to do? Should they just ignore the commandment that they love with all their heart—that has kept them and their ancestors through all their sufferings over the centuries—that alone has preserved the existence of Judaism to this day?"

"That's sacrificing the spirit of the law to preserve the letter!" Chana exclaimed, upset. "Can there be anything more disgraceful and sillier than to take the bread from the mouths of sixty Jews only because they're Jews? To keep the Sabbath holy—to preserve the Sabbath!—Herr Germersheim really thinks he's doing something that pleases God?"

"If my father is doing this," Germersheim junior said, "then it's certainly right! What he's doing is exactly according to the law!—You can count on that!"

"But the important thing is the spirit of the law!"

"That's not our concern! We're Orthodox!—We have to obey the letter of the law; what is permitted by the Holy Torah cannot be bad!—But why are you getting so upset?—You probably know how becoming it is when you look angry!"

Chana stared at Germersheim in astonishment; she lacked all comprehension for this sort of compliment and this easy manner of handling problems.—

Amanda carried in a tray with glasses and a teapot and put it on the table; she openly looked over Chana with a critical eye. As she passed Germersheim on her way out, she snatched Germersheim's large round yarmulke he had just put on to say the blessing before drinking. She remained standing at the door and played ball with the yarmulke to show Chana by making faces that she was making fun of Germersheim.

"Stop that nonsense, Fräulein!" Germersheim said and chased her. "Give the yarmulke back! I need it now!"

"Come in with us!" Amanda said, hiding the yarmulke behind her back as she leaned against the door posts. "Ilonka is just crazy about you!"

"Give it to me!" Germersheim said as he encircled her with his arms; they briefly but vigorously wrestled and pressed against each other until Amanda tossed the yarmulke into the room, and with a laugh she shut the door behind her.

Germersheim picked up the yarmulke, hurriedly brushed it off, put it back on his head, went to the table, and, still out of breath from the struggle, said the required blessing.—

Meanwhile, Joelsohn had come to the table; Löwenberg sat there with head bowed over his folios, impervious to everything going on in the room.

"What do you say to this, Joelsohn?" Kaiser asked.

"To what?—to what you said there?—You know what I think! There's only one thing to do: the Jews must go back to the ghetto!"

"Your old hobbyhorse!" Kaiser laughed, annoyed.

"Hobbyhorse or not a hobbyhorse!—It's true! I couldn't care less about emancipation and everything!—Our law, our Torah alone has preserved us, and in our lives today you *are forced* to do clever things with forms and with Kluck and the key belt!—You can't really observe the law—you turn everything into a symbol, into a reminder! You don't have the Sabbath anymore, but if you carry your key on your stomach instead of in your pocket, you say to yourself: today is *really* the Sabbath—you aren't *really* supposed to carry anything!—The technique of mnemonics! All Jewish life is mnemonical technique! Don't forget your Judaism—think of Palestine—remember what you really are!—You don't live as a Jew should—you almost stop being a Jew; but you remember: you *really* ought to live differently—but you *really* are a Jew!—It's a farce!"

"But you don't have to cooperate!" Chana said. "At home in Russia you're either a Jew or you aren't!"

"That's what I say! Because you still have a ghetto.—A Jew lives in a ghetto like a person.—I know: he was a poor, miserable, hungry person and always afraid for his little bit of life! But he didn't have to play a farce his whole life until he has no idea anymore what his true self is and what's a mask.—A Jew is forced to be a fraud today—and the worst thing is: he knows that doesn't help. You can't live on symbols. You're drinking from empty cups the way actors do in the theater; and they act as if it tastes good.—But they are still sober and hungry and empty!"

"Well—you're generalizing way too much!" Kaiser said. "Ultimately there's some Jewish substance even with German Jews. There are still—"

"*Still!*—That's just it: *still!*—They say of a pious Jew in Germany: he's *still* religious—and of a lapsed Jew: he's *already* liberal! *Still* and *already*! It's only a matter of time—a matter of two or three generations!—Everyone is leaving! And the

Orthodox Jew who thinks about things—I don't mean you, Germersheim!—who knows exactly where the road goes. He goes reluctantly—he drags his feet, but it's no good.—It's just a matter of which direction. One will go straight ahead—another goes back—he looks to one side and goes to the other!—Another one clings with all his strength to everything that somehow is within reach! A drowning man grasps at straws; he knows it won't help; but he still holds fast; a straw is somehow a symbol too!"

"It seems to me," Chana said, "a young man would just be repelled by rigid adherence to all the rules!—So does a wig stand for all of Judaism?"

"That's exactly what I say!" Joelsohn exclaimed. "What's happened here had to happen, that a wig is more important than the person who is underneath it!"

"Well—just listen now, Joelsohn!" Germersheim said angrily. "Perhaps you want to get rid of the sheitel? Our law says that a married woman may not show her hair in order not to be pleasing to any man but her husband!—Would you destroy our morality?"

"You don't need to be afraid of me!—Otherwise I'll still have to deal with Amanda!—It's already bad enough to live with all these thousands of rules nowadays!"

"So you are perhaps thinking of reforming things?" Germersheim said patronizingly. "Herr Joelsohn—the new reformer!"

"Me?—God forbid!—Who am I?—and who could reform anything these days?—We all already know what comes of all these reforms!—Someone cuts out this—someone else cuts out that—and in the end there's nothing left!—and the worst thing is that Judaism will soon be different in different places. Nothing in common remains—nothing to identify the community—no hope for the future of the community!—No!—There's nothing to do but to conserve everything without making distinctions!"

"But you say yourself that that doesn't work in today's world!" exclaimed Chana. "You admit that even the Orthodox are subject to reform and progress!"

"Exactly!—and therefore I still insist that we must go back to where preserving ourselves is possible—where our entire existence doesn't otherwise come in contact with the world—into the ghetto!"

"No!" Chana said. "That's absurd!—and to think we have to hear this in Germany; we who fled the Russian ghetto to get here—to freedom. We thought a Jew can't be a Jew there—that is, oppression prevents him from showing what he can do. But here abroad—in the West, someone who's Jewish can develop freely and can earn the honor and respect of all people instead of the contempt that is the lot of ghetto Jews!"

"And I tell you—if new emigrants weren't leaving the ghetto in the East to go to the West there wouldn't be any Jews by now in Germany. Those over there think that their fortune lies here—you want to leave the ghetto to reach freedom—and we who live here in what you call freedom—we have come to see that we cannot live without walls; we should return to the ghetto!"

"Well, fine!" Germersheim said. "Then return to the ghetto! I like it here! What don't I have here?—and I know we are pious enough in our villa in Grunewald. You can be pious here too; we fulfill every word, every letter of the law!"

"I know!" said Joelsohn. "Every letter!—You don't even drink wine at the house of a non-Jew—as it is written—and you don't touch money on the Sabbath. That's why at every nightspot where you go you've set up a Sabbath account, and that's why you always are in the company of those sorts of women who drink the wine for you!"

"Herr Joelsohn!" Germersheim said loftily. "There's a lady present!—and I think you should be happy that there are well-off Jews who are still pious and who regularly study the Talmud like me and Löwenberg!"

"Do you want to suggest that I must live from teaching the Talmud?" Joelsohn said. "Without the income from my Talmud lessons you would be a fine sight at the balls in your villa—in Grunewald!!—or out there in Halensee or wherever it is that you go dancing!—Why don't you go over there to the next room and dance with those broads—with Ilonka and Amanda and Frau Deneke—as you do every day?—That's your Talmud lesson!—You dance and Löwenberg sleeps!—Such an ass as Löwenberg has never walked the earth before! He doesn't comprehend a single word!—But he comes punctually to study the Talmud because that's the commandment.—Even learning has already turned into a symbol!—"

From the next room came squeals and laughter—an angry yelp was followed by the sound of a hard slap!

The door jerked open, and Amanda stumbled in.

"Herr Kaiser!" she exclaimed. "I'm coming to you!—Herr Sonntag is getting fresh!"

Behind her came the man whom Chana had seen sitting on the sofa between the two young women; his left cheek was bright red. He walked to the window, trying to appear nonchalant, and bent over his books.

"How far did we get today?" he asked.

"We got through the tractate about moral purity," Joelsohn said. "The Talmud lesson is finished—wake up, Löwenberg!"

Figure 1.

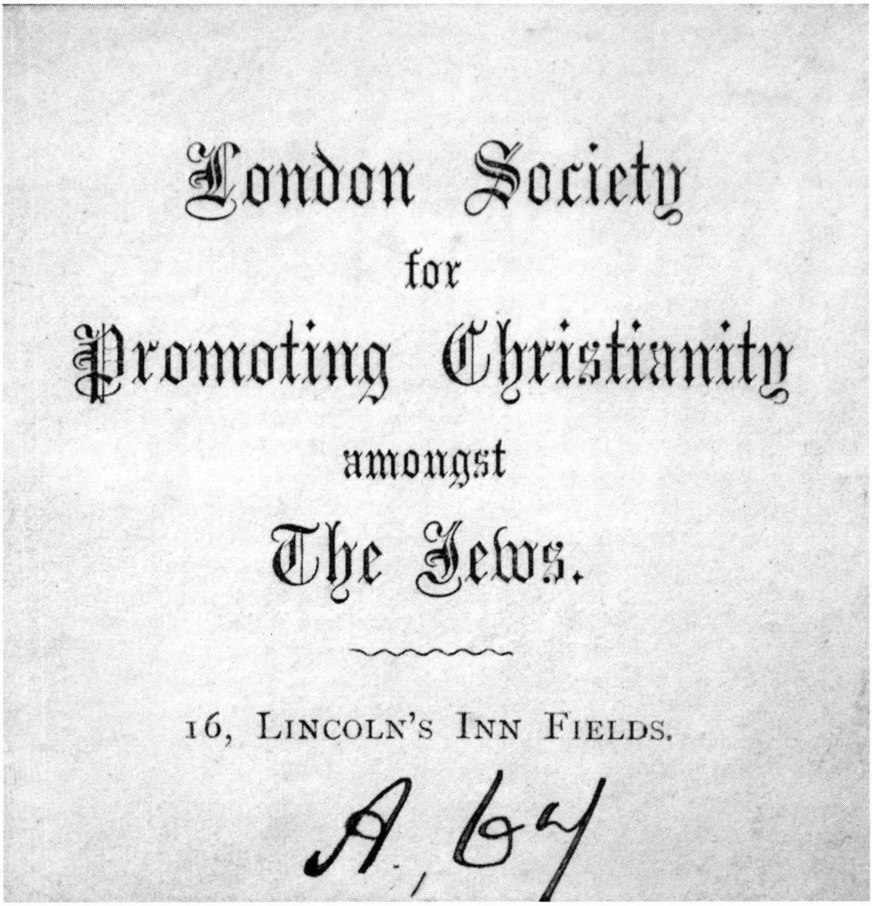

London Society

for

Promoting Christianity

amongst

The Jews.

16, LINCOLN'S INN FIELDS.

A. 64

Figure 2.

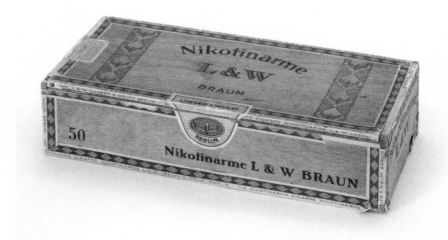

Figure 3.

„Warum haben Se sich denn katholisch taufen lassen?" — „Ach wissen Se, bei den Protestanten sind mir zu viel Juden."

Figure 4.

Figure 5.

Figure 6.

Figure 7.

Figure 8.

Johann Andreä Eisenmengers/

Professors der Orientalischen Sprachen bey der
Universität Heydelberg

Entdecktes Judenthum/

Oder

Gründlicher und Wahrhaffter Bericht/

Welchergestalt

Die verstockte Juden die Hochheilige Drey-Einigkeit/
GOtt Vater/Sohn und Heil.Geist/erschrecklicher Weise lästern
und verunehren/ die Heil. Mutter Christi verschmähen/ das Neue
Testament/ die Evangelisten und Aposteln/ die Christliche Religion
spöttisch durchziehen/ und die gantze Christenheit auff das äusserste
verachten und verfluchen;

Dabey noch viel andere/ bißhero unter den Christen
entweder gar nicht/ oder nur zum Theil bekant gewesene Dinge
und grosse Irrthüme der Jüdischen Religion und Theologie/
wie auch viel lächerliche und kurtzweilige Fabeln/ und andere
ungereimte Sachen an den Tag kommen.

Alles aus ihren eigenen/ und zwar sehr vielen mit grosser Mühe
und unverdrossenem Fleiß durchlesenen Büchern/mit Ausziehung
der Hebräischen Worte/ und derer treuen Ubersetzung in die Teutsche
Sprach/ kräfftiglich erwiesen /

Und

In Zweyen Theilen

verfasset/

Deren jeder seine behörige / allemal von einer gewissen Materie
aussführlich-handelnde Capitel enthält.
Allen Christen zur treuhertzigen Nachricht verfertiget/und mit
vollkommenen Registern versehen.

Mit Seiner Königl. Majestät in Preussen Allergnädigsten
Special-Privilegio.

Gedruckt zu Königsberg in Preussen/im Jahr nach Christi Geburt 1711.

Figure 9.

Figure 10.

Figure 11.

Figure 12.

Metamorphose

(Zeichnungen von Th. Th. Heine)

Moische Pisch handelte in Tarnopol mit abgelegten Kleidern,

als Moritz Wasserstrahl siedelte er nach Posen über und handelte mit Pariser Modewaren

jetzt lebt er als Maurice Lafontaine in Berlin, wo er eine neue Kunstrichtung gegründet hat und mit abgelegter Pariser Kunstmode handelt.

Figure 13.

Figure 14.

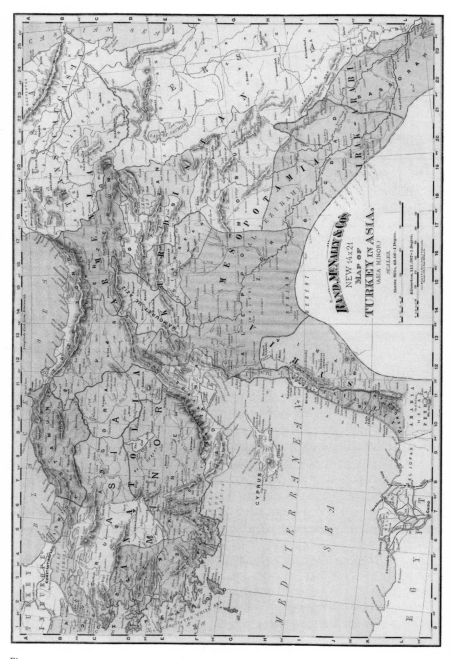

Figure 15.

Der

Verzweiflungskampf

der

arischen Völker mit dem Judentum.

Von

Hermann Ahlwardt
Rektor in Berlin.

Greif niemals in ein Wespennest,
Doch wenn Du greifst, so greife fest.

Berlin 1890.

Verlag von F. Grobhäuser.

Figure 16.

Figure 17.

Figure 18.

Figure 19.

Figure 20.

Gesamtansicht der Hauptfabrik in Elbing

LOESER & WOLFF ∗ BERLIN
Größte Zigarrenfabrik des Kontinents
und Rauchtabakfabrik

Figure 21.

Figure 1. Sammy Gronemann (1875–1952). *Portrait by J. Alexander, Central Zionist Archives, Jerusalem, PHG/1095056/Portrait by J. Alexander.*

Figure 2. "Berl Weinstein had himself baptized again, and this time with great success. All in all, he probably made about eight hundred marks. . . . [by] showing up at the mission society's large meeting in Whitechapel." (p. 1) *Bookplate of the London Society for Promoting Christianity Amongst The Jews (est. 1809) (date unknown). Courtesy of the Shimeon Brisman Collection in Jewish Studies, Washington University Libraries, St. Louis, Missouri.*

Figure 3. "'You know Loeser & Wolff!' Heinz said gravely." (p. 36) *Cigar box of the firm Loeser & Wolff, ca. 1871–1918, Berlin, wood and paper, © Jüdisches Museum Berlin (B 12342), photo by Jens Ziehe.*

Figure 4. "'I didn't subscribe to any dogmas when I converted. I believe no more and no less than hundreds of thousands of Christians and Jews here in Berlin. —The state in which we live is, after all, a Christian state; with no pressure on my conscience, I could have my name assigned from one enrollment register to another.'" (p. 49) *"How is it you converted to Catholicism?" "Oh, you know, because the Protestants have too many Jews." Drawing by Eduard Thöny (1866–1950). From* Simplicissimus. Illustrierte Wochenschrift, *vol. 3, no. 19 (August 6, 1898).*

Figure 5. "'That's it—kosher,' the Baroness said. 'I knew that: kosher—and in German that means 'meat grocery.'—Do you still buy your meat there?'" (p. 51) *Kosher shop, Berlin, Germany, 1900, © Image Works, ESVB0041190, photographer SV-Bilderdienst.*

Figure 6. "[The case is a]bout a shipment of a type of fruit called esrogs or 'apples of paradise,' which seem to be used during the Jewish Feast of Tabernacles, where the congregants shake them in the synagogue—there seems to be a sort of dervish dance performed—and a number of stems seem to have fallen off with this shipment. The defendant refuses to pay, because he claims that the fruit cannot be used for this ritual if the stems are missing." (pp. 53–54) *Etrog container, maker: KB, Augsburg (Germany), 1674–1680. Silver: chased and gilt, 7¼ × 9 × 5½ in (18.4 × 22.9 × 14 cm). Gift of Dr. Harry G. Friedman, F4390. Photo by Malcolm Varon. Photo credit: the Jewish Museum, New York / Art Resource, New York (ART52844).*

Figure 7. "Yossel was standing on the other side of the Oranienburger Strasse in front of the synagogue, where a crowd of curiosity seekers watched elegant couples dismount from carriages pulling up in front to hurry into the building." (p. 61) *Exterior of the New Synagogue in the Oranienburger Strasse, ca. 1900, Berlin, copper etching and print, © Jüdisches Museum Berlin (T1J1927), photo by Jens Ziehe.*

Figure 8. "About twenty definitely older men were sitting or standing around the long table in front of the window; their eyes were staring into books or into the distance or were closed now and then for several minutes in deepest thought; all were rocking back and forth either slowly and deliberately or rapidly and nervously." (p. 133) *Auerbach-Levy, William (1889–1964). Men Studying Malachi, 1921. Etching on paper, 8 ⅞ × 12 in. (22.5 × 30.5). Gift of William G. Golden, JM5-62. Photo credit: the Jewish Museum, New York / Art Resource, New York (ART495074).*

Figure 9. "[Candidate Ostermann] had quoted from Justus Brimann and Rohling and had gone back to Eisenmenger's *Entdecktes Judentum* or *Judaism Discovered.*" (p. 146) *Johann Andreas Eisenmenger, title page* Entdecktes Judenthum/Oder Gründlicher und Wahrhaffter Bericht, *1711, Königsberg, © Jüdisches Museum Berlin (PE100456/1), photo by Jens Ziehe.*

Figure 10. "Have you never been to Herrnfelds' theater on the Alexanderplatz?" (p. 150) *View from Alexanderplatz station in Landsberger Strasse, Berlin, 1905. Berolina statue and the Grand Hotel (left), restaurant and beer hall Aschinger in the former royal theater (right). Photograph. Photo credit: bpk, Berlin / Art Resource, New York (ART495049).*

Figure 11. "It is, God knows, a difficult step for all of us when we marry into a Jewish family. If your life were differently—no, never mind! We have made our decision like so many of the noblest families. I stepped over the chasm when I entered his house to at least see if the woman you wished to take as a bride would not personally bring shame on us. And as I said—there is nothing to object to there. And also she's blond!—So in principle, the deed is done with my visit—Nevertheless, if we have taken this step, we must secure the essential boundaries all the more so.—If we are already compelled by circumstances to bring an alien member into our family, we must be doubly clear who we are and who they are.—" (p. 156) *And you, Lieutenant, who have always been against marriages for money, is it true that you have become engaged to the daughter of Commercial Councillor Baruch?" "Well, it can sometimes happen that one falls in love with a rich girl." Drawing by Eduard Thöny (1866–1950)* Ein weißer Rabe, *cover of* Simplicissimus. Illustrierte Wochenschrift, *(1897/98), vol. 2, no. 20, (August 8, 1897).*

Figure 12. "As [Heinz] turned onto the street that had been completely foreign to him until now, his eyes widened, and he asked himself whether he wouldn't be asked to show his passport here. He was apparently no longer in Berlin or Germany but somehow had been magically transported to a Russian or Galician Jewish town." (p. 163) *Facade of Fashion House Israel with passersby, ca. 1900, Berlin (assumed). Black-and-white photograph, gift of Monica Peiser, © Jüdisches Museum Berlin (T1J1922), photo by Jens Ziehe.*

Figure 13. "Here [in the Dragonerstrasse] an old man with a worried look who could have been a model for Moses, was holding up a gray plaid pair of pants by the legs as he stood in a doorway and spoke sternly to a young man who was foppishly and raffishly dressed as he chewed indecisively on the knob of his walking stick." (p. 163) *"Moische Pisch buys and sells second-hand clothing in Tarnopol, he moves to Poland as Moritz Wasserstrahl, and deals in Paris fashions, and now as Maurice Lafontaine in Berlin, where he established a new art movement, he deals in second-hand Parisian art fashions." Drawing by Theodor Thomas Heine (1867–1948),* © ARS, *New York. Metamorphosis. From* Simplicissimus. Illustrierte Wochenschrift 8, *no. 10 (June 2, 1903). Photo credit: bpk, Berlin, Art Resource, New York (ART49501).*

Figure 14. "At the entrance he had to get past a cordon of very young people, almost children, wearing the blue-and-white emblems, who were holding out their collection boxes, flyers, brochures, or newspapers to everyone passing by." (p. 176) *Collection box for the National Jewish Fund, Palestine or Germany, ca. 1920,* © *Jüdisches Museum Berlin (KGM 98/1/0), photo by Jens Ziehe.*

Figure 15. "Furthermore, he declared Zionism to be a utopian chimera, because Palestine would never be handed over to Jews, since it was the jewel of Turkish lands, and besides, it was the Holy Land of all Christian peoples." (p. 179) *"Turkey in Asia" from Rand, McNally & Co.'s New 14 × 21 Map of Turkey in Asia. (Asia Minor.)* © *1895, by Rand, McNally & Co. (Chicago, 1897).*

Figure 16. "'Well, the ol' hoopla begins again!—I know that lot of anni-Semites from the days of old Ahlwardt. Always Germany!—Germany! I tell 'em'—he leaned confidentially towards his passenger—'that we wouldn't still have the whole misery with the anni-Semites if there was no Jews.'" (p. 180) *Title page of Der Verzweiflungskampf der arischen Völker mit dem Judentum (The desperate struggle of Aryan peoples against the Jews) by Hermann Ahlwardt, (Berlin, 1890), from electronic copy in library of the University of Frankfurt/Main, Germany*

Figure 17. "[I]magine, for the evening of the seder, the evening that begins the festival of Passover, on which every Jew wants at least to be a guest at the festival meal." (p. 185) *Seder meal of Jewish soldiers in the First World War, Mitau, April 6, 1917. Gift of Lore Emanuel,* © *Jüdisches Museum Berlin (FOT97/9/2).*

Figure 18. "[Heinz], a member of the Feudal Club on the Nollendorfplatz—the envied friend of posh Tilly—the alumnus of the fraternity Roswithania—who was now sitting here in Borytshev at the table of Moische Schlenker." (p. 193) *Group photo of a Jewish fraternity, 1908. Photograph. Photo credit: bpk, Berlin, Art Resource, New York (ART 495049).*

Figure 19. "[Heinz] heard only confused shouts and thought he was seeing an utter chaos of excited white figures, with no one taking anyone else into account." (p. 221) *Etching by Ernst Oppler, The Great Synagogue in Munkácz, ca. 1915. Gift of Ellen M. Ansprenger,* © *Jüdisches Museum Berlin (GDR79/8/0), photo by Jens Ziehe.*

Figure 20. "Squeezed in the alley, the mob was sweeping back and forth, without anyone being able to say what was actually happening—A few thugs in peasant blouses, trailed by females, their faces flushed with excitement, were running . . ." (p. 226) *Caricature by Henryk Nowodworski (1875–1930), Tsarist thug (cockade in hat) in the Bialystok pogrom. Cover of* "Dzięcioł" *[Woodpecker] no. 12. (1906). From the collection of the Museum of Caricature and Cartoon Art in Warsaw), photo by Katarzyna Majek.*

Figure 21. "Apropos—you have dug up the most completely fabulous character of a cigarette man. Isn't he the same as the creator of the brand Klatzéki, which suddenly became so popular? Brussow swears by this brand and says this is the only Papyrosse suitable for a civilized person—people say Papyrosse now!" (p. 237) *Otto Bolhagen, "Werbepappe der Firma Loeser & Wolff," ca. 1920–1930, Bremen,* © *Jüdisches Museum Berlin (Ni675), photo by Jens Ziehe.*

FIVE

Paradise Apples

I

"Kahn!—Kahn!—Colleague Kahn!!—Colleague Siegmund Kahn!!!"

Justice Councillor Wenzel had been bellowing for half an hour for Kahn—shoving his bulky figure through the bustle of the chambers of the Regional Court on the Grunerstrasse.—He was wandering up and down the long corridor, peering right and left—he looked into a number of cubicles and inspected the groups of people at the broad tables between the coat racks—he looked through the glass door into the legal library, whose somnolence and silence strangely warded off the surrounding atmosphere of a stock market—he blared his battle cry into the chess room facing the library to summon the missing party to appear. There several games were under way that held the attention not only of the players but also of the kibitzers—he called as he walked past the row of telephone booths—he bellowed his "Siegmund Kahn!!" across the steps and the colonnaded corridor, planted at the main entrance of the attorneys' room.—But no Siegmund Kahn could be found!—He found Leopold Kahn and various Kohns—even Siegmund Kohn, who had hastily come running to follow the Justice Councillor storming along the winding stairs up to and into the courtroom; only there and only after Kohn had looked through all twenty-three files that had been delivered to him as notice of the court date by the Berendson Trust did the error come to light, and he left greatly exasperated.—But Siegmund Kahn did not come to light!—

Meanwhile, the attorney Sigismund Hank sat in the chess room, squeezing his slight figure behind a group of kibitzers who were staring as if hypnotized at the chess board, at which two hopeless chess bumblers were brooding over the most boring of all possible games—and he had fallen deaf and dumb. He knew why Wenzel was looking for him; it was the cursed lawsuit over the esrogs, which he as the plaintiff had lost at trial level. He had had to file an appeal at the insistence of his client but was mostly convinced of the uselessness of the law. Indeed, he had little sympathy for the matter for many reasons, and, even more unfortunately, it had been assigned to the bench—of all people—of the notorious Bandmann to adjudicate. He firmly resolved, if he could escape the opponent who was searching for him and if he could get a continuance in this way, he would dump the files on a colleague for transmitting legal notice of the court date.

But fate was approaching in the form of a courier; he stopped as Wenzel bellowed again his "Siegmund Kahn!!" as he passed by. The courier tugged at the Justice Councillor's robe whipping past and asked: "Whom are you looking for? —Kahn?—Siegmund Kahn?—But Herr Justice Councillor—he doesn't exist anymore!—By virtue of a journey of grace, he has been granted by a decree most high a further penance with his name.—You know—during the recent great boom: from Saul to Paul—from Levysohn to Lehnsen—and from the ashes of Siegmund Kahn arose the phoenix Sigismund Hank!"

And so he belted out: "Attorney Sigismund Hank!"

"The devil alone knows who these Israelite colleagues are!" Wenzel said, annoyed. "They have a different name every time you turn around!"

"Hank!—Colleague Hank!" he shouted, his hope revived.

Sigismund Hank had to respond to the call now, for better or worse; he pulled his files together and pretended to hastily come from the chess room.

"Look—there he is!" exclaimed the courier. "Herr Justice Councillor Wenzel is killing himself looking for you!"

"Was I called?" Hank asked innocently. "Herr Justice Councillor Wenzel?— Over here—my name is Hank! You're finally here! I've been waiting for you for at least an hour!"

"Really!—Excuse me?" Wenzel said, outraged. "I've been bellowing for three hours like a crazy man after you!"

"So sorry!" Hank said. "I certainly would have heard that if you were calling my name.—I only heard my name just now for the first time!"

"Really—if it has the charm of something new to hear your name—my voice is completely hoarse.—Well, come along, then, so we can get our paradise apples safely in the bag before Easter."

They hurried up the stairs to the third floor and entered the council chamber of Bandmann, feared for his eloquence and malevolence, enthroned between the Regional Court Councillors Schlüter and Bernstorff. Because the proceedings in the case of *Romanov v. The Prince of Wales* had taken so long, a rather large number of attorneys were gathered in the room, all waiting impatiently until it was their turn. Both newcomers were greeted with dirty looks, and the usual sort of discussion ensued about who was first. According to the appointment slips, next up was the case of *Pfeffer v. Boruch;* the other attorneys grumbled and reluctantly moved to the back.—Wenzel and Hank posted themselves nonetheless next to both desks affixed to the right and left of the judge's bench to have their case announced the moment the court clerk in charge cleared the field before any attorneys could rush in at the last moment with an even better number on their slips that could postpone the case again.—

The parties, however, emerged from the crowd of onlookers on the back benches—Herr Pfeffer and Herr Boruch in person, who had been there since the first call of the courier, that is, almost three hours—the appointed time had been nine o'clock, and now it was almost twelve—they had been sitting on the wooden bench the whole time, exchanging black looks. The fury pent up in each party, as well as in their own attorneys, who had left them there for hours to stew with impatience, now gave way to somewhat friendlier feelings; full of hope and ready for battle, they planted themselves next to their advisors, giving the opposition's attorney black looks.

The Romanov case against the Prince of Wales was still not entirely finished, yet the head of the court was already dictating to the law clerk the settlement by which the leather merchant Wolf in the Romanov firm and the shoe merchant Rosenbaum in the Prince of Wales firm buried their axes.

Finally the time had come; the settlement agreement was read aloud and approved. The two attorneys, having finished, rushed out with their files, and Wenzel and Hank took their place.

"The next case on the docket!" the Justice Councillor said. "Number 286— *Pfeffer v. Boruch.*"

"I already see," the president of the court said, casting a quick glance over the parties as he took the files from the hands holding them, "that this is the case with the paradise apples, which have turned into the apples of Eris. The milk of human kindness has fermented into dragon's venom.—Herr Law Clerk Lehnsen—that is just your sort of case! Please take down the transcript."

II

"The matter is ready for disposal!" Justice Councillor Wenzel said. "It has been carefully documented in the briefs; do we still need to have oral argument?"

"The gentlemen are prepared on the matter with all serious attention to detail in their written arguments," the Director said. "We can probably accept the speeches as having been savored and decide according to what's in the files."

"I would like to add something," Hank exclaimed.

"Fine—right! Your client himself is here in person."

"That has absolutely nothing to do with how I do things!" Hank said, annoyed.

"And why should it?" Bandmann asked, apparently puzzled. "How do you even think such a thing?—Let me finish! I wanted to say: since both parties are here in person, perhaps the dispute can be settled through a compromise.—"

"A compromise seems to me to be out of the question!" Hank said hastily; he had already made efforts to no avail at trial level for an amicable settlement of this dispute, which he found most unpleasant. Efforts that failed due to the stubbornness of his client. He didn't mind at all stretching out this pointless appeal about this matter.

"As you wish!" the Court President said coldly. "Well, then, first of all the transcript, Herr Law Clerk.—Call the parties, who are here! Appearing with the plaintiff and the appellant"—he glanced at the file label—"whose legal representative is Attorney Kahn—"

"Hank!"

"I beg your pardon?"

"Attorney Hank for the plaintiff!" the short man said, turning red.

"You are—? Pardon me! I can't personally know who all the attorneys are!—I thought you were Kahn—how appearance deceives!—Shall we, Herr Law Clerk? A new transcript: with the plaintiff whose legal representative, Attorney Kahn, is represented by Attorney Hank as substitute."

"No!" Hank groaned. "Not a substitute—I myself am the legal representative!"

"Sooo?—Oh, sorry!" Bandmann said with exaggerated politeness. "Please, Herr Law Clerk, a new transcript: with the plaintiff the Attorney Kahn with the remark that he has been authorized to be the second legal representative along with Attorney Kahn."

"Absolutely not!" Hank exclaimed—apoplectic over the laughter he could hear beginning to spread in the audience behind his back. "I am indeed the legal representative—Attorney Hank—I am the only legal representative!"

"Ahh!" Bandmann said with undiminished politeness. "That was another misunderstanding; I beg your pardon.—So, Herr Law Clerk, please, a new transcript: with the plaintiff whose legal representative is Attorney Hank—who informs us that the client relationship with the previous legal representative Attorney Kahn has been dissolved."

"That is just—!" Hank was ready to throw the files on the floor and storm out. "I am one and the same—Kahn and Hank, that's the same.—I have been the legal representative from the beginning!"

"Oh?" Bandmann said very graciously. "I still don't understand; please be so good as to explain all this to me."

Hank pulled himself together and said as calmly as possible, "I changed my name with sovereign permission: my name is now Hank!"

"Ahhh!—Indeed. Why didn't you say so right away!—Herr Law Clerk, a new transcript please: with the plaintiff whose legal representative is Attorney Kahn—"

"Hank!!" the attorney shouted frantically.

"Just keep calm—a moment!—One thing after the other!" Bandmann said gently. "Got that, Herr Law Clerk? With the plaintiff whose legal representative is

Attorney *Kahn.*—Attorney *Kahn* explains that he since recently no longer bears the name of *Kahn* with sovereign permission but now calls himself *Hank;* Attorney Hank now files an appeal.—Have you got that, Herr Law Clerk?"

"Yes indeed!" Heinz Lehnsen said without looking up, writing busily; he did not share in the general mirth.

"And with the other party," Bandmann continued, "Justice Councillor Wenzel. —The name is correct, no?"

"Correct!" the Justice Councillor chuckled jovially.—"Still August Wenzel— from baptism to today!"

"So a settlement is out of the question?" Bandmann said with regret. "Pity! The matter is so well suited for it.—It's a question of objects for an Israelite ritual; it should be important to both parties, who are of the Mosaic faith, not to let such disputes come to this extreme if they couldn't help but litigate the matter.—What does the defendant have to say?"

"Well—open your mouth!" said Wenzel, pushing toward the judge's bench his client, who was wearing a thick fur coat despite the mild spring weather.

"Herr President!" Boruch said. "I am a peaceful man—but in this matter I've had so much trouble: I'm supposed to pay still more money?—The fruit can't be used in the synagogue if the stems are missing—"

"Ah, well!" Bandmann said. "Personally, I don't quite understand, of course, just why the integrity of the stems should so impair the ritual use.—Back then in paradise the apple no longer had a stem when Adam took a bite—but we have to go along with the greater expertise of the rabbinical report. Still, the matter isn't completely legally clear.—Wouldn't you rather pay the plaintiff half of your own accord?"

"Why?—For the stems that were ripped off?"

"Did I sell the stems?" Herr Pfeffer suddenly interjected. Pfeffer was a thin, pale little man with a narrow goatee and large glasses. "I sold fruit!—If I buy pears and the pears are good, I can't say there's something wrong with the pears—and then refuse to pay!"

"I've bought the pears?" Boruch exclaimed. "Is an esrog a pear?—You knew that I wasn't making esrog jam!"

"Why do I care why you bought them! You can eat them with whipped cream for all I care!"

"Herr Director!" Hank exclaimed. "The settlement hearings really are useless."

"But why?" Bandmann said. He had leaned back comfortably and was contentedly following the discussion of the quarreling parties. "You are now on your way to coming to an understanding here. Just let them continue talking, Herr Attorney Kahn!"

"Hank!" the little attorney shouted, beside himself.

"Hank?" Bandmann said, apparently completely surprised. "But this time you are *wrong*! You just put into the transcript yourself that you changed your name with sovereign permission and now are named Kahn!"

Hank gasped for air.

"Please check, Herr Law Clerk Lehnsen!" Bandmann said solicitously. "What was it exactly?"

Heinz bent low over the transcript; he had to look twice before he found the answer.

"Attorney Hank—formerly Kahn," he finally said in the most official tone possible.

"Ah, really?—Then that's it!—I must ask you to excuse me. It's truly—an understandable error? It could just as easily be the other way around.—Hank! I shall certainly remember the name now!"

"I most urgently request that you do!" Hank said angrily.

"But why so offended?" Bandmann asked innocently. "I merely made a mistake and acknowledge that I did so.—I remember now that you said Hank; and added that was so since your baptism to today!"

"Well, that was probably me!" smirked Wenzel.

"Possibly, possibly!" Bandmann said. "So that takes care of that contretemps!—Now once again to the paradise apples at hand.—You, Herr Boruch, had religious reservations about the devaluation of the stemless fruit?"

"Without stems the fruit is useless!—No one would buy them from me, because you can't pray with them at all!"

"How does the plaintiff answer?"

"This point is totally irrelevant," said Hank, who was sensing the need to play a somewhat less passive role. "I don't even want to respond to that; I personally don't understand a thing about that, but—"

"What?" Boruch interrupted. "You don't understand anything about that? And the late old Leiser Kahn was the prayer leader in the temple in Wongrowitz!"

"I must ask that I be spared these insults!" Hank exclaimed.

"Herr Boruch!" Bandmann said earnestly. "Stop interrupting and cease your inappropriate comments about the plaintiff's legal representative.—The late Leiser Kahn from Wongrowitz is of no concern to this court, nor does he concern Attorney Hank.—Do you understand?"

"But Attorney Kahn—Hank—knows perfectly well—every Jew knows—"

"I'm a Protestant—if you don't mind!" Hank said sharply.

Boruch looked him in the eye and suddenly became very quiet.

"I don't mind!" he said and stepped back. "I didn't know that Herr Pfeffer's attorney was baptized!"

"I can't do anything about that!" Pfeffer exclaimed heatedly. "He only went and got baptized after the proceedings started! I'd already paid the retainer!"

"What effrontery!" Hank protested. "I resign my brief if you say another word!"

"But Herr Attorney!" Bandmann said gently. "Don't get so excited! A bit more Christian charity!"

"I must protest these continued anti-Semitic and insulting comments directed at me on the part of the President of the Court!" Hank shouted, now completely beside himself.

"Anti-Semitic? Insulting?" Bandmann exclaimed in a tone of complete surprise and looked as if thunderstruck at his colleagues beside him, who were looking indignant themselves. "Anti-Semitic and insulting?—But are you even an Israelite yourself, Herr Hank?"

Hank was incapable of any further reply; he hastily gathered up his files and stormed from the room.

"Have you ever seen anything like that? What's wrong with the man?" Bandmann asked and looked around him.—His glance fell on Lehnsen, who was bent far over the table, still writing.

"You have put the claims into the transcript, no?—Herr Justice Councillor Wenzel has requested the appeal be denied!—The date to announce the decision is in eight days!"

III

Heinz Lehnsen left the court in a sullen mood to go home; he carried under his arm the portfolio with the files for the miserable case of *Pfeffer v. Boruch.*—His vote on the appeal had been overruled, and now he had the task to draft the opinion in the next few days. That was, incidentally, not treacherous in any way, and his thoughts for the moment were concerned less with the legal issues of the case than with today's hearing, whose witness and chronicler he had been forced to be.

The manner in which Bandmann had handled the attorney disturbed Heinz and angered him; Bandmann's malice was surely directed at him too or even mainly at him. He had, after all, changed his religion and name at the same time as Kahn; he had had to keep calm throughout the hearing and transcribe what was said, while it remained open to the attorney to appropriately object to the spite in the allusions.—Now this newly minted Herr Hank certainly did not possess the personality to defend his position with dignity.

Heinz was almost angrier with Hank than with Bandmann; Hank had made him, along with himself, look ridiculous, Hank had become the attorney of his case too by chance and through his ineptitude had gotten him mixed up in this too.

Heinz mentally put himself in Hank's shoes and asked himself what he would have said in Hank's situation.—He was convinced that he would not have let himself be as caught off guard as Hank and that he would have stood up to the judge's arrogance with suitable vigor.—But that certainly did not take care of the issue; the unsuitable behavior of one could be energetically resisted without having to take a position oneself.—Heinz, however, recognized all too well that beneath the surface of that conversation between judge and attorney, between the innuendos and banter, there was something else, something more serious.—He had a definite feeling that it wasn't only the lack of snappy repartee or dignity in demeanor that caused Hank to make such an unfortunate impression in the eyes of everyone watching.

How would Hank have been able to defend his position, his change of name, and everything that went with it if he were seriously accused of what Bandmann had garbed in malicious digs?

Heinz was seized by a simmering rage at Hank; he saw in his mind's eye Hank's small, slight figure—his narrow, slack face—his restless eyes—his hooked nose, and the blood rose to his face when he realized how this repellent wretch had writhed under Bandmann's jibes. Would not Bandmann and most everyone else see him as they saw Hank—with the same disgust—with the same contempt?—

But what right did these people have to their snotty judgment, these elites who rewarded those who converted. His father owed his promotion to his baptism after all, which had been advised so urgently by an authoritative office.—What the state considered as a condition to attain a higher post could not be immoral in and of itself. And how many noble men, moral beyond a doubt, did he know who had followed this path.

It was likely that the case of Kahn—Hank's case was different, completely different from his case and the cases he had just thought of.—What Boruch had said was probably right: Kahn really did come from a Jewish family, knew something of Judaism, of Jewish customs and Jewish sensibilities, and still had taken the step—had been able to deny his past.

On the other hand, he—Heinz Lehnsen! What did he deny?—What ties had he torn?—He had never had anything Jewish around him; he hadn't known his grandparents, even though the memory of his mother's father had been particularly esteemed. His picture hung in the dining room, and the story of his rise from a poor immigrant teacher to a wealthy entrepreneur had impressed him. In his parents' house nothing Jewish had been cultivated or even tolerated. Jews who came to the house did not have anything recognizably Jewish in their manner. At best, Dr. Magnus! But even he had spoken no word that a Christian theologian wouldn't have said. Tact for Christian company dictated that perhaps!—The children were really aware of their Jewishness only in that they weren't in their schoolmates' religion class in school and they didn't go to church.

Heinz had only been in a synagogue once—for his sister's confirmation; they both had had confirmation lessons. He retained only a dim concept of ethical obligations sorted by a, b, and c.

Consequently, he had rejected nothing when he converted from Judaism—he had not committed any deception when he changed his name; on the contrary, he had shed the name of Levysohn and of being a Jew as a particularly misleading designation.—Only a false impression of who he was had long been indicated by these terms—he was identified with a category of community that in truth had nothing to do with him.

But Hank, on the other hand!—

But perhaps the matter was different, and maybe he was being unfair to Hank! —What if this Hank had turned his back on Judaism out of his very knowledge of it! What if he had come to judge Judaism on the basis of serious study! While he, Heinz, had taken this step without any knowledge, with no basis for judgment.—What had actually happened was that he had accompanied his father without any particular interest to the chamber court to hand in the declaration.—

Wouldn't he come off worse than Hank if he were seriously questioned in a hearing? What could he say?

Strange!—Heinz knew only enough about Jewish history to know that baptism had always opened the way to freedom for a Jew, that for centuries those who held fast to Judaism were threatened by death and torture.

How was it even possible that there were even still Jews!

Whoever was weak or fearful in any way, whoever wasn't endowed with the strongest will to live had to be overlooked back then. Even more: if even one single person in the subsequent generations succumbed to the pressure, then all his descendants would be lost to Judaism, and the family would be stricken forevermore from membership in the scroll of Jews.—

In modern times really only a selection of the strongest and bravest were saved.—

Heinz stood there shaken when this thought occurred to him.

But that was the aristocracy—aristocracy in the best sense of the word!

In contrast, what were the Stülp-Sanderslebens, who traced their title back to a crusader and for whom aristocracy had always smoothed the way. When had this aristocratic family been forced to struggle for existence?—When had courage been required to profess its membership in this aristocracy?—

Just how did it happen—Heinz continued his slow way home through the Tiergarten—just how did it happen that in modern days when danger to life and limb now no longer threatened—that the sons of this old aristocracy converted en masse, that they almost all had wanted to disappear without a trace in the crowd, to relinquish what marked their identity?—For a pretty fraternity ribbon, for a pair of epaulettes, for a miserably remunerated position they gave up what the fear of mortal danger and torture had not been able to extort from their fathers.

How pointless history is when something was preserved and held onto for thousands of years with infinite tenacity and then was tossed aside like rubbish the moment the danger had passed.

Is history, then, really so pointless?—or is the present day supposed to be the greatest test from which only a few, the best, would emerge once again as the greatest and last elite!—

The best—where the Hanks and the Lehnsens didn't belong!

Possible—even probable that his forebears had clung to an old superstition long since overcome—that couldn't obligate him, a modern, enlightened son of the present day.—But he should have had knowledge of what it was—to make his own judgment.—

But now it was, of course, too late!—He had taken the major step without giving the matter any sort of consideration.—and he wasn't able to defend what he had done—if anyone questioned it.

But was it really too late?—Would it not be worthwhile, even now—particularly now—to review the matter, to find evidence as to how morally justified conversion was and be able to face any hostility and doubt with a free conscience.—

But what if the result would be different from what he expected?—

Heinz burst out with an angry laugh; on what kind of crazy path was the incident in today's hearing taking him! He, who not only absolutely had no religious needs at all but also undeniably possessed no trace of comprehension for things such as "belief," was figuring on the possibility of landing in religion by way of investigating it—and even an ancient one putting up with fantastic and tasteless forms like the Jewish one.—He imagined himself parading with the esrogs among a crowd of old men, all with beards.—That would be something for Elsa!—

He suddenly remembered that today was his sister's birthday, and guests would already be at home. He hurried home along the last stretch.

As he crossed the street to arrive at his door he saw a group in the entryway that made him pause for a moment.

There stood a pale young Jewish man, his dress obviously of decent but Eastern Jewish origin, about his own height, exchanging words with the porter.—He was in shirtsleeves, having come directly from the cellar, and had taken up a position to block the door. He was waving his muscular arms wildly, and when he saw Heinz approaching, he shouted: "I tell you again: go away! No Levysohn lives here! Here comes the young master—you can ask him yourself!"

IV

Heinz slowly approached the door; meeting a Jew of the old-fashioned sort just now seemed to be a remarkable coincidence and prophetic. He watched the young man, who had turned around and was walking toward him pensively and with a smile on his face. Was this the representative of the ancient aristocracy? Was this one of those who was said to have withstood trial by fire, whom he so failed to measure up to in the same way as Hank had failed?

He was so deep in his own intricate musings that he didn't hear Yossel's greeting.—

"What do you want?" he asked, shaking off his thoughts.—

"And I'm bringing back your money," Yossel finished the explanation that Heinz had missed.

"What money?"

"The ten marks!—"

Yossel held a ten-mark coin in his hand—in the other, a money order receipt.

"Ten marks?"

"Yes—the ten marks for Lifschitz at Bornstein's!"

Heinz remembered now the schnorrer letter and his philanthropic impulse. He looked at Yossel with astonishment.

"You are returning the money to me?"

"I don't need it!" Yossel answered with embarrassment.

"You're Lifschitz?" Heinz asked.

Yossel turned red and looked at the ground.

"You're Levysohn?" he replied.

Heinz also turned red and looked at the sky.

At that moment a carriage came around the corner from the direction of the riverbank and slowed down as it approached the house.

"Come along!" Heinz said brusquely as he glanced at the conveyance and hurriedly went inside.—Yossel followed behind.—

Regional Court Director Lehnsen and two younger gentlemen stepped from the carriage.—Lehnsen paid the coachman under protest from the two men, who each wanted to pay his share.

"But absolutely not, Herr Lieutenant!—I grabbed you and brought you along.—Please, Herr Assessor Borchers—Herr Lieutenant!—What's the matter, Böhme?"

The porter had emerged again from his cellar when the gentlemen went inside, and his red face expressed outrage.

"Herr Director!" he huffed in agitation. "I just want to say: I couldn't do anything about it!—The young master—Herr Law Clerk Lehnsen didn't let me—I wanted to throw him out!"

"What?—Who?" Lehnsen asked, mystified; the two young gentlemen watched the agitated Cerberus with amusement.

"Why, that damned Jew scoundrel! The one who comes around begging!—Now he's up there with the Herr Law Clerk! He's called—Lifschitz or Bornstein or something like that; that's what he said—an' I said: No Levysohn has been here for a long time, and Jews don't have any business here anymore!"

Both gentlemen began to converse loudly with conscientious discretion as they slowly went up the steps.

Lehnsen looked angrily at the porter and shouted in a voice loud enough to be heard at the top of the stairs: "Fetch a policeman and have the fellow arrested!"

Then with repressed rage he hastened up the steps, trying in vain to compose an unconcerned and happy face.

V

Holding the coin and the money order receipt in his hand, Yossel followed Heinz up the steps with a sinking heart. Heinz opened the door with his latchkey; a parlor maid in a white cap and a skimpy apron appeared and observed the unusual apparition of Yossel with curiosity.

"Is my father already home?" Heinz asked.

"Herr Regional Court Director hasn't returned yet," the maid said. "There are already lots of guests inside—"

From the salon one heard the buzz of voices.

Heinz opened a door on the left and waved to Yossel to follow him.—They entered the study of the young law clerk; Yossel shyly remained standing at the door while Heinz put his things down and then, as was his habit, emptied his briefcase.—He picked up a file, thumbed through it, and asked with a slight smile: "Do you know what esrogs are?"

Yossel looked him so helplessly that Heinz had to laugh.

"I asked if you know what esrogs are—paradise apples—the fruit that one takes to the temple during the Feast of Tabernacles."

"You mean—I know—you're just pronouncing it differently—ethrog and lulav!"

"Lulav?"

"Well, yes—for Sukkos!"

"Sukkos?"

"The plants you shake during the holiday?"

"Yes—right—what were the words again?—Doesn't matter!—So you know what I mean?"

"Of course I know."

And with that the conversation reached its provisional conclusion. Heinz went to the window and looked out. He fell into his old train of thought and asked himself whether he should use this opportunity that had so fortuitously been handed to him to learn something about Jewish things.—But was this person really the right teacher? His face was pleasing enough; he found it trustworthy enough, in any case, it was a sympathetic face; the man didn't really look like a schnorrer and certainly not as if he were capable of writing such lamentable letters.—Right! He was returning the money after all; that had to be clarified before anything else.

He turned around.

"So, what's the story with the money?" he asked. "Why are you bringing it back to me?"

In his astonishment over the questions about the esrogs with which he had been received, Yossel had entirely forgotten why he had come. Now he was even more frightened.

"I'm returning the money to you," he said and put the money and the money order receipt on the table. "What else do you want?—There was a mistake.—It was nice of you, but I don't need it."

He tried to quietly get to the door.

"Stop!" Heinz said, and Yossel stood there. "Not so fast!—If you don't need it, why did you write in the first place!—"

Yossel started to sweat, he twisted this way and that and then finally said with downcast eyes: "But I didn't write it!"

"You didn't?—So you aren't Lifschitz at all?"

"No!"

"Who are you, then?"

"Who am I?"

"Yes! What's your name?"

"Schlenker—Yossel Schlenker!"

"Schlenker?—Where are you from?"

"Borytshev."

"Borytshev in Russia?"

"Yes."

Heinz had sat down on top of the desk during this interrogation and lit a cigarette; he stood up now and paced up and down the room.—Then he went to the window and pulled the curtain open, and daylight flooded in. He gestured to Yossel to approach.

"Come here!—Take a seat here!"

He shoved a chair next to the window for Yossel, and, feeling rather uncomfortable, Yossel sat down—awaiting the subsequent questions with trepidation.

The longer Heinz was silent, observing him with a strange curiosity, the more discomfited Yossel became.—Finally he couldn't stand it any longer and asked in a tight voice, "May I go now?"

"Go?" Heinz started as if awakened out of a dream. "Oh yes!—No—On the contrary! So—where were we? Right—so, now tell me, Mr. Yossel Schlenker: who is Lifschitz?"

That was a mean question, and Yossel made no answer.

"Who is Bornstein?"

That was easier to answer.

"That's the landlord from the Dragonerstrasse."

"Now who wrote the letter?"

"Why are you torturing me?" Yossel said after a moment. "I've done nothing wrong; you have your money back. It's only because I didn't want anyone to cheat you that I brought it back.—How am I involved otherwise?"

"Look!" Heinz said. "Someone wanted to cheat me!—Who wanted to do that?—The letter was a con, then?"

"Herr Levysohn!" Yossel said, standing up. "Excuse me! But I can't say anything more.—I certainly didn't intend to do anything wrong; otherwise, I wouldn't have come here. And I don't want to say anything more! Do what you want with me!"

"I don't want to do anything to you!" Heinz said softly and felt a strange sympathy with the poor man whom he had caused such embarrassment. "I think you are an honest man. Otherwise you really wouldn't have brought back the money.—It seems to me you wanted to stop something fraudulent, and I am thankful to you for that.—But what have you to do with all this? How did you get the money? You are, after all, not Lifschitz but Yossel Schlenker!"

"I must ask you, dear sir," Yossel pleaded, "let me leave. I don't want to harm another person!"

"I promise you that nothing will happen to anyone!—But I want to know what's behind all this."

"You absolutely promise me that?" Yossel said hesitantly, looking Heinz directly in the eye.

"Here, you have my hand on that!"

"As truly as you are a Jew?" Yossel asked insistently.

Heinz was silent with embarrassment.

"As truly as I was born a Jew!" he finally said.

Yossel now began to tell what had happened a few days ago in Bornstein's pub, described what Klatzke did, repeated the arguments of Berl Weinstein, and reported how he and his wife had objected in vain.—

Heinz listened intently.

"No blame attaches to you!" he said. "It is commendable that you are returning the ten marks to me. But now go on. Tell me what brought you to Berlin and what you've been doing here."

Yossel spoke, and Heinz interrupted with lots of questions until he knew in broad outline not only the result of Yossel's and Chana's visits to Berlin rabbis but also about the Borytshev *Faust* studies.—Yes, he was even interested in Yossel's family—he asked about Yossel's father, whose brother had disappeared abroad many years ago, about Chana and her sisters, and many more from the chronicles of the Borytshev community.

To be sure, he was listening with only half an ear at the end and began to pay attention to his own train of thought as he looked down on the street from the window. Something there suddenly seemed to catch his attention. He saw the porter walking with the policeman toward the house, and, flinging open the window casement to lean out, he saw both of them disappearing through the front door.—Hastily he shut the window, went to the door, and opened it softly; he heard the heavy steps of the men coming up the stairs, and then someone was knocking on the hall door.

The maid opened the door, and Heinz heard the porter speaking to her softly: "I just want to say that I got a policeman; he can wait out here only so long."

As the maid, her eyes greedy for sensation, was trying to find out more, Heinz withdrew.

He paced up and down in agitation; the connection was obvious to him, and he was angry and upset.—All the anger accumulating in him since this morning's hearing in the case of *Pfeffer v. Boruch* now came to the fore and overwhelmed him.

He stopped in front of Yossel and seized him by the arm.

"Come on!" he said roughly.

Frightened, his eyes wide, Yossel stood up and looked at Heinz.

Heinz stood there a few moments, gripping Yossel's arm—his eyes close to Yossel's.

At that moment he was overwhelmed with hot and almost painful shaking as he peered into the deep and pure eyes that now looked at him questioningly and with fright—similar perhaps to the feeling he had once experienced as a little boy when he held a baby bird imprisoned in his hands.

Making a rash decision, he tore open the door to the next room without letting go of Yossel's arm and dragged him into the chamber.

VI

Many guests were already gathered in the salon when Heinz was still on his way home from court through the linden trees and the Tiergarten.

Elsa's friends were sitting in the bay window; Erika Gerson and Hedwig Blumenfeld were excitedly talking in lowered voices with a short Hussar lieutenant of jaunty mien and a skinny attorney who was struggling to adjust his appearance, expression, and character to the demands of the monocle jammed in his eye with a nervousness that elicited sympathy. Martha Mertens, a tall, grave blonde with a sober, unselfconscious air, was sitting silently and quietly as she closely observed the group on the sofa across from her. Others also turned their attention to this group—Hedwig called them the "chamber of horrors"—while they exchanged comments about them.

There were indeed great things happening over there; Joseph had succeeded for the first time to get his family patriarch, the old Baron Anselm von Stülp-Sandersleben, into the Lehnsen home, with whose family he was to become allied by marriage; as long as the house still went by the label "Levysohn" it had been absolutely totally unthinkable, and even so, it had cost enough effort.—The dignified old gentleman was now sitting happily between his niece, the Baroness, and the wife of the Regional Court Director and was talking in a friendly fashion with Elsa, who was sitting across from him.—Upon entering, he had scrutinized the room, glancing over the austere and unobtrusive furnishings as well as the gathered company and was now focusing on Elsa, whose pretty, pert face had naturally begun to blush under his serious, probing look; nevertheless, she bravely continued to stare innocently into his eyes until she had to cast down her eyes and managed with an effort to give modest and calm replies, concealing any signs of her disposition and scintillating wit. She showed just enough understanding along with just enough of her own opinion to comport with what she thought would be a German maiden's sincere naïveté and innocence. One could see in all this that her morally steady character and her profound respect for all that was good, noble, and beautiful constituted a pledge to any husband who took her as a wife that he would find in her full compensation for any moral heft that he himself lacked and that all guarantees for solidity in life and for the proper continuation of good and ancient traditions had been vouchsafed to him.

The manner in which she conversed promised all of this; the conversation seemingly ranged across every possible subject, theater and music, sports and travel, lectures and charities.—However calm Elsa forced herself to be, under her lace collar her fingers fiddled nervously with the cross she had been given today. Without consciously knowing why, she instinctively tried to always keep the piece of jewelry under her lace collar, which she had, by the way, added to her toilette at the last moment just for this purpose.

The other guests who generally sat at the table understood very well that what was going on here was a kind of test, and they weren't participating at all in the conversation, following the two in their dialogue only with obliging smiles—with the exception of Leah, who was sitting rigid and stiff in her chair and staring blankly with an ostentatious lack of interest.

Joseph was standing behind Elsa's chair, his hands resting on the backrest. He had a cheerful expression, looked at the old Baron triumphantly from time to time, seemed quite proud of Elsa and confident about his case.

Indeed, it was clear that the old gentleman was completely charmed by Elsa and had noticeably perked up.

—Everything was going according to plan.—

"Just look at Elsa!" Hedwig Blumenfeld said softly. "How innocently she casts her eyes down!—See, children—we can learn something from her!"

The lieutenant whispered something in Erika Gerson's ear, whereupon she suppressed a squeal and over her shoulder pressed the hand that he had rested gently on her back. He could just about suppress a gentle yelp.

"Children—you're ruining the whole ensemble!" Hedwig said. "No canoodling here! We don't want to spoil our sisterhood of bridesmaids!"

Whereupon the lieutenant began to gently tickle the back of her neck under her hair; she tilted her head and furtively gave him a nudge with her fist. But she also managed to maintain a properly modest expression as she did so.—

The Director entered accompanied by both gentlemen whom he had picked up along the way. He and the old Baron exchanged greetings with ceremonious solemnity; Lehnsen apologized for being so late on account of his duties at work, and so began a serious and measured conversation between the two about the organization of Berlin courts. This was a topic the Baron knew little about and about which the Director vividly expounded with great expert knowledge.

Baron Anselm took the first opportunity he could to engage Elsa again in conversation, spoke almost exclusively with her for some time, and then stood up. Everyone got up at the same time, and suddenly the group at the bay window fell quiet. Everyone looked expectantly in a vague way at the old gentleman, who took a few slow steps into the room with a pensive expression.

"I must say good-bye for now," he said slowly to Elsa's right hand, which he held between both of his own. "But I believe we shall see each other more often —quite often—and I hope we will perhaps get to know each other better." He gave his words significance and some warmth. "I am genuinely thankful to my great-nephew that he has allowed me to meet you. It is permitted an old man to say how much I like you, my dear Fräulein! Your family is surely quite proud of you! And Herr Director!" He released Elsa's hand and turned to Lehnsen. "I am very happy if our two families share special friendly sentiments for your young daughter so that they can be unified in this respect.—In any case, I am very happy to meet you and your wife today too and at least part of the family, in which—"

At this moment a door behind the Baron opened.

"Here's Heinz!" Frau Lehnsen cried. Her hands folded in front of her, she glowed as she listened to the Baron's words. Then, horrified, she stepped back with a short scream of fear when the figure of a Russian Jew appeared next to Heinz in the doorway.

Interrupted in the middle of his sentence, the Baron slowly turned around and stared with surprise and displeasure at the group standing in the doorway.

Heinz stood a moment in the doorway; he was flushed and excited—his eyes wandered over the guests and all the eyes that were focused on him. Then, still clutching Yossel, who was limply following along, by the arm, Heinz came forward and said in a slightly quivering voice as everyone stared at him silently: "Permit me, dear Mama, to introduce to you your cousin—Yossel Schlenker—the son of your uncle Moische Schlenker from Borytshev!"

SIX

The Sounds of Easter

I

In the end, Pastor Bode was more aware of Pesach this year than even Rabbi Rosenbacher; in any case, of the two school friends Marie Lodemann and Hilde Lilienfeld it was only the Pastor's wife who even saw matzah at all.

"For God's sake, what have you got there?" she scolded the little maid, who was sitting contentedly in a corner by the stove and stuffing the crumbly crunchy bits into her mouth, grinding them thoroughly with her healthy jaws. "What in the world is that?" and with sharp scrutiny the alarmed housewife swept the shiny scoured floor, which now looked as if a snowstorm had hit.

"Matzah," Liese said reluctantly as the notion of having done something wrong began to dawn on her, "from Baker Schnerson."

Frau Marie gasped for air.

"Get rid of this stuff immediately," she said briskly. "This has no place in a Christian household—that nasty garbage! Didn't you know that at Easter, Jews—" She recollected herself and stopped; but it wasn't her fate to hold back something that burned on her tongue. She sailed into her husband's study. There she burst into a vigorous exchange between the Pastor and Dr. Strösser. The high school teacher was sitting in the corner of the sofa smoking, while Bode was standing on a chair in front of the bookcase, feverishly rummaging on the top shelf.

This annoyed the housewife afresh.

"How often do I have to tell you, Johannes—don't stand on the leather chairs. Papa never did that; and besides, no one has touched the books on the top shelf for a year. You can put what you need down below where you can easily reach them. At my house we always had the worldly books on the top shelf—the classics and such.—You know how Papa always said: the greatest adornment of a German home! Just what are you looking for?"

"I've already found it," Bode said as he stepped off the chair and guiltily brushed off the upholstery. "Here's *The Rabbi of Bacharach*! How did Heine land in the back row?"

"I did that during spring cleaning; Papa never tolerated Heine in the house at all, and Papa was certainly quite tolerant; but he said: a Jew does not belong in a German home."

"My dear child," Bode said with a smile. "This Jew, who by the way was baptized, did give us some lovely ballads. Look—you yourself loved singing the 'Lorelei.'"

"Heine wrote that?" Frau Marie said, her eyes growing large. "Really, Herr Doctor? Well, he must have done so after he was baptized. Strange!"

She looked so upset that Dr. Strösser asked: "What's so strange about it?"

"I don't know how I should put it—I've often sung the 'Lorelei,' and it never occurred to me that someone 'made' it. You shouldn't have told me, Johannes; now I'll always have to think of that and how these Jews just push themselves forward into everything. Couldn't this Heine have left this to a real German poet—Körner or someone?—and what's this about *The Rabbi of Bacharach*?"

"It's sort of an Easter story," said Strösser, who had begun to thumb through the book. "We were just discussing the Jewish Easter customs, and we wanted—"

"Stop right there. I just came in to see you about that!" Frau Marie exclaimed.— "Now just think, Herr Doctor—Johannes, can you imagine what just happened to me. I'm going all innocently into the kitchen, and there's Liese sitting next to the stove stuffing herself with as much of that horrible matzah as she can. What do you say to that?"

"But my dear child," Bode said, a bit surprised. "I don't see anything so terrible. Quite frankly, I wanted to get a few pounds myself."

"You want to bring that stuff in here and eat it?" Frau Marie asked, outraged. "Everyone knows perfectly well that Jews put Christian blood in their Easter bread."

"Marie!" the Pastor, his face bright red, protested with a vehemence that was unusual for him. "I forbid you, yes, I forbid you to say something like that! Don't say such irresponsible nonsense! This stupid hogwash—"

"Hogwash? But just think of Ernst Winter! Papa was very tolerant, but he always said—"

"Once and for all, I don't want to hear anything more!" Bode said firmly. "I know that this superstition is widespread. This matzah has already cost enough blood! Not Christian blood, of course, but Jewish. It looks as if we are going to have a new edition of this story. This unconscionable baiting and incitement in flyers surely affects simple-minded people!"

"Not only them," Strösser said. "There's tension in the so-called better circles as well, Herr Pastor! Even your own flock! Many a mother accompanies her children to school every day now just out of fear that they could be kidnapped."

"There's not a Christian child to be seen on the boulevard," Frau Marie said with emphasis.

"Marie," cried the Pastor, interrupting his excited pacing around the room, "now I see! That's why our Bertha hasn't left the garden the last few days! This must stop! Let there be no more of this! I'll tell the maid myself that she must start her usual walks again to the Governor's garden."

"But, Johannes, I implore you—"

"No more of this! People must have noticed—as well known as our little Bertha is in the city—"

"Yes," Strösser laughed. "She already is one of the most popular personalities here—thanks to her companion; up until now no one was familiar here with the native Spreewald dress."

"I like showing my Germanic pride!" Frau Marie said with emphasis.

"So that explains the Wendish dress!" chuckled Strösser. "That's how it's come back into the Slavic milieu."

"People recognize it from afar, and I can keep an eye on her better," Frau Marie said with concern. "Do you really insist that I take the child along the old path, Johannes?"

"Not you! The maid will take the child on exactly the same walk as she did earlier. For heaven's sake! If I hear that you contribute to this—you must forgive me, Marie, that I became somewhat vehement, but now, when everyone in the city is so upset and there may be a riot at any moment, we have to be all the more careful about what we say. If stupid old women frighten themselves with such stories, that may be fine, but if the young, educated pastor's wife herself endorses—"

"I'm only talking to you and Dr. Strösser," Frau Marie said a bit meekly. "You know Jews better than I do, of course. But tell me, dear Doctor—is Johannes right to be so angry? Maybe there's something in it; and Papa always said: the voice of the people is the voice of God."

"Yes, dear Frau Marie," Strösser said good-naturedly. "You are the uncontested authority in all matters of cooking and baking, but your matzah recipe just happens not to be true. Jews don't even eat animal blood, and their matzah is entirely harmless and digestible food. I personally prefer other Jewish dishes, such as cholent, to which your friend Heinrich Heine after his conversion dedicated ecstatic verses, or the Shabbos kugel or gefilte fish—"

"I do believe that you are a good Christian. Are you secretly eating nothing but kosher food?" Frau Marie said, outraged.

"Why not? Whenever I can get it," Strösser laughed. "A true German man can't stand a Jew, but he likes his fish. But do calm down, dear Frau Marie, I have still retained my liking for ham. Ever since I prepared a couple of Jewish boys for their exams, the various mothers have tended to make culinary attacks on me from time to time to conquer my heart by way of my stomach in favor of their darlings. That Jacob Schlenker brought me a box of matzah today and moreover taught me the art of matzah coffee grounds. That's not a simple matter. Pay attention. First you take—"

"Would you please be quiet," Frau Marie said angrily. "I'll have no such thing here; whether it's Christian blood in the matzah or Jewish blood, as Johannes says—"

"Hold on!" Bode cried. "What did I say?"

"I just don't want to hear anything more about this stuff, and it won't be brought into my house. We haven't come to that yet!"

And she angrily left the room.

II

Now out of sorts, Bode paced up and down in silence.

"I've always said, Herr Pastor," Strösser said after a while, "keep away from the Jews. You will have no reward, not even in your own home! And what do you achieve? What was the effect of your *Faust* lessons with your Yossel Schlenker? Did he come any closer to belief in salvation? He went to Berlin; he'll probably become a heathen there, but definitely not a Christian."

"I am greatly indebted to those lessons," Bode said thoughtfully. "I admit that things developed in ways I didn't originally anticipate; but I certainly got a lot from them. I came into contact with a Jewish soul.—I have gained unexpected insights.—"

"Do you understand things more clearly than the time when you worked at the Berlin Seminar for the Jewish Mission?"

"Actually, no!—I would have to say, on the contrary. The situation is really much more complicated than I thought at the time. But even this insight is something positive, and then: a gap has been breached. Many of the more understanding Jews learned from Yossel Schlenker's example that contact with modern culture does not have to mean betraying one's own community. The best proof of that is, of course, that you yourself have a number of Jewish pupils."

"That's true! Yossel's brother, little Jacob, was the first—now there's almost a dozen."

"And they bring you joy, I believe."

"Of course I'm pleased if I can pocket some tuition fees."

"Strösser, Strösser—didn't you yourself say how bright—"

"I should be pleased about that? Well, yes, to some extent, because it confirms an old observation of mine. I strictly follow the normal German curriculum, and I take devilish pleasure whenever I have an eight-year-old little rascal who is conversant in the most complex questions of marital laws and civil disputes, saying, 'A little sheep, as white as snow.'"

"Well, in any case, you are working on building a grand bridge between people, and I'm happy that I contributed to that with my effort with Yossel Schlenker to span the chasm here. You can imagine my anxiety when I now see that what little I have achieved has been compromised here by this insane rabble-rousing. You must put yourself in my place! I am very concerned!"

"Leave the Jews alone!"

"Can I? Am I supposed to stand by, doing nothing, when the members of my own congregation believe this ritual murder nonsense? Shouldn't I do something about it if I see that this terrible lie will spill blood again?"

"Oh, you know that's silly!"

"What is?"

"That an accusation of ritual murder is always followed by persecutions of Jews."

"What? And the massacres in the past—the persecutions that always occurred at Easter—the rabble-rousing that we have now again here?"

"I am familiar with all that. But Jews aren't killed because people believe that Jews need Christian blood but because they want to kill, because they hate them, because they think that they are cannibals. When they wanted to exterminate Christians in ancient Rome the exact same things were said about them. So to offer a rational rebuttal is useless. Logic has never defeated unreason."

"It's hatred itself that you have to fight!" Bode cried. "You cut the ground out from under hatred by destroying every pretext it invents.—You have to rip off every mask it hides behind.—You have—"

"What do you have to do?" Strösser interrupted, standing up to leave his corner. "Strip hatred bare to make it visible to every eye? What would happen if people see themselves as they really are? Everyone hates everybody! At least they are still ashamed and have pulled on a coat of love and other coats as well over their nakedness. The fig leaf was the first lie!—to eat from the Tree of Knowledge meant recognizing the necessity of lying!"

"You are speaking blasphemy, Strösser!"

"I speak no blasphemy!" Strösser said more calmly after a moment. "How does man differ from a beast? By the ability to lie, and above all to lie to himself. A cat kills a mouse without telling itself that this is a socially beneficial deed or that it is dispensing justice; if we want to kill someone, we must tell ourselves all sorts of things or even perform a comedy of justice. Logic and justice are fictions, even completely splendid fictions, and I understand we need them."

"It is the basis of our culture."

"And the culture reflects that! These are illusions, nothing more, but they control our instincts, which would otherwise run riot. Louis XVI, before his judges! —All the sentences of the revolutionary tribunals! You have an example there! Woe to the judge who would decree an acquittal; but the comedy of justice had to be performed!"

"In such troubled times—"

"—What would otherwise better remain hidden rises all the more noticeably to the surface. Basically it's always one and the same thing. They are just as determined to kill Jews as they were determined to kill Louis whether or not the Jews eat small children. I'm not someone who wishes to deny others their illusions; I only want none as far as I'm concerned. I consider the traditional illusions of humankind, such as justice and brotherly love, to be a blessing, for without them it would be much worse. If people knew how they hate each other!"

"And the doctrine of love?—Love thy enemy! Has that been taught in vain?"

"That's a good phrase, but it will always be falsely understood! Love thy neighbor—"

"That's still insufficient. The Old Testament even teaches that. But love thy enemy! That is directed against the hatred you are speaking of."

"Excuse me, Herr Pastor! In my opinion it is exactly the same thing. Your neighbor is your enemy. Neighbor and enemy are identical concepts. Whom am I supposed to love, for heaven's sake, if not my enemy? I don't need a commandment to love my friend? I'm supposed to hide my hatred and show love where I hate, where nature itself presses me to hate, do good instead of evil. Thus the lie becomes the highest moral principle! Love can be commanded or forced as little as hatred or any other feeling. What one does is the important thing, and that is dishonest, and it's *supposed to be dishonest*. Truth is debased!"

"Unfortunately not for the first time I'm hearing these sorts of thoughts from you!" Bode said, shaking his head. "But fortunately you contradict yourself often enough."

"I am proud of the fact that I don't have a system! I also do not submit to the gods of logic. I simply look at the facts as they appear at the moment.—We started with the matzahs and the blood libel and have digressed a bit; I only wanted to make the simple point that there is no sense, no sense whatever, to think that people who have decided to murder and will murder under any circumstance also honestly believe that they are carrying out a just and pious deed."

"You are a victim of that pedantic logic that you so often preach against!" Bode retorted with heat. "I shall do my duty without brooding over things and without sophistry! I must bear witness for the doctrine of love, and I shall do so!"

"What do you plan to do?" Strösser asked apprehensively.

"I shall speak to my congregation on Sunday and give myself and my word as pledge against this fabrication of lies!"

Strösser was silent, but his expression showed concern.

"Herr Pastor!" he then said carefully. "I don't want to interfere with your official obligations, but you realize that the government is behind the agitation for a pogrom and that one doesn't joke with our Governor General."

Bode angrily raised his eyes.

"An appeal to fear?"

"No!—But let me remind you of many tasks that are given to you here, and carrying these out would perhaps be made complicated, if not impossible, for you. Your congregation surely must be of more concern to you than the Jews; they will spread what you say beyond the church—"

"That's my intention! People should know here in the Lutheran Church the way to bar this superstition and hatred from our congregation. We want to be able to lift our hands without stain! I have seen what my duty is and shall do it."

III

Spring cleaning before Passover can deliver many a pleasant surprise to the Jewish housewife. All sorts of things are found as she ransacks everything, even in the darkest corner of the house, in her search for "leavened" foods to be cleaned out, foods that have mysteriously disappeared over the course of the year: like a flash, memories emerge that illuminate puzzles long since abandoned as insoluble. Of course: the diapers that had long since vanished had been unthinkingly stuffed into the large closet when there had been an unexpected visitor and no other choice was available in the rush—the thick letter from America, for which one had hunted for weeks until one was half dead, was jammed under the leg of the eternally wobbly laundry table—and thus many a seemingly supernatural thing found a simple and rational explanation, even though it will probably remain forever unexplained how a pair of glasses came to be under a cleaning rag or even how the silk yarmulke came to be in the leaky waterproof boot. A person who keeps her household in pedantically boring order will never feel the tingly sensation that all these entertaining and occasional surprises provide; in any event, it is a beneficent effect of Jewish law that once a year all households undergo the inexorable spring cleaning at Easter time because of the strict taboo against anything leavened. Here, as with many rules of Jewish ritual, the thought is unavoidable that for many rabbis who have recorded every stipulation under the commandments, the means is at least as sacred as the purpose and that they were quite excellent psychologists who used holy purposes to guarantee quite profane but very useful things about hygiene and cleanliness for all times and in all places.

In Moische Schlenker's home the regime was reasonable during the year; nevertheless, Frau Beile Schlenker had had several surprises during spring cleaning over the last few years, especially when she did the children's rooms. Every time she had put back into place the many German books whose incomprehensible script she observed with deep distrust, sighing and shaking her head. Last year the foreign books had found their way into her house just as they had in many other Jewish houses; thus there was no way to anticipate what sort of surprises would blossom.

And, yes, there was one for her like none previously—for a long time she couldn't get over the shock. She shook out a bedsheet from a drawer belonging to her daughter, Rivka—and something bounced out onto the floor; she looked down and, terrified, sank onto a pile of laundry. With a beating heart she stared at the mysterious, shiny little thing with nickel fittings that lay in front of her.

How did that get into her house—into her Jewish house? How did that get into her daughter's—into a Jewish daughter's—trousseau?

What a world—what sort of times!

In the house of Moische Schlenker, the Torah scribe, a revolver!

After Goethe a Browning! European culture and European barbarity penetrated through the high walls of the large ghetto in the East. Jewish youth in Borytshev weren't willing to let themselves be slaughtered without a fight should there be a pogrom; and it looked very much as if there was going to be one. Hadn't it already come to bloody excesses in some cities? The elderly of course shook their heads—a pogrom in Borytshev—ridiculous! Here, where Jews always lived together so peacefully with non-Jews? In Kishinev the circumstances must have been otherwise. The poor people there! There were collections for the unfortunate victims whom fate had driven into the arms of such terrible people. You could count yourself lucky that you had chosen so wisely to live here.

But the young men couldn't believe there was no danger and were busy organizing an underground self-defense force, which was now happening everywhere. There was great enthusiasm, but it was almost the only accomplishment of the troop. There were very few weapons, and for those they had even fewer volunteers who understood how to use them. Furthermore, the young men often lacked the most primitive ideas about organization and discipline, and enthusiasm substituted most unsatisfactorily for everything else. That they would stand their ground if things became serious was not in doubt, but just as obviously one couldn't deny that they wouldn't be able to do anything if, as had happened elsewhere, the military itself had a hand in carrying out the pogrom. In some places the police had rendered the self-defense force harmless by searching all the Jewish homes beforehand for weapons—the minimum sentence for possession of a weapon was three months in prison!—Searching for weapons in this way secured a double advantage for the pogrom organizers, first by ensuring no danger to themselves and further by allowing them to add to their own store of weapons. Because they greatly feared a weapons sweep in Borytshev, they had distributed the weapons among as many houses as possible and hidden them in the most improbable places.

Frau Beile Schlenker shuddered herself back to life with a deep sigh; she bent over and timidly picked up the weapon with disgust as if she were holding a revolting insect, holding it by the handle between her thumb and forefinger. And holding it this way in front of her with outstretched arm, she carried it into the corridor. She looked around confused because she didn't know what to do with it; in no event should the maid find the thing. As she was standing there—the instrument of murder was burning in her hand—the entry door opened quickly. Thank goodness it was only Rivka, who had just stepped out only to immediately return. When she saw her mother with the revolver in her hand she stopped in consternation but then had to burst out laughing at the unusual sight.

"You laugh! Fine thing!" Beile said bitterly. "Take the thing so I won't see it anymore. All of you will bring misfortune on all of us with your guns!"

"That's why I came back," Rivka said, taking the revolver. "I suddenly realized that I had forgotten it."

She stuffed it under a white cloth in the market basket on her arm.

"God in heaven!" Beile cried. "How the girl says that; as if she had forgotten her umbrella. She has to take a revolver when she goes to market!"

Rivka had already disappeared. She was in a hurry to make up for lost time. There was a meeting in the new study house with the leader of the self-defense force that she wanted to take part in. Normally women were strictly prohibited from entering rooms of study or prayer; but now people ignored a great deal, obeying the demands of the moment. They had, after all, to choose the most inconspicuous places for these meetings so as not to arouse the suspicions of the police.

Rivka went through the archway that led into the courtyard of the synagogue; in the second courtyard was the meat market, and one could therefore assume that she was going there to buy something. But when she saw all was safe, she quickly turned to the right behind the small temple building and entered the half-dark little room next to the large prayer hall.

She was very tense. Electrifying rumors were circulating in the town about a clash reported in the area between the members of the self-defense force and police the previous afternoon. The police could easily use this as an excuse to search for weapons so that all the work of the self-defense force would be endangered.

And so she expected to find a mood of dread; instead, while still outside she heard the happy, excited voice of Benjamin Schapiro. When she opened the door, he immediately jumped up to approach her.

"Rivka! You already know? Splendid great news! Wonderful prospects!"

"What prospects?" Rivka asked with a beating heart.

"The harvest prospects in Palestine!"

IV

"So is it possible to work with you Zionists?" Meier Kaplan asked, tossing his cigarette on the ground angrily. "We have a thousand worries—death and disaster could swallow all of us at any moment—and he dances with joy because the prospects for the harvest are good in Palestine."

"In my Palestine—mine!" Benjamin cried angrily. "All of you have already heard it—as if it isn't the Palestine of all of us!—Our homeland!—Our fatherland!"

"My homeland is Russia!"

"A fine homeland!"

"Our homeland isn't Russia and it isn't Palestine!" said David Perkovsky, a pale, thin man, lame and slightly misshapen. "Our homeland is not even any existing country; our homeland is the entire world! Proletarians of the world are our brothers!"

At this point a general debate began; there were about a dozen young people present, almost all puffing on cigarettes, making the air almost unbearable in the small room. Everyone talked at once; everyone defended his philosophical point of view with fervor and zeal and vigorous gestures.

Finally, the lanky Mendel Friedmann rapped a few times on the table, and the noise died down.

"We didn't come here today to plan our programs!" he said, vigorously shaking his thin face with its short, brown beard. "I am as good a Zionist as you are, Benjamin; you know that. I love what is good in Russia, as you do, Meier, and that I stand on the side of the oppressed, you know that too, David. But we are all Jews and want to help our people. Today we are faced with things that are of immediate concern, not our ideal future. You all know, I think, about yesterday's catastrophe.—"

"I still don't know anything certain!" Rivka said. "Is it true that Esther Neumann was murdered?"

"She isn't dead!" Mendel said. "But she's seriously hurt—someone cut off her finger."

"For God's sake!" Rivka cried, horrified. "A finger? How did that happen? Who did that?"

"Who does that sort of thing?" David said, shrugging his shoulders. "Our dear police!"

And now Rivka heard about the sickening attack. Esther Neumann and two young people were attacked and robbed by some peasants close to town; the brutal dismemberment had happened then. To more quickly snatch a small diamond ring they had hacked off the finger. Everyone suspected that the perpetrators weren't peasants at all but police spies in disguise, like those Police Lieutenant Kujaroff, considered to be the leader of the agitation for a pogrom, attracted in large numbers. The city had recently been crawling with outsiders and suspicious persons. The attack might be a prelude to a worse disaster. Everyone turned serious; the fate that was approaching suddenly stood vividly before their eyes. Accustomed from childhood to concern themselves with spiritual matters and possessing an aversion to any sort of raw violence or spilling of blood, an aversion that was deeply rooted in all Jews, these young people shuddered and fell silent for a moment.

"If I see something like that with my own eyes, then even I will be able to use my weapon," Meier said in a constrained voice. "Otherwise, I could never shoot someone."

"So innocent blood must flow first?" Benjamin cried. "I won't wait until it is too late for some of us. If these murderers even try to enter our houses or shops, we must give the signal to fight."

"We aren't there to protect the capitalists!" David said. "Jewish capitalists or Russian, they're all the same! They're all bloodsuckers. When they lay hands on the lives of people, then we shall know how to fight and die!"

"My God!" Rivka said and sank down on a bench. "Poor Esther! What have these people done! Is everyone around us a criminal? Or are we the criminals?"

"Not us and not them!" Mendel said. "Our enemies are probably unhappier than we are. What hopeless darkness they suffer! We at least have a light in this night! We have the hope of Zion and Palestine! What sort of hope do these backward people have?"

"When the hour of liberation comes for all those oppressed," David said softly, "light and freedom will come to these unfortunate lands. We, the most ancient and most free of all peoples, now have the duty to free all humankind and to break all the chains of slavery. Moses was the first who brought slaves into freedom—Marx and Lassalle were Jews—"

"But first we must liberate ourselves!" Benjamin cried. "When we have a Jewish kingdom in Palestine we shall show the world what freedom is. There will be no slaves with us!—No proletariat!—and no bloodsuckers! Light will go forth from Zion—the word of God from Jerusalem!"

"Zion can be anywhere!" Meier cried. "The light of freedom can be kindled anywhere! To bring our teachings to the Russians we don't need to emigrate! We must demonstrate here in this land what we are! If our Jewish people reflect on themselves, on our national dignity, it will be a power here. A power of the spirit!—A moral power!—and the spirit triumphs over violence in the end!"

"Just get Kujaroff with spirit and morality!" Benjamin cried with heat. "Only in Palestine, in our own ancestral land, when we are free from the stranger's oppression can we live our own lives. Here we betray our own ethics—we take on the soul of a slave! Here, read in *Die Welt*!" He rattled the yellow newspaper that was the organ of the Zionist movement known to all. "How our settlements there bloom—how our Hebrew tongue awakens! A healthy, free life develops there! The World Zionist Organization is growing day by day! Dr. Herzl is now in negotiations with the British government and the sultan. Not much longer and the Jewish nation is fact! What does it matter if we're all killed here!"

"Why are we even trying to defend ourselves!" Meier shouted. "Let's just all be slaughtered!"

"We work for all humankind, not for a part of humankind!" David shrieked. "We want to build a Zion for everyone. There will come a time when all national differences will cease, such as the differences in religious beliefs, in birth, and wealth."

"There won't be any more Jews by the time that beautiful dream comes to pass who are able to rejoice in it, if things continue as they are!" Benjamin declared.

"We must at least live to reach our goals!" Mendel said quietly as he rapped on the table to call for quiet. "We are agreed that we want to defend ourselves and our town if the Kujaroff thugs attack us. We need our ideals, no matter how much they differ. We defend our ideals with our lives. We can continue these discussions when Easter is over. Now we must get to work. We have a lot to do. Here's the list of people in our self-defense force. We now have to decide on the places where our units will meet and where we can give the alarm when the time comes."

"Just a moment!" David broke in. "Is there anyone in the next room who wants to join us?"

He limped to the door of the adjoining room, opened it a crack, and poked his head in. The buzz of voices that had been heard all along now became louder.

"Oh dear!" he said after a while, closing the door again. "They are debating how to examine witnesses before the Sanhedrin in Jerusalem. Something of importance!—Those old men!"

V

The question under discussion in the study room was not a simple one. How hard their brains were working could be seen in the furrowed brows and faces taut with the prodigious effort of thinking. About twenty definitely older men were sitting or standing around the long table in front of the window; their eyes were staring into books or into the distance or were closed now and then for several minutes in deepest thought; all were rocking back and forth either slowly and deliberately or rapidly and nervously.

"So here's the point," said Moische Schlenker, who had studied ahead, scratching his beard vigorously, and every time he hit the wall behind him as he rocked back he let his head rest there a few seconds. He spoke in that singsong that was a part of Talmud study. "Two witnesses are necessary to sentence someone on the basis of their testimony—now the two witnesses have given their testimony; they have seen how Ruben murdered Simon—on such and such a day and at such and such a place. And now two other witnesses step forward and say: you have sworn false testimony; on such and such a day you were nowhere near the place, but you were with us at a different place—and the law says: both the first witnesses are false witnesses, and both these false witnesses are sentenced to death, and they are executed—they are executed—they are executed, and—they are both executed together, because one may not execute just one. If one of them dies in the meantime, you must let the other one live, because alone he could not bear false witness—testimony from one person alone is nothing—one must have testimony from two witnesses. Therefore, both together have sinned, and only both together can be punished."

"And how can you punish the first two on the basis of the testimony of the two new witnesses?" someone interrupted. "Over here are two witnesses and over there are two witnesses, it's two against two. Who says that the two new witnesses are telling the truth? Perhaps they are lying, and the first two spoke the absolute truth."

"Right! Truth!" many voices cried excitedly.

"That's a good question!" said Moische Schlenker and pushed back his peaked cap. "It's not a new question. Many commentators have addressed this—Rashi and others too. The point is this: each of the two first witnesses is examined separately so that one witness doesn't hear what the other witness said, and then the second two witnesses, the new ones against one—so that it is always two against one—they also must be separated. But we will see what Rashi has to say about this!"

"I have another question!" someone shouted from the far end of the table. "You say, Reb Moische, the law demands: if one of the false witnesses dies, the other one cannot be put to death. Now I ask you: How is it now if the one witness kills the other witness? They go to the place of execution, and on the way one of them picks up a stone and kills the other; he has to go free, right? He has to go free? Heh, can that be right?"

Hostile murmuring could be heard.

"Reb Chaim," Moische Schlenker said in a deprecating tone, "what kinds of questions are those—how does that help anyone? He would of course be put to death for murder. So not any sort of question, so—there are two witnesses contradicting two witnesses, but really there are two times two witnesses against one witness every time."

"Reb Moische!" exclaimed Chaim, who was offended by the curt dismissal. "Your answer isn't an answer. Because he killed the second witness he can't be put to death. That is not murder!"

General hostility was directed at Reb Chaim, who was interrupting everybody's train of thought by butting in with a question.

"And why not? Why isn't that a murder?" Moische Schlenker asked calmly.

"Because it is written that only he commits a murder who destroys a life; but whoever kills a dead man, that is to say, one who is as good as dead, whose life is done, and for whom there is no possibility of saving his life, he commits no murder. Here we have a person who is about to be put to death—he is already on his way to the place of execution—there is no possibility at all that his life can be saved—he is already as good as dead! How can the other man then be put to death if he kills him? He is killing a dead man!"

Reb Chaim had succeeded in awakening everyone's interest in the question. Everyone was staring at him, and a new wave of rocking back and forth betrayed how intensely everyone was thinking about the problem.

Moische Schlenker was taken aback; he repeated the case.—

"That's correct! Someone who is led to the place of execution is already as good as dead—he is a dead man—is a dead man—a dead man! He who slays him commits no murder—no murder, so he cannot be punished for murder—he is free, and he cannot be executed either on account of his false testimony—he is free again—truly! Reb Chaim is right; he is free; if a witness who gave false testimony murders the other witness who gave false testimony, he frees himself."

A great buzz arose. "That's impossible! A criminal evades punishment by committing another crime! The law cannot intend that."

Suddenly Moische Schlenker slapped the table.

"Quiet! Be still! I've got it! What is Reb Chaim telling us for nonsense? The second witness, he says, is a dead man—is already as good as dead because he's already on the way to the place of execution. But one witness is situated exactly as the other is; both are being taken to the place of execution. Both are lost. Now one slays the other—slays him and he should go free? Right? Now if the one can do that, the other can do that as well—the other witness, the second one, could slay the first witness; then he would go free! Right?"

He made a long pause and looked triumphantly around at everyone.

Everyone was holding his breath.

"So!" he finally continued. "So the other one also had the means to free himself—so he wasn't a lost man after all, he wasn't as good as dead; he wasn't a dead man but a living man. Then the first witness has slain a living man, has definitely committed murder, so he can be executed, and the whole affair doesn't help him at all!"

There was great joy around the entire table. Everyone shook his head in acknowledgment. A fine mind—a sharp mind—Reb Moische Schlenker! Only Reb Chaim wasn't satisfied.

"It seems to me," he said, "that the question is still a question. If it is as Reb Moische says, that it doesn't benefit the first witness who slays the second at all, not at all, and if he is executed all the same—then it wouldn't benefit the second witness either if he had slain the first witness—he would then also be put to death. So there is no way he can free himself—he will be executed no matter what. But then he's once again someone who is as good as dead, and the first witness has not murdered a living man but a dead one. And he goes free."

"Then the case can never be resolved!" Moische Schlenker cried. "If he is free, he must be killed—if he must be killed, he is free! A difficult case!"

The round table sank again into a sea of doubt.

A man in a coachman's uniform, a long whip in his hand, who had entered a while ago and was waiting unassumingly by the door, now stepped forward and asked if it wasn't time to say the afternoon prayer, his hackney was waiting in the courtyard.

That was the signal to pause a moment. With heavy heads they stood up and went to the east wall to pray.

"Maybe there's someone in the next room who wants to join us in prayer," someone said as he opened the door to the adjoining room.

He quickly slammed the door shut in annoyance.

"Do you know what they're talking about in there? About pogroms—about self-defense! Something of importance! Those young folks!"

VI

When Pastor Bode was on the pulpit and wanted to know if his words were understood and taken to heart, he looked at the elderly. The younger folks sat stiff and motionless in their seats, staring at him with expressionless eyes. But the elderly had the habit of showing their approval from time to time by nodding. This happened every Sunday so regularly and without exception that this constant and persistent approval struck him at times as somewhat suspicious, and he asked himself on occasion if there wasn't something mechanical at work here, leaving him with no firm conclusions about the impressions his words were making.

This Sunday, however, could give him the reassuring certainty that it wasn't the case this time, for the nods of approval were absent—for the first time since he had taken up his work in Borytshev. That happened toward the conclusion of his sermon; he spoke about the ringing of the Easter bells from the many church towers for the last few weeks announcing the message of the Resurrection and reminding the faithful now to reflect and pray. As long as the Pastor talked about these topics, that the bells were bringing the message of love to all Christians, to the Protestants as well as to the Roman and Greek Orthodox Catholics, the elderly nodded in their usual tempo. But when he continued after a short pause and demanded with raised voice that this love also be directed to the people from whom the Savior had come—the Jewish people—a marked commotion went through the congregation, and when he turned against those who were agitating and fomenting fear and hatred—it seemed as if everyone was holding his breath—and not a single friendly smile encouraged him. Undeterred, he continued his sermon against hatred. He who preaches the doctrine of hatred has revoked the right to call himself a true Christian. The disciples of Satan, however, can be recognized by the methods they use. Only the archfiend, the father of lies, could make use of the demented accusation of using Christian blood. "We have been put here to announce the doctrine of love; how are the Jews, for whom we want to open the path to salvation, supposed to believe in us if we, who call ourselves the disciples of love, preach hate?" He closed with the prayer asking the Lord to keep the congregation from the spirit of hatred and lies forever and to give everyone the courage to fight against this libel and lie.

This time there was no approving murmur muted by respect that he was in the habit of hearing when he left the pulpit. There was a lot of whispering in the church, more perhaps than was appropriate for a house of God, and when the service was finally over everybody hurried out the door. Outside, people gathered in groups to energetically discuss the sermon.

As the Pastor left the church with his wife and Strösser, everyone fell silent for a moment, and everyone respectfully bared his head; but no one stepped forward as usual to shake Bode's hand or to thank him in particular for the sermon.

Silently, they entered the vicarage in deep thought. Frau Marie hurried into the kitchen to prepare dinner, for which Strösser had a standing invitation for Sundays, and the two gentlemen settled in the study to light their cigars. They puffed away in silence for a while.

"It seems they aren't happy with me!" Bode finally remarked to break the ice, in a joking tone but still somewhat uncertain. "Now go ahead and shoot!"

"I don't want to take up our recent conversation again," Strösser said, shaking his head. "You've had your way now. I hope nothing bad comes of it."

"Again, you're fearmongering; that at least worries me," Bode said, distracted.

"I would be unfair to hide my concerns from you. Without a doubt the Governor is being informed right now of the content of your sermon today."

"The Governor is way too important to be concerned with a minor German pastor's sermon," Bode suggested, smiling incredulously. "Besides, I wouldn't mind if he took notice of a truthful word in this way. Moreover—how could he do anything to me? He is, when all is said and done, a cultured man, so I hear.—He's even studied in Germany."

"Better not count on that; he's the very definition of an autocrat.—Ivan the Terrible in the provinces. He won't do anything directly against you as if you were a local peasant, but he still has enough ways to make carrying out your duties difficult if not impossible."

"He could expel me from the country, but he wouldn't dare!"

"I think that myself; there would be implications. But he is capable of every possible villainy and brutality! He whips his peasants bloody. They are maltreated as only the serfs were and, moreover, apparently are quite happy. Last year he locked a young girl in a dark cellar for six weeks; she came out half-crazed."

"Do you want to scare me with such bandit tales?" Bode laughed, somewhat annoyed. "Let's wait to see what happens."

"Yes, but I am still blaming myself that I didn't try hard enough to prevent you from making that sermon. Quite frankly, I think that goal you aimed for in the church was not at all worth the risk."

"Look, that is exactly what interests me far more than your provincial tyrant. My congregation! God knows I spoke from a full heart today, and today it was that I missed the human contact."

"Yes, you mustn't demand too much from people."

"Demand too much? I've never preached anything but active human kindness as daily Christianity."

"But today you gave them a specific task. Look, Herr Pastor, nobody has an objection to ideals. Who doesn't like to flee the gray monotony of daily routine for a short hour in heaven? But you are relieved when you return to the ground of reality again and are happy that heaven is so distant and pretty!"

"What's that supposed to mean?"

"That every day isn't Sunday, that your lambs do not have wings, and that people aren't angels. All due respect for the apostles and saints, but they wouldn't fare well if they were to walk among believers today."

"You lack faith, Strösser!"

"Faith in what?—In God or in humans? There are many more people who believe in God than those who believe in humans!"

"And what does that mean now?"

"Do you know Saint Crispin? Do you want to know him? He lives right on the bank of the river, in the old Fish Alley; there he sits, mending his shoes in a damp hole. You can find a whole group of apostles here in town who have a family resemblance that makes them easy to recognize, whose very existence provokes; you can find all your Christian ideals embodied there: chastity, human kindness, the spiritual life, joyful poverty, the sense of self-sacrifice, and martyrdom."

"Yes, if there are really such ideal people among the Jews, as you claim—and one really must believe you, the anti-Semite—it should be easy to find a path to them through love."

"It's just these people who arouse the most discomfort, just because they are real saints and not humans.—They're confusing!"

"Confusing? If they match your descriptions, then they would indeed be true Christians!"

"The rest you can read in Lessing's *Nathan*! We normal humans don't want to see these ideals embodied in every cobbler and tailor. We can only bear that if it rarely shows up; we render them harmless by making such people into gods or saints. They are only slightly more bearable for us if they at least really sinned in their youth. It's always the same story in Catholic legends. First a sinner, then a perfect person, then martyrdom, and finally official sainthood. Heaven for them, the earth for us. A saint who runs around uncrucified contradicts our natural sensibilities and awakens hostile feelings."

"That's not fair!" Bode responded, annoyed. "Would your splendid Governor then be right if he locked me in a hole on account of my ideas? What is it?"

Frau Marie had appeared in the doorway, pale and upset.

"From the Governor!" she said in a thin voice. "A policeman. You are to go with him at once! Oh, Johannes!"

Sobbing, she threw her arms around him. Bode stared incredulously at Strösser, who had stood up, terrified.

"That isn't helping!" Bode gently disentangled himself. "Bring me my good coat! He's not going to eat me! This will be over by the time dinner is ready. Herr Doctor, please stay with my wife until I return."

"I'm coming with you!" Frau Marie cried. "I'm going with you!"

"Impossible! You can't go out on the street in your state. I'll be back in an hour at the latest. You two must stay calm. I'm certainly calm."

But he wasn't entirely all that calm, although he gave no sign of distress. A police officer was slouching outside the front door and indolently touched his cap as the Pastor walked by, checking him up and down with a sidelong glance. Bode clenched his umbrella a bit harder and hurried to cross the street; something like pride came to him as he strode along. Perhaps he was being summoned to champion the cause of righteousness and reason before the powerful.

When he went through the Governor's garden he saw flashing brightly from afar the colorful dress of the nanny. He turned aside for a moment in her direction. Then he saw the police officer sauntering about fifty paces behind. With a jerk, he turned and strode off in the direction of the Governor's mansion.

The Swiss officer at the door seemed to be waiting for him; without asking, he ushered him into the waiting room. The spacious room was empty. In one corner an oil lamp burned in front of a large icon. The servant went on through the room and disappeared behind a door; he returned immediately and, without saying a word to the Pastor, walked past him and exited through the entrance.

Bode stood at the window and looked out over the garden and the boulevard that led up to it, where the corner of his own house could be seen; he would have so much preferred to be home again.

He waited a long time, and waiting always made him nervous.

Two gendarmes with impressive bushy beards suddenly entered the room. They looked fiercely at Bode and took up positions by the door. After a while Police Lieutenant Kujaroff entered from the room beyond, glanced at the Pastor, gave a fleeting greeting, and spoke softly and urgently a long time with the two police officers, all three frequently glancing at him with suspicion. Suddenly a bell rang short and sharp somewhere inside. Kujaroff went in, came right out again, held the door open, and nodded to the Pastor.

Bode gave a start and crossed the threshold. The door closed behind him.

He was alone with the powerful man.

The Governor stood behind his desk in a white jacket with gold buttons, looking colossal. Both hands rested on his desk, his bald head reflected the light, and with his eyes that almost disappeared under his bushy eyebrows he sharply observed the man who entered. His head was somewhat bent forward so that his long graying beard, groomed into two portions, tumbled onto his breast. Bode made a respectful bow; the Governor didn't move for a long time.

Suddenly the stiffness in his face gave way to broad, friendly laughter, and the powerful man approached him with outstretched hands.

"My dear Herr Pastor, how happy I am to see you here. Now take a seat, and let us chat comfortably."

VII

The Governor lit his Papiros cigarette with a great deal of fuss. He pushed forward the cigarette box to invite his visitor to take one. The visitor, confused, declined. Then the Governor leaned back comfortably in his chair and said cordially: "So, my dear Herr Pastor, I am happy to finally see you here. Until now I've delayed making your acquaintance. Quite honestly, I know Germany and Germans somewhat—I couldn't know what sort of views you have. But since today—since your sermon today that has somewhat changed. I am charmed to become acquainted with a German, and a German academic at that, who holds such liberal views—really charmed and surprised!"

Pastor Bode's face showed complete bafflement. The Governor moved his chair right next to him and slapped him on the knee, mischievously looking him in the eye.

"You see, I am well informed—I am generally rather well informed. So— you have given me a happy surprise, I can tell you. Anyone who experienced the Konitz affair in Germany knows how widespread stupid superstitions about the grisly tale of blood libel there are. I knew many of your so-called educated men who were convinced of the truth of ritual murder. Such a thing is impossible here with us. Anti-Semitism is so deeply rooted with you Germans.—You're barbarians!"

He slapped Bode on the knee again, laughing; he exuded such joviality that Bode couldn't be angry.

"Your Excellency," the totally confused Pastor stammered. "Our German culture—"

"Oh, don't bring up your German culture with me!" This time for a change the Governor slapped him on the shoulder. "We are alone here—we are talking as good friends!—Your so-called culture is nothing more than cultural white-wash!—You Germans possess nothing but what you've studied. There's nothing left once that disappears. You have machines—technology—organization—the devil knows what all. Every German hackney coachman reads the newspaper and does politics. We don't have that here—thank God! But we do have culture, as do the Jews, of course. Moreover, they also have skills and education—things we encounter in few people among the Russians—fortunately! What's the result of all that general education? Discontent—increasing demands! Education has not made people any happier! And that's how it should remain in Russia, that's why the Jews are a threat here, and that's why one must oppose them. But Jew hatred or even contempt for Jews—there's no such sort of thing here among educated Russians. Your Bismarck invented anti-Semitism. Your Stöcker created the movement in Berlin. Your marvelous theories have by now been translated into violent actions here after anti-Semitism was imported from Germany. But there's no educated Russian here who would seriously fall for such a crude lie as ritual murder—not one! My word of honor!"

"Excellency!" Bode said nervously as he struggled to collect himself. "On the one hand, I'm deeply pleased that you agree about the matter of ritual murder that I find here, but on the other hand, as a German I cannot accept everything you say without contradiction. Especially in Germany, Jews enjoy full equality and—"

"Pfff, equality! But only under the condition that they deny their Judaism and even then—they demoralize the few Jews whom they have over there, and they're already so happy that they are ashamed of their own brethren, and they try to blend in as a sort of church congregation. That's why I praise my dear Russian Jews! They are at least real men!"

"Excellency—may I speak freely?" said Bode, who had in the meantime collected himself.

"But of course, my dear friend!" the Governor said with effervescent cordiality. "Entirely free and open—as I have done. We are speaking as friends.—I am not the Governor now.—I'm happy to be able to chat with an educated and liberal person for once."

"So, completely open, then! I am enormously surprised, not only because I encounter such views here that are completely new to me and that are incomprehensible to me for now—up until now I thought that Russians were fanatical anti-Semites to all intents and purposes—"

"How little you know us, you Germans!" the Governor said, smiling as he shook his head.

"But above all—people even told me Your Excellency was a rabid anti-Semite. And now I'm hearing that ideas I explicated in my sermon today not only displease—"

"Displease!—But I'm thrilled, delighted!"

"I'm happy from the bottom of my heart to have you praise my sermon, and I promise that along these lines in the future—"

"Just a moment! Not so fast!—Do have a Papiros.—No?—So, your sermon! We are in total agreement in our views, as I said—but whether it is right to proclaim it, this enlightened view of ours, from the pulpit is perhaps another question."

"Is it not my duty to enlighten? Especially now, when people are talking of a pogrom—"

"Who's talking about a pogrom? A pogrom? Here? In my city? Who's pulling your leg?"

The Governor's face showed complete astonishment and outrage. Bode looked at him unbelievingly.

"People are generally talking about it," he said, confused. "People talk a lot, of course. People have even said that Your Excellency yourself—"

"You see what kind of evil people there are!" the Governor said, shaking his head. "It's sad! Now you have gotten to know me! I tell you: if it should come to a pogrom here—it isn't impossible after all—the spark could only come from the German side."

"Then it will never come to that!" Bode cried. "I can vouch for my parishioners!"

"It is better that you do not speak with such assurance, my dear Herr Pastor. It's already difficult enough to vouch for oneself. But if you think so—why do you preach against a pogrom? Why are you exposing yourself with superfluous comments? Who forces you to take a position? You place yourself in contradiction to the general mood of your compatriots, and you are trying to anticipate a higher power. One must leave things to fate. Everything that happens is good in the end. From time to time a wave of pogroms passes through our Russia. Yes, bless me! The mob seeks a vent for its wild instincts. A wise administration must take care that the destructive rage wreaks no irreparable harm or destroys irreplaceable possessions. Who is supposed to be the target of this frenzy? The church—the state—the government? Dear friend! We are speaking confidentially here. We are familiar with these institutions. Could they withstand the storm? They would crumble—they stand on hollow foundations. The Jews—they're something else! They can withstand any storm and any fire. For thousands of years they have suffered every persecution and vicious force, and they have survived everything, without any damage to what they are. So therefore it is for the best if the inevitable storm is directed against the Jews. Noblesse oblige! They can do that and survive even worse without any danger to what they are. What I am saying: they only increase in inner strength. You in Germany with your so-called equality are dismantling the barriers that have preserved the Jews from total assimilation, from absolute destruction. Pogroms and special laws are basically the greatest act of charity for the Jews. The life of the nation is saved by the deaths of the victims of the pogroms. Am I supposed to resist that? Can I? Can you? Can I sacrifice an entire people to save the lives of a few individuals? No, my dear friend, we must suppress our personal feelings. It's a question of the whole! We protect ourselves and our culture, and in doing so we don't in the least harm the Jews as a whole."

"Your Excellency must like to joke!" Bode said after a moment. "I am unable to credit the sincerity of this logic."

"You will have to credit it whether you want to or not, dear Herr Pastor," the Governor said with emphasis.

Suddenly he stood up and looked down at the Pastor meaningfully. The giant figure of the Governor was so close to him that the Pastor couldn't rise from his armchair.

"You will have to learn to keep the larger picture in mind. Everything in Russia must subordinate itself to the great Russian soul—even the Jews—even the Germans.—I would be truly sorry if the tolerance I've generously shown until now toward the Lutheran Church would lead to dissension."

He gave a significant nod and stared down at the Pastor for a few seconds; then he slowly turned to pace silently back and forth in the room. Finally he approached Bode, who had stood up, pale and confused, and said sternly: "Herr Pastor, you are a very good German, you even consider your obligations as a German! Don't confuse your simple parishioners! Every German is fundamentally an anti-Semite, you too—of course, even you! Your views are from your head, not from your heart. You are not at all capable of that enlightenment, that freedom of intellect as we are, not even of that depth and generosity of a worldview. When it comes down to it, in the end you are still personally capable of believing in the fairy tale of ritual murder and starting pogroms."

Bode looked around, dazed. What could he reply to these palpable contradictions?

"Herr Pastor," the Governor continued, cutting off any reply with a wave of his hand, "I have spoken with you frankly, with the honesty of a true Russian. I have a request! I, the Governor, to a German pastor: next Sunday you will declare from your pulpit—without having to withdraw anything about your views on Christian love—that you have the greatest confidence in the government and that you are convinced that the government of the czar conducts itself with justice and wisdom in all it does for all his subjects—and that it is presumptuous if a single person dares to question or criticize the motives of the authorities."

"I cannot and may not say that!" Bode said steadily.

"It was friendly advice—you are free to act on it or not!" the Governor said curtly. He pressed his lips together, and his eyes flashed for a moment. Immediately the dark face gave way again to the jovial and open expression. The Governor bid Bode farewell, shaking his hand with a smile, and escorted him through the antechamber to the door. In the antechamber, the gendarmes stood at attention and saluted.

At the door, the Governor stopped.

"Isn't that your little girl back there?" he asked with a smile. "Everyone can recognize her from afar by her brightly dressed companion. Do you have any more children?"

"No, our Bertha is our only child."

The Governor smiled.

"So, Herr Pastor," he said, "I will say one more thing to reassure you: if a pogrom isn't caused by Germans, there will be no pogrom."

He nodded pleasantly to bid farewell to the Pastor and watched him as he went down the garden path to the gate. Bode flinched as he heard the Governor calling in Russian something in a threatening voice behind him that was directed to the guard on the street. The guard ran quickly to his sentry box next to the door, and as he passed Bode he presented his weapon.

Embarrassed, Bode doffed his hat.

SEVEN

The Trumpet Sounds

I

With a beating heart, Candidate Ostermann mounted the narrow, dirty steps of the house to the rear of the Lindenstrasse. The stairwell was already dark by midmorning and barely lit by a low gas flame throwing a flickering light on the filthy plaque with the inscription:

To the Editorial Offices of *The Trumpet*
2. Étage

The word "Étage," however, had been vigorously crossed out with a red pencil several times and replaced in large letters with the word "Floor." It could not be more plainly expressed that this was the way to a stronghold of remorseless advocates of Germanic pride and unswerving slayers of everything un-German. The "Floor" over the second story indeed told the story of William Tell.

Slowly mounting the stairs, Candidate Ostermann timidly clutched his black overcoat to keep it from brushing against the cracked whitewashed walls. He certainly was not in the frame of mind to appreciate such subtleties of presentation. He was about to enter these mysterious rooms for the first time, where men sat who represented public opinion—he was about to come face to face with those brave protagonists of Christian-Germanic bloodstock and heritage, with those who had taken up the fight against the increasing decadence in the Jewified and corrupted babel of voices and who sought to tumble the walls of heathen strongholds with the echo of the trumpet anywhere false priests of Baal worshiped the gods of Mammon.

Only after much indecision and hesitation did he have the courage to send in his manuscript "The Demoralizing Influence of Jewry." He could admit to himself, of course, that the work wasn't bad—it even surpassed most of the essays on this topic in scholarship and in the number of footnotes. He had carefully studied the relevant literature—naturally only those authors with a strictly anti-Semitic point of view that guaranteed reliability and lack of bias—he had quoted from Justus Brimann and Rohling and had gone back to Eisenmenger's *Entdecktes Judentum*, or *Judaism Discovered*. In its organization his essay faithfully followed the customary structure that had been the basis of his essays in high school in Probstweida and that he now strictly required of all his pupils, why the Rhine was the favorite river of the German folk or when they had to draw parallels between the structure of *The Maid of Orleans* and that of the *Anabasis* by Xenophon. The essay also did not lack a certain moderate verve in its language or a sparingly applied enthusiasm easily understood by anyone at the conclusion of every paragraph, which not every speaker or author desiring an effect could always apply. And the frequent literary Teutonic heartiness evoking fundamental values was directly reminiscent, as Ostermann told himself with justifiable pride, of Martin Luther. Had he not quite industriously extracted a long list of expletives and organized them systematically according to categories in a table so that when he was overwhelmed by the holy zeal as he wrote he only had to look up in his list to find the right expression for his emotion?

He had carefully withheld the manuscript at Leah's urgent request as long as he was hoping for the scholarship. But on the afternoon of the day the committee met, whose outcome Leah had told him at once, he had precipitously without saying a word taken the manuscript to the Lindenstrasse and had slipped it himself into the mailbox of *The Trumpet* with a cover letter. He walked away with the long, proud steps one takes after a liberating act; finally he had been able to vent his rage against this clutch of Jews; his anger against this people who had carried so much guilt since the days of Golgotha and had increased at least tenfold through this newest incident, the denial of the scholarship.

The euphoria he felt soon evaporated; the same evening he had already realized it had been presumptuous of him to think his work would be accepted. How many well-known men were eager to see the output of their pens published in *The Trumpet*.

The men who presided over their sacred office could choose among the best, they who had the task of judgment over the life and death of the spiritual offspring of the best—they could choose; would they even have the time to read his manuscript? Indeed, could they, whose time and effort belonged to the public and the Fatherland—would they even waste their time reading every scribble sent to them? How much chaff must have accumulated; could they and would they squander precious hours to discover even one small gem?!—

But after only a few days he received a postcard bidding him to appear at the editorial offices as soon as possible—"for the purpose of a conference in person in the matter of the contribution most kindly submitted."

And so he was now knocking—a few hours after receiving the card—on the door that led to the holy shrine. He felt the significance of the moment; a new chapter was beginning for him; in a few seconds he would step into the circle of august souls, hoping to join the ranks of their crusade.

"Come—in!"

Ostermann straightened his shoulders and turned the doorknob; the door stuck a little and then suddenly burst wide open.—Somewhat taken aback, he stood in the doorway, holding in his hand the hat he had removed before knocking. He was so stunned, even blinded, by the sudden brightness that it took a few moments until he could see the room and differentiate among those present.

Moreover, neither of the two people sitting in the room took notice of him at first. They looked very busy. Ostermann glanced wildly at the sign on the door, which still stood open, to check again whether he was really and truly standing on the threshold of *The Trumpet*'s holy of holies. Then he turned to stone again.

"Close the door, hang it!!" bellowed the voice that was the same jarring voice that had shouted "come in"; Ostermann quickly and deferentially obeyed and tried to see the speaker's face. At first he saw nothing of this personality but the lower part of his large checked trousers and enormous yellow shoes and a gray-green right sleeve and a huge paw. Mighty clouds of smoke, which were fitfully emitted, allowed the approximate position of the mouth to be ascertained. Moreover, the smoker was concealed by an ample red-blond lady of indeterminate age who had settled herself familiarly on his lap and was leaning against the gray-green arm as comfortably as if sitting in an easy chair. Lying in front of her on the broad table, unbelievably piled with a jumble of papers and newspapers atop a pile of books, was a notebook she was using to take dictation from the jarring voice.

A bright blond tangle of hair was only intermittently visible behind the lady whenever she turned her face briefly toward the visitor. Then she stretched her right leg so vehemently that her skirt and petticoat flew up to a discreet height, reached artfully with her foot for the chair, knocking it over to spill the books lying there, and flung her leg with admirable dexterity that suggested long practice toward the visitor, hitting him in the shins.

It was an invitation in pantomime but an effective one to take a seat.

Ostermann sat down, totally confused; he felt dizzy; what he saw corresponded in no way to what he had expected, either in general or in detail. He felt dimly that it would be rather difficult to describe his visit to the editorial office to Leah by going into detail with any exactitude, which he had originally promised himself to do.

"Damn it—these constant interruptions!" it growled in annoyance.—"Of course, right in the middle of all this craziness!—Emmy, light of my life—the last paragraph again, please!"

"Hang on, Chubby!" said the well-nourished lady trumpeter, flipping through her steno pad. "Where is the nonsense?—Ah—here it is: When will the healthy spirit of our still-unbowed folk in its boundless primal force finally have the courage to sweep away with the mad rage of our ancestors of old those pasha manners and harem morals reminiscent of the Orient in more than one respect and unnatural to every Germanic being? Should it come to pass, moreover, before the eyes of German men and women—German fathers and mothers that—well, Chubby, what happens next?"

"Right, wait a second—what really should come next?!—Damn it—let's sprinkle a little pepper on the salad—so: further, should it come to pass that—blond German girls and maidens are at the mercy of the lecherous desires of their pashas with their black curly hair—meekly awaiting with trepidation the moment when the almighty lord of the seraglio tosses his less-than-clean handkerchief? Further, should the pomaded libertines who use cologne to mask their nauseating, tear-inducing odor, an odor from the East that clings to them, where their cradles stand—and further, should they really so increase the demand in the shops for cradles in the West, their very own invention against the healthy middle class that—"

"Hey, now just stop it!" the lady trumpeter said and roughly poked the man with her elbow as he was dictating. "You're getting tied up in knots!"

"Yes. Indeed! You're right!—The mood has passed! Go away—Emmy, my life's light, and smarten up the Cardinal's existence! Go check if the swine has slept off his hangover yet!"

The trumpeter's angel snapped her notebook closed, thrust her hand into her blond tangle of hair, roughly shook the source of the incomprehensible grunting noises a few times, and threw herself with the full weight of her charms into a drawn-out kiss, while he focused on securing the safety of his pipe—he clamped it in his left hand, stretched toward heaven. Then she suddenly jumped down from his lap and disappeared noisily into the next room.

Candidate Ostermann and the editor were alone.

"Heavens!" said the large blond man with a bushy full beard, now visible as he puffed on his pipe to get it going again. "Heavens! She's a thoroughbred bitch! The swine can squish you to death!—That's the sort of freedom of the press I love!"

His pipe was working; he turned around, and for the first time he noticed the candidate. He scrutinized with some astonishment the figure who was all frock coat and ceremony.

"Who in the world are you?"

Ostermann was so taken aback that he couldn't say a word; he extended his hand, holding out the postcard he had received.

The large man didn't even bother to take the card but read it from afar still in Ostermann's hand.

"So," he said and slowly let his gaze wander deliberately over Ostermann's figure once more. "So, that's you!—Hang it!" He slapped himself so hard on his knee with his right hand that there was a resounding pop. "And you look exactly as I thought you would!"

II

They sat there awhile, looking at each other—Candidate Ostermann and Dr. Schliephake, the editor in chief of *The Trumpet*.—Ostermann was trying to decide if the words were actually flattering, while the other man continued to stare at him with swollen eyes as he puffed away—opening his mouth a few times as if he wanted to say something.—But some time passed before he spoke.

"Now, just tell me, man of God—I'm supposed to print the entire drivel?"

Ostermann shot out of his chair, red as a beet.

"Please," he managed to say, "give me the manuscript back—I see I was mistaken —I am not at the right place.—Not at all!" he concluded with a sidelong glance at the door through which the divine nymph of *The Trumpet* had disappeared.

"Always gentle with young horses!" the other said, calmly continuing to puff away. "Now sit down again nicely on that part of your body Providence loaned you for the purpose and don't forget to carefully spread the skirts of your youngster's coat.—You're a main feature! Man of God, now don't behave like a sulking liverwurst; if we hadn't liked your submission a lot, I wouldn't have had you gallop over here but would have dismissed you with an expression of deep regret on account of a backlog.—I'm supposed to touchingly shake your paw by greeting you as a new comrade-in-arms? What?"

Ostermann's expectations were in fact in that general direction; he sank back into his embarrassment.

"You can have that too, honored benefactor," the other man continued. "Everything you could wish—through that door through which you saw the buxom she-devil disappear, which seemed to endanger your senses so, O errant and virtuous knight.—Ye are errant, thither is no Venus or Witch Mountain, but there the most honorable Cardinal, alias Dr. Phil. Hesse, sits and awaits a joyful resurrection.—So all sanctimonious jabber and stupid rubbish belongs in his portfolio. I don't mince words.—So, tell me, really: What do you think you should be paid for this article here?"

Ostermann had taken his seat; it dawned on him that his article must have definitely found favor. Why had they told him to come there? The last question caused him to blush again, this time with pleasure.

He made a half proud, half modest, generous gesture.

"I don't write for material gain—I do not hesitate to ask you to decide the honorarium yourself."

The other man looked at him silently for a while again.

"Do you have a criminal record?" he finally asked.

Dumbfounded, Ostermann stared; it was difficult to follow these leaps of thought.

"Do you know *The Game of Klabrias*?" was the next question. "Have you never been to Herrnfelds' theater on the Alexanderplatz?"

The connection of this question to the topic at hand also escaped him.

"No, never!" Ostermann said but still shook his head vigorously. "I don't go to those sorts of places!"

"Too bad! It's really required if you want to study Jews.—I go to every play at least three times—my sense of Prussian duty!!—So a coffeehouse patron asks: Whaddya think I can get for the coat?—and the other noble coreligionist answers: A year in jail.—You can get three months for the item!"

Horrified, Ostermann shot up.

"Stay seated—you have to gradually become used to sitting.—Judah's anger shall burn fiercely, and they will deliver us to the Moabites. That makes no difference. We have needed that for a long time.—Mocking religious institutions—lots of fuss—investigations—experts' reports—long summaries of trials—it is published and known—and then the dough for Emmy still must be there so she can shell out in the end for her silk blouses she so dearly covets.—Thus Israel shall have its joy!"

"Israel?" Ostermann babbled, confused.

"Namely, N. Israel on the Spandauer Strasse!—Indeed, you had probably no idea about the effect of your appearance in literature?—Your laurels are crooked!"

"I thought—not far—and besides: I wanted the article to be printed without my name!"

"Oops?—Nay, my most honored sir! I'm supposed to face your music?—You can put that idea out of your head right away! Nip that in the bud!"

Ostermann reached for his manuscript.

"I will forgo having it printed," he declared. "It's not cowardice on my part. There are personal relationships—I simply cannot have my name published— and then—it's that everything is different from what I thought."

Again he involuntarily glanced quickly at the door to the next room.

"Ahh, you youth with the coat of virtue!" the editor said as he stood up. "As soon as you appeared, I should've probably thrown Emmy, that creature of the devil, to the ground, and as for you, the honest and virtuous knight without fear or blemish—wait! We'll be right with you—"

He opened the door to the next room and bellowed: "Cardinal!—Does Your Eminence wish to bestir yourself?"

The being conjured up appeared on the threshold; it emanated not so much an odor of holiness as an odor suggesting a serious use of alcohol. The being was a rather stocky, corpulent gentleman in a somewhat greasy jacket. His short neck, which scarcely bubbled up from a black scarf, seemed greasy too, as did his badly shaved beardless face with its snub nose and round eyeglasses. His appearance had on the whole the aura of something of a spiritual warning, especially as a bald spot crowned him as if he had been tonsured. He moved slowly and with a certain solemnity; his speech was measured and sanctimonious.

"Cardinal—I have done my part—do yours," Dr. Schliephake ordained. "This child, pure as an angel—is Candidate Ostermann, who wants to sexually enlighten us about Jews. He has handled the topic so that he delicately remains in the background, and we're supposed to natter on for him.—"

The Cardinal sorrowfully swayed his head.

"Furthermore, he feels morally compromised by the sight of Emmy's legs and seemed somewhat perplexed about the manner in which she took up her post on my lap. Who the devil am I supposed to put on my lap? The holy ecclesiastical council perhaps? So this one falls into your department, Hesse—schmaltz and butter!"

He sat down again at his desk and began to tamp his pipe afresh.

"Yes," the Cardinal said, smiling gently. "Sometimes it's difficult to get along with our good Schliephake. Don't let that bother you, my young friend!—You must judge him according to his articles; that's where his soul really is. What does one detail matter! We are all in the service of magnificent ideas! Right?—The greatest ideas! Truth—Fatherland—Folk—right, my young friend?"

"Of course—of course," Ostermann stammered. "That's exactly why—"

"There you are!" Hesse said emphatically as if everything were now completely clear, and he looked at Ostermann as if he were sorry that he had given the Cardinal occasion to reprimand him on account of his moral behavior. "Right! Now let's drop it!—What's a detail? What am I?—It all depends on the larger perspective! Whose concern is it if our friend here has his little weaknesses?—or what difference does it make if I, for example, got miserably drunk every evening? Who is so petty as to bother about it! Who among us is so presumptuous as to assume his private little life is somehow important?—What matters is what we write! That goes out into the world and rattles the soul of the indolent!—Ye shall know them by their fruits! Who asks how the soil is fertilized, from which the fruits grow—what filth lies there where the most beautiful trees sprout.—Never judge by appearance!"

"Man!" Schliephake said. "You must be in a foul mood!—Enough with the sermon!—Get down to business!!!"

"I too have read your manuscript—great talent—great talent! And a painstaking piece of work! We must delete a bit—the main points can remain—and so we won't have to worry about a jail sentence—maybe it would be better—but I think that with no extensive changes at all I can bring the matter down to a fine of about five hundred marks.—I am somewhat acquainted with the schedule of charges!"

"But that's quite out of the question!" Ostermann shouted. "My name cannot be published under any circumstances! For personal reasons!"

"I do understand," Hesse said. "I suspected as much. You are still a student. You are thinking of stipends, and since almost all stipend funds flow from the Jewish purse—"

"No!" Ostermann said bitterly. "I have no hopes there! That's over and done with!"

"Over and done with?" the Cardinal asked sympathetically. "You were rejected? Which stipend was it?"

"It doesn't matter!" Ostermann said. "Two rabbis against me, and the third trustee is a baptized Jew."

"Two rabbis together with a baptized Jew?—Who was it?"

"Regional Court Director Lehnsen!"

"Hey!" Schliephake exclaimed, jumping up. "My friend Levysohn? The fellow who gave me two weeks for that stupid prank in a café with the Jewish girl and her father? He's sitting down with rabbis? I thought he was living Jew-free!"

"That would be difficult for him," Ostermann laughed grimly. "His Polish family is arriving at his house now."

"You have to tell us more details, dear sir," Hesse said with increasing interest and glancing meaningfully at Schliephake.

"Oh, it's not of any interest," Ostermann said. "Only that just in the middle of the birthday party for the young lady of the house, right in the middle of all the guests, appears—there was even a baron's family there—a young Jewish man, actually mumbling genuine Yiddish and with a long beard—it must have been quite a situation. But that can't possibly interest you."

"But it is of colossal interest to us!" Schliephake exclaimed. "That will be a fantastic prank and is worth ten essays on morality!"

"But gentlemen!" Ostermann stammered, turning pale and looking from one to the other. "That's strictly private what I happened to tell you—you won't put that in your paper—who would be interested in that—"

"My young friend and colleague—I may call you that now," Hesse said with a certain solemnity. "In the difficult and holy struggle that we fight, as conscientious workers, we must not let slip any opportunity to investigate the numerous ramifications of Jewish life and their subtlest psychological motives. It is strictly only for our personal information, not for the paper—"

"If you don't tell us now everything that you know, most honored sir," Schliephake said harshly, "I will put together a ragout out of what you've said so far for the next number that Herr Lehnsen can digest for a long time. If it's not correct, he can address our source—Herr Candidate Ostermann!"

"But on the other hand," Hesse said gently to the completely dazed Ostermann standing miserably before him, "if you give us your information—you also give us evidence that you consider yourself fully and totally as one of us. And then, of course, we will consider your wishes and publish your article about morality without naming your name—right, Schliephake?—You don't need to even pay one penny for this!—"

"And you will not publish my name even if later unpleasant consequences actually ensue?" Ostermann asked uncertainly.

"We pledge the honor of our paper and our own," Hesse said solemnly. "Consider—editorial confidentiality!"

"And what I tell you—I have it from my—from someone who was at the birthday party—remains among us—will not appear in the newspaper?"

"Absolutely not!" Schliephake said. "The story is valuable to us only if it isn't printed!"

That was somewhat unclear, but Ostermann felt reassured and told the attentively listening Hesse of Yossel's appearance in Lehnsen's home.—

"Well, there isn't much to make of that!" Schliephake grumbled. "But what happened that day with the boy?"

"Well, I don't know anything else. My—the guests left quickly, and I don't know what happened after that!—When will my article probably come out? And without my name! Editorial confidentiality!"

"Strictly anonymous! Tomorrow the first part goes to press!" Hesse said. "So, dear Herr Candidate, we hope to have more contributions from your valuable pen and to enjoy your interesting conversation more often."

They shook hands to say good-bye.

"It will be a hit!" Hesse said.

"Like a stink bomb!" said Schliephake.

"Onward—for Germanic breeding and morality!" said Hesse melodramatically.

"Pithy—courageous—forceful!" Schliephake said.

"And anonymous!" said Ostermann and departed.

III

It is not always good to be too careful.

On occasion it is even careless.

That is what Regional Court Director Lehnsen must learn.

When the Rabbi informed him by telephone that Kaiser had declined the stipend and confirmed that Ostermann could now be awarded the stipend, the Regional Court Director was of course not a little happy. But just as he was about to go to the ladies to deliver the good news, he had second thoughts. May the devil put trust in the dear Magnus! In spite of himself, Elsa's pet name came to him during the telephone call, and as he hung up he had the feeling that he had had something unpleasantly sticky in his hand. If the raving Professor would persuade the Rabbi one more time, he would finally fold. Lehnsen therefore decided to avoid more vexation and additional disappointment—better to say nothing to anyone about the newest twist before the final outcome was definite.

He circulated the files again after he had given a brief notice that Kaiser had declined the stipend. He requested the formal declaration to award the money to the only remaining applicant, Ostermann.

The files arrived at the Professor's on Friday and, since he did not transact any business on the Sabbath, remained unopened until Sunday. They only reached Dr. Magnus on Monday; beneath the notice written by the Director, the Professor had written in enormous letters:

No!!!—I don't agree!!!—
In violation of the bylaws!!!—Hirsch

The whole thing was underlined in red three times.

Dr. Magnus ran around his room in distress. He had actually, perhaps somewhat rashly, already confirmed with the Director—but he was also not a little intimidated by the Professor. Hadn't he taken the position in the meeting that awarding the stipend to a non-Jew was in violation of the bylaws? What was to be done now?

The file sat on his desk for three days, annoying him. Finally he wrote down his vote after he had torn up several false starts; he thought his final version masterful and breathed a sigh of relief as he shoved the file into the envelope.

His vote, however, read:

Expressly reserving the freedom in future cases to decide and noting with the strongest possible emphasis the will of the deceased founder A. as the definitive factor in all decisions of the board on the one hand—and on the other hand with respect to the extraordinary set of actual terms and conditions of this particular case I can, after considering all pros and cons of the relevant reasons, only come to the conclusion to abstain from voting.

Dr. Magnus,
Rabbi

Lehnsen smiled derisively as he read this; but he understood Magnus very well, who knew very well that in the case of a tie—and that was now the case—the Director's vote decided.

As the bearer of good news he hoped to erase the remaining bad feeling that may have persisted in the Baron's family from the troublesome event at Elsa's birthday party. In general it had gone better than he had thought in the first panic. He had had the happy notion of letting Heinz travel for the time being to prevent any new caprices or irksome arguments. Joseph came every day as usual, and the official engagement approached; even Baron Anselm seemed to want to mask the existence of the unfortunate cousin Yossel with the mantle of Christian love.

IV

The bolt of lightning that had struck the Lehnsen family when the exotic guest appeared thus seemed to have been a blunt bolt.—After Heinz's spectacular introduction of Yossel, the party guests had sort of turned to stone for a few moments—Baron Anselm and the Director even stood convulsed, holding each other's hand—and everyone stared thunderstruck at Yossel, who for his part was no less confused than anyone else. But even Heinz had turned red, astonished and shocked at himself about his impulsive act and its paralyzing effect.

It was Leah who finally broke the tension; she had the talent to find the inappropriate word in any situation and said with frosty charm: "I think we should really take our leave now! We don't want to disturb the reunion of beloved relatives."

And so the spell was broken: a rather confused round of hearty handshakes began. Outside, the Director had to hustle off the policeman waiting on the landing.—After he had cheerfully bid everyone good-bye and had opened the door to the salon again, he found only Martha Mertens and Yossel; he angrily slammed the door shut once more and went to his study.—His wife was sobbing in her bedroom.—Elsa and Heinz had locked the doors to their rooms.—

The guests parted ways outside without mentioning what had happened. Joseph accompanied Baron Anselm; they walked slowly along the bank of the canal toward the Lützowplatz.

A deep silence on the part of the old gentleman unsettled Joseph more than a little. Damn it! Everything had started so well until that disgusting Jewish lout had burst in on everything. That nice Heinz, whom he otherwise liked well enough and whose baroque ideas had amused him often enough, now seemed to have gone totally and completely mad. What was he supposed to say to the old gentleman now! This bearded cousin from Polackland could not be easily argued away.

Finally Baron Anselm began cautiously: "That young lady didn't make a bad impression on me. A well-brought-up, darling child—she has good manners—really, actually behaves quite nicely. You can see: the parents have apparently done everything in their power to—umm—make you forget her origins."

And to Joseph's great astonishment there followed a detailed description of Elsa's merits in the warmest terms, as if it were a matter of overcoming Joseph's objections to the engagement.

"If circumstances prove otherwise satisfactory—" Baron Anselm concluded.

"The situation of the family is splendid!" Joseph said ardently.

"—then I probably think that this girl can certainly be a good and honest wife."

"So you will give your blessing?" Joseph cried with joy. "Well, thank God! You can rely on that too—that this unfortunate Oriental cousin no longer enters the house!"

"What cousin?" the old gentleman said slowly. "That young man that looked so crude? How does he upset you?"

Joseph looked at him blankly.

"If he doesn't bother you—I assume—he's really impossible—one will have to hustle him off—I don't believe that the Lehnsens were very delighted about him."

"That could be. That's a matter for the Herr Regional Court Director, of course. Might I ask what that has to do with us?"

Baron Anselm stopped and peered sternly at Joseph.

"What sort of false path do I see you taking, Joseph? It is, God knows, a difficult step for all of us when we marry into a Jewish family. If your life were differently—no, never mind! We have made our decision like so many of the noblest families. I stepped over the chasm when I entered his house to at least see if the woman you wished to take as a bride would not personally bring shame on us. And as I said—there is nothing to object to there. And also she's blond!—So in principle, the deed is done with my visit.—Nevertheless, if we have taken this step, we must secure the essential boundaries all the more so.—If we are already compelled by circumstances to bring an alien member into our family, we must be doubly clear who we are and who they are.—"

"Certainly!" Joseph said, bewildered. "That's exactly why I thought that this exotic young man—he's certainly outrageous—in the family—"

"Outrageous! Of course!—But more outrageous than the Herr Regional Court Director himself? More outrageous for us?—Joseph—you've become unsure of yourself—you don't know where the boundary line is anymore. The chasm is between us and the Director, not on the other side of him, not between him and the cousin in the caftan. A Jew's a Jew! It doesn't matter if he's baptized or not—if he wears a caftan or a smoking jacket. They don't get closer to us with the help of tailors, barbers, and interior decorators—not even with the help of the pulpit or professor's lectern. They remain what they are, and we remain who we are. Anybody can put on a mask; I almost want to say that the masked Jew is to be spurned all the more because he's more dangerous. I see that now in you!—A pill is a pill, and you sugarcoat it only for children.—Marry your Elsa, and we'll see about getting over everything else; we want to receive them in a friendly way and make sure of turning her into a brave little Christian German nobleman's wife. But the family!—Keep away from them!"

And so Joseph got the blessing he wanted from the head of the family.

V

Yossel Schlenker was standing where Heinz had left him in the Lehnsen salon just as everyone whose cynosure he had abruptly and unwillingly become suddenly disappeared through the various doors. He was completely dazed by all the bizarre events he had just experienced, especially the manner of his introduction into Berlin society.—That fat and elegant lady was supposed to be his cousin— these elegant and fine people his relatives? He had known that an older brother of his father had come to Germany many, many years ago—his name was rarely mentioned; he was considered a renegade and had surely gone to rack and ruin somewhere—and now he was rediscovering his family here, and under such circumstances! His head spun!

When he regained consciousness, he noticed he was alone in the room; there was only a young lady standing at the window who was watching him carefully. His adroitness with women since the time he had had the momentous argument with Chana about carrying an object on the Sabbath had barely improved, and the entire situation wasn't suited for helping him with his awkwardness. He had only one desire, to disappear from this uncanny house as quickly as possible, to get back to his familiar surroundings, to his wife, where he could put his tumbled thoughts in order in peace and quiet. He made a half-attempt at a bow and, to spare the costly carpet as best he could, tiptoed to the door.

He had almost reached the door—he was stretching out his hand to grab the doorknob—when suddenly the door was ripped open from the other side; filling the door frame was the same stately gentleman with a short, graying moustache who had shaken hands so amiably before with the other old gentleman. Now his face was scarlet and angry, and he pierced Yossel with so furious a look that he fell back, terrified. In the next moment, the door was violently slammed shut, and the apparition disappeared.

Yossel became nervous; he concluded he had fallen into a madhouse. He stood there, not knowing what to do.

A hand gently touched his hand, and a quiet woman's voice said: "You probably want to go too, Herr Schlenker. Come with me."

He looked at the lady and had the feeling that he was dealing now with a sane person. Her calm, clear, oval face—gray eyes—smooth blond hair—the firmness in her voice—everything promised safety. He quickly and happily followed her to the street.

"Where do you live here?" the lady asked quietly as she continued to walk, as if it were a matter of course that Yossel was still with her. Yossel told her—the lady took him to the streetcar stop and made sure that he got into the right tram car.—

He had scarcely departed when Heinz Lehnsen hurried along; he looked around and turned toward Martha when he saw her.

"Excuse me, Martha—did you see that young man?"

Martha pointed to the streetcar disappearing in the direction of the Potsdamer Platz.

"He's going by streetcar; I put him on the tram."

"You took care of him?—Of course, you are the only one who thought of what should be done."

"Yes," Martha said, smiling. "It seemed to me that he needed some protection, and your lively interest in him had flagged so suddenly that he was standing all helpless and alone in your salon. So I just jumped in for you."

"Oh, well—Christian duty and so forth! You just can't expect that I have the right training in that respect."

"It seemed to me for a moment this morning as if you might even be feeling some un-Christian impulses now and then."

"Ah, well, perhaps I'm once again becoming the Tolstoy of Berlin West."

"In any case, it seemed to me that you have shown something of a sense of family today for the first time. Even if the peculiar form of it didn't improve Elsa's party."

"Do me a favor, Martha—scold me properly; I'm serious!"

"If you think that you deserve a scolding, then you don't need a sermon from me. You can reprimand yourself quite well!—What were you thinking?"

"It was only a thought—and really a childish one, too. I was excited, and the young fellow—I had quite a day today that set my nerves on edge. I was just tempted again to start something to turn the philistines into a pillar of salt—of course in principle I don't have the least desire for half-Asian cousins!"

"And why are you now running after the young man?"

"It's beginning to occur to me that I've thrust him into a most unpleasant situation—in addition to Elsa. I can apologize sooner to someone I don't know—it's going to be more difficult with Elsa.—You know that I have difficulty even talking seriously with Elsa—indeed, with anyone in the family or among good friends—except you, of course!"

They walked along the canal toward the Lützowplatz; he had hooked his arm in hers in an intimate gesture.

"It's terribly sad," Martha said after a while, "that you and Elsa can't speak seriously with each other. Each of you is embarrassed by your feelings, and you both avoid each other with flippant remarks and jokes.—It's as if you are afraid to look things in the eye and also—to look each other in the eye. You both are unable to speak unselfconsciously and to call things what they really are."

"What do you want?—That's what we happen to be. All of you are different!"

"Us?—Maybe! You two often make me so terribly sad—you don't have the best things in life.—At the same time, I envy you two for so much. I've been really fond of Elsa ever since we knew each other in school; I've always admired her. Everything has come easily to both of you, without work or study; but she never considered it important to her. And I'm often worried about her—I must say, she's always trying to flee from herself, just like you."

"Martha," Heinz said quietly, pressing her arm lightly, "that's just what we love about you—what we lack. How is it that I can talk with you as with no one else?—I've often thought there's a deeper reason why so many young men of Jewish background don't marry Jews—"

"What are you going to do now after what happened today?" Martha asked quickly. "Your splendid prank could have annoying consequences."

"Yes—there could well be some painful discussions at home," Heinz said morosely and dropped Martha's arm.

"And this young man—don't you want to find him?"

"What am I supposed to do with him?—One visit was enough. Although—I heard interesting things, and if it weren't unfortunately a genuine cousin—"

"So it's true?"

"There's really no doubt. Listen."

And he told her the adventure from beginning to end; Martha listened with interest and posed many questions about the Borytshev background. Heinz had to admit that he didn't know much more than what Yossel had said.

"Strange!" Martha said. "It's strange to think how very close relatives live in such different worlds! There in Borytshev—that must be a completely different world. Maybe the real Jews are there—I had no idea of such things."

"What I'm concerned about is basically the split in the family."

"Aren't *you* here the ones who have been split off? You were torn off from there—and it seems to me that you are still trying to flee. What I said before: you are fleeing from yourself—that has even more significance in the end than I understood myself."

"What are you saying? I should go to Borytshev? I should grow sidelocks?"

"Not that at all. But I think if I were you—I would take an interest in these things—I would look for an opportunity to go there. It must have its charms—to see one's ancestors alive on earth. It would almost seem to me to be a duty. Noblesse oblige."

"That is strange!"

"What?"

"You're saying what I was thinking early today, before this miserable contretemps. Am I not ultimately from the oldest aristocracy? You've seen what happens when one of our ancestors becomes alive and appears in the flesh in our salon.—I would be quite curious how strange a Stülp-Sandersleben ancestor would look in Berlin West—a beefy, illiterate, brutal highwayman—"

"Maybe something like that could be scraped up nowadays. I don't know who would emerge looking better.—But here's my streetcar. I have another hour to go.—But do think about the problem!"

"About my aristocratic heritage? Please, Martha—I beg of you to keep it confidential so that my newly discovered aristocratic descent won't make me arrogant. I shall continue to sit with the young lords from the time of the Crusades and the Landknecht without prejudice in any discussions just as before and even spare you a kind word now and then. And if I don't go directly to my ancestral home in Borytshev—I shall seek my noble cousin Yossel from the house of Schlenker at his residence among the nobles on the Dragonerstrasse. By my knight's honor!"

VI

Heinz had steeled himself for a well-deserved dressing-down when he heard from the maid on his return home that his father was waiting for him in the study. Feeling guilty, he decided to let everything pour over him with downcast eyes. But to his surprise, he found the Director sitting rather calmly reading a file, and what he heard made him raise his eyes in astonishment.

"You have often said," the Director said, "that you wanted to go to the International Union of Criminal Law conference, which is coming up in Petersburg. Up until now I have not agreed because, on the one hand, I've never seen any particular interest on your part for the topics on the program, and, on the other, I believe that you have plenty to amuse yourself with here in Berlin.—I have reconsidered the matter. You can get a passport and a visa tomorrow, and it is all right with me if you leave quickly. Hand in a request for a vacation for three weeks; I will approve it if necessary. You can visit Moscow and anything else in Russia that interests you.—You don't need to thank me; you understand that in no way is this a reward. I think it better if you disappear for a while."

Heinz left with a red face and a sense of embarrassment; he had ardently desired this Russian trip and had been thoroughly annoyed by his father's veto. Now it just fell into his lap. No doubt his father was worried about more pranks from him. Finally, he even realized that what had been nothing but rash improvisation was actually the result of a careful plan. In any case, the Petersburg trip was the happy result of a stupid prank, a reward for inept virtue.—

The next day Heinz went to the police headquarters to get his passport and then went to the Russian consulate to pick up the mandatory visa.—First he had to wait in the office for other passport holders ahead of him to finish. The consulate clerk was talking at the moment with a quite elegantly dressed lady who seemed to be greatly upset; she crushed her handkerchief in her nervous hands, dabbing her eyes from time to time, and, trembling with impatience, kept an eye on the slow and phlegmatic movements of the clerk. In front of him was a thick ledger in which he registered the information the lady was giving him, every so often carefully checking the papers that she was handing him.

"So—what is the name of the company for which you are traveling to Moscow?"

"Friedrich Schmolke," the woman said with a sigh. "It's right there—in the statement."

"Friedrich Schmolke. Margarine *en gros* and *en detail,* 43 Köpenicker Strasse," the clerk slowly read aloud from the paper. "That checks so far; that's in the commercial registry of the Royal Court of the District of Central Berlin."

He held the document up to the light as if he doubted its authenticity.

"And now your power of attorney."

This document too was subjected to a careful examination.

"According to this document—the power of attorney—signature notarized by Notary Dr. Berger—you are traveling for the Schmolke Company as traveling sales representative—fully authorized to purchase for cash. Is that correct?"

"My God!—Yes! Yes!" the lady said, suppressing a sob. "For God's sake, hurry. I have to catch the train today!—You know after all—I wanted to leave yesterday—I've been running around since early yesterday!—"

"So sorry," the man behind the counter said indifferently. "I'm bound by the rules."

The lady sighed deeply.

Heinz was wondering not a little in the meantime about this elegantly dressed margarine sales representative and even more about what could be so heartrending about this sober commercial sector and what could be the source of the lady's distress. He was just considering what in the world a margarine firm could be interested in buying in Russia when he was catapulted into a state of even higher astonishment as the clerk read out the name of the traveling sales representative from the passport.

"Frau Privy Medical Councillor Dr. Mandelbrot, Hannah, née Brudskus."

Heinz looked up, surprised; now he even recognized the lady, whom he had met now and then at social gatherings. What could have happened that this stinking rich and well-known spouse of a famous specialist was dealing in artificial butter?

"So you can pick up the passport when it's ready," the clerk said. "The fees are four marks ninety for the visa—six marks fifty for approving the power of attorney—a total of eleven marks forty.—Thank you.—I do urgently advise you to get a notarized translation of the documents into Russian so that you don't have any difficulties at the border—that costs ninety-one marks eighty. It will be ready in three days."

"Three days?" the lady exclaimed, horrified.

"Yes, it can't be done any faster.—But if you wish, you can pay the ninety-one marks eighty now and have someone pick up the documents when convenient. You get the passport in this case right away."

The lady sighed and paid. The clerk disappeared into a side room, and she sat down next to Heinz on the bench. Heinz was somewhat confused: he didn't know if the lady would appreciate being recognized as a traveling sales representative in this odd situation. But she recognized him and held out her hand.

"You here?—You want to get to Russia too? Ah, these difficulties with passports are terrible. What goods are you traveling for?"

Extremely astonished, Heinz said: "Excuse me, madam! I'm an attorney."

"Yes, but—ah, a thousand pardons. I forgot.—You've been baptized."

Now both parties were somewhat embarrassed.

"But our sort!" the wife of the Privy Councillor continued. "Of course, our children were long ago—but I didn't have the heart as long as my mother was still—"

With her handkerchief she dabbed her eyes.

"Yesterday I had a telegram from Moscow—Mother desperately ill—now I have to run from Pontius to Pilate to make this journey. You are lucky: you show your baptismal certificate, pay your four marks ninety, are handed your visa, and can travel. But Jews can only cross the border if they can prove they are representing a company. Fortunately, my cook's father has a small business; so I'm traveling now as his employee. But not until I've gotten all these documents together! It's extremely embarrassing to lie like this—but what can you do? And then all these deceptions and the extortions!—Now I'll finally most likely get the visa. But it has certainly cost enough money!"

"I had no idea about any of this!" Heinz said, astonished. "But at least you are going to get your passport for certain? The clerk did say that just copying the documents would take three days."

"A lie!" The wife of the Privy Councillor laughed grimly. "They never make copies, and no one ever asks to see them—they are totally and completely superfluous. It's just another method for those scoundrels to extort a bit of money to line their own pocket. If I don't pay, I have to wait a week!"

"But that's outrageous!—Are Jews completely defenseless here?"

"There's always baptism," she said with a shrug. "Oh God! I'll probably not see my mother!"

She sighed and dabbed her eyes with her handkerchief.

"So—this time is probably the last time—if one still has a mother—isn't that so, Herr Doctor?—one gladly makes the sacrifices!—Today my religion has cost me almost one hundred and fifty marks."

The clerk's reappearance brought the conversation to an end. Heinz told the lady, who finally had her passport, that he wished her a pleasant journey and his hopes for her mother's recovery, and it was his turn at last—

In a few minutes he had his visa.

He had to admit that possessing a baptismal certificate had its advantages.

VII

Heinz started to do what he had intended to do, visit his cousin. He set out toward the Dragonerstrasse. As he turned onto the street that had been completely foreign to him until now, his eyes widened, and he asked himself whether he wouldn't be asked to show his passport here. He was apparently no longer in Berlin or Germany but somehow had been magically transported to a Russian or Galician Jewish town.

To the right and to the left there were Hebrew letters staring down at him from the storefronts; at cellar entryways Oriental-looking women wearing long shawls were yelling out the food for sale or other unidentifiable wares. Men with corkscrew sidelocks in long caftans were in deep debate in the middle of the street, which had lost the character of a roadway and had taken on the character of a general meeting place, and myriads of children, competing in picturesque filth with those of Genoa and Naples, blocked the way everywhere.

Amazed, Heinz made his way through the crush of pedestrians, stopping every now and then to peek into open doorways. On the worn steps in front, dark-eyed children bartered with serious little faces. He was taken aback by the number of expressive faces of the older men whose spiritual, patriarchal expression didn't really comport with what they were doing. Here an old man with a worried look who could have been a model for Moses was holding up a gray plaid pair of pants by the legs as he stood in a doorway and spoke sternly to a foppishly and raffishly dressed young man as he chewed indecisively on the knob of his walking stick—and there a group of martyr figures standing together in a window, examining a pair of diamond earrings in the sun. The women definitely looked more mundane; thick and fleshy figures that waddled across the street, they certainly would have, as Heinz noted to himself, fit quite well in a salon on the west side of town without causing comment if dressed differently.—It was sad to think that many quite pretty young women with their deep, dark eyes reflecting the sorrows and knowledge of a people with a thousand-year-old history should have sunk to the vulgarity of their mothers.—

At last he reached the Bornstein Pub and stepped up to the bar. The landlord was leaning against the counter. He was a muscular Jew with a short curly beard, his coat and vest unbuttoned. He was talking with two young people who were obviously not from this part of town. The young man wore the colors of a fraternity; the lady with him gave the impression of being a conservatory student.—The landlord snarled at them rather rudely: "So why should I care? Rubbish—A Shekel Day!—What's that, then—shekel?"

"But you must have heard of Zionism," the young man said calmly. "Shekel—that's the name of our yearly contribution—a mark."

"Well—and what's this about the mark? If I give a mark—what happens?"

"The Zionist program is to create an officially, legally recognized homeland in Palestine for the Jews."

"With a mark?—A new sort of schnorring! Now the fine ladies and gentlemen from the Tiergarten are coming to Russian Jews to get money!—That's a topsy-turvy world!"

"We aren't schnorring," the young lady said. "We are going to every Jew—German as well as Polish, it's all the same to us. As long as they're Jews. Today is Shekel Day. So we're asking for money. There should be no more schnorrerei anymore, but a job for everyone."

"Did you hear that, Brandler!" Bornstein bellowed with laughter and slammed his fist on the table. "No more schnorrerei! And your business?"

From the table at the window a corpulent, red-nosed man stood up and shuffled closer.

"For all I care! Shekel! Palestine! Zionism!—No business for me!—That's something for rich people—getting rid of schnorrers! The world depends on charity!"

"You don't want to, then?" the student snapped, annoyed. "Fine, we don't have time to talk for long."

"So just listen, young man!" Bornstein said with a grin. "I've never seen such fine schnorrers. You've got something here!"

With that he scrabbled around in his vest pocket.

"Thanks very much," the young lady said. "We don't accept any gifts. We only accept a shekel from Jews who agree with our program. We are looking for people, not money!"

They tossed a few printed flyers on the table and passed Heinz, who was standing in the doorway, as they left. Bornstein caught sight of him as he watched the two Zionists leave and immediately approached Heinz with oily courtesy. His little puffy eyes took on a nervous look. He obviously didn't know what to make of the visitor.

"The gentleman wishes—?"

Suddenly he became suspicious.

"So you too are here for a shekel?"

Heinz reassured him.

"No—not that. I wanted to ask about one of your guests—"

"Several have already been here today—these Zionists are running around the whole town today.—The gentleman is looking for a guest of mine?—You're not from the police?"

"No, no!—I'm looking for Herr Schlenker."

"Oy!—Yossel Schlenker!" Brandler cried. "He's probably living with Klatzke now—do you know Klatzke? A real human being too! He had wanted to write letters! He thought it would be something easy to do, writing letters!—The idiot!

He was going to take bread out of my mouth! Do you need a letter? What am I saying? He probably wrote to you?"

"I'm not looking for Herr Klatzke," Heinz said, looking at the furious red-nosed letter-fabricator with amusement. "I'm looking for Herr Schlenker."

Meanwhile Bornstein had emptied his pockets, pulling out a bunch of paper scraps onto the counter, and finally found a crumpled note with Yossel's new address on the Auguststrasse.

As Heinz turned to go, Bornstein held him back; it seemed he was afflicted with pangs of conscience for letting the fine gentleman go without getting anything useful from him.

"Excuse me," he said. "Perhaps the gentleman is a doctor; I have a chest with surgical instruments for sale—like new—and cheap."

Heinz declined and left.

"Could you use a small steam plow?" Bornstein called after him. "A silver pocketbook?—Shoelaces?"

Heinz hurried to escape to the street. In the doorway some young people were studying the flyers the Zionists had distributed. One was reading aloud; random words reached him:

"Shekel Day—Basel program—the answer to the Jewish question."

Heinz smiled; when would there be an answer to that question? His eye fell on a piece of paper lying on the sidewalk, and he saw the large print:

This evening 8 o'clock sharp
The Answer to the Jewish Question

EIGHT

The Minyan Man

I

"Erich Schmidt says—"

"I don't care what Erich Schmidt says!"

"Please, Hamburger! The person who discovered the *Urfaust*—"

"Oh, Goethe himself didn't care for Kleist—how could his epigones care either! The Great Elector absolutely did not ever seriously want to kill the prince. His monumental character construction would have been destroyed if he had been persuaded by Natalie or the officers to change his mind. He surpasses them all intellectually by far—he takes what they think into account right from the beginning. His aim, however, is to educate through a radical cure the one person who isn't like himself but could be. He therefore uses the fear of death, a powerful psychological means, with the carelessness of powerful people.—In that way he compels the prince to consider things, to analyze things—he compels him to come to his point of view. After he has achieved that—and not before—he grants the mercy he had always intended to grant!"

Jacob Kaiser and Fritz Hamburger had been wrestling with the problem of the Prince of Homburg for over a week now. Both students had attacked the topic with equal zeal, the likes of which only the audience of Moische Schlenker could bring to a question on a point in the Talmud. Yossel Schlenker and Klatzke, who had just entered the room, were not a little astonished to hear the two arguing the topic once again.

"Odd folks!" Klatzke said. "You're arguing about what the author of the play was thinking. I'd love to have your problems! What's the final result? If I am going to argue about a book, I'll take a page of Talmud; you can never get to the end of it."

"And what is the final result?" Kaiser asked with a smile.

"Those are certainly practical questions—things one uses daily," Klatzke said naively.

"For example," Kaiser said, "the question of when the spring sacrifice in the Temple in Jerusalem can be made is a very practical question. Or the argument about the digestive product of a goat that ate from the priest's tithe—those are the sorts of things that you can use every day."

"But how can you even compare that!" Yossel said nervously. "I understand completely that one reads a poem or a play slowly and wants to completely understand it. But the Talmud—which is of course not simply entertainment—that's our whole life after all.—Why have we been studying day and night, then, for centuries in our houses of study, and that is more important to us than eating and drinking?"

"Indeed, why?—Who can answer that?" Fritz Hamburger said. "We German Jews don't do that anymore; I believe there aren't many students like us who study Talmud—"

"And certainly not medical students!" Kaiser interjected.

"Right! At least you want to become a rabbi—so there's a reason. I'm studying Talmud with pleasure because it's the most amusing and intellectually challenging thing there is. But how does it happen that an entire people—especially of whom it is said that it is eminently focused on the practical—can spend its life crouching over tomes."

"But the people wouldn't exist anymore without studying the Talmud!" Yossel declared. "It gives them strength as a people—that's what it's supposed to do—"

"Now you are saying it's only a mission!" Kaiser exclaimed. "It's true—the Talmud is splendid intellectual training—but I'd only like to know to what end the intellect is trained? Only to learn again how to learn new details? What does the world or humankind profit from what's bred behind ghetto walls? What's the point of all that?"

"I'd like to have your problems," Klatzke said again as Yossel thrashed around in his mind for a reply. "It is what it is, and the good Lord will know why he made us as he did. And what do you do when you aren't studying Talmud—you study then the Prince of—what's he called—of Hamburg. I thought Hamburg was a republic and didn't even have a prince."

Everyone laughed.

"Fine—go ahead and laugh! I'll learn these things too when I have time.—Now come over to my office. It's all set up, and now business can begin."

Everyone betook himself into the next apartment, where there was a splendid placard on the door of which Klatzke wasn't a little proud:

II

Klatzke decided on the spur of the moment to give up his letter-writing work to move in with Yossel and Chana and begin a business with better prospects. Manufacturing letters to beg for money did not offer career development for someone with higher aspirations. He had decided on the letter writing as a stopgap choice right from the start. When Yossel, his old student, had arrived, he was forced from his routine, and the chance acquisition of several hundred cigarettes, which Gurland had used to pay his debt, had turned his vague plans into a definite plan. Why shouldn't he try cigarettes? Of course, he had no expertise at all, but then he didn't have that in any field, and he could certainly develop some in the course of time. The main thing was the business sign and an office. He made the sign himself, and furnishing the office presented no difficulties. He suggested to Yossel and Chana that he move in with them on the Auguststrasse. He took the large front room, and they moved into the small back room. He paid the rent, and in return they received the customers when he was absent. Chana was also to help with the correspondence.

Now the students admired the business quarters. Klatzke had figured out well how to arrange the furnished room with the inevitable suite of plush furniture into a sort of business office. On the walls were large colorful posters of tobacco companies that he had gotten ahold of—heaven knows where. On the desk were piles of paper around a colossal inkwell.—The bed had been put into the back room—Klatzke slept on the narrow sofa. One couldn't make out the washbasin during the day; a wide, long cloth covered the sink top, and resting there were the volumes of the Talmud that he had borrowed from the students. From afar they really gave the appearance of business volumes and promoted the deferential impression of respectability and the scope of the business.

"Well, didn't I make this look nice?" Klatzke said. "Now I only need customers and inventory. The main thing is the customer! I'm going to the officers' barracks—it's a good thing I still speak terrible German—they'll easily think I'm a foreigner. I'm blond—otherwise, that wouldn't work so well.—Maybe I should get a red fez. It will all work out somehow—tiny profit and good product—that's the main thing.—I must order an elegant suit—that's very important. I'll have to eat cheese—but I have to look like a count."

"Yes, but who is going to come here on the Auguststrasse?" Hamburger said with a laugh. "Is it a home for elegant foreigners?"

"I'll say to the gentlemen: 'What's the advantage to you of an expensive location for which you have to pay after all? I want to live modestly to serve my customers better with cheaper prices.'—and no one will ever come here and check. If anyone does come, you are my young people, and the Talmud volumes are my ledgers. You would do me a favor if you would play my clerks."

The young people were laughing heartily about this obligation when someone knocked at the door. Joelsohn, Germersheim, and Löwenberg walked in.

"Where have you been?" Joelsohn asked peevishly. "And where are the books? We've been waiting half an hour over there. It's already time for our Talmud lesson. You're not there—the books aren't there. Finally Amanda tells us that you're over here. Do you want to study here?"

"Sure!" Klatzke cried with enthusiasm. "It's even a Jewish custom to study Talmud to consecrate a new place. We can consecrate our new business office and new apartment."

"Don't we want to pray first?" said Germersheim. "Doctor Pinkus, the chemist, stopped me below on the stairs—I told him he should come on up—it's his father's *yahrzeit* today."

Yahrzeit, the anniversary of the death of a close relative, appears to be a sacred duty for even otherwise nonreligious Jews. On that day the person tries to join a service in order to say the special mourner's prayer, the Kaddish. If it's in any way possible, he also tries not only to attend a service but to act as the prayer leader. This honor is seldom possible in the regular services in a synagogue on account of the competition alone. Accordingly, he prefers to gather the required ten men, the *minyan*, himself and improvise a service. No Jew would refuse the duty to join such a service where he was needed to complete a group of ten men. It is even a special source of income for poor Jews who are available to serve as "minyan men." The liberal synagogues are forced to hire minyan men even to hold their regular services.

So the young people were immediately willing to help Doctor Pinkus fulfill his pious duty without being put out about the fact that as the president of the Association for Cremation and as a socialist he was a continual thorn in the side of many Orthodox Jews.—Klatzke took out a prayer book and his prayer shawl, the long woolen cloth with the dark-blue stripes and the special corner fringes, the *zizit,* and held them out to the chemist, whose angry voice could be heard from the stairs. Pinkus entered with his assistant, Dr. Cohn, a young man who wore on his lapel a silver Magen David, which was formed by two intertwined triangles, the Star of David, the Zionist insignia.

"And I tell you," Pinkus shouted, taking the prayer shawl and unfolding it, "there is no greater nonsense than the sentence: religion is a private matter. That's the cowardice of social democracy, and the Zionists imitate the same nonsense. Backwardness must be fought and destroyed! Down with all superstition! Away with religion!"

He wrapped himself in the prayer shawl and, following ancient custom, mechanically covered his face for a moment.

"Stop!" Joelsohn cried. "We don't have a minyan! We're only nine! We're missing one!"

"I'll go get a minyan man," Klatzke offered obligingly. "I'll surely find a Jew on the Auguststrasse.—In the meantime, maybe the gentlemen would like to try these cigarettes. I can accommodate your every wish."

As he hurried out the door, he bumped into a tall young man inspecting the sign on the door.

"Is here the apartment of—?" the stranger asked after he had regained his balance.

"Excuse me!" Klatzke interrupted. "Are you Jewish?"

The stranger looked at him with embarrassment.

"A stupid question!" Klatzke cried. "You can tell. Come in—you're in luck—we were just about to pray. We were missing the tenth man for our minyan!"

With that he boldly grabbed the man's arm and pulled him into the room.

"Herr Levysohn!" Yossel cried with astonishment and stepped toward him.

Doctor Pinkus, however, brushing off his speech against religion, had already taken his place at the east wall and begun to recite the opening psalm in Hebrew in a loud voice. Everyone fell in—with no consideration for harmony or rhythm—and the wild murmuring made it impossible to understand anything for the moment.

Heinz Lehnsen mechanically covered his head according to the example of the others and tried to make himself worthy in his new dignity as a minyan man, whose functions weren't yet at all clear to him.

III

Heinz was thrust without ceremony so quickly into the group of men praying that he had no chance to protest, even if he had decided to correct the error in this delicate matter about his religious affiliation. Now there was nothing to do but to see how things developed. He squeezed into a corner and watched the meeting with curiosity.—

The opening psalm had ended; it had been muttered rapidly without any particular form. Some of those praying walked around the room as they prayed, with their arms clasped behind their back, or they sat somewhere. One of the young people even sat on the table and hastily finished smoking his cigarette during the prayers.—Suddenly it now became quiet: the prayer leader rapidly recited a prayer solo, bowing frequently; every now and then the choir interrupted with a confused response. Then a rather long, quiet prayer followed with everyone taking part as they looked in the same direction while standing, feet together on the spot. First one, then another bowed. Yossel and the man who had introduced Heinz rocked the upper part of their body back and forth, while the others stood almost motionless. Bowing was done in different ways: some snapped like a pocketknife closing while bending deeply in the knees—others executed a conventional dance lesson compliment.—After a rather long time first one, then another took a few steps back, nodding in all directions. Finally the prayer leader did so and began to recite a new prayer.

Heinz observed the proceedings, which struck him as rather incomprehensible, with astonishment and curiosity. In its amazing absence of any apparent form, this service, held in a room filled with cigarette smoke between advertising posters and plush furniture, had absolutely no similarity to anything he understood as a church service.—Indeed, there are scarcely any points of resemblance between celebrating a solemn ceremony in a church or a synagogue in the western district of town and the rushed completion of a prescribed prayer curriculum by a Jewish minyan such as the one gathered in Wolf Klatzke's room.—The observant Jew must say certain set prayers three times a day. Not only the words but how one stands, facing east—in the direction of where Solomon's Temple stood—are fixed. At certain phrases one strikes one's breast in penitence, at others one bows in deference. After a while the habit and practice of these movements become mechanical; the hand goes to the breast, the neck bends automatically as the words fall from the lips without the brain having anything to do with the matter. The prayer is muttered in most cases completely unconsciously so that the person praying is brought back to consciousness only with the automatic movement of his feet stepping backward, and he knows his assigned prayer stint is finished. There's nothing preventing him from indulging his own thoughts during the prayers; the prayer is purely a bodily function without any engagement of intellectual capacity. Of course, there are people who pray, who are sensible of what they are saying, and who try to steep themselves in devotion, but for one thing the number of those in the West who even understand the text is comparatively small, so that in the final analysis it comes down to jabbering a completely incomprehensible string of words, and for another thing it is almost impossible for people with a professional life to suddenly switch themselves fully spiritually every few hours. A person at prayer might well really feel reverence, but then there is still the question whether this is connected to the spoken words in any way.—

During the silent prayers Chana entered the room; she had bought all sorts of things for the new room and was weighed down with packages. When she saw what was happening she tried to tiptoe softly into the back room. The packages slipped from her hands, spilling onto the floor. They landed near Yossel and Kaiser. Frozen into prayer, they made no move to help her. The only one who moved to spring to her aid was Heinz. She looked at him in astonishment and was slightly disconcerted. Thanking him only with a nod of her head, she disappeared into her room.—Heinz easily guessed whom he had helped, and, pleasantly surprised, he watched Chana go. He had long since drawn himself a picture of a female Russian student that was a caricature, that didn't match reality at all.

Meanwhile, the prayer service drew to a close. Doctor Pinkus hastily said the final prayer, the Kaddish, while throwing angry looks at Hamburger and Cohn, who were chatting only a few feet away. It was clear that he was in a rush to jump back into the debate that was annoying him. He said the last words of the prayer in one breath so that what loudly followed sounded like a continuation in German.

"You could be quiet when I say Kaddish for my deceased father. And how academics, educated men, can believe in the immortality of the soul and such nonsense is a puzzle to me." He angrily tore the prayer shawl from his shoulders. "This heap of superstition must go! Down with religion!!" He angrily crushed the shawl into a ball and shoved it into his pouch. Then he seized the prayer book and shook it violently. "So-called religion must be extirpated root and branch!" With a grim expression he put the book to his mouth and kissed it. "This backwardness is the disgrace of our time! I tell you!" With that he tossed the book on the table and left.—

IV

As the room was clearing—Joelsohn and his Talmud pupils moved into Kaiser's room, carrying the volumes under their arms—Yossel greeted Heinz and introduced him to Chana, who had returned.

"I'm afraid this came at an awkward time," Heinz said.

"Why awkward?" exclaimed Klatzke, who took a lively interest in the visitor and was measuring in his mind Heinz's probable tobacco consumption. "We just needed a minyan man.—and if that was awkward, then we now are quits! Yossel will be all the less awkward at your house!"

"I'm afraid that Herr Schlenker ended up, in fact, in a somewhat embarrassing position at our place," Heinz said, looking at Klatzke with some ill will and somewhat disconcerted, "as this gentleman indicates—"

"But I'm Klatzke," Klatzke said, smiling in a friendly way, "Wolf Klatzke—cigarettes wholesale and retail. Without my letter you wouldn't have become famous at all. I don't write letters anymore now: I only do cigarettes."

"I think the gentleman wants to speak with us," Chana said in mild rebuke.

"I know," Klatzke said, unfazed. "Don't let me disturb you, Herr Levysohn. Yossel and I are old friends, and you are even related to him. Chana will put the kettle on, and we will have a nice cup of tea together."

It turned out that the kettle was already boiling. Heinz thought that first they should return to the incident at his parents' house.

"I came here to ask your forgiveness for putting you into an unpleasant situation."

"There's no need to apologize," Chana said softly. "I don't think that you wanted to embarrass my husband. Klatzke, in fact, is probably right. Yossel doesn't fit in your house, just as you don't fit in our minyan. I noticed that you didn't even join in the prayers. It's two different worlds that have little to do with each other."

That did not sound all too inviting, but Yossel gripped Heinz by the hand and said warmly: "But I'm still glad that you've come. That's very fine of you. After all, we are relatives, and above all, we are all Jews!"

Heinz felt himself turning red; he couldn't bring himself to disclose just yet the fact that he was baptized. The thought crossed his mind whether his participation in the service in such circumstances would appear as intentional blasphemy to everyone.

"Unfortunately, I know little about Jewish things," he said carefully. "I really didn't pray just now because I don't know the text at all. That's all strange to me. We avoid all these things completely in our house."

"Well," Yossel said, smiling, "that's certainly a pity. That really doesn't matter. You can be just as good a Jew as all of us, anyway."

"How is that possible?" Heinz asked uncertainly. "You probably misunderstood me! I don't know a word of Hebrew—I never put foot in a synagogue—I don't observe the Sabbath or the holidays—I have no connection at all anymore with your religion. So I can't possibly be a good Jew."

"What remarkable ideas one finds among German Jews!" Chana said. "In the few days I've been in Germany, I've heard more talk about religion and Judaism than in my whole life. I would like to know if non-Jews are always talking about their Christianity or their Germanic heritage."

"And I will tell you something," Klatzke exclaimed. "If you get to Russia someday, you will find a picture of Theodor Herzl in every Jewish home, and if you ask any Russian Jew who is the greatest and most important Jew, the best Jew in the world, he will tell you: it is Dr. Herzl in Vienna. And there are certainly Jews more pious than he is. Dr. Herzl probably doesn't pray any more than you do!"

Heinz knew dimly that he had heard or read the name of Herzl somewhere, but he didn't want to ask.

"Are there, then, no good Germans or Russians without religion?" Yossel asked. "Why can't there be any Jews without religion?"

"In Germany," Klatzke said, "it's like this: a Jew must either have religion or act as if he does."

"But a Jew without religion is monstrous to me," Heinz exclaimed. "Just like a Christian—"

"A Christian?—But that's something completely different," Klatzke exclaimed, upset. "How can you make such a comparison? Excuse me, but I don't think that you ever go to synagogue. If you've never heard German rabbis preach, you could never hold such wrong notions. That's first of all an invention of German rabbis, that Judaism is a religion just like Christianity."

"And what do your Russian rabbis say?—How do they respond when asked what Judaism is?"

"No one would ask such a question at home," Yossel said. "Everyone just knows that on their own. A Jew is a Jew and a Russian is a Russian!"

"I think," Chana said, "you misunderstand me. You must be as disconcerted about us as I was about German Jews at first. Here it seems that Jews must declare a religious belief in some sort of way, and if someone has lost his belief, he entirely loses his Jewishness."

"And then he goes and gets baptized," Klatzke shot back. "To be a Christian, that's what not believing anything anymore means. They only act as if they believe in something, something new. And those who don't, go and get baptized; they act as if they believe in something, and no one can say what that is! Frauds, all of them!"

"I don't know if it's all a fraud," Chana said, thinking it over. "The only reason for this strange notion is that to be a Jew has something to do with belief. People believe what they hear: if they are shaken in their belief, they always think that they are still Jews despite everything. They can't do anything else now but try to lie to themselves and others that they've lost what is considered to be the basis of their Jewishness."

"Exactly!" Yossel said. "They are told that without religion, no Jew. Nonetheless, they feel like Jews—so they say we have to be religious even if we don't feel religious ourselves."

"And the others go and get baptized," Klatzke said. "They tell themselves: if we have to act as if we believe, then we prefer the group with an advantage."

"I am always surprised here," Yossel said, "when I see what German Jews consider as religion. At home in Borytshev no one would think of praying if he didn't really believe what he was saying—and here—"

"Here," Klatzke exclaimed, "you find people who pray three times a day for the return of the people of Israel to Palestine and at the same time fight against the Zionists—who say publicly that what they are praying for would be a disaster—and who even say that there is no such thing as a Jewish people."

"There's nothing like that in Russia?" Heinz asked.

"There are many Jews who aren't Zionists," Yossel said. "But of course there isn't anyone who will say we are not a people. In any case, you find there that one does not pray for something and work against it at the same time.—There a person stays who he is, and here he becomes someone different when he goes to temple.—"

"I'm going to Petersburg this evening," Heinz said. "Perhaps I'll become familiar with things there."

"To Petersburg?" Chana said. "There are scarcely any Jews there; only the very wealthy ones, merchants of the best guilds, are allowed to live there."

"Know what?" Yossel asked excitedly. "Take a small detour to Borytshev. Visit my parents there. You will be a good guest for a celebration. With us a guest, especially one who is a relative, is cause for great joy!"

"Even if he's a heretic like me?" said Heinz with a smile.

"That won't matter to us," Chana said earnestly. "No one will ask you to act like a pious Jew."

"Excuse me," Klatzke asked, "how did you get a passport? You have to go as a company agent. What kind of company do you have?"

Heinz gave some ambiguous reply about margarine and asked about the connections to Borytshev without having actually decided at the moment to make the detour. Still, the opportunity was tempting. He would glance into a new world that was unfamiliar to him, and this interest had been greatly increased by the conversation, which continued to keep him at the tea table.

He parted as a good friend; even Klatzke, whom he had promised the possibility of being a customer and a source of recommendations, was satisfied.—

"You know," he said, "your cousin has given me a good idea. I'll register my firm with the authorities. There must be a lot of Jews who want a passport to Russia and need a power of attorney. They're well paid, and I can print up 'Special Agent for Russia and the Orient.'"

V

Heinz had already sent his luggage ahead to the train station and was considering how he wanted to spend the time until his train left. As he walked around he saw the poster again announcing a public discussion of the topic "The Answer to the Jewish Question." He decided to see the meeting for himself one day.—

At first glance this type of meeting differs little from other presentations of the sort, in which the current "burning topic of the day" is discussed along with the intake of immense quantities of beer. To be sure, the difference can most likely be measured in just this respect, namely, the consumption of alcohol. Substantially less is drunk than otherwise at political gatherings; that is only partially due to the fact that participation of the female variety is incomparably greater than at other such gatherings; further, the male participants drink almost nothing at all, and only some of them order a glass of beer more for reasons of propriety than with enthusiasm; in any case a serious consultation with the waiter starts with what kinds of beer are highly recommended today, and then the order follows as the considered result of a thorough and earnest reflection. With great dignity the head on the beer is observed, the patron blows into the glass, and then he takes the first sip while concentrating most carefully all his critical faculties. Much indeed depends on the result of the sample taste, as much for the speaker's success as for the party's; if the result even partially fails to meet expectations, then many more orders certainly follow the first one, and the waiters must constantly schlep their trays, heavy with beer steins, across the meeting hall the entire evening.—Here their work is a contemplative one; the beer glass stands there untouched for a long time, the head collapses, and the drink has long since gone flat by the time the guest finally remembers and, not to waste his money, slowly takes a sip without enthusiasm. He mechanically pushes the barely touched glass away—he tries a few times more to ingest the value of his coin, but he doesn't force things, and after the meeting is over the sour remains are scattered everywhere.—Thus, after delivering the drinks ordered at the beginning, the waiters lead a tranquil existence and observe the auditorium with scorn, apart from the fact that their dignity is wounded by the plentiful orders for lemonade and seltzer water, drinks that tolerant hosts essentially keep on hand only in deference to their Jewish guests.

Further, it is a particular characteristic of these kinds of meetings, one of which Heinz observed today with curiosity, that here it wasn't only people of a given social class coming together, as was typical almost everywhere else. As he tried to get closer to the speaker in the packed hall, Heinz noticed that the audience came from all sorts of trades and professions and all levels of affluence.

The strong and active participation of young people also struck him. At the entrance he had to get past a cordon of very young people, almost children, wearing the blue-and-white emblems, who were holding out their collection boxes, flyers, brochures, or newspapers to everyone passing by. In the hall other functionaries, mostly young women, were going from table to table with their receipt books, lists, and membership cards to enlist the souls of the visitors.

But none of that stopped the audience from paying careful and eager attention to the speaker. On the stage there were six or seven mostly young people; the chairman was the only older member, and because of his long, graying beard and of course because of his attractive personality, he had been entrusted with leading the meeting. With both hands he grasped the sign of his office, a bell, and seemed to be looking up at the speaker standing next to him whose lively gesticulations did indeed threaten the dignity of his person and his office at any moment with one blow.

The speaker was a tall thin figure with a thin small brown beard but with a compensatory thick head of hair. He spoke at a dizzyingly fast clip, and it took Heinz a long time to understand more than a word here and there. He repeatedly heard "Palestine" and "Zion," and almost each time there was loud applause that broke off quickly, since the speaker didn't slow his pace at all, unconcerned about the noise that made him absolutely incomprehensible, as he continued to speak at the same tempo. That he continued to speak was noticeable only from the fact that his mouth and hands kept moving.—He was already at the end of his speech and now finally concluded—very much to the relief of the chairman—with words that even Heinz could understand.

"The yearning for Palestine has sustained our people through the centuries! The yearning for Palestine has held us together—Jews from the East and from the West, wealthy and poor—educated and simple people—the pious and not pious! We all—we want to return—to our land—to our homeland—to Palestine!"

A storm of riotous applause broke out that recommenced again and again, seemingly without end. The speaker stood up repeatedly and bowed with an abstracted and preoccupied air as he mechanically wiped the sweat from his brow. Every time he stood up was a signal for a fresh ovation.

Heinz watched the tempestuous crowd with amazement. All these people wanted to go to Palestine—thought of Palestine as their homeland? Here sat apparently dignified and philistine bourgeois citizens, matronly thick good housewives, young women with fashionable hairdos, students with their fraternity facial scars, old Russian Jews with yarmulkes—bespectacled doctors or engineers, young and old elegantly dressed gentlemen, among whom he recognized with astonishment an attorney from the chamber court—they all clapped wildly, clapped for this obstreperous speaker who seemed to him like an apostle of a fanatical sect. Palestine? My God!—Did that even still exist? Far away, deep in Turkey? The word "Palestine" evoked in him reminders of Bethlehem, Golgotha, the Mount of Olives—then the lunacy of the Crusades. The Palestine of today was, as far as he knew, a dreary lost desert filled with dangerous, thieving Bedouins, a land sought out, in any case, by Nordic and English sectarians, Russian pilgrims, and Jewish beggars, where now and then a tourist with his Kodak visited under the protection of a Cook's tour guide, or where a bold archaeologist looked for material for his dissertation.

The applause gradually died down, and Heinz now heard behind him an audible hissing. He turned around and saw at a table to the side a group that was apparently the opposition—young students who could have just as easily stood on the other side, according to their dress, if the empty beer steins somewhat ostentatiously on show hadn't indicated that at that table one cultivated the pure Germanic style. A large man wearing dark-rimmed pince-nez on his hooked nose seemed to be the center of the group. He called using his hands as a megaphone something basically incomprehensible up to the stage. Heinz thought he heard the words "Leave for Palestine!" His friends laughed, clapped wildly, and banged their beer steins on the table.

Meanwhile, the second speaker to the left of the chairman stood up. He was a thickset man of medium height whose clean-shaven dark face had energetic and sharp features.—

Heinz braced himself for a fresh outbreak of fanaticism and was quite shocked as the speaker started in a completely different style. His speech was sobriety itself, almost all facts and figures. The speech sounded like a board report at a general stockholders' meeting. The speaker gave an overview of development of the Zionist movement to date. Heinz learned about the founding of the organization by Theodor Herzl, and now he remembered where he had heard the name. He had read some of the writer's feuilletons and had enjoyed the elegance of style, the clarity of argument, and the melancholy humor that reminded him of Heine. He was quite surprised that this man Herzl, who had seemed to Heinz according to his writings to be a representative of the best of German culture, was turning out to be the founder of a movement whose fanatical acolytes had astonished him as much as they had disconcerted him. He examined again the program formulated at the Zionist Congress in Basel, which he had already heard of on the Dragonerstrasse, and he learned that there had already been serious negotiations with the Turkish government and the political leaders of all the relevant European governments. He heard of the first settlements in Palestine, of experimental farms and banks being established, of scientific expeditions and reports, of estimates and industrial projects—there was talk of sanitary utilities, improvement projects, and settlement cooperatives. The speaker discussed the question of imports and exports, of raw materials, of natural sources of energy, of artificial fertilizer and establishing a school system.—Without transition, he spoke of one thing after another—all with equal clear-headedness. Without clichés, without pathos or sentiment, he discussed the questions in a strictly informative way, reading the statistics from notes. The auditorium also followed this speaker attentively, as if everyone wanted to imprint all the numbers in their minds.—Only at the table where the opposition sat did they seem to be bored and talked rather noisily among themselves.—This speaker too was rewarded with loud applause.

Heinz was struck with amazement by the first speech and even more so by the impression that it had made on the audience; the second speech increased his astonishment and even upset him a little.—Fanaticism, that seizing on an idea to the exclusion of everything else, even if it was for a far-fetched, crotchety idea about the world, had something noble about it; the thought that a crowd of people—millions, if the speaker were to be believed—could seize on an idea was almost exhilarating in today's materialistic culture. But a coldly calculating zealotry, ardor that calculated with statistics and was based on preliminary estimates, struck him as self-contradictory, almost degrading.—He saw with satisfaction that the leader of the opposition, now sitting next to the chairman and getting ready to speak, was greeted with vigorous applause from the speaker's friends.

The speaker began by explaining that he considered himself completely and totally a German, a member of the German folk, and as a German he would always try to fulfill his duty to his German Fatherland!—Already at this point the hall had become restless, and a fat man jumped up, his face bright red, crying, "Us too! That's an outrage!" Everyone was standing to see who was interrupting. Some were applauding him—the opposition was screaming, "Order! Order!"—and some were adding to the racket by screaming, "Quiet! Quiet!" The chairman calmly continued to ring his bell with a perseverance that betrayed that he was used to such scenes, while the speaker exchanged obscenities with one of the gentlemen at the head table but couldn't be heard above the noise. Gradually it became quiet, and the speaker could continue. He repeated that as a German nationalist he had to fight against Zionism.—He was, he continued, against this Jewish nationalist movement since he was a cosmopolitan and couldn't support chauvinistic movements. Furthermore, he declared Zionism to be a utopian chimera, because Palestine would never be handed over to Jews, since it was the jewel of Turkish lands, and besides, it was the Holy Land of all Christian peoples. Even if it were handed over, it was worthless land, a bleak, desolate, barren area unfit for settlement. Moreover, Jews were incapable of any sort of colonizing work—they weren't any kind of People.—The Jewish People had been scattered across the world to serve as teachers of their holy truths to other peoples. This was its mission! He fought against Zionism because it was a reactionary movement, contradicting all modern, liberal trends. He spoke a lot about the Enlightenment, equality, fighting any sort of bigoted hypocrisy and superstition, and closed with these words: "Let us be mindful of our sublime mission and of our Germanic soul! Let us put away from us all special wishes and habits so that we can no longer be distinguished from the totality that surrounds us! And let us not forget the principles of our venerable religion, which teaches us to wait in patience until the Messiah of which the prophet spoke leads his people back to Zion."

This last turn of phrase by which the speaker wanted to perhaps ensure himself a soft exit from the angry majority—of course with no success, as energetic hissing and howling drowned out the applause of his allies—particularly annoyed Heinz. He had quickly gotten the impression that this opponent had made things quite easy for himself and took the arguments as they had offered themselves but without one that was thoroughly convincing. Toward the end he had rather hoped that in his fight against reaction the speaker would honestly demand a renunciation of stubborn adherence to a discredited faith; instead, there was even a kind of acknowledgment of the very discredited faith, of the opposed tradition.—And it seemed tragic and comical that the speaker, every time he brought forth a fresh argument, whether it was from the arsenal of nationalists or cosmopolitans or freethinkers or the Orthodox, was applauded by his hangers-on and was hissed by his opponents.—The stormy drama recurred almost after every sentence of the speech with practically no variation.—Both parties had apparently decided to weigh each argument not according to its objective weight but only according to the extent it fulfilled their personal desires.

Now a Zionist was up to speak, a blond student with his pince-nez perpetually sliding down his nose, who tried to give proof, with lively agreement from the audience, that a Jew as a Zionist could be a true German patriot, whereupon the opposition table brought forth a loud shout that once again triggered utter outrage among those who had raged loudly before. "Every honest man must consider anyone suspicious," the speaker shouted, "who lacks nationalist feeling or is ashamed of his people!—Nationalism and religion have nothing to do with citizenship; but if we Jews, who consider ourselves as the oldest nobility of humankind—"

At this point a noisy gale of laughter broke out at the opposition table; the gentlemen roared with laughter and banged their beer steins.

"Nobility! Blue blood!—Hurrah!" they bellowed. "Hear hear! Herr von Cohn! Count Levy! Nobleman Levysohn!"

The blood rushed red into Heinz's cheeks. He plunged toward the table and shouted: "What are you laughing about, gentlemen? About yourselves? You are laughing about your own mothers!"

His words disappeared into the hellish racket that had broken out; he himself was deeply affected by the explosion of kindling that had accumulated in him whose existence he himself had scarcely been aware of. A moment before he had composed to himself how he would have answered the Zionist speaker on the stage. And now this furious breakdown toward the other side!—Deflated, he pressed through the excited crowd to the exit. Everyone was standing up and screaming into the bedlam. The chairman had finally stopped ringing the bell, since it was pointless, and left the stage. Everyone understood that the meeting was over, and gradually the hall emptied.—The young gentlemen of the opposition stayed together and shoved their way steadily to the door, and as they went out, they began to sing "Deutschland, Deutschland über alles."

Heinz stepped into the street and hailed a hackney. He had just gotten in and told the coachman to go to the train station when the singers appeared with the crowds streaming out, and now they continued to sing as a choir under the portal.

The old coachman turned around as he drove and said, shaking his head as he pointed to them with his whip: "Well, the ol' hoopla begins again!—I know that lot of anni-Semites from the days of old Ahlwardt. Always Germany!—Germany! I tell 'em"—he leaned confidentially toward his passenger—"that we wouldn't have the whole misery with the anni-Semites now if there was no Jews."

NINE

The Firstborn

I

Little Jacob Schlenker bit happily into the piece of gingerbread, although he had no actual claim on this treat, which had been distributed early this morning at the house of prayer. These were strictly for the firstborn sons, and besides his big brother Yossel, Jacob had an even older sister, Rivka.—He was crouching on a step to the *bimah*, the large podium in the middle of the room, and thus was out of view of the participants in the common meal, especially that of his father, who were eating the gingerbread meal.—

He didn't need to hide. Everyone crowding along the long table set against the windows—only a few had found a seat on the two benches—was very occupied, above all Moische Schlenker himself, who was holding forth again. They hadn't paid much attention to the cake and schnapps that were waiting for them on the bimah but had eyes and ears only for the folios on the table. Today's study had a particular characteristic: it was the customary event on the day set aside to prepare for the Passover holiday, the celebration of the Fast of the Firstborn.

To remember that once in Egypt when the Angel of Death had slain the firstborn but passed over the houses of the Israelites, all the firstborn sons were to fast on this day according to Jewish custom.—There are quite a few such special fast days in addition to the High Holiday when everyone fasts—so many that it seems almost impossible without serious danger to health to refrain from partaking of any food or drink on so many days. People take wise precautions. It's understood that whoever has the chance to take part in a meal expressly arranged for this sacred reason on such a holiday is excused from fasting. There are all sorts of these special meals—when there's a wedding or bris feast or, most importantly, the meal that celebrates concluding the study of a Talmud portion. There is a feast that has a special role and takes place, when it occurs every few years, in a house of prayer when the Talmud has been studied from beginning to end. It's a feast that includes the entire town. To finish a single portion doesn't take all that much time, and a few months before Passover groups of firstborn come together with a teacher to study such a portion, and they arrange things so that the conclusion falls just on the day of preparation, which is one day before the holiday itself. After the last words of the lesson some gingerbread and schnapps are handed out to symbolize the festive meal; in this way, what is enjoyable is combined with the useful, and instead of an unpleasant fast, all the participants have the happy feeling of having a portion of joyful intellectual work behind them.

This custom had, strangely enough, taken deep root and is even practiced in places where otherwise not much enthusiasm is found for Talmud studies; and many Jews, who had otherwise given up on almost everything, insist on taking part in these events, even getting their oldest son used to it from a young age.—

In Berlin too this is the custom; there it has, of course, taken on other contours.—There the meal has become the main point, and learning the Talmud is only hinted at.—There it has become an opportunity for social clubs; there is even a genuine Association of the Firstborn, with bylaws, membership dues, and entry fees, and, of course, most important, there are chairmen and officeholders.—The association meets once a year, of course on the day one prepares for Passover, very early in the morning. First, the morning prayers are said—then, the rabbi hastily reads the concluding sentences of a Talmud portion that he has studied on his own—none of those present has taken part, and almost no one is listening to what is going on—most don't know the tradition or the meaning of the event anymore; then, after this boring ceremony is taken care of, everyone sits down to a generous breakfast set out with coffee. Some even show up after people start eating. While everyone is seated, there are treasurer's and president's reports—the actions approved by the board and elections—there is a series of speakers, in which all the honored persons in the association are praised in the long-accustomed form, and the merits of the association, its high ideals, and its successful activities are praised—the appeal to all firstborn sons is not overlooked; furthermore, they are urged to remember their noble mission and to join together with greater solidarity during the coming year to achieve their aims and to further their common cause. The deceased are remembered, and telegrams with greetings from absent members are read.—Then the association disappears again into total nonexistence for a year.

Now Heinz Lehnsen, even when he was still Levysohn, hadn't ever heard of the existence of such associations or of the special duties of the firstborn. So he watched what was happening before him entirely disconcerted and ill at ease as he entered the house of prayer in Borytshev on this morning of the day of preparation for the Jewish spring holiday. He had arrived late the evening before, and, full of curiosity, he had awakened very early to go out to look around. The loud murmuring and the singsong chanting coming through the gate had shown him the way.—He had passed through the gate, through which old, bearded Jews, each with a bag under his arm, were entering and leaving, and had found himself in a tiny, rough, cobblestone courtyard bordered with sundry small buildings in random order. A babble of voices reached him from all the houses. He approached an open window and saw men veiled with a long, dirty blue or yellow shawl in the crush. They were bobbing their upper body rapidly, not unlike a rhythmic choir, frequently interrupting the prayer leader. Many, the prayer leader too, had drawn the shawl over their head to hide their face; others, hurriedly preparing to pray, unpacked their prayer shawl from their bag and draped the shawl around their shoulders, or they laid the black straps with the box around the head or around the bared left arm.—Groups of Jews stood around in the courtyard itself, talking nervously or excitedly. Heinz climbed the few well-worn steps into one of the prayer rooms, where it seemed to be a bit quieter, and thus landed in the Celebration of Firstborn, over which Moische Schlenker presided.

The room, not very large, was dimly lit; the small windows at street level, opaque with filth, didn't let in much light—and on the table where all the students were gathered two tallow candles burned in a candelabra. Everyone was so absorbed in study that no one paid attention to the stranger dressed in European fashion, which in itself stood out here.—Heinz observed the men pressing close to the table with amazement; from his position at the door, he couldn't make out what was the center of their animated attention; the packed mass of men barred any possible view of the table. He was involuntarily reminded of a quite similar image he had often seen—although he couldn't think just then where he had seen it. Where in the whole world was there in the West, in Europe, the same thing: a crowd of men pressing around a long table, everyone close together—most of them standing, bending over the few who were sitting—everyone filled, it seemed, with extreme heightened tension, as if under a spell as they followed what was happening on the table?—Finally it struck him, and, dumbfounded, he pushed to the table in a few strides: in Monte Carlo—at his club in Berlin, too—at the green table where roulette or baccarat was played there was the same thing.—Could there be here—? Not possible!—He couldn't believe that anything besides gambling could evoke such focus. Eagerly he mounted the podium in the middle of the room, and only then did he see the thick tomes over which the heads were bending.

Something tugged at his coat; looking around, he saw a small boy of about ten years old who was feeling the material of his suit with solemn expertise.

"That's good material—very fine material!" he said admiringly and nodded gravely when Heinz turned around to look.

II

Heinz became aware that he had become the object of intense curiosity for the packed room. About two dozen boys surrounded and boldly examined him—his face, his clothing, his shoes. He apparently was the star of a show, a magnificent attraction.—Heinz in turn examined the children with equal interest; they were a sensation in their own way for him too. The solemnity in their large dark eyes, the calm certainty with which they withstood his gaze seemed almost uncanny. But no one could say that the physiognomy was rather unchildlike. They totally lacked that doll face that he knew well from the West; they were already sentient beings, only small and undeveloped, whose expression already manifested a certain impenetrability. They really didn't look like dolls; those who were better dressed wore a long black *kittel* and stiff round hats—many were barefoot, and what they wore were truly rags; tatters hung from gaping holes. A few wore dirty battered hats that were far too large. The most striking thing above all else were the solemn eyes, which made one instinctively ask how the children could have such old eyes.—

One of the boys approached Heinz and stretched out a rather dirty hand, saying something in a foreign tongue.—When Heinz took the hand, suddenly the entire throng pressed against him, everyone repeating the same words, which gradually rose to a cry, as each one wanted to drown out the others. And everyone wanted to shake his hand; many tried to do so a second or third time. It began to be something of a game and gave the children great fun, as with the children who shook hands with the tame chimpanzees in the Berlin Zoological Garden.

"Say aleichem shalom!" one of them called.

"And shalom aleichem!—aleichem shalom!—sholem aleichem!—aleichem sholem!" they chorused.

Heinz began to feel uncomfortable, even if the children's mischievousness, which replaced their earlier solemnity, was almost a relief.

Suddenly a short, red-bearded Jew darted between him and the children and with a great deal of yelling and a large expenditure of scolding scattered the circle that had formed around Heinz. Then he neared Heinz and extended his hand.

"Shalom aleichem!"

And now even Heinz understood the ancient Oriental greeting of peace, the salaam aleikum, "peace be with you!"—He had not read his Oriental fairy tales in vain.

"Aleichem shalom!" he murmured, well taught, and in that moment he found himself quite interesting.—He had frequent opportunity to apply this newest linguistic acquisition, for now all the Jews were streaming over to him from the long table, and each one eagerly stretched out his hand and offered the ancient greeting of welcome. They surrounded him and began to appraise him with no less interest than the children had.

Meanwhile, a sharp interrogation began; where did the gentleman come from —where was he staying—whether he had business here—what kind of business was it and all sorts of such questions.—

Heinz was surprised how well he mostly understood the sense of the words, which sounded like strange German; his replies were generally vague, but in the press of the questions raining down on him no one was really listening.—

Out of the flood of questions there was one that was asked again and again whose meaning eluded him for a long time: "Where is the gentleman going today for the seder?"

"Seder?" he asked, baffled.

"Yes—this evening is the seder."

And when it finally came out that he wasn't going anywhere that evening— imagine, for the evening of the seder, the evening that begins the festival of Passover, on which every Jew wants at least to be a guest at the festival meal—shouting really began that apparently turned into an argument.

Heinz stared with utter amazement and almost with concern at the bizarre commotion. It looked as if at any moment violence could break out. He couldn't understand for a long time what in all the world could be the object of the conflict. He did notice that it was about him; they were pointing at him or in the heat of the argument even grabbing one arm or another and were trying to pull him to their side like a piece of goods whose possession was in question. Others shouted their names again and again and their addresses into his ear. He looked around helplessly.

But it wasn't a trivial thing at all for the Borytshev patresfamilias. Here was a stranger, a Jew who was apparently entirely unknown here—that he was not a Jew at all was a possibility that no one in the synagogue considered; what would a non-Jew be doing at the celebration of the Firstborn in Borytshev?—So, a foreign Jew, probably a "Taitsch," a Deutscher, a German, maybe not a learned or pious Jew, but still a Jew. He appeared to have been sent by heaven to bestow a special honor on one of the Jewish families this festival evening. Hospitality, which among all virtues of the Jewish people is the highest virtue, is in remembrance of the flight from inhospitable Egypt, still a special obligation. And in Borytshev there had scarcely ever been a more interesting object of hospitality than this finely dressed stranger who had shown up at just the right time.—What a triumph for the paterfamilias who brought him home to the family table; how envied he would be by all the less lucky competitors! So everyone wanted him, and no one would yield.

Finally, the reasonable view prevailed that the stranger himself should decide.

Gradually, the matter became clear to Heinz: people were scrambling to have him as a guest at their dinner table. His European sensibility flinched a little; but apparently the rules of etiquette, like the concepts about hospitality and treatment of strangers, were quite different here from those prevailing in the neighborhood of the Potsdam Bridge. There could be no question here about debut, introduction, initial visits, or similar ceremonies. The prospect of being a guest of one of these men seemed somewhat tempting if in this way he could hope for a closer look into the circumstances that he found so fascinating here.

Among the names shouted out to him he heard a name he knew: Schlenker. Could that be—?

"Come to our house," one of the boys said, echoing the invitation of his father in passable German. "Moische Schlenker—8 Vilnius Strasse. I'll come fetch you at your hotel—I can speak High German. My brother is in Berlin."

He said that with great pride.

Heinz gave a hearty handshake to accept.

"If you wish," Jacob said happily, "I'll show you around. Perhaps you would like to see the town? I don't have school today."

And thus Heinz Lehnsen took off with his little cousin Jacob Schlenker to see Borytshev, the city whose narrow confines his grandfather had once fled to seek German culture and freedom.

But Moische Schlenker hurried home to prepare his wife for the splendid guest the good Lord had sent them.

III

It was no small disappointment to Jacob Schlenker that the sights he thought would be the most sensational completely failed to impress the guest.—Neither the boulevard nor the Governor's garden, not even the new dragoons' barracks or the Alexander monument impressed him. Most peculiarly, what did interest him were completely ordinary and everyday things. He just wouldn't leave the smelly Fish Alley, which Jacob wanted to pass by quickly and Heinz absolutely wanted to enter. He stopped at every shop and stared into the holes overflowing with filthy, murky junk whose owners waited patiently for customers who were possibly absentminded enough to buy their wares.—The bustle of the market, which was especially crowded today, the day before the holiday, then captivated him for a long time.—When Jacob pointed out to Heinz with a mixture of pride and respectful reserve an old man who knew the entire Talmud by heart, Heinz barely glanced at this paragon of learning, but he couldn't get enough of the beggars in rags at the fountain.—And at the brandy shop, protected by a monopoly, where schnapps was available, he was astounded at the virtuosity with which peasants understood how to pop the stoppers out by slapping the bottom of the bottle with one hand, a skill that was surpassed only by their skill in emptying the bottle.

"An odd person!" Jacob thought, but he didn't give up showing all the sights.— He was also fighting a bitter battle against a regiment of small barefoot boys and girls running behind the stranger, stretching out their hands to beg and mechanically repeating their pleas unceasingly in whiny voices. Heinz had long since given out all the change he had, but it took Jacob a long time to get some sort of peace for Heinz.—The child chattered the whole time without stopping, talking about himself and his family and whatever stories seemed interesting to him about what they were passing and the people they were meeting. It was obviously a great deal of pleasure for him to use his German.

Thus, during his walk Heinz learned not only much about his relatives and the history of the community, he also learned much of the town gossip and even became familiar with the nicknames of those he was meeting; bestowing nicknames is especially popular among Eastern European Jews.

Jacob mentioned with special pride over and over again his big brother in Berlin who was studying there—that's what he wanted to do himself; he was now taking lessons from Doctor Strösser and already was able to read and write German pretty well.

He was in turn teaching his sister, Rivka; the gentleman would see for himself how well she understood German, maybe even better than he did—no, not really better, but at least as well!—The man over there in front of the junk shop, in the police uniform, that was Pristav Kujaroff, who wanted to start a pogrom now, and the two young people opposite who were pacing back and forth, they were from the self-defense league—the man with the odd face and the prominent forehead was Noseless Rosenfeld, the *shadchan*, the matchmaker—he visited them often— his sister was ready for marriage, but she didn't want to—he was an odd person, by the way; he knew the Talmud so well that if you put a volume in front of him and stuck a needle somewhere in the book, he could tell you exactly what word the needle penetrated on every page—the house with the large gate was the fire department; it was very good. The head of the fire department had gotten many awards because he was always so quick to arrive with his fire hose; of course, it was said that he always knew ahead of time where there would be a fire. He had been investigated twice.—The monument to Alexander III had cost 80,000 rubles; the money came from voluntary contributions of Jews; that man had been a bad person, the old czar, and a great enemy of the Jews! But the money was raised anyhow. At first there wasn't enough, but then the Governor sent a commission of physicians, and they had said all the houses in the Fish Alley and almost all the schools were derelict and dangerous to health and had to be closed. The money was collected quickly after that so all the poor people wouldn't be thrown out on the street and we had to have schools. And so the Governor was merciful again. He got a big medal because the city was so patriotic!—The red brick building was the high school where Doctor Strösser taught. A son of the wealthy Berelsohn was also there, that was a bad thing, because he had to write on the Sabbath. And it cost Berelsohn a lot of money. Only five percent of each class could be Jewish, and now in Sasha Berelsohn's class there were eighteen pupils altogether, so he wasn't allowed to stay in the class. So his father had no choice but to bring two poor peasant boys and pay for them, so they went to the high school too, and now there were twenty pupils in the class. But both of them were very stupid and lazy, and Berelsohn had to pay for expensive private tutoring for them and pay the director something in addition so that they would pass and his Sasha wouldn't be thrown out.—The funny person with a pipe was Boruch, the Commandant. Jacob's father claimed that Boruch had been very smart some time ago and very learned. He had just wanted to command everywhere and especially during prayers; so they named him the Commandant. Only he wasn't right in the head anymore from too much studying. And once he was a court witness in an important trial in Moscow; the Governor had sent him there, Boruch was supposed to testify that the Jewish woman who had sued the pope because he had wanted to harm her, that this woman was an immoral woman. And then someone asked him what he was, and he replied: Commandant of Borytshev! The court laughed and sent him home!—Many people with the large sacks were strangers; nobody knows who they are. People think that Kujaroff had brought them in to start a pogrom.—Jacob wasn't scared; the self-defense league was there, and Passover was this evening. You didn't need to be afraid; you didn't need to say the evening prayer once on this evening.—Over there was their house, and the woman standing in front of the door and giving out money, that was his sister, Rivka. She took care of giving out money until now, but now it was his turn, because now she had to go into town; she would take Heinz to his hotel.—

Heinz couldn't tear himself away from the picture that he saw in the entrance of the Schlenker home and that he had seen repeated in front of many doors as he made his way through the streets.—In the hallway stood a small table on which there were many little heaps of money; behind the table sat a young girl of about eighteen with dark, naturally curly hair and with delicate, thin cheeks red from effort. A crowd of men and women, poorly dressed, crowded around the table where the young girl handed out the money. It resembled a payday for workers, but there were differences. A short old woman was just complaining that she had a claim to a larger sum, while the person in front of her was distrustfully checking the coins he had just received. "Hinde Rashe is right," Jacob declared. "I know she's supposed to get double since the last time, Mother said."

"Fine," Rivka said, laughing. "I didn't know that."

She pushed a few coins over to the old woman and apologized in a friendly way about the mistake. The old lady grumbled, took the money, and hobbled quickly off as she gave vent to her bad mood about the wasted time.

Jacob took his sister's place after he had whispered to her what he knew about his guest. Rivka put on her hat, which had been lying on the table, and went up to Heinz with a forthright smile, offering her hand.

"I've heard we have a special guest this evening. It's nice that I meet you now.—If you want to go to your hotel, we go the same way. I have patrol duty now."

IV

These last words—spoken in all seriousness—completely confused Heinz. He thought he hadn't heard right.

"Sorry!—What do you have?"

"Patrol duty.—Jacob can take care of the money now; you've seen that he knows how as much as I do. People are very impatient today because it's payday everywhere."

"On account of the coming holiday?"

"Certainly. Usually Thursday is payday for us, but today's not normal. People have to hurry, and they aren't patient about waiting."

"Yes—are people then employed in several places at the same time?"

"Employed in several places? I don't understand."

"I mean, do the people work for you and elsewhere at the same time?"

"Work?—These people would all love to work, but there aren't any jobs. They don't work at all—only if something comes up."

"Now I don't understand—you were paying wages to them, right?"

"Wages?—No, not at all! My father doesn't have a factory!—These are all poor people."

"Good Lord! You aren't saying that all these people have received alms?"

"Nothing but. That's what everyone is doing today in families here who can somehow give something."

"But the people behave as if they are entitled to demand money."

"Don't you have that?—They behave differently where you come from?"

"Where I'm from—certainly! There are scarcely any beggars who go house to house: we give to associations, and on the door there's a plaque that says you are a member of the association against begging from house to house. Rarely does a beggar even dare ring the bell, even if the porter would let him in the door."

"That's peculiar!—We have many such associations for taking care of the poor, but what you have would suit no one here."

"You mean the poor people?"

"No—the others too! You have to give something, after all; the poor have that right. You must give a tenth of what you have; that's Jewish law. And how could you give gladly and from your heart if one didn't know who received it? I've taken part in this payday ever since I was little."

"You actually have paydays?"

"Of course! Otherwise you'd constantly be interrupted, so every family has its own day during the week, its general reception day.—You don't have this?"

"Our Berlin *jour fixe* has a very different character."

"People become accustomed to this, and they know: you go to the Schlenkers on a Thursday. Of course, there are still special cases. But on that day everyone gets only a few kopecks. Everyone is relying on that, and if someone is unable to come, he asks for double the amount the next time.—It happens that people even go on strike."

"Strike?"

"Indeed! In the case of one family—I don't want to say which one—too little was given. Then they just stayed away. That was such an embarrassment for the family—a real scandal! They apologized and had to plead for a long time before the people would come again."

"I find that just incredible. At home begging is legally prohibited, and a beggar is the most contemptible thing in the world."

"Maybe you have work for everyone!—We don't hold the poor in contempt! On the contrary! If a poor stranger comes, everyone scrambles to invite him to come as a guest for a meal."

"That doesn't seem to be limited to a poor man, as I saw today."

"Every guest is a joy for us; I hope you aren't sad about not being poor."

She smiled.

"I really am not responsible for that," Heinz said ruefully.

"And to have a guest today for the seder is a great fortune!"

"Excuse me! I have to admit that I don't even know what a seder is. I should like to admit right away that I am completely ignorant in Jewish matters."

"Well, you'll soon find out! As a child I always considered the evening the loveliest of the year, and it is the essence of everything splendid.—But it has always been a dangerous one for us Jews. Who knows what this year will be. You can see what I'm doing now: I'm about to go on patrol."

"Then I did hear correctly! I must admit I can't imagine what that actually means. Even in my military country women are exempt from military duty."

"I'm a member of the Jewish self-defense league. It isn't news to you that we expect a pogrom here—"

"I heard someone mention it on the train. Is there really anything to this?"

"We have to be prepared just in case; that's why we started our self-defense league."

"And young girls are supposed to fight too?"

"Not exactly that, although—it would be nice if every woman had a weapon—not to fight, by the way.—But our men are almost all without weapons.—And even the weapons we do have are taken away beforehand; there are house searches."

"So you think you will be disarmed? And what then?"

"We are hoping we can keep our weapons. We've put all the munitions and weapons outside of the actual Jewish part of town, and the self-defense league will gather there when it's time.—Meanwhile, we patrol all the streets here—which look quite harmless. We young women are really good at this. If something threatening happens, we give notice at certain checkpoints where there are a lot of messengers waiting to give the alarm."

"That's a strange mission for a young lady. Don't you find that awful?"

"How so? Our whole situation is awful—the whole Golus, our Exile. We are in a strange land."

"I pity you from my heart; you feel yourselves to be strangers here, you must feel you are strangers. You are without a homeland, which we have in Germany."

"I think you deceive yourself if you think that you are more loyal to Germany than we are to Russia."

"Don't we have to?—You have no homeland, because you are without legal rights and considered to be outlaws; German Jews have equality, they are citizens like other citizens and share the joys and sorrows of everyone in the country."

"I don't know personally how things are there, so I won't contradict you. But does love for one's country depend on how good or bad things are for us?—You misunderstand me; I don't want to say that you don't love Germany; I don't know anything about that, but I do know that I love Russia."

"You love this land where you are persecuted, deprived of your rights, murdered?"

"Yes," Rivka exclaimed with emphasis. "I love the Russian people, these warm-hearted, good-natured, dreamy people—I love the wide spaces of the steppes—I love its songs and its poets, its history and its dreams. I believe in the future of Russia, in its liberation from the czar's yoke; I believe that it promises something of immense importance for humankind—treasures that the degenerate and over-cultivated West has no idea of and that will rescue it someday after it has frittered away its portion."

"So you are a true Russian patriot," Heinz said, strangely moved as he looked at his companion, who spoke with great enthusiasm and flashing eyes of the Russian people, on account of whose murderous designs she was going to her patrol duties. "I wouldn't have imagined this. I don't know whether I could've ever heard a young woman speak so lovingly of the Germans. So you are true to your people?"

"What are you saying here?"

"I'm saying I am surprised to see such a patriotic Russian in you."

"Me, a Russian?—Oh, how you misunderstand me!—I'm not a Russian at all, I'm a Jew."

"And your homeland is—"

"My homeland is Palestine. Ever since I was a child I've known that we come from there and that we must go back there. Since I was ten years old I've had my Palestine collection box next to me, where I put every kopeck I can spare."

"So you can buy Turkish land?"

"Go ahead and joke! There are hundreds of thousands of such boxes. And the main thing is the enormous desire of millions of people whose little children are doing without treats, sacrificing for their people and their land. I feel strongly that Palestine belongs to me, personally belongs to me."

"And Russia?"

"Can't one love both mother and father?—I don't fool myself that I have Russian blood in my veins just because I am so attached to both the land and the people.—If a woman marries, she remains a member of her family, and she cannot be divorced from her *family*."

"I was at a Zionist meeting in Berlin for the first time a few days ago. The question whether the Jews were a people was—"

"What question? Whether Jews are a people? What are they, then?"

"Well—in Germany they are primarily considered to be a religious community."

"Indeed, are the German Jews, then, all so religious?"

"That's scarcely the case. Still—in Germany they are defined as a people—the definition isn't really so simple. The Germans are definitely a people, and so are the Russians."

"Definitely?—But certainly not as long as the Jews have been!—Scarcely any people have survived in Western Europe as perfectly as Jewish stock—"

"Missing is a country—"

"Even without land and without many other things that make their continued existence easier for other people, we have preserved ourselves as a people. No other people has survived such trials to their strength and will to live.—I don't know what scholars hold to be a people, but if someone were to ask me what a people is, I would only give them the example of our people—the only people, the Jewish people."

A young man, limping badly, came toward them and spoke a few words softly with Rivka while Heinz slowly continued on.—She quickly caught up with him.

"For now everything is calm in town; that was the post whom I relieve.—Over there is your hotel, and I say good-bye until this evening at your first seder!"

She shook hands with him; a police officer sauntering by who had just walked out of the hotel gave Heinz a sharp appraisal as he went past and greeted Rivka with casual courtesy. Rivka looked after him and bit her lip.

"Do you know who that is?" she asked. "That is Pristav Kujaroff, the man who is organizing the pogrom."

V

This is the bread of affliction eaten by our ancestors in the land of Egypt.—Whoever is hungry, let him come and eat. Whoever is in need, let him come and join in the observance of Passover.—This year, we are here. Next year, may we be in the land of Israel!—This year, we are slaves. Next year, we will be free men.

Heinz Lehnsen was looking around in constant amazement, and every now and then he clutched his head incredulously to convince himself that the velvet-black yarmulke was enthroned on his head. Was he really—Law Clerk of the Court of Justice Heinz Lehnsen, who lived on the Matthäikirchstrasse in Berlin, who just a few days ago was draped in the judicial robe of a Prussian court reporter, transcribing the proceedings and drafting the decisions—he, a member of the Feudal Club on the Nollendorfplatz—the envied friend of posh Tilly—the alumnus of the fraternity Roswithania—who was now sitting here in Borytshev at the table of Moische Schlenker, which was set with old-fashioned silver dishes and unfamiliar things?—He sat—no, he reclined, resting on a settee made of two chairs covered with a blanket, his head resting on his left hand, which sank into a pile of pillows. Across the table, resting on a similar seat, was the host, who resembled an Arabian sheik this evening. He was dressed in a snow-white garment, a long, embroidered garment without buttons belted with a white cord, and on his head he wore a broad, white, turban-like cap with silver embroidery. On his right sat Frau Schlenker, whose dark wig could be seen peeking out from a huge white bonnet. To the left of his father, on the right of Heinz, was Jacob, who wore a dark yarmulke, and on the other side of Heinz, between him and her mother, sat Rivka, whose dusky skin, almost black hair, and deep dark eyes above her white dress made an exotic Oriental impression. Lying open in front of each person was a little Hebrew booklet, the Haggadah, that curious ancient work that guided the complicated ceremonies of the evening. The new, prettily bound Haggadah that Yossel had sent from Berlin as a present for the holiday and whose German translation next to the Hebrew text made it possible for the ignorant guest to follow the holiday ceremony, was given to Heinz.

Rivka was just going around the table to refill the cups—the men had beakers and the women had glasses. Heinz indicated he didn't want any, because he had just sipped at the wine as he had seen everyone else doing after the initial sanctification.

"My cup is still full."

"That's no excuse," Rivka said with a smile. "You have to follow all our customs tonight. The cup is filled to the rim four times—so it is written. Not before the cups have been filled twice can Jacob say the Four Questions."

Heinz acquiesced, not a little astonished to discover here fraternity drinking rules apparently going back an even more respectable length of time than the list of rules of the Kösener SC, and now it was Jacob's turn, who was ready and waiting impatiently. As the youngest among those present he had the task of asking the Four Questions, which were the introduction to the service.

"How is this night different from all other nights?"

Heinz followed with the German text what Jacob was asking. He wanted to know why on this night only unleavened bread was eaten, what the bitter herbs were, what the custom was for drinking, and what the meaning of the comfortable reclining at the table meant.—

Heinz found that for his part he could have asked considerably more questions.—

Now the answers, which take up the greatest part of the Haggadah, were to begin; but Moische Schlenker stroked his beard in thought and started speaking to Heinz with a smile: "Four sorts of children know the Haggadah, and we must tell them tonight the story of our people's liberation—the wise one and the wicked one, the simple one and the indifferent one.—God has given us this day a foreign guest, a dear guest—but we don't know to which of the four categories he belongs. The wise child, it is said, wants to know the meaning of all these things that we do today—the wicked child too; it is just as important to him, but he is like a stranger, not one of us; he asks what does all this mean *to you*—he cuts himself off from his brothers. One should care for the simple child and teach him like someone who doesn't ask anything at all, who has no interest at all. Only to the wicked child should one say that there is no place for him among us.—

"We don't know who you are," Moische Schlenker continued after a short pause. "You come from abroad, and we see you don't know our holy tongue or our customs. Perhaps you know something of all this, perhaps you know nothing because there was no one who told you and awakened your interest when you yourself had no interest in these things—and no one explained to you what you didn't understand. Maybe you have thought that there are things that are none of your concern, and maybe today, after what you hear and see today, you will want to learn everything down to the last detail.—

"Today it is our duty to tell the story of the flight of the Children of Israel, our history and our beliefs. Whoever is hungry, let him come and eat with us. Whoever is in need, let him come and join in the observance of Passover!

"Avodim hoyenu."

And he began to read the words from the Haggadah: "We were slaves—"

After almost each paragraph he interrupted his reading with his own commentary.

"Here we have the story of the men of Bnei Brak," he said at one point, "who sat the whole night together and spoke of freedom such that they didn't notice that morning had come until their students came and told them. Are we not all like the men of Bnei Brak? We have sat the long, long night of exile in the house of study and talked and talked of freedom. But young people, the new race that didn't sit there and didn't talk and study there, they see the light and bring the news to the old men that the night is over and that it's morning. Perhaps—"

He shook his head slowly; then he began again to read from the page.

Heinz heard the strange singsong as if in a dream; it was as though he was hearing wise men from a far-off time, as if in another life, unreal, yet it sounded as if he knew it well; a warm feeling burned in him, it seemed to him as if from far away he saw something long lost but only forgotten, something that he would have liked to grasp and take ahold of at all costs and that nonetheless was lost to him forever. Was he exiled from his own kind? Was his presence here defiling the perfect peace of this home?—He bent further over the Haggadah and read: *And it is this that has preserved our ancestors and us; for not just one alone has risen up against us, but rather in every generation they rise up against us; and the Holy One, blessed be He, saves us from their hand.*

Pointing with her finger to the lines in the book, Rivka showed her neighbor, who was leaning on the pillows with his head almost resting on her shoulder, where they were. It was a strange book: melodramatic and lofty passages alternated with funny tales; there were strange, convoluted question-and-answer games. Riddles that seemed half simple-minded and half mystic and that then gave way to impressive quotations from the Bible and the psalms. Something from all epochs and nooks and crannies into which the Jewish soul had once been confined had shown up in this curious yet sublime book.

And there was just the same mixture of high ethics and scurrilous low tales in the remarks made not only by Moische Schlenker to proudly show off his learning but even by little Jacob every now and then. Even Rivka threw out a comment from time to time that wasn't really relevant.—The essence of everyone here seemed to be like the Haggadah, the result of many periods and many fates.—

"What does this mean," asked Jacob, "when it says here: *If He had led us to Mount Sinai but had not given us the Torah—it would have been sufficient?* Why would that have been sufficient? What were we doing then at the mountain? Standing like oxen at the mountain!"

Heinz looked at his host nervously; wouldn't he be angry about what seemed to him a very irreverent question about a holy book? Moische Schlenker, however, nodded his head and smiled, looking at Rivka: "Well, Rivka? A good question! You can answer: What would we have done if God had led us to the mountain but hadn't given us the revelation?"

Rivka blushed and desperately looked at the book: then she exclaimed happily: "I know! We would have fetched the Law ourselves! We would have pulled it from the clouds!"

Moische smiled with satisfaction and continued to read: *Had he given us the Torah and not brought us into the Land of Israel—it would have been sufficient.*

The Haggadah spent a long time on the plagues that afflicted the Egyptians. And as the ten plagues were counted, everyone took up his wine cup and sprinkled a drop of wine on the table. Heinz felt himself to be right at a banquet of classical antiquity, making a libation of the sacrificial drink as he stretched out

on the pillows and Moische explained the custom: "We are not supposed to completely relish joy, because people have been destroyed. We were guests in the land
of Egypt, and the Egyptians persecuted and oppressed us, but the Torah teaches
us not to hate them. We were guests in their land!—"

Finally they had gotten far enough along that the second cup of wine could
be drunk, and then the festival meal began. It was introduced with a number of
strange rituals.

First, Rivka went around the table with a basin, a pitcher, and a towel, and
everyone carefully washed his hands while a special blessing was said. Then the
host placed a large dish filled with many strange things in front of himself, and
he began to hand them out to everyone at the table—first the matzah, the bread
of affliction—then the bitter herbs, the symbol of the bitter work of slaves—then
the dark mixture of apples and almonds, which was supposed to remind one of
working with mortar—and then horseradish between two pieces of matzah—
next a dish that actually didn't seem to be part of a ritual but was customary in
general for this evening, eggs in saltwater—then the famous gefilte fish—then a
soup with the tasty matzah dumplings—and then other typical accomplishments
of the Jewish Passover kitchen. While they were eating, the conversation turned
more casual and was buoyed by an unspoken cheer that surprised Heinz anew
and wasn't the least of the evening's surprise. Outside lurked rape and murder—
the pogrom could begin at any moment; but here inside reigned peace such as he
had never known. This absolute self-assurance had been missing in his parents'
home; some sort of latent nervousness, an internal urgency, never let them fully
enjoy the sweetness of the present, of the moment. Something undefined was always chasing them; neither joy nor sorrow was fully felt—they never fully understood a single feeling.—These people here had an inner homeland—he belonged
to the restless, the eternally wandering folk.

He was by far the most silent person at the table after the hostess, who scarcely
spoke a word, and the others, noticing that he was busy thinking, didn't disturb
him. Gradually, however, as Jacob reported about today's walk, Heinz too began
to talk of his life in Berlin, and his descriptions produced great astonishment.
Moische Schlenker diplomatically asked about Jewish matters in Berlin, such as
whether Passover was also celebrated there the way it was here, and, somewhat
embarrassed, Heinz had to admit that he wasn't qualified to say.

"I only know," he said, "just from my school days that all Jews who were still
observant were scared just before the holidays. They missed school days, later
they missed work days—they couldn't ride on those days and had to go by foot
over long distances; they even had ten times more work and difficulties on holidays than they otherwise did."

"But the joy of the mitzvah—didn't they know that?" Moische Schlenker asked
with concern.

There was a rather long pause until Heinz could process this word—mitzvah—into German. And even when he realized what the word meant, namely, a commandment, obligation, or fulfillment of an obligation—he was only able to vaguely guess the meaning of what Moische Schlenker was saying with the joy of the mitzvah. The word, however, made an impression on him; here seemed to be the key to many a mystery.

Rivka guided the conversation to another topic and asked Heinz to talk about university and the life of a student. His reports of the customs and practices of the students in fraternities, of the commercia, or students' academic feasts, and the *Mensur*, or the fraternity students' traditional fencing match, of the drinking customs and obtaining satisfaction stirred puzzled amazement, even a little suspicion about his adherence to truth. In any case, there was no trace of that enthusiasm seen in Rivka that such customs usually bring forth in young ladies.

Heinz suddenly stopped and cleared his throat a few times; behind the host's seat something strange was going on. With the gestures of a secret conspirator, Jacob had crept behind his father and was trying to secretly extract something from the pillows. Heinz definitely saw that the mother and Rivka had noticed these goings-on without doing anything to stop them; Rivka even nodded encouragingly to her brother. And Moische Schlenker himself seemed to suspect that there was something going on; but instead of grabbing the miscreant, he leaned forward even farther to let Jacob gain possession of the object of his thievery, an object wrapped in a napkin, with effortless triumph into his hands.— Again classical memories came to Heinz; weren't little boys brought up to thieving dexterity in Sparta?—He soon discovered what this was all about.

As soon as the meal came to an end, the traditional dessert that plays a large role in the Haggadah was served. At the start of the evening the host breaks off a piece of matzah, wraps it in a napkin, and puts it back. At the conclusion of the meal he passes to each person a tiny piece of this matzah, after which it is forbidden to eat another bite. The custom developed so that this important ceremony would never be overlooked and thereby damage the ritual at a vital moment, a custom that is a jealously guarded privilege for the children, to steal this piece of matzah—called the *afikomen*—and only release it to the host for a ransom. The thief anticipates the ransom at the right time, of course, and even reminds the host if necessary.

The little comedy plays out in the usual way; chuckling, Moische Schlenker played his role as unsuspecting victim, searched for the stolen treasure, accused everyone at the table, one after another, and was most shocked when Jacob confessed to being the malefactor. The negotiations for the ransom went smoothly at that point; only Heinz was surprised when Jacob demanded as his price nothing other than Goethe's *Faust*—which he was promised. But Rivka protested and declared that Jacob had stolen on her behalf; she wanted as her share a special contribution for Palestine. That too was granted, and everyone should have been able to eat the afikomen if Heinz hadn't suddenly discovered that the piece he had been given had disappeared. There was much laughter until finally Rivka, whose blushes raised the suspicion of her hand in this, produced the piece of matzah. She refused to accommodate Heinz's desire to fulfill a wish and didn't want to hear of a ransom. But Heinz protested vigorously, and a war of innocent banter continued between them for the rest of the evening.

The Haggadah was taken up again; an inordinately long grace was recited, psalms were recited in an unfamiliar melody, and the last two cups of wine were drunk.

There was another incident that made a deep impression on Heinz. A large cup that had sat there unused was placed on the table filled to the rim, and at her father's command, Rivka opened the door to the room and then to the house.

"For the Prophet Elijah!" Moische Schlenker said solemnly, "the redeemer who will take us back to Palestine," and everyone stood up and looked at the door as if they expected the prophet would come to empty the cup.

The doors stood open for a few seconds, and they heard muffled shouting in the distance.—Then the door swung closed, and Rivka returned to the table. She calmly encountered questioning looks as she took her place.

"Drunken peasants!" she said. "Kujaroff's rabble.—They are fortifying their courage for a pogrom with drink!"

"A real Passover—a real seder!" Moische Schlenker said. "Tonight has often been the signal for murdering our people.—But we shouldn't forget that we are guests in their land!—"

The door was closed; all that was unholy or discordant remained outside. They turned again to the Haggadah and continued to sing until the final cheer: "Next year in Jerusalem!"

At the very end the Haggadah offered some silly songs to close the ceremony.—

Rivka stepped into the street with Heinz to show him the way to go to the hotel.—He clasped her hand, hesitating a little.

"Good-bye for now," he said hastily. "I must pay my debt.—Take this and think of me!"

With that he adroitly slipped a small pretty ring on her finger and hurried away before she could recover from her surprise. He felt himself to be remarkably young this evening and was actually surprised that he wasn't at all ashamed of his behavior, which would not have been suitable at all on the Matthäikirchstrasse and at the Stülp-Sanderslebens.

Rivka stood in the doorway for a little while and then, full of her thoughts, turned to go, twisting her ring.

It was a beautiful, clear, starlit evening; far off one could hear Kujaroff's peasants howling.

TEN

Resistance

I

"Your dear Magnus proved reliable again, Elsa," Lehnsen said, pleased; they were sitting again at the breakfast table, but this time without Heinz, and were studying the morning post. "Ostermann is sure of the scholarship now. Magnus's vote is worth reading. You can have the Baron send Ostermann a preliminary notice."

Frau Lehnsen said in a satisfied tone: "Well, at last! It's a disgrace in front of everyone that this has taken so long! Such a good person, Magnus, who helps out with everything.—I see that the Baroness is on the committee to provide edifying reading material for the army and navy this afternoon; I shall bring her great joy.—What else was in the mail? Nothing from Heinz?"

"Only printed matter," the Director said, leafing through a brochure. "Here are the topics for the Petersburg congress—an extensive agenda—if they get through all of this between the banquets, receptions, and sightseeing, they'll have to work hard.—Reform theory—the international fight against trafficking young girls—increased penalties against blackmailers.—"

"I hope Heinz doesn't overexert himself," Frau Lehnsen said with concern.

"Don't worry," the Director laughed. "At least not on account of the congress meetings. If I know our gentleman son, he will be busier with the bright lights of Petersburg nightlife than with the dark side of human lives. When I was young I didn't have it as good; there wasn't enough for me to go to international congresses.—I had—well, if I were in Petersburg, I would finally get to say a word or two!"

He pushed his book aside and with a flourish poured himself a fresh cup of coffee.

Frau Lehnsen looked at her husband in some surprise.

"Maybe you can write to Heinz what you have to say," she said. "It would be very nice if he shows up in the report. If you have a good idea, it would be a shame not to exploit it."

"And thus it remains in the family," Elsa laughed. "Really, Papa—I'd like to see Heinz as a legal star. Law Clerk Heinz Lehnsen of Berlin has the floor.—"

"Just what we need," grumbled Lehnsen. "It's better he strolls through all the Petersburg nightclubs than opens his mouth there at the congress and ruins his career once and for all with his paradoxical manner."

"By presenting *your* ideas?" Elsa asked a little scornfully. "Did you give him then such subversive tips?"

"That's just it!" Lehnsen said in a good mood, buttering his breakfast roll. "The boy has his character from somewhere; I always knew how to control myself. But there's a huge amount of explosive material still stored in me. I sometimes feel an almost irresistible desire to jump up and smash everything to smithereens."

"Please!" Frau Lehnsen said, shocked, and shifted the coffee machine to the side.

"Papa!" Elsa exclaimed with surprise, clapping her hands. "Go on, and you can be sure of my sympathy. What I'm learning about you!"

She was so interested that she was still holding the folded newspaper in her hands that she had just taken out of its wrapper without looking at it.

"Yes," Lehnsen said, not without complacency, standing up to walk around the room. "My children consider me the quintessential philistine, the writer of nothing but dry legal clauses, and the dutiful Prussian civil servant. That's true in a certain sense; I don't seem to be anything else. But I was indeed once something else; I was indeed and I am still something else in a certain sense—I was—"

"A Jew," Elsa said.

"Elsa!" Frau Lehnsen exclaimed, outraged.

Lehnsen was a bit thrown off his stride.

"I wanted to say I was once young," he said, a bit distracted; he seemed to be embarrassed about the interruption. "Besides, maybe—doesn't matter! I wanted to say something else: yes—when I had to play the criminal judge in Moabit during the last court recess, that was something especially powerful for me. I had to control myself now and then not to burst out in the courtroom in the middle of the trial. What sort of shameful handiwork are we doing here! What daft comedy are we performing here!—Well, fortunately I didn't do or say that but only continued to speak in the name of the king's law, protecting Church and Fatherland—but at least I didn't delude myself that morals and scruples can be improved by the penitentiary."

"You are quite a revolutionary, Papa!" Elsa cried, delighted.

"Yes, but very much a secret one!"

"Herr Actually Privy Revolutionary Councillor Lehnsen—or, if it is truly se-cret—shouldn't one really say Levysohn here?" Elsa laughed, throwing herself, newspaper still in hand, into the rocking chair.

"Elsa, you're terrible!" Frau Lehnsen exclaimed.

"We are all revolutionaries!" Lehnsen said. "We're not so completely stupid as to fall for the swindle!—I come across all these things as I read these program topics about blackmail. The whole thing ends up protecting criminals, idiots, or cowards!—Increased penalties for the blackmailer are called for; that's the bo-nus for society's hypocrisy and mendacity! The poor wretch who *lets* himself be blackmailed should be punished! But many prefer to surrender to the caprice of a notorious scoundrel than to trust justice and the morals of society and the state.—Is that not absurd? I once had a wretch who ten years ago had served a ten-year sentence—he had long since paid, as one so delicately puts it, for his crime—I think it was perjury. And he had bit by bit tossed his entire fortune at a blackmailer, fully ruining himself, just to prevent this sin of his youth from being known.—Pitiful!—"

He sat down again and grabbed the newspaper; Frau Lehnsen had sat down in front of the window with her embroidery.

"It's not right of Heinz, not even sending us a postcard while traveling—from the border or—Elsa! For heaven's sake! What is it?"

Elsa was pale and upset, staring at the newspaper that she had taken from the wrapper.

"What is it then?" the Director asked, now nervous too, and grabbed the pa-per. "What? *The Trumpet*? How did that gutter paper get into our house?"

Elsa pointed mutely to the place marked in red.

With a furrowed brow, Lehnsen read: "The demoralizing influence of Jews.—Yes.—How is that our concern?"

"The introduction!" Elsa groaned.

"The introduction? What is—?"

He quickly read a few lines silently, and his wife watched with growing alarm as his face grew red with anger.

"That bloody gang!" he furiously exploded, hurling the crumpled paper to the floor. "This rabble! These blackmailers! Blackmailers!—Vile blackmailers!"

He angrily stomped on the paper.

"Damned pack of Jews!"

II

The editorial staff of *The Trumpet* had provided an introduction to Ostermann's article that read as follows:

We are publishing soon a highly significant essay from the pen of one of the most knowledgeable experts of Jewish-Talmudic literature who wishes to remain anonymous for reasons we have fully examined and understand, and this essay may be followed by others from the same author. We have, as our readers know, always made an effort to be absolutely objective toward even our worst enemies, even Jews. To protect our threatened German morals against the penetration of Oriental ideas, if we proceed uncompromisingly with total clarity and severity today, that will not stop us, even as an exception, from considering sporadic, more conciliatory sides of Jewish life. We might even offer our readers as early as our next issue a small episode not without its own piquancy from the salon of a baptized Berlin-West Jew that clearly proves how the Jewish sense of family and appreciation of Jewish community triumphs over social and other barriers. Imagine a reception salon decorated with paintings of the Crucifixion and living officers and barons belonging to a freshly converted Berlin person of title, in which at a family gathering the honoree, resplendent in his sidelocks—but we do not want to anticipate the article but refer you to the next issue and the feuilleton "The *Mishpocha* of the Director," or "Blood Is Thicker than Water."—Today we only wanted to show that we too acknowledge Jewish virtues. It is hoped that the intense sense of family will be appreciated by the baronial family that plans soon to become related by marriage with that of the Director. We shall accordingly report the nuptials and the subsequent brotherhood of tailcoat, uniform, and caftan in due course.—

"Oh good Lord!" screeched Frau Lehnsen when she realized what the situation was. "Dreadful! We've been destroyed!—and there's another article to come! You must stop that, Adolf! The police must forbid that!"

"The police are completely powerless!" said the Director, who had recovered from his fit of rage and was staring out the window.

"Well, what are the police there for?" Frau Lehnsen cried, beside herself. "Someone can mock us with impunity and plunge us into ruin?!"

"We don't have any way to challenge them yet," Lehnsen said somberly. "Should I perhaps go there and declare publicly that I'm the one in the article? We haven't been named yet; that's going to come! The police can't do anything—afterward, when something has happened—yes! If we want to sue, it's ten to one that the wretch of an editor is untouchable, but the trial will be a pretty show! With you two and Baron Anselm as witnesses! You can practice now all you want in swearing!"

"Are you serious, Adolf?" Frau Lehnsen asked, confused.

Elsa, who had been sobbing to herself, sat up.

"Father! Can't you talk with the editor—explain things to him? Surely he'll be open to a sensible explanation of what happened!"

"Of course!" Lehnsen said grimly. "You can depend on that! They will be open to reason made of gold. The whole thing is nothing other than the usual sort of blackmail by this gutter press!—If I only knew what scoundrel gave them the story!—and that Heinz—who has cooked up this pretty mess for us, is amusing himself in the meantime.—He could really satisfy his Jewish feelings now! We all now have the prospect of becoming victims of anti-Semitism!—and he's off gadding about somewhere and has no idea about these things!"

"But Father!" Elsa said, who was now calmer and held him fast as he was striding angrily around the room. "Something must be done! If something can be done with money, then it isn't so bad!"

"Am I, Regional Court Director Lehnsen, to throw money down the throats of this gang so they'll keep quiet? I should negotiate with these bandits?—Aside from my views about blackmailers and their so-called victims?—I would become an accessory!—Just recently at court I publicly characterized such a coward in announcing the verdict. It was a question there of a merchant who had molested a minor girl and was in fear of going to prison—"

"But our case is much worse!" Frau Lehnsen exclaimed, wringing her hands. "Just think! We should let ourselves be dragged through the press as Jews? We are ruined—we won't be able to show ourselves!—and our child! If Baron Anselm hears the story, that's the end!"

"It's a cursed business!" the Director said darkly and again stared out the window.

Elsa came near and put her arm around him.

"Father," she said softly, "you have to make the sacrifice! You have to go to these people and negotiate with them! It is shameful—I understand that very well. But—you see—if one considers things right—Heinz spoke about this recently—and I thought it over; it is after all just the newest link on an old chain. It isn't the first attempt to blackmail us! From the moment we decided to deny our Judaism we have been subjected to blackmailers.—We have to constantly pay so that others will forget our origins and be humiliated. We are no longer free human beings! Those contributions to build churches, the scholarship for Ostermann—my large silver cross, your dinners, whom we choose to see, our reading material, participation in political parties, denying all our basic feelings—eternally being on the qui vive—isn't that all blackmail too? And doesn't everyone know that? And aren't all the Jews here in the hands of usurers and blackmailers? Mustn't the Jew achieve every accolade, every miserable title with ten times the effort in comparison to others? What just falls into the laps of others doesn't happen at all or happens for the Jew only with enormous struggle.—There are Jews who don't bend under the pressure—right from the beginning—and the stubborn Jews insist on living their own lives. But it's too late for us! There's no stopping once one is on that path.—We have taken this path—you chose it with good intentions. Maybe if you had had an inkling—it's too late now. Look—I certainly seldom say a serious word—we certainly don't usually talk about it at all! But if I have thought through these things, then they are certainly not new thoughts for you! Nothing can help now—we have to go on to the end! We have to bear the burden!—and we are prey for every blackmailer!—But finally—it seems to me—the gentlemen of *The Trumpet* aren't even the worst! They are still the most honorable and want nothing more than money!"

The room fell silent for a long time; only Frau Lehnsen was weeping bitterly in the corner of the sofa. Finally the Director stirred; he disengaged himself from Elsa and went to the door, his face turned away.

"I'll go right now to *The Trumpet*," he said calmly and left.

III

"Have him come in," Assessor Borchers said with a sigh in the Prosecutor's Office at Superior Court I, having examined for a long time almost with surprise the card a bailiff had put on the table in front of him:

> Dr. phil. Josef Magnus
> Rabbi
>
> In his capacity as acting president of the General Association of Mosaic Subjects in the German Reich requests a meeting on a pressing matter.

"Just a moment, Starke," the Assessor called as the bailiff grasped the doorknob. "Does the gentleman really mean me?—After half an hour it will finally turn out in the end that I'm not the right person at all!"

"But Herr Assessor knows me. I do know what's what!" the old man said in a confidential tone. "I wouldn't burden the gentleman to no avail, and of course I asked what the matter was; he said there wasn't any file started—a new matter. But he was referred by the administrative office here, since it is a matter of the Herr Assessor's special department. So should I let him in or keep him waiting a bit longer?"

"Fine—let him come in!" Borchers, said giving up.

The Rabbi entered—in a dark overcoat with a velvet collar and brown kid gloves, a shiny top hat in his hand. Under his arm he carried a bright yellow glossy portfolio of impressive dimensions.—His face was arranged in dignified wrinkles, announcing things of the greatest importance.

"Rabbi Doctor Magnus," he said, introducing himself.

"Borchers," the Assessor said, standing up. "How can I help you?"

"I wouldn't like to unreasonably take up much of the highly valuable time of an important prosecutor for anything unnecessary," Magnus said, treating every word so tenderly that it came out as a perfected acoustical work of art and awakened anticipation of significant depth of thought buried beneath it. "That is not my custom, since I myself, out in the world—in the public world—and also even in a narrow circle, represent public interests. No one knows better than I that we are all slaves to work—but still I consider it my duty to speak at an opportunity of unusual significance, which led me here—significant not just for the community in whose name I have the honor to speak, but significant first and foremost and above all for our beloved Fatherland and its cultural development—I consider it, as I said, to be my duty to draw your attention from the beginning that I will probably have to explain a bit first, and it isn't possible to settle in the twinkling of an eye, so to speak, in passing. I—"

He looked nervously around the room.

"Please, take a seat," the Assessor said with resignation and gestured to a chair while taking a seat himself. "I would be grateful if you could really—I am very busy."

"I come right away in medias res!" Magnus said. "Allow me to spread out my material."

From his portfolio he took out some books of threatening size and a pile of brochures and newspapers and arranged them all on a file trolley, which stood between him and the Assessor. As he was arranging things, he frequently pulled out and consulted a small notebook.

Disconcerted, Borchers watched these preparations.

"Would you please be so good as to tell me what the matter is?" he said politely with some emphasis.

"Just a moment—I've just prepared everything systematically—so that I won't be disagreeably interrupted in the course of my account—time is money—my work tools, so to speak.—There, I'm finished! I come, as I said, in medias res!——The word of the immortalized imperial silent sufferer, that anti-Semitism is the shame of our century, has been newly confirmed in a way that is deeply tragic and shames me sorely as a German. One of those city organs—which can be called poisonous mushrooms in the German forest of publications—a paper that is likely not unknown in the course of his duties to even the Royal State Prosecutor—namely, *The Trumpet* has published in its most recent issue an article entitled 'The Demoralizing Influence of Jewry,' which makes the most sacred and intrinsic venerable institutions of the Jewish religious community contemptible—drags it in the dirt, I can indeed say—and offends us Israelites as a whole and every single one of us in the most serious of our most hallowed feelings."

"Hold on!" the Assessor interrupted. "You want, if I understand you correctly, the state prosecutor to proceed against *The Trumpet* on account of its anti-Semitic article?"

"I am completely correctly understood, and I—"

"Do you have the article here?"

"Here's the corpus delicti. I have taken the liberty of marking in red in the margins the relevant passages, and I may probably—"

"Permit me to see for myself."

Borchers read the marked passages with a practiced eye, skimming quickly the rest of the text while Magnus carefully observed the effect of the material. But the Assessor's face retained his cold expression.—He shrugged his shoulders indifferently.

"And these books here?" He pointed to the material piled up on the file trolley.

"By means of this literature I take the liberty of objectively proving not only the untruth of these accusations, step by step and line by line, but also the evil intention of the writer of this shameful article.—It's a matter of the evil compilation of all the material ever accumulated over the course of time and centuries of fabrications and slanders. The author repeats here, for example, Rohling's forgery, long since refuted, with respect to the passage from the—"

"Excuse me, Herr Rabbi—there's really no point in showing me this material. It would be a waste of your time and mine. If you will just leave everything with me, if necessary for an impartial expert—"

"Herr Assessor! Scholarship has long since through its appointed representatives, of which only Christian theologians with the eminence of a Strack, one of—"

"That would be a concern later. But first the question must be settled whether there is even an actionable act and if so—whether it is in the public interest justifying action by the state prosecutor—"

"Public interest? Indeed, Herr Assessor, I wonder—is that even a question?—It is indeed of the most important public interest, I should think, that inciting hatred against citizens, the provocation of the basest instincts, is sufficiently punished. An intelligent domestic policy is the best way to enlighten—"

"We have nothing to do with politics or enlightenment," Borchers said stiffly. "We need only to examine if the statutes of the criminal code and which ones have been violated."

"Definitely, definitely—I don't deny that. But my intentions were that the general interest—"

"Herr Rabbi—you must admit that you aren't objective here and can't be objective at all. You as an Israelite—"

"Herr Assessor," Magnus said gravely, "I would like to emphasize that I am here not only as an official of Israelite cultural affairs and a pastoral worker—but first and foremost as a Mosaic subject in the German Reich."

Borchers cast a confused glance at the card.

"Ah yes, you are—"

"Acting President of the General Association of Mosaic Subjects in the German Reich," Magnus said with dignity. "Our first president is Herr Privy Commercial Councillor Maier—I am the person who is actually concerned with ongoing business. And as a subject, albeit a Mosaic subject—but still as a subject in the German Reich I have to say that it is, most certainly, in the interest of the German citizen to fight this incitement and stultification. We rejoice in the broadest forbearance and tolerance under the glorious reign of the ruling house, if I am not mistaken. And even if now and then there is unfortunately still irreconcilable prejudice, then those are just remnants that will melt away under the sun of enlightenment like—like shadows on a wall. If I may perhaps use an ingenious image from the treasury of ancient Jewish wisdom: our wise men say—"

"Excuse me, Herr Rabbi—as much as the ingenious comparison would interest me—work presses. And it is important to you too that a quick decision is taken in this matter—"

"But of course! *Bis dat qui cito dat!* An immediate confiscation of the paper to prevent further dissemination seems to me to be the most important thing right now."

"I'll look into the matter! I leave it to you to formulate your views in writing. It's best that you take your materials with you for writing your document."

"Yes, but—so much time is lost."

"What you submit will all be properly taken care of in order.—Besides, especially in this case, any overly hasty action would be a mistake. An unnecessary action in the freedom of the press needs to be avoided wherever feasible. Even the press favorable to you—"

"Favorable to me?"

"Of course, I don't mean you personally. But just the principles of tolerance, the right of free expression, which you should represent—"

"Tolerance—for the hatemongers and mudslingers? That is certainly no longer an exercise of the right of free expression if one class of people is incited against another.—The article was shouted out on the Friedrichstrasse; every decent Israelite must be insulted when—"

"The question of an insult would have to be carefully examined. Just for that reason, I leave it to you to include a complaint in your document, although presumably the case may be referred for private legal action, as it is lacking public interest. The question too of the standing to sue is very doubtful, particularly as to whether the Association of Subjects Mosaic—I mean, the association with the long name—is really entitled to represent all German Jews. As far as I know, you have a number of such coreligionists who consider it better if attention is not directed to Israelite affairs through public trials—who prefer that nothing is mentioned about the Israelite and Mosaic faith."

"I assure you—"

"Please, put your views in writing. I will then look into the matter. I certainly can give you little prospect of intervening after my cursory review."

The Assessor stood up. Magnus pleaded with raised hands.

"But, Herr Assessor, I find this point of view incomprehensible. Our first president, the Privy Commercial Councillor Maier, the well-known industrialist on whose behest I'm here, has not doubted for a moment that the Royal State Prosecutor's Office would make an example in just this case with special diligence just to give fresh proof of its objectivity—and even more so when it concerns a paper of the caliber of this *Trumpet*."

"What is required will be done, according to the regulations that are relevant for us," Borchers said impatiently and turned to read his files. "I cannot say anything more to you; I first await your submittal."

"I must accept that," Magnus said sourly and slowly packed his materials back into the portfolio. "But I must emphasize again—a negative result would pain me more deeply as a German than as a Jew.—There are already serious disturbances; if it comes to excesses, which I by no means rule out—"

"If you show me such a case and can bring concrete evidence that because of this article one of your coreligionists was insulted and was injured in his bodily integrity such that he could not find remedy through private legal action, you will find me fighting your cause.—"

He now bowed so curtly that Magnus willy-nilly had to take his leave. He put the portfolio under his arm, the top hat in his hand, and after a polite, cold bow he left the room.

He looked around in the long hallway to orient himself. He tried going to the left, but after only fifty paces he heard someone call his name. Looking around he saw the Assessor, with *The Trumpet* in hand, hurrying after him.

"Just a moment, Herr Rabbi! Would you be so good as to come back to my office.—I just thought of something.—I have to talk more with you about this matter."

Astounded, Magnus turned around; the Assessor was completely transformed, pulled up a chair, and was politeness itself.—He explained to him that he had just now come to the conclusion that immediate action and a quick confiscation were definitely called for. He would arrange at once for everything necessary and even personally lead the raid. To get the necessary leverage, he was now asking for immediate documentation for some sort of explanation—particularly what had disparaged religious beliefs and the like.

Dr. Magnus started unpacking his portfolio, even though he was totally bewildered by the abrupt change of heart, and gave the documents demanded to the Assessor, who was now eagerly writing the notices. After a quarter of an hour the gentlemen went their separate ways in the corridor, where the Assessor had brought his visitor to graciously show him the way, shaking his hand firmly.

Dr. Magnus sought out a coin-box telephone in the basement—happily excited but still brooding over what could have brought about the change so quickly in the Assessor's heart. He telephoned Privy Councillor Maier to report the result of his efforts at the State Prosecutor's Office.

Privy Councillor Maier was deep in his work and didn't have enough time or interest to listen to the detailed report the Rabbi wanted to give. Magnus had just begun to tell how cold and hostile the Prosecutor had been about what he wanted at the beginning and then wanted to dwell more on how he succeeded in shattering this position with his forceful presentation when Maier interrupted him.

"I don't have any time now. Get to the point. The outcome?"

"The outcome is splendid!—When I arrived, he barely offered me a seat—when I left, he accompanied me to the corridor and shook my hand."

IV

The policeman standing in front of the entry to the building where *The Trumpet* had its office had taken up his post. He glanced, full of official mistrust, at the gentleman with the red face who seemed excited and in such a hurry, as if he were on a dangerous street, getting out of a taxi, who ordered the coachman to wait as he hurried into the building. His mistrust would have no doubt instantly changed into the official posture of standing at attention had he known the gentleman was a regional court director; but even this official posture would have been inappropriate, because the Director was absolutely not visiting the editorial offices of *The Trumpet* in his official capacity but solely for personal reasons.

"What's going on in there?" asked the greengrocer. The busybody stood on the basement steps, swiveling her tousled black Gypsy head back and forth from the entry to the building and the file transport van standing off to one side.

"Press offense!" the policeman said gravely. "Newspapers confiscated!"

"Oh, those newspapers! I tell ya'!" the woman said. "Those Jew papers!"

The policeman only nodded silently; he was on duty here and had to avoid expressing any political opinion.

The door to the editor's office was open; Lehnsen saw a man sitting at a desk who was bent over, busily writing, while another man stood at the desk, dictating, his back to the door.

The Director hesitated a moment, then stepped forward firmly, went up to the man who was dictating, and brusquely said: "I must speak with you, Herr Editor!"

The man addressed slowly turned his head, then turned around quickly and stretched out his hand to the Director.

"Good morning, Herr Regional Court Director!"

Disconcerted, Lehnsen took a step back and stared at him. He saw a familiar face.

"Herr Assessor Borchers!" he murmured, unpleasantly surprised.

"You are surprised to see me here? I can imagine.—You see, the Royal State Prosecutor's Office works swiftly. I am officially here on the basis of a complaint made by a Jewish party to confiscate the entire number of copies published of the most recent *Trumpet* on account of disparagement of the beliefs of the Israelite culture."

He wallowed a moment with a slight smile in the stunned amazement of the Director. Then he called to his court stenographer: "You can close the record. Have the cited materials brought down."

The court stenographer disappeared into the next room, and Borchers turned again to the Director, who had lowered himself onto a chair.

"So here's the explanation. Usually the matter doesn't proceed so swiftly; under normal circumstances the order, if there is one at all, would only come after a few days if the brave little Trumpeters had had a proper paragraph. Fortunately, I saw this morning, just as the gentleman from the Jewish Defense Association was leaving, the editors' preface. Since I had only recently had the good fortune of extending my good wishes for your daughter's birthday, I was definitely a witness of just that incident that the paper was publicizing. Their intention was definitely clear, and I am happy to be able to give this troupe a lesson and at the same time, by vigorously pursuing my duty, to do you a little service."

"Very good of you—indeed," Lehnsen said, blushing and biting his lips nervously.

"I called the Herr Rabbi back—by the way, a very well read gentleman with astonishing knowledge in his field of expertise, only not really cut out for people who don't have much time, a certain Dr. Magnus, in case you know him—and I had him give me some information. So really—what the man knows is incredible. He had even brought the books with him—some in Hebrew—that he could read off-the-cuff—I'm dizzy just looking at the letters—and he was able to convince me that action really was absolutely justified. This type of incriminating article, this scurrilous tone is the sort that compromises all serious anti-Semites.—So I have now carried out the preliminary confiscation."

He diligently continued to allow the embarrassed Director time to make sense of the new situation. Lehnsen reflected quickly and then stood up.

"It was indeed very kind, Herr Assessor," he said cautiously, "that you also thought of my personal situation. That this had absolutely no influence on your official decision is naturally a matter of course. But naturally I am pleased that the scurrilous notice is not going to find an all-too-wide dissemination."

"I am probably not incorrect in assuming," said Borchers, who had anticipated more enthusiastic thanks, "that the very reason you have come here was to stop the distribution?"

"That would scarcely have been in my power anymore, but I wanted at least to see if I could negotiate with the editors to prevent the second article that was promised from appearing."

"If you want to speak with the gentlemen, you'll find them in the next room, where the confiscated copies have just been packed up. I don't have anything more to do with these people; I can only wish you the best success."

"Again, many thanks, Herr Assessor, for your intervention."

"It was nothing, Herr Director. I only regret that we have no official means to stop the article. But you yourself will surely succeed. You should have the necessary means at your disposal."

V

Lehnsen stepped into the next room, where two policemen were just hauling out a huge laundry basket filled with issues of *The Trumpet,* while a third policeman, along with the court stenographer, filled another basket. A fat, squat gentleman was busily helping them.—On a desk off to the side sat a tall man with a blond beard holding a long-stem pipe, as well as a woman with light red hair smoking a cigarette who had crossed her legs and seemed to be enjoying herself.

Lehnsen looked around uncertainly.

"Just look, what an honor!" the blond man exclaimed, climbing down from the desk and waving his pipe. "Herr Regional Court Director Levysohn—I mean Lehnsen—gives us the pleasure. Schliephake is my name, editor of *The Trumpet*—and this is my colleague, Dr. Hesse.—Yes, we're old friends, Herr Director. You don't recall anymore? I can imagine! The two weeks in the Moabit sanatorium that you were so kind as to prescribe for me at the time made a deeper impression on me than on you."

"Dear Schliephake," Hesse said disapprovingly and dragged up a chair. "It would be more fitting to offer the Herr Regional Court Director a seat. Please—"

"Don't disturb yourselves," Lehnsen said with contempt. "I can finish my business while standing. You know quite well why I'm here. We want to talk business."

"If you have a business concern," Hesse said with a worried look, "you have chosen a bad time. The authorities have ordered a completely incomprehensible measure that will certainly not be upheld, one that damages us materially and morally. It forces us to accelerate publishing our next number. Fortunately, we already have a number of contributions set up in type—still, it is quite a burden on us."

"Let's be brief," Lehnsen said brusquely. "How much do you want for suppressing the printing of the article you announced today about—you know which one I'm talking about."

"Dear sir!" Hesse said, deeply offended. "You are talking to us as if we are blackmailers!"

"That's what I'm doing," Lehnsen said.

"You are doing us a serious injustice," Hesse said gently. "With the publication of our paper, we fulfill a moral duty from which your desire cannot deter us. We fight the demoralizing influence of that community from which you yourself have contritely divorced yourself in justifiable revulsion.—We would only agree to not publish this article—and then of course without a penny recompense, without any payment—if you prove to us that our information is false—"

"One thousand marks!" Lehnsen said, looking past Hesse.

"You remain of that opinion, Herr Director?" Hesse calmly went on and sadly shook his head. "You misapprehend us—your interpretation proves how falsely you misjudge us. If we have made an effort and incurred considerable expenses to research this information—if we pay the author a significant honorarium—he would, by the way, I know him, demand considerable recompense if we did not keep the duty we undertook to publish—that happened—"

"Who is your source?" Lehnsen asked, still staring at the ceiling.

"You wouldn't presume to violate press confidentiality," Hesse said contemptuously. "Should you wish to buy the article yourself, purchase it from us—"

"Five thousand marks!" Schliephake said pitilessly. "You can stop your drivel now, Cardinal. Yes or no?"

"That's an outrageous demand!" Lehnsen flared with anger.

"We're not haggling Jews!" Schliephake said scornfully. "You want to buy—we set the price."

Hesse had retreated, shaking his head reproachfully. Lehnsen thought for a moment.

"If I pay, will you name your source?" he asked.

"Out of the question!" Schliephake declared. "He can still bring us other good information. So—do we have a deal?"

Lehnsen took out his checkbook and began to write while still standing.

"And who guarantees me," he said, pausing, "that the article or anything similar isn't published?"

"Herr Director," Hesse said with the mien of a martyr, "the word of two honorable German gentlemen is your guarantee."

Lehnsen laughed disdainfully and threw the check on the desk.

"There's your money, my Herr Men of Honor!—Ugh, disgusting!"

He went to the door. Hesse jumped up and elaborately held it open for him.

"Thank you, Herr Director!—Don't stumble—it's rather dark in the stairwell."

"Honor us again soon, Herr Director!" Schliephake called threateningly after him.—The dame squealed loudly with laughter.—

Lehnsen hurried to get away—but crashed against a gentleman on the landing who was storming up the stairs in a panic and with his eyes focused downward on the steps, bumping directly into the Director's stomach. The Director's hat fell off. Hesse sprang down the steps to help, but Lehnsen was there before him. As he stood up, he saw the terrified face of Ostermann.

The two men stared wordlessly at each other.

"So it's you?!" the Director said, shaking with anger.

Ostermann fumbled in high confusion with his battered hat.

"I—I," he stammered. "I only wanted—I wanted—to thank you so much for the scholarship."

VI

It was Candidate Ostermann's special bad luck that Hesse witnessed this encounter. Now the editors of *The Trumpet* insisted that Ostermann relinquish to them the amount of the scholarship as compensation for the damages his article had caused them and to offset the expected penalties and court costs. Otherwise, they threatened him with turning over his name to the State Prosecutor's Office. When Ostermann reminded them of their word of honor they had given him Schliephake only laughed derisively. Thus he departed very sad from the editorial offices that he had entered with such proud hopes only a few days before, he who had come to protest the indiscrete preface to his article. And with that his journalistic career ended.

"It's not always good to be overcautious!!"

We have seen above how that is and have proven that sentence with the example of Regional Court Director Lehnsen, who after the telephone call with Dr. Magnus had hesitated out of an overabundance of caution to immediately mention to his ladies the new chances of Candidate Ostermann. The truth of our maxim has now been demonstrated. Had Lehnsen not hesitated back then in disclosing the news, Ostermann would have been told in time, and he would never have crossed the threshold of *The Trumpet,* the Lehnsen family would have been spared much trouble and would also have happened to save a nice round sum, and Assessor Borchers's department would not have had an additional workload. Candidate Ostermann also would not have had to make such a terribly stupid face when he saw his learned article stashed in the file transport van as he left the editorial offices. To be sure, then, the red-blond Emmy, who sweetened the prickly existence of the warriors of *The Trumpet,* would not have so quickly managed to get ahold of the furniture of N. Israel, Spandauer Strasse, which, thanks to the five thousand marks of the Herr Director and thanks to the magnanimous foundation of old Schlenker, Frau Director's father, had finally turned into a reality. And Dr. Magnus too and the General Association of Mosaic Subjects in the German Reich would not have had the opportunity to succeed in giving to its board the especially touching expression of a vote of thanks, and especially to its outstanding executive director a few months later at the general meeting of the association.

At this meeting the president, Privy Commercial Councillor Maier, read a detailed account of the events, giving particular attention to the services of Dr. Magnus, that Dr. Magnus himself had drafted. In closing, he could make the announcement, noting with great satisfaction, that the responsible editor of *The Trumpet,* a certain Schliephake, had been ordered to pay a monetary penalty of five hundred marks plus legal costs.

Thereupon there was a motion for a vote of thanks, which passed unanimously. Then Herr Dr. Magnus asked for the floor to make an important announcement.

After he emphasized again how this very case had manifestly illuminated the necessity and the blessed effect of the association—it was only, according to the speaker, the effect of perseverance on the state prosecutor and, naturally, the force of incontrovertible arguments, which had been put forth by him, that the initial reluctance of the department had been transformed into the most stirring zeal-ousness and the most far-reaching fervor—he now would address the main point. He elaborated:

In court, as everyone knows, the editor had refused to name the author of the article. To know that person, however, the one who was truly guilty, was exceed-ingly important for the association even if justice had been served in the penalty that had been imposed and had provided a deterrent. But they must know their enemies, these scandalmongers of the Mosaic Subjects in the German Reich, in order to watch out for them, to monitor their activities, and, in the relevant case, to be able to act quickly. Now a member of the editorial staff of *The Trumpet,* a certain Dr. Hesse, had visited him, Magnus, a few days ago. (Commotion.) This person, who made the impression of a serious, apparently well-meaning, but mis-led man of not unsteady moral quality—(Catcalls: Yeah! Yeah!) People had to credit at least this much knowledge of people to him, the speaker! One must be fair too with respect to his opponents and be careful not to generalize in the anti-Semitic manner. (Vigorous bravos.) That gentleman, Dr. Hesse, confided in him that the editors of *The Trumpet* truly regretted having been misled themselves; it was a question here of a topic in which they weren't knowledgeable. (Hear, hear!) In the future, they hoped that similar "misunderstandings," as Dr. Hesse put it, would no longer occur and that they would not happen anymore, and they were ready, because they were appealing to the famous sense of sacrifice and generosity of their fellow Israelite citizens, to disclose the name of the author of the article if the association would pay from its purse the monetary penalty of five hundred marks and the court costs. (Outrageous!—Insolence!—Great gen-eral commotion.) He, the speaker, had not wanted to take the responsibility of responding himself but was leaving the decision to the meeting. Dr. Hesse had agreed and had allowed himself to say that he had infinite confidence in the un-derstanding of the Jewish notables gathered at the meeting, on the one hand, and in the sense of honor of a Jewish pastor, even if he was de facto his opponent, on the other hand. As a sign of which he had presented him with a sealed envelope that contained the name of the author and empowered him, in the event that his suggestion was accepted, to open said envelope and make its contents known to the meeting. He was now handing over this envelope to the honored president: herewith his mission was done for now.

That final effect brought about a general commotion. Everybody was obvi-ously practically devoured with curiosity to open the envelope to quench his curiosity. Privy Commercial Councillor Maier, who had followed what was happening half-distracted, accepted the envelope from the Rabbi's hands somewhat confused and turned it over indecisively a few times. From all sides came impatient cries to open the envelope, but a debate, to be sure a short one, nonetheless started. One speaker, who vigorously reproached the Rabbi for falling into negotiating with that pack of rabble and for even serving as Dr. Hesse's representative, was forced to sit down by the stormy calls to stop, and Dr. Magnus received great applause when he called out: "We are playing politics here! In politics all means are justified!"

The next speaker, from Frankfurt, tipped the balance with the argument: "Five hundred marks is nothin'! On account of five hundred marks we don't need to turn ourselves inside out gossipin'."

Dr. Hesse's suggestion was accepted, and no one breathed as the president opened the envelope. He pulled out a piece of paper, carefully set his pince-nez on his nose, and shook his head as he read what was written, then he gave the piece of paper to Herr Dr. Magnus so that he could announce the name.

Dr. Magnus stared at the piece of paper so long that the meeting began to get nervous.

"Read it aloud!" people called out from all sides.

The Rabbi gave a start; he nervously grasped his collar and in a constrained voice said: "The author is a certain Candidate Ostermann."

The name roused no recognition at all in anyone present.

"Do you know him?" someone asked.

"No! I do not know him!" Magnus said, red faced, and sat down.

"Then I will end the meeting," the president said, "by expressing again all of our warmest thanks to the honored Herr Dr. Magnus. May he long and often always be effective on our behalf."

ELEVEN

Pogrom

I

"Wherever can Bertha be!—"

Annoyed, Pastor Bode looked up from his desk; his wife was storming in from the kitchen every few moments this morning to look out the window of his study for the child.—

"Whatever is the matter with you?" he asked, putting down his pen. "The maid probably went a bit farther in this nice weather—toward the river—or she's gossiping—"

"She knows that she's not supposed to go beyond the Governor's garden, and whom would she be gossiping with? Just look outside! The streets are completely deserted. Where have all the Jews who usually stand around making a racket suddenly disappeared to? It is positively uncanny! There aren't even any hackneys at the corner! The coachmen are Jews, of course! Jewish coachmen! Dreadful! All the work is done by Jews! And today everything is empty and deserted!"

"But dearest Marie! You usually are upset that too many Jews are running around in the street—"

"I can't abide these do-nothings! Father always said—"

"Please! You just said that all the work—"

"For God's sake, Johannes—no silly speeches now!—I'm dying of anxiety because of the child! I must—"

She stormed out of the room, calling loudly for Liese.

Bode looked at the clock. It really was alarming that the nursemaid hadn't yet returned with the child. He stood up and stepped to the window. No one could be seen: only Police Lieutenant Kujaroff, who was just sitting on a bench across from the house smoking a cigarette. He half stood up and politely greeted Bode with a gesture. Bode thanked him coldly and stepped back from the window.

From the house all but a small portion of the Governor's garden could be seen, and the Spreewald dress would have been visible if the maid had stopped between the Governor's palace and the vicarage. There was still the one possibility that she was in the part of the garden hidden by the Governor's palace. But what in the world could have delayed her! Bode felt himself infected by his wife's nervousness and was just considering how he could go over there himself without letting his wife know he too was nervous when the house door opened and Liese ran down the steps to the front garden. Frau Marie appeared in the open door and watched the maid, who was quickly running barefoot, her head scarf flapping, toward the Governor's garden.

Bode breathed a sigh of relief and followed the maid with his eyes; he noted that Kujaroff was watching too.—Maybe the person had, after all, discovered a sweetheart, and they had forgotten everything around them as they were billing and cooing. Of course, that was it! The park was deserted today, and the pretty spring day made it all too conceivable. But he would scold her until her head spun for the anxiety she had caused his wife. And the bizarre terrifying stories of Pesach victims were surely surfacing again in his wife's mind even if she hadn't said anything. It was an opportunity to demonstrate to her afterward her own silly terrors, how such stupid and dangerous suspicions—

At last Liese appeared in the Governor's garden; she was certainly out of breath and was walking, not running. How slow she was! Bode felt to his chagrin that he was increasingly agitated. The only thing possible was that the child and nanny were sitting on the other side of the house. Only a few steps more, then Liese would be at the corner, and her gestures, her waving to the hidden two would clearly show how silly all this anxiety had been. But if there was no sign?!—Bode's heart stood still. He glanced quickly at his wife, who had gone out into the street and then looked anxiously at the corner where Liese, who had probably caught her breath by then, was running across the lawn.—

Now she was there—now—

What was that?!

He tore open the window and leaned out as far as he could.—Frau Marie was convulsively grasping the garden railings—the Police Lieutenant over there rolled himself another cigarette. All this Bode had mechanically noted as he had unlatched the window. Liese had stopped at the corner, looked around, and then turned back; she returned slowly, waving her hands in the air, pantomiming unmistakably that she had found no one.

The Pastor's wife detached herself from the railings and ran toward the maid, waving frantically to her as she in turn began to trot. Bode remained at the window—frozen—and tried to collect himself. Missing! Child and nanny! How could that be! What could be the natural explanation, if not—

He saw how his wife and Liese met and now, looking around in every direction, returned to the house together. When they reached Kujaroff's bench, he raised his hand to his visor and looked closely into Frau Marie's face. She stopped and addressed him, apparently forgetting in her confusion that he couldn't understand German. Bode saw how he politely stood up when the lady spoke to him and quizzically turned to Liese. She looked as if she was translating the question, and now a short, lively dialogue began, accompanied by gestures, which the Pastor's wife followed, darting her eyes back and forth anxiously between the two speakers. She plucked at Liese's arm, impatient and upset. Finally Liese turned and exclaimed a few words to Frau Marie while clapping her hands in the air, a gesture that Bode couldn't understand from his window.

Frau Marie, however, emitted a shrill scream and sank down on the bench.

Bode stormed out of the room and into the street.—

In the few seconds during which Bode left the window and hurried to the street, the scene outside had changed.—Suddenly a crowd of alarming and threatening figures had appeared; carrying truncheons or thick, heavy wooden clubs in their hands, they ran from all sides to the bench where Frau Marie was sobbing in the arms of Liese, who was at a loss. Bode had to press through the throng.

His wife sprang up when she saw him and threw herself sobbing into his arms.

"Our Bertha! The Jews have dragged our child away! They are butchering our child!"

"Marie! For God's sake—Marie!—What is it? Calm down!"

Now howling loudly too, Liese recounted, in the midst of the almost unintelligible and incoherent screaming and shouting of the crowd, that Kujaroff had seen an old, unidentified Jew standing with the nanny an hour ago, and they had been whispering together.

"They're butchering our child!" Frau Marie screamed, wringing her hands frantically. "Johannes, do something! They have to look for our child!—Everyone help if you are Christian!"

Liese screamed, gesturing Russian words with her hands. The rapidly growing commotion of the crowd intensified even more. Cudgels were swung, and some young lads scattered in various directions while grunting loud sounds, apparently to spread the news of the Christian child who had disappeared.

Bode forced himself to gather his wits; he took Liese by the hand and turned to Kujaroff. Using the maid to translate, he demanded that Kujaroff undertake the necessary measures to investigate.

The Police Lieutenant politely but dismissively shrugged his shoulders. If a complaint were to be properly filed, naturally everything possible would be done that was required in such cases. A notice in the official gazette would probably be the best.—If they couldn't give him something to go on or the basis of their suspicions, there was nothing he could do. He could hardly undertake a search of every house in the city.—The Herr Pastor would have to do that personally with his friends.

The mob was bellowing and bawling. Bode looked about in helpless dismay and saw his true savior, Strösser, who was making his way toward him.

"Strösser! Help us, for heaven's sake!"

"I know everything—there's already rioting in town. Keep calm!—Above all, get your wife into the house! You aren't helping here at all, Frau Marie!"

He nodded to Liese; Frau Marie, sobbing brokenly into her handkerchief, let herself be gently walked to the house. But on the doorstep she turned around with a fresh outburst of agony: "Everyone help! All of you! Search for my child!"

She broke down at the door, whimpering.

Strösser now turned to Bode, speaking gravely: "Don't do anything hasty! The disappearance will resolve itself in due course. There is some sort of devilry! An unidentified Jew!—Kujaroff knows absolutely every mouse in town! And that rabble just happened to be standing by!"

"Where is Kujaroff? I want him—"

Bode looked about wildly, but the Pristav had vanished. Meanwhile, a few members of Bode's congregation had shown up. One of them approached.

"Herr Pastor!" he said. "Those are the worst sort of people. Absolute foreign riffraff!—They say they want to check every Jewish house, but only if Herr Pastor wishes. I would advise you not to have anything to do with that mob—"

"But what should I do?" Bode cried. "My child could be killed at any moment! Wherever could she be, if not—"

"Yes, that is also possible," the man said. "If Herr Pastor means that Jews—"

"I know nothing and mean nothing," Bode shouted wildly. "But whoever brings my child back to me, he is my savior and redeemer!"

"So—then!" the man said and translated the last words of Bode to those standing there.

"Bode!" Strösser gripped him by both shoulders. "Herr Pastor! What are you doing!—Think of your sermon!—Do you want your own teachings—"

"Leave me alone," Bode cried, beside himself, and tore himself free, pushing away the hands that wanted to hold him back. "Now is not the time to think of sermons and theories. I am searching for my child!"

Then Dr. Strösser turned away, struck the pavement sharply with his walking stick, and went home. On the corner he turned once more to look back. The Pastor's wife was still sitting at the door, whimpering, with Liese standing next to her, bawling loudly. But Bode was running bareheaded after the mob, which was rolling on in the direction of the Jewish ghetto.

Once home, Strösser closed all the shutters and locked his doors. Then he filled his pipe and lay down on his bed. He was determined not to leave the house again today and not to think of anything that might be happening in town.

II

"Good that you're finally here, Herr Doctor," exclaimed Herr Hansemann, the bustling landlord of the hotel, a Russian German from the Baltic region, to Heinz Lehnsen, who was slowly approaching, hat in hand in the warm weather. "Did you find the large synagogue?—I'm sorry I didn't warn you. It can break out at any time."

"What?" Heinz asked, distracted. The greeting had shaken him out of a deep dream.

"Why—the pogrom is almost here. The soldiers are standing ready to march in the courtyard of the barracks."

"So they will intervene in time," Heinz said and peered at the doorway across the street, where, day and night, he had convinced himself that some young Jewish people were on patrol.—Even now there were two of them who were hardly past boyhood, and then one was just leaving in a hurry.

"Intervene? Sure—certainly!" the host smirked. "It's only a question of against whom.—It's better if you stay here inside, although you personally are probably safe. The Pristav checked with me yesterday to see your papers and make sure Herr Doctor is no longer Jewish. Good thing your baptismal certificate was attached to your passport! But still, I urgently advise you to stay inside today. Mistakes could easily occur and—"

"Nonsense!" Heinz said, annoyed. "I don't believe in the disturbances!"

"What? You don't believe?" The host seemed almost offended. "I tell you, in two, three weeks I will have good guests in the staterooms on the second floor!"

"What does that have to do with a pogrom?" Heinz said in surprise.

"Oh, please—quite a bit!" the other replied with heat. "You must know that Jews stick together everywhere. Anytime there's been a pogrom and there's a lot destroyed and demolished and the Jewish population is starving, then collections are taken up over there in Germany and everywhere. And afterward a commission of wealthy Jews travels to where the pogrom was to make a report and distribute the money. They are welcomed by the government, they get travel visas and passports—they bring money into the country, after all.—I've already gotten the rooms ready for the gentlemen.—"

Heinz had heard enough and went to his large room on the ground floor. He felt the need to think undisturbed about what he had experienced that morning.

He had not gone to the holiday rooms of Moische Schlenker on purpose but had asked the way to the large synagogue because he hoped to disappear into the crowd and remain unnoticed.

The exotic scene had riveted him from the moment he entered. The long, narrow room was filled to overflowing with men and boys—there were no women to be seen. The men were wrapped in their prayer shawls, the long white or yellowish cloths that resembled togas. Many had pulled their shawls far over their head so that neither face nor figure could be distinguished; when they rocked back and forth these figures offered an uncanny sight. Others wore the shawl coquettishly folded over their shoulders—dimly Heinz recalled a verse of Heine. —Most wore the shawl in the manner of a classical garment so that the folds fell picturesquely.

That was the garb preserved from time immemorial to the age of machines and the cutaway—the real clothing of a Jew in which he wrapped himself when he was tired of the comedy of pretending to be what the oppression of the day compelled him to be. Heinz found the garment a sign of the incredible miracle that a piece of ancient spirituality had remained alive to this day—Jerusalem, Athens, and Rome wove it into a unity. After the decay of all ancient cultures, when feeble and artificial attempts at revival in the Renaissance and in the period of humanism—still after all this, the ancient culture was still alive, rescued, and preserved in the poor, filthy, and scorned homes of the pariahs among all people.

For what possible purpose?—

Heinz gave a start and stood up from his comfortable chair at the open window. He got a cigarette and paced up and down the room. He didn't want to lose himself in the infinite, and he forced his thoughts back to the scene at the prayer house he had visited that morning.

First it had seemed to him as if there was no coordinated action at all in the room, in the crowd standing shoulder to shoulder around the roomy elevated platform in the middle. He heard only confused shouts and thought he was seeing an utter chaos of excited white figures, with no one taking anyone else into account. Here some were praying softly and intensely with eyes closed—many had laid their faces on a desk, others shouted loud words to the heavens as they beat their breasts, stretching their fingers oddly heavenward and then suddenly clenching them as if they had caught something in the air; often the wild gestures made the impression that the person praying wanted to pull with all his strength something to him that he wasn't able to grasp.—Unaffected by everything going on around them, many sat behind thick books, sunk in their studies. Some were making their way through this tumult, mechanically it seemed, for their lips were moving in prayer without pause, pushing through the crowd with an effort—the inner movement did not seem to allow them to rest in one place.—The murmuring of prayers, the groaning and moaning, the shouting and the singing created an utter chaos of sounds that was confusing and overwhelming.

Heinz was first compelled to think that it was not a question at all of a group praying, that it was really everyone for himself, praying his own prayer. According to Western European notions, a service mainly consists of everyone singing or engaging in silent prayer. The entire congregation stands up as one or sits down as one—the organ's notes carry along the choir of those praying—the choir's song fills the hall with harmony. Here anything like that was absent, nor did priests officiate to celebrate their holy service separated at a distance from the people. As he reflected now, Heinz asked himself whether the carefully rehearsed congregational singing and what went with it didn't belong, whether the deferential and pedantic observation of form in the service, the uniform standing up and sitting down, the kneeling didn't express something of military discipline—whether every primal feeling didn't ossify there in the technique of the ritual. The person praying couldn't and shouldn't freely surrender to his fervor—he wasn't alone with his God but was supposed to fall into formation at all times with everyone else at prayer to maintain the right direction and feeling. Heinz thought then of those praying solo whom he had seen now and then in Catholic areas around the cathedral or in front of a saint's shrine on a country road. He was inclined to see in the Jewish temple here an abundance of such people alone in prayer who only happened to be crowded together in a space without having anything to do with one another—who were just pressing against each other and were forced to distract themselves.

But then it occurred to him how the source of all the power and fervor of each person only lay in being a community, in deeply rooted conviction. To belong to the whole, to be tightly linked in the chain from generation to generation. There in the prayer house, where all the cries that escaped a person and carried his suffering and very own wishes to the heavens, the essence of this singular folk found expression. Simply beings of the most distinctive idiosyncrasy, differentiated in the smallest detail, they were united outside of time and place, bound to each other independently of human desire and judgment, and only thereby did each one have a soul and strength. There, where they converged again and again and again their whole life long, day after day, and at almost every hour—where their real being pierced through the veil of the mundane, each person had to become aware that he, with all his personal strengths and abilities, with his work and all his activity, was only a tiny part of a vast whole. It seemed to Heinz that he had really seen something today, perhaps for the first time, that could truly be a divine service—a mass of people that became one by leaving behind all earthly burdens only because of their collective yearning upward to reach transcendence. For the first time in his life he understood the concept of a praying community.—

What a commotion had seized the crowd when the scrolls of the Torah were taken from the Ark and were carried to the platform! The men carrying the scrolls could scarcely move forward, so pressed were they from all sides. Everyone wanted to press a kiss on the Torah mantles that wrapped the scrolls or at least touch them with their fingertips.—Fathers held up their young sons so that they could learn the pious custom now—careworn workmen nestled their pale faces against the cloth for a moment, smiling happily at the Torah scrolls; these people held fast to the Torah with all their might and all their heart! What was life's suffering—what were pogroms or persecution—what were the centuries of misery—here was happiness, the eternal, the sublime, which was outside time and space—the treasure of the people that no thief could take from them. The pride of the chosen people, who were intended to protect for all eternity their treasure there, shone from all eyes.—

Never, so it seemed to Heinz, had he seen a crowd of happier people, sure of themselves and content with themselves, as he had in that moment.

And outside loomed blood and thunder!—

Heinz had listened to the reading from the Torah, had seen how the scrolls were dressed again in their jewels and brought back to the Ark, and then he had turned to leave—the air had been unbearable for a long time—when a sudden stillness, followed by a strange, soft song, forced him to turn around, surprised, as he was already on the top step of the stairs leading to the exit.

The singer stood on the platform in the middle—it was a man still quite young, with a short curly beard, singing liltingly with an unschooled but amazingly soft voice that now and then somewhat abruptly rose in an immense crescendo as he sang a prayer, rocking back and forth. Everyone listened silently without moving as if under a spell. Then suddenly the voice blew like a sudden blast of wind over the congregation. All the figures in white shook themselves back and forth, and a wild tumult roared from a thousand throats into the air. The clamor lasted only a few seconds, and then again the echoes of the prayer leader's song joyfully rose alone upward through the silence. Again the wild and tumultuous chaotic choir broke in, and again the singer waited for the noise to die down. But then, when he finished, there began again that strangely charming conversation of each person with his God, and the earlier utter chaos took over again. But now Heinz knew that a spirit presided over this utter chaos.—All these people at prayer, all of them looking in their books, all of them speaking the same words, each one for himself, saying the text prescribed for everyone; each person carried the prayers of the whole together to God's throne, each in his own way, at his own place, and at his own time, the prayers fixed for all times and all places.

The last impression that Heinz was left with was the sight of the mass of figures wrapped in their white prayer shawls, undulating back and forth.—

His thoughts wandered back to the annoying improvised prayers on the Auguststrasse in Berlin in which he had unwillingly taken part a few days ago.—That was only a few days ago!—He easily recognized in the service there the distortions and masquerade of what he had experienced here. Or—had he perhaps only seen everything there in the false light of an unsuitable setting—maybe he had only noticed what wasn't important, while the core had remained closed to him?—In the end there was the fundamental source of an enormous error in judging Jews and everything Jewish in that the Jews always found themselves perforce in the wrong place and in unfavorable circumstances! What made them seem repugnant, strange, picturesque, ridiculous was perhaps not them at all, not through any fault of theirs, but was only the awkward position in which they lived, a people without land, a community dispersed and scattered like grains of sand.

So then was all anti-Semitism, the miserable Jewish question that never seemed to find an answer, only an enormous misunderstanding? People couldn't get to know Jews as long as they didn't know themselves.

Was there an answer? The unnatural circumstances had to be changed to natural ones.—That means—

Irritated, Heinz jumped up from the easy chair where he had been sitting.

Just where were these thoughts taking him? He was all ready to move to a place that was contrary to everything he had ever learned and to his customary setting. On account of his understandable interest he had, really more out of curiosity than scholarship, observed the customs and the way people lived in the milieu his family came from. This effort had offered him interesting things aplenty. He could be and had to be content with that! What concern were Jews to him? They could take care of their own affairs! Yesterday evening he had felt quite dazed by the strange atmosphere in Schlenker's house—who knows whether his pretty companion hadn't had more influence than he had wanted to admit yesterday.—Now it was time to think about the criminal law congress and Petersburg. In the Hermitage he would probably soon smile at the culture of Moische Schlenker.

He picked up the railway guide to study the train schedule.

The sounds of disorder in the street brought him again to the window. Herr Hansemann and the hotel servants stood on the sidewalk and looked to the left down the street, as did some passersby standing there. From here one heard a clattering racket and yelling. Heinz leaned out the window, and in the distance where the lane curved he saw a dark mass of people.—A platoon of soldiers came running across the street on the double and disappeared around the corner.—The entry post was empty, but Heinz saw the young man who had last been standing there just coming out a different door; several young people followed him, and all of them were rushing down the street in a hurry. Heinz realized that the self-defense league had been alarmed, and now it was getting serious.—Across the way the café owner was battening down his shutters.

Heinz grabbed his hat and hurried out into the street.

"It's started!" Herr Hansemann said, scurrying after him. "They're already looting on Fish Alley.—Don't go out! Fortunately, it doesn't concern the gentleman anymore."

He recoiled with horror; in the distance a gunshot rang out.

Heinz hurried off, paying no attention to Hansemann—who was trying to catch up with him without success.

"But they'll think you're a Jew!" he pitifully cried after him. "At least take a crowbar with you or a pickax so they know you're a Christian when they see you!"

III

Before he knew it, Heinz was at the end of the street and had caught up with the mass of people. He was acting purely from instinct and had hurried from the hotel and down the street without thinking what he was actually going to do.—Now he was pressing through the crowd that was standing around nervously whispering and staring at the line of soldiers with rifles in their arms, forming a chain across the street. Between them and the crowd there was an empty space of about twenty feet. The cordon, however, had been placed so that it cut off the curve in the street, and no one could see what was happening on the other side.

Confidently and quickly, Heinz strode across the empty space and approached the soldiers.—Running past him were five or six men in peasant garb, carrying picks and axes in their hands. The cordon of soldiers immediately opened to let them through. The soldier standing in front of Heinz said a few words roughly to him in Russian and pointed his weapon.

Heinz stopped short and fell back; now he could get a look past the cordon. There was yet another row of soldiers there, its back to the first row and in effect sealing off the Jewish ghetto. On the other side of this cordon but at a short distance many Jews were helplessly running back and forth. Dragging packages and boxes, confused and frightened, the pitiful people, including many women and children, filled the air with their screams. A man with a large wooden chest panted across to the right, a young woman followed with a child on her arm and holding behind her another by the arm. The throng of peasants was just coming through the cordon as the man was dragging his chest past; in fright, he dropped the chest, screaming as he ran off. The chest broke open; Heinz saw one of the peasants approach the woman, who couldn't run away on account of the children, and then saw her face distorted with fear for a moment—then the soldiers began to threaten him with their clubs. Heinz shrank back, and the houses blocked his view.

He looked around, confused; the people behind him watched him silently with curiosity. But no one made a threatening move. He walked through them without resistance and hurried into a side street to make a detour to the large square and from there to get to the house of Moische Schlenker.

He walked through the quiet, deserted lanes to the square and had an extensive view, since the square sloped up along one side.—Here too a double cordon was set up at the level of the well house standing in the middle of some shrubbery. He could see the Vilnius Strasse off behind them to the right, while just ahead was the house where yesterday evening he had spent such happy hours. The mob apparently hadn't reached the house yet; the street was as if dead, all doors and shutters were closed. To the left, however, the poor, narrow, and dark Fish Alley led off from the square. The looters were busy there. He heard piercing howls followed by the tinkling of smashed windows.—Squeezed in the alley, the mob was sweeping back and forth, without anyone being able to say what was actually happening.—A few thugs in peasant blouses, trailed by females, their faces flushed with excitement, were running to a pile of cobblestones lying in the middle of the square. The officer, who was leaning on the well house and playing with his riding crop, called something to the soldiers, whereupon some of them put down their weapons and tossed stones already there between the two cordons to the mob. They ran off quickly with the stones and set to work. Again the shattering and tinkling of window glass, loud howling—there were some gunshots fired—the screams of fear coming from women suddenly drowned out all the noise, only to fall suddenly silent again.

In a couple of strides, Heinz crossed over to the officer, who recoiled, gripping his saber. In his hand Heinz had the Russian permit that he had received when he had presented his credentials.

He only wanted to get past—to be over there—with his relatives to whom he belonged—among the Jews—the persecuted—with the self-defense league!—

Yes—with the self-defense league! Where was it?—

The plan of the self-defense league, as Rivka had explained to him, wasn't bad. To avoid a premature seizure of arms and to prevent the weapons from being discovered in a predictable search in Jewish houses, they had hidden the weapons they had—there were few enough—in a safe house outside the actual Jewish ghetto. After the alarm had been given, all the members of the self-defense league were to gather there to go armed and in closed ranks to the scene of attack.—The alarm had worked—every member of the self-defense league had shown up; they quickly hid the weapons in sacks, set out, and—bumped into the cordon.

Kujaroff had seen through the plan and had quickly known how to skillfully thwart it. The entire Jewish ghetto was ringed by soldiers who had strict orders not to let any Jew pass—from any direction. So the members of the self-defense league, since all the young, able-bodied Jews were prevented from passing through, since the targets of the pogrom were without weapons, were prevented from helping, and any possibility of defense was cut off.

The little troop of members of the self-defense league gathered, terribly agitated, to hold a war council. Any attempt to break through the regular troops equipped with modern firearms was, of course, totally hopeless. Nevertheless, they voted unanimously to undertake the effort.

"We shall die!" shouted Mendel Friedmann. "We shall not die in vain! Our death will be a living testament for our people and against our enemies! Forward!—"

But it happened differently. Suddenly, soldiers were pressing in from all sides into the narrow lane where they were standing, and before they really knew what was happening, the soldiers showered them with blows from their clubs.—They were thrown down and tied up and led away. Some of them were dragged away unconscious, and one, Meier Kaplan, lay dead, his skull shattered.

Benjamin Schapiro started to sing the song of Zion, the Hatikvah—but a club that struck him heavily across the shoulders dropped him to the ground, ending the song in a whimper.—

When Kujaroff, who had personally led the successful lightning attack, crossed the square he saw Heinz Lehnsen, whom he knew by sight. When Kujaroff had seen Heinz walking with Rivka Schlenker, he had become suspicious after seeing Lehnsen's Jewish physiognomy and had checked his papers in the hotel.

Heinz spoke rapidly and desperately to the officer—nervously thumbing through his little dictionary; he continued to speak German unconsciously while he was checking the dictionary. The officer looked distrustfully and doubtfully at the paper that Heinz was showing him, impatiently striking his riding crop against his tall boots. Puzzled, the soldiers watched the well-dressed foreigner and smirked about his funny way of speaking.

Kujaroff stood at some distance and watched the group.—Suddenly straight across the square ran Pastor Bode, alone, distraught as if crazy. He was waving his hands wildly and screaming from afar something incomprehensible. Behind him, running and trying to catch up with him, were two men from his congregation. Kujaroff frowned and hastily called in Russian to an officer: "Let the young man pass!—He's German and a Christian. Baptized last year!—"

At this moment the black figure of a Jew who had apparently forgotten what was happening shot out of the bushes behind the well house, leaving his hiding place to stare wide-eyed at Heinz. The apparition was so unexpected and surprising that everyone froze for a second—the lieutenant handing the paper back with arm outstretched—Heinz stepping forward toward the Jewish ghetto—the soldiers with their smirking grins.

Then one of the soldiers, with a filthy curse, dealt the Jew a kick in the stomach so that he flew back a few steps and collapsed.

Heinz, having been given permission to go, leaped forward and bent over the man lying there.

IV

Berl Weinstein had checked his earthly belongings for the tenth time that day after returning from the prayer house that morning to pack anything valuable and easily transportable in his pockets. He wanted to hold himself in readiness just in case he had to flee; he hadn't had a wife for many years, his daughters were all happily married. So he was all alone and had only himself to worry about. And he was, after all, near and dear to himself.

As he was rummaging around in his papers, which he carried around tied into numerous bundles in his breast pocket, he even found, besides many valuable documents and addresses, a collection of letters of recommendation and testimonials from all over the world, including a letter from Reverend Hickler of London. This letter on stationery of the English mission society and in three languages—English, German, and Hebrew, the last being according to a draft by Berl Weinstein—most urgently commended this brother, who was well read in God's Holy Scriptures and who was converted and true and pious in spirit to the truths of the Gospel, to all charitable Christians working in the vineyard of the Lord, especially and first and foremost to all servants of the Church.

Berl Weinstein had stored this letter at the bottom of his coat pocket archive. If it appeared inopportunely, this letter could bring scorn and hostility upon him from his community. On the other hand, he had never been able to bring himself to destroy this dangerous document. He had never used it outside of London, since there was always the possibility that something of his putative conversion could trickle down into the circles he depended on. But a day could come when this letter might be of use to him.

Was today the day? If it went really badly, he could put himself under the protection of the Christian Church with this document, or perhaps the personal protection of Pastor Bode, whose gentleness and humanity he had heard much about from his son-in-law.—But that would only happen in an extreme case, if danger really threatened. Then such a step couldn't remain secret, of course, and meant a final break with all his friends. No Jew in Borytshev would want to have anything more to do with him, and the Pastor, on the other hand, would try to exercise his right to the new little sheep of his church. He was resolved that he would not participate in any way but that he would have to leave his home and seek a new one where no one knew him, where the Pastor couldn't lay claim to him or a Jew would show him the door.—

Just in case, he put the document away so he could easily pull it out and went out to look for news in the lane. The tumult in front of the large synagogue, the main school, was scarcely different from the usual scene at such a time. The schoolyard, circled by most of the prayer houses, was filled with men dressed for the holiday, who were chatting with each other after the service before they went home to dinner. From an open window of a classroom could be heard the singsong of the students there.—

Berl Weinstein went from group to group to pick up news. At some places he could profit from the expert critiques that today's singing of the prayer leader was subjected to—here they were arguing again which of the various lectures announced for the afternoon was preferable—only seldom was there talk of danger from a pogrom. But what was said about that was so absurd that there was nothing to be learned there.—As those praying gradually took off for their homes, Berl hurried on and dared instead to leave the ghetto, since he had learned nothing unsettling. But when he reached the large square two boys ran screaming across in different directions. Berl heard their cries and became frightened. A Christian child was said to have been killed—the Jews were the murderers.—The messengers from the self-defense league were already running through the lanes and raising the alarm—the crush of people in the Jewish streets precipitously cleared, and the streets were swept empty in the blink of an eye. Doors and window shutters slammed shut, and only here and there a delayed self-defense league member, breathless, ran to the collection point.

Berl Weinstein had observed everything from the thick shrubbery next to the well house, where he had plunged when the lads had come storming with their alarming news.—Now he didn't dare move but watched everything, shaking with fear.—Then the thuggish mob appeared, howling wildly, rushing into Fish Alley.—A little ways behind a few stragglers followed; among them to his astonishment he recognized Pastor Bode, who was rushing along without a hat, his face contorted. Now would be the right time for him to hurry forward with his document and commend himself to the neighborly love of the person who from now on would be his pastor. With a shaking hand he reached for the important document, but still he hesitated—and then it was too late. Bode was already beyond calling distance.

Then the military commandos could be heard, and soldiers marching in double time turned into the square. Berl gave a sigh of relief. How fortunate that he hadn't given himself away too soon! The military was going to intervene! But what he felt when the soldiers, instead of intervening, formed cordons across the square apparently with the intention of protecting the pogrom perpetrators and making it impossible for the Jews to escape. And the commanding officer moreover had planted himself only a few steps away from him, Berl!—

In acute terror, Berl crouched there and listened to the tumult that was coming from Fish Alley, to the wails of lamentation and howls of rage, the shattering of windows, the screams of terror, the gunshots, and the splintering of furniture.—Away from this hell! At any price! If only Pastor Bode came by again. If he could reach him, he would be safe. The Pastor would protect him from the soldiers and peasants. He himself knew very well the joy with which these Christian clergymen received every convert. He had often taken advantage of that when it hadn't been a matter of life or death, as it was today, but only to make a nice profit. He had never felt a pang of conscience at the time—he had just given upright people a downright priceless joy with little effort. But strange! Today, since he was going to—forced to—act under duress, it seemed to him to be a cowardly act. In the crucial moment he hadn't been able to run to Bode.—Now it was totally too late. The opportunity would scarcely come again!—If it did— if heaven would give him another chance, then he would know how to use it! Several gunshots rang out; he squeezed his eyes shut, quaked in fear, and swore to himself to make generous contributions for Palestine—he promised himself to be more punctual in the future on his travels with the afternoon prayer than he had been up until now—from now on he wanted to observe more carefully all the commandments of the Holy Law—he wanted to devote an hour a day to the study of the Talmud—in short, from now on he wanted to behave as a Jew was supposed to behave. But in order to be able to do that, God had to perform a miracle and send the Pastor to him! In his case he could be discovered at any moment and then—

There!—Had God performed a miracle?—Pastor Bode himself came storming along—right toward the shrubbery and the well house, where the officer was talking with the young German man. Berl carefully pulled his paper from his pocket with shaking fingers and held it clenched in his hand, waiting for the right moment to jump out.—Suddenly he froze at a new terror; over there stood the worst of the worst, Pristav Kujaroff.—But the Pastor was already panting closer. What was he screaming? "Stop! Stop the killing!" That was the man who could save him.

He trembled. Kujaroff waved and called out something. Had he seen him? Thank God, no! He was waving to the young German. But what was that?

"Baptized last year!"

A *meshumad*!—The young man was a meshumad—an apostate who had betrayed the beliefs of his fathers, who had betrayed and abandoned his people. And Berl Weinstein, who had just wanted to throw himself at the feet of the Pastor, clutching the attestation of his baptism in his hand, was seized by the enormous instinctive revulsion and loathing that every Jew feels in the presence of a meshumad. Forgetting everything—his situation and surroundings, the danger and his plans—he shot up, rigid, out of his hiding place and stared, terrorized, at Heinz.

The well-aimed kick of a soldier's boot to the stomach hurled him back to earth.—

Pastor Bode had by this time reached the officer and was panting as he leaned against the well house. He couldn't speak a word for a moment; the men following him had gathered around to help. Kujaroff approached and spoke roughly to the men: "Take your pastor home! He can't complain; he's the one who caused the whole riot and must bear the responsibility.—We can't do anything now. Translate that to him!"

With that he turned to the officer, and both left without looking back.

Bode listened, apparently without understanding anything, as they translated for him into German what had been said. He straightened up and wanted to rush after them, but his strength failed, and finally he allowed himself to be led home, a broken man.

He had witnessed unspeakable things; as the mob fell upon the Jewish homes and began to pillage, he awakened from the confusion that had started with his child's disappearance and that had left him acting out of pure instinct without reflection. He had stood between the mob and the victims, had thrown himself into the tumult without considering the danger to himself—in vain! No one heeded him. He was shoved aside, and his friends only barely rescued him from the swirling hell. When he saw the soldiers and the officer, he wanted to make one last effort, using all his strength to put an end to the terror for whose outbreak he felt partly responsible.—But now his strength had collapsed, and he passively let everything wash over him.—

Heinz was looking after Berl Weinstein, who was slowly coming to. The scene with Pastor Bode had diverted the soldiers' attention, and that was perhaps Berl's good fortune.—He half sat up, supported by Heinz, and looked about, confused. He looked into Heinz's face, then at the paper still in his hand. Then he suddenly remembered everything; angrily he shoved away the hand supporting him. He twisted away hastily, stood up with an effort, and slowly and thoroughly shred the paper into confetti. Still gasping for breath, he stood bent over and stared with hatred into the eyes of the stranger Heinz. Then he hurled the confetti into his face, spit, and shrieked: "Meshumad!"

And he ran off in long leaps, holding his throbbing stomach with both hands.

Heinz looked at him in amazement; he had fathomed the meaning of the foreign word.

V

Desolate cries, which this time were not coming from Fish Alley, startled him. At the end of the street, where the Schlenker house stood, there was a howling mob beginning to destroy and pillage there. Heinz flew over the square into the street and rattled on the Schlenkers' door.

He heard the window shutters cautiously open, and he stepped back into the street so he could be seen and recognized.

Immediately he heard the bolt thrown back, and the door opened a crack. He entered quickly, and the door was closed at once. The entryway was dark, and he could barely see Rivka's slender figure.

"You came," she said softly. "You came—to—with us—"

She fell silent, and Heinz tried in vain to find words. The young people found and grasped each other's hands. They stood silently in the dark. Then a door to the right opened.

"Who's there?" Moische Schlenker's calm voice asked.

Heinz was too upset to answer and stepped through the door. Moische Schlenker, who was sitting in an upholstered, high-backed chair, deep in a folio, stood up, surprised, to greet the guest.

Heinz looked around, embarrassed and greatly flabbergasted. Even today the room still made a thoroughly peaceful, festive impression, and it seemed improbable that the inhabitants knew that in a few minutes murder and devastation would descend on them. Because the window shutters were closed, there were candles burning in the silver candelabras that threw a hallowed glow over the dishes on the table, which Frau Schlenker was just clearing.—Jacob sat next to his father with a book; Rivka, however, was standing at a window, and, turning her back to the room, she diligently spied through a gap in the shutter.

Everyone was dressed up for the holiday.

"Did you bolt the door again?" Moische Schlenker asked. "The door is always open for everyone. Now we've bolted it.—You look around and are surprised? It's not as joyful as a holiday usually is, but nevertheless, today is a holiday, and we won't let ourselves be disturbed. We have eaten and prayed as usual, and now I'm studying with Jacob as I always do. What happens will happen! If we are chosen to die in honor of the Holy Name, it will happen no matter what we do.—But you shouldn't rush into danger in vain. We remain where we are. But you? Why did you come?—You cannot help!—Is it fair to your parents and friends if you put yourself into such danger here in a strange land?—"

Heinz spoke firmly: "I shall stay with you. Give me a weapon."

He turned to Rivka, who without altering her position said: "We have no weapons! The self-defense league has been cut off with all the weapons!"

"Weapons!" Moische Schlenker said disapprovingly. "What do we need weapons for! This here is our weapon!—You cannot use this weapon. Go!"

He pointed to his books.—

"I'm staying here," Heinz repeated.

"I cannot allow that," Moische Schlenker said. "I would be guilty if something happened to you. You are disturbing our peace.—We are where God has placed us, and we await what He has decided for us.—But you? This is not your place, and you do not belong to us!—You can surely still achieve much good at home. The German Jews have nothing to fear, praise God, from pogroms; they have all long since forgotten the terror; only they shouldn't forget their Judaism. Go and remain a good Jew! I saw yesterday that you have a Jewish heart and that you come to us now in our need to be with us in danger—it is very, very noble of you.—But you do not belong here. You are from another world. I thank you, and God will repay you—the intention is as important to Him as the deed. But—go!"

He began to rock back and forth over his book, pulling a lamp closer.

Heinz went to Rivka.

"Do you also tell me to go? Am I a stranger to you too?" he asked softly.

It was completely silent in the room; a narrow strip of sunlight shone through the heart-shaped cutout in the shutters into the half-darkened room, lit only by flickering candles.—The mob's howling as it looted seemed to have moved into the distance.

Without turning around, Rivka slowly reached out her hand to Heinz. Then she said, pressing his hand hard: "You are a good person, a dear, dear person!—But you don't belong to us! Your fate isn't our fate!—Go!"

"Fine!" said Heinz truculently, taking his hand back. "I shall prove to you all that I belong to you. I am one of you!—I belong to this family!—You had a brother, Herr Schlenker, who left you years ago. He went to Germany—he fled from here. I am his grandson; I am the son of his daughter, and now I return to share your fate. I've never known just where I belong; now I know! Do you want to drive away your own nephew and cousin—do you want to throw me out of this house?—I have the right to stay here!"

He had seized the heavy poker from the stove and wildly swung it about.

Rivka had turned back to the room and now looked at him, her eyes glistening. Moische Schlenker, deeply moved, started to stand up.

"Chaim's grandson—the grandson of my older brother Chaim, the one who disappeared—? Where is—does he live—?"

He stood up, going to Heinz with outstretched arms.—Jacob got there first and leaped with joy.—For a moment everything happening outside seemed forgotten.—

Then there was loud shouting at the back of the house, and someone rattled the door. Everyone stopped and listened in terror.—

"That's Berl Weinstein!" cried Frau Schlenker. "I'm opening the door."

She ran out of the room, and before anyone could hurry after her, she returned with Berl, who looked pale and confused. He sank into a chair; then everyone tried to help him. They gave him a glass of wine. Finally, he recovered enough to tell them what had happened.

He had been dreadfully ill used by soldiers and almost beaten to death. He had barely escaped and had been wandering around aimlessly. He didn't dare go back to his room; in the streets everything had been destroyed and looted. Finally he had managed to crawl here to get into the house from the back, to be with friends. But they should flee; the mob was coming closer.

Moische Schlenker sat down again with his book.

"We are not running away," he said. "I want them to find me at home in my chair—my home and me."

Again, just as Heinz had been reminded at the seder yesterday of images from a bygone classical era, he saw the Roman patriarchs before his eyes as they sat on their chairs to await the barbarians.

Berl Weinstein emitted a sudden shriek, pointing to Heinz.

"How did you get here? Who is he?" he screeched.

"He belongs to us," Moische Schlenker said, trying to calm Berl down, "even if he wears different clothes from us. He's a Jew like us."

Rivka went to Heinz's side and put her hand on his shoulder; perturbed, she looked at Berl Weinstein's choleric expression.

"A Jew? Him?" Berl Weinstein shrieked in rage. "He's a meshumad! Baptized last year!—"

Turning pale, Rivka stepped away. Horrified, everyone stared at Heinz.

"Listen!" Heinz said hastily. "It's true! I've been baptized! But it's not my fault! I didn't know anything about Jewish things—"

"Enough!" said Moische Schlenker as he stood up. "It's enough! No one has the right to judge you!—We aren't judges! But it's time to stop!—You must get out while there's still time!—You can't stay here with us now—not today. Your blood mustn't mix with ours if God has decreed the worst for us.—Go!"

Heinz looked around again. He saw nothing but cast-down eyes. He approached Rivka. She retreated and quickly left the room; he followed without a word. She opened the door a crack and squeezed into the corner of the entryway. He wanted to step close to her, but she retreated farther back and waved him fiercely away.—

He pushed off into the street, and the door was closed at once; the bolt was thrown. It seemed to him that he heard a sob. He looked around. The street seemed empty. The mob, which could be heard nearby, had disappeared into a side street.

He took a few steps toward the square, where the soldiers had been posted before—then stopped to lean against a wall of the house that he was leaving.

Expelled from his family—from his people! Where did he belong?

Suddenly, a few rocks clattered against the wall close by. Startled, he straightened up. Part of the mob was just breaking forth from the lane across from him, and the leaders assumed that, standing there alone by himself at the house wall, he was a good target for their stones. Instinctively, he began to run to the square; he saw the Pristav screaming loudly as he hurried toward him. A hard blow against his left leg made him collapse. The fellow leading the mob dropped to his knees and aimed his revolver at him. He looked—but did not understand or even recognize the danger—down the barrel of the gun with no sense of fear.

Above him the shutters opened; in the window there stood—he glimpsed only for a second like a vision—the figure of Rivka. She seemed to look down on him calmly, without moving. The sudden blast of the shot grazing him robbed him momentarily of consciousness, and he saw, as if through a haze, the figure in the window silently collapse.

Then he was carried from the melee by Kujaroff's soldiers. Kujaroff had intervened just in time to avoid the annoying consequences that killing a foreign subject could have had.—

While this was happening in the Jewish ghetto, the Governor's carriage with its attendants was drawn slowly through the main street. The Governor himself was sitting on the front seat, while Pastor Bode's maid in the Spreewald dress and little Bertha sat on the back seat, looking with astonishment at the excited crowd pressing both sides of the coach and cheering them.

And while the news spread throughout the city that the Governor had single-handedly snatched the child about to be killed from the murderers, the Governor stood before the stunned Pastor and his wife and said with a gracious smile: "Your child is quite charming. I had the greatest pleasure in the few hours she was my guest and I could extend to her my hospitality."

TWELVE

The Grand Festival Week

I

Tromsø, August 3, 1903.

Dear Heinz!

Our postcards will have convinced you that even up here nature is generally quite pretty and clean but definitely feels kitschy. We assiduously finish our meals and participate in the daily activities scheduled by Hapag, having expressed the required enthusiasm when meeting the HMS *Hohenzollern* the day before yesterday, and last night as we arrived we fell under the spell of the obligation of continental pleasures. Joseph has started—as I say, sighing hard but with the long-standing sense of duty of the Prussian nobility—the customary night journey under the proven guidance of Count Brussow. I accompanied him a few stations along the way (the version for the more mature youth). After my lord and master convinced himself by thorough local studies that lasted until morning that there is no significant difference for the gentleman traveler between Cairo, Budapest, or Tromsø, he is now recovering from the glorious excursion, and I am using this rare moment of leisure to write a properly addressed letter for fraternal greetings.

Not that I promise myself all too much from this—it isn't and it won't be any outpouring of my heart. There's nothing to pour out there, or I would have to go at it with a scratch brush or a crowbar, which is better left undone. But perhaps another time! You never know! It looks as if an oral report is probably forever out of the question, so I must rely on the efficacy of a written channel, even if such apparently is never used. You of course have had no need of such a channel since you found your confessional box.—Calm down! Martha has not violated the seal of confession. But I have definitely noticed that she is the only one who knows what really happened to you on your mysterious Easter trip and changed you first into a great moorhen and then by way of the sanatorium to something rough around the edges of the first order (without being convincing). Of the hypotheses that were suggested around the family table in your absence there were quite a few, but not among them was one that explained where you were until your de-layed arrival in Petersburg. Mama's outrage about your life of pleasure in Peters-burg and its corrupting influence seems to me to only touch the surface; thinking back to your famous birthday surprise, Papa thought it might be a gentle case of religious insanity; he was already speaking of having the half-Asiatic cousin deported as the bacillus carrier. Now I don't believe in the kind of religious ec-stasy that runs riot in nightclubs. I would sooner believe in lo-oo-ve, which by itself never suffices for happiness—also, who knows what Slavic beauty on the Neva mourns you—if the choice of a blond mother confessor weren't perplexing! Or is there yet another secret concealed perhaps behind the confession? That is fine with me—more than that! And that way Joseph would have, completely un-earned, a peasant sister-in-law from genuine Aryan nobility!

Isn't it too stupid that I am now giving the impression that I want to meddle in your secrets, since I even aspire to keep secrets from myself and not only from you and my husband—who would richly amuse himself about these analyses of the soul that we are so fond of and would certainly find here new grounds for amazement. That Joseph admires me is certainly no secret. But what he admires about me and the manner in which he courts me are both so grotesque that I often don't know if I should laugh or be angry. So usually I do both. What these people notice and what impresses them—what these people have been told!—and what doesn't matter to them and what they do not understand is a study in itself.

I half feel I am being watched in a panopticon or like a wild Hagenbeck animal for a zoo, a half-civilized person among fire eaters.—Do you know this feeling? I imagine you must have felt something like that on your sentimental journey into the eastern realms of Berlin, of which I know more from Martha than I do from you. Apropos—you have dug up the most completely fabulous character of a cigarette man. Isn't he the same as the creator of the brand Klatzéki, which suddenly became so popular? Brussow swears by this brand and says this is the only Papyrosse suitable for a civilized person—people say Papyrosse now! He is proud to have discovered them and introduced them to his club and tells of miracles about the mysterious importer, who he thought was a disguised Magyar nobleman because of his accent and appearance, whose services by the way he is inclined to consider much better by far than the Drakes.—If it makes him happy! Thackeray would have loved him.

Among other things we found a letter from my dear sister-in-law Leah. Os-termann has prospects for a place. A provisional position for now is budding at a small Lutheran church in Russia in a town that, by the way, has a large Jew-ish population. His predecessor had a problem on that account; there was a pogrom there, and either the good man caused it or was somehow involved—in any case, he suffered a nervous breakdown, wanted to leave no matter what, and was searching desperately for a successor. The situation isn't entirely clear to me despite Leah's comprehensive account. She certainly managed in her telling to use the word "Jew" as often as possible.—She graciously added that Ostermann would absolutely not be attracted to such byways but would strictly limit himself to his official duties. He has my blessing.

Our parents wrote from Karlsbad; I think Mama's illness has an atavistic cause. According to the array of guests, there seems to be a causal connection between ritual diet and gallstones. Or is the sudden change in diet after two thousand years supposed to have an ill effect?

You happy man, you don't need to undertake either a diet cure or a honeymoon—at least not this time—I wish you much joy on your Swiss journey. That you want to spend the week beforehand at the Grand Festival Week in Baden-Baden is smart. Ice Wind will probably be in the races there, Joseph says, to which I want to contribute something in this respect.—Brussow swears by Graditz; there's lots of talk about Faust. I am composed about how it comes out, give you full powers, however, to risk a blue one for me on the most blatant outsider, or let's say fifty marks. If chance decrees, I shall stand before the experts and earn new laurels. If it comes to nothing, it remains just between us.

So, take care—life is kitsch! Say hello to Martha!

Your Elsa.

II

Martha Mertens slowly and carefully read the letter to the end while Heinz smoked a cigarette on the steps of the sleeping coach, watching from above.— They had met at the Anhalter Railway Station a half hour before the train left—at Martha's request. She had wanted to see Elsa's letter, which Heinz had mentioned to her when he telephoned to say good-bye.

"Are you finished?" Heinz said as Martha was irresolutely thumbing through the letter, apparently confused. "Then let's walk up and down a little bit."

Silently they walked along the platform back toward the gate barrier.

"Don't you have anything to say?" said Heinz carelessly.

"I actually have a lot to discuss with you," Martha said softly, her head bent down as she played nervously with her umbrella. "But the worst thing is just that no one can talk with you anymore.—After your journey you at least gave me a complete account—but since then you have moved further and further away."

"Oh, rubbish!" Heinz threw his cigarette away and took a new one from a small wooden box he had brought back from Petersburg as something typically Russian. "You've persuaded yourself that's true."

"You know I'm right.—You used to always say that I was the only person you could seriously discuss things with. Elsa still thinks even now that you've confessed to me—"

"Elsa thinks more than that.—She thinks—God forbid—it would be so nice!—God forbid—"

"It shouldn't be!—Heinz—what's the matter with you?"

"Absolutely nothing! Nothing's the matter with me!—Elsa is right insofar as you are the only one who knows my Borytshev adventure, and it is nice of you, Martha, that you didn't laugh at me."

"Laugh at you!—Heinz!"

They were standing now at the barrier and were watching the passengers pressing through the platform barrier gate.

"Ah well—I even laugh myself sometimes and am properly ashamed of myself. Such kitsch as I've experienced is outrageous! Elsa is entirely right. Nature and life are terribly like a garden bower—and I am too. Even the whole idea of going to Borytshev—I should have known myself better. Naturally, I am like a boarding school gosling entrapped by a few sentimental songs, a half-darkened room full of atmosphere, a pair of gypsy eyes and accessories—"

"Heinz! Please—don't talk like that!—You can't seriously make fun of yourself for having once found yourself."

"In this case, I won't argue. But after this experiment, I've lost the desire to get to know me. I have almost decided to break off the connection with this traveling companion. One way or another! I don't know where my real self is hiding. Am I the person who knew myself at Easter this year, or am I the person who suddenly appeared there?"

"In other words, are you a German or a Jew?"

"Clumsily said, but you could put it like that!—"

"You are neither one nor the other, Heinz!"

"So what am I, then?—Am I even truly a person?—You can't be just a man—as long as others see differences.—It's probably best if you just mindlessly doze along, which I cannot do anymore and which I am trying to do again."

"Is that conceivable?"

"In that case, there's just one alternative—generally to not give a damn—just enjoy life—just enjoy life—think only of oneself, only of the moment—brazenly and with deliberate icy egoism.—I can still do that and—it's not right to try to stop me."

They slowly walked back. Martha seemed concerned but was silent a long time.

"You've never talked of your experience again," she said after a while more brightly. "Did you ever find out what happened to Rivka?"

"I know nothing and do not want to know anything!" Heinz said roughly. "I saw her sink—" He choked a moment. "Perhaps I only imagined it. I was probably feverish. A half hour later I was sitting in the train, and I have heard nothing more since. From the newspaper I know that the pogrom lasted three days, and there were many dead and wounded. Enough!"

"With the girl's brother here you could have—"

"But, Martha—what for? Why? I couldn't have helped her, and since in the meantime people here must have seen me as one of the apostates too, I would have only conjured up more pain.—The episode is closed and over without a trace."

"Definitely not without a trace!—You've become someone else. But I now believe you will yet find yourself."

"Possibly! But I'm not looking."

"You really have become rough around the edges, as Elsa writes," Martha exclaimed angrily. "And the nicest thing in all this is that you think you can lose yourself in the very moment when you seem to have finally come to yourself.—Let me finish! Now I want to confess for once!—We have always gotten along well, and I was immeasurably proud when you spoke seriously with me. I was indeed the only one, you said!—and still there's something strange in this. When you suddenly got the impulse for—let's call it your 'Jewish period'—it seemed to me that changed. It seemed to me that the outer shell would crumble now—you would become now a freer, more natural person—like all normal people. You would, I thought, recognize your own worth, finally taking your proper place. That is, find your true home here as a German—"

"And to do that, you are saying, I had to first become a Jew?"

"In a sense, yes!—The first thing is to find oneself, one's own nature, one's worth. Then one can bring something to the community—take one's place—feel truly equal."

"Well—possibly! But for that it appears to be a bit too late, thanks to paternal precautions. The way is blocked.—I don't belong with the people in Borytshev— Moische Schlenker was completely right when he showed me the door—and I don't belong—I don't belong anywhere. Enough! Enough! Enough!—It's a matter of killing time and eternity as pleasantly as possible.—Should I bet something for you too in Iffezheim?"

Martha shook her head, displeased.

"I am not giving up on you yet.—When are you going to be in Baden-Baden?"

"Tomorrow around midday. The sleeping coach is uncoupled in Frankfurt early in the morning. I'll be lucky to get a place in another car in time. The train is remarkably full."

They noticed just then what a strange crowd had filled the train.

"They don't all want to go to the races in Baden-Baden," Heinz said, puzzled, and stared at a group of old Russian Jews walking along next to the train, carrying heavy suitcases, and looking for empty seats.—In front of a third-class car a large group of young people had gathered; they were talking animatedly with others leaning out the window. Everyone was unmistakably Jewish. Many wore the Zionist insignia—Heinz recognized it from the meeting.

"Has the spirit of sport suddenly fallen on Judah?" he asked again.

Now someone in the group of young Jews noticed the old people with their suitcases, and some students, identifiable by their bands of fraternity colors, hurried over to carry the suitcases and accompany the confused men, who were helplessly looking around in the noisy crowd.

Heinz suddenly started and quickly pulled Martha away. He had recognized Yossel and Chana in one of the windows. They were outwardly somewhat changed, Europeanized. Yossel had cut his beard short and wore a dark suit; Chana wore a small waterproof hat and raincoat. They were talking in a lively fashion with a gentleman standing on the platform who wore a striking plaid coat and a tall top hat. They didn't see Heinz.—

"Where are all these people going?" asked Heinz of a young man who was carrying a large bundle of papers in yellow sleeves—Heinz assumed they were a sports newspaper—that were literally being torn from his hands by the passengers. "But surely not to the Festival Week?"

The young man, who also wore the Zionist insignia, looked up, surprised.

"The Festival Week?" He looked at Heinz without comprehension; then he seemed to understand and smiled confidentially. "Sure, for the grand week in Basel—for the Zionist Congress!"

III

The train arrived. Heinz, who had walked with Martha to the end again, swung himself into one of the last cars and now, standing at the window, watched the crowds lingering on the platform. Through the confused sounds on the station platform suddenly a lusty chorus could be heard; the singers glided past, and Heinz glimpsed for a moment the almost sacred expressions of the young Jews as they sang their hymns while standing bunched tightly together on the platform. The melody rose to a climax and ended with resounding cheers, the echoes awakening some sort of vague memories in Heinz. He almost forgot to wave good-bye to Martha, who was already disappearing into the crowd; then the chorus broke into groups to leave—the noise and the singing suddenly broke off, and the train chugged through the evening quiet between the silhouettes of chimneys and factories slowly slipping past into the darkening landscape.—

To reach his sleeping car, Heinz had to walk almost the whole length of the train, passing through the third-class car. He could only proceed very slowly, because the corridor was blocked by suitcases and packages, and many of the passengers were busy sorting their things or were milling about in excitement.—He was able to scrutinize the unique group of travelers.

The Zionists had quickly found each other and filled almost two cars. The few non-Zionist passengers who happened to find themselves there looked on in bewilderment, wondering how people from all possible regions and countries, apparently totally unknown to each other—different languages, clothing, educational background, and social standing—could become friends with each other in a few minutes.—Almost all of them were carrying as their emblem the yellow newspaper, *Die Welt*, and the young people even stuck a few copies of the newspaper into the window frames to show anyone looking in who they were. A linguistics scholar would have rejoiced to see how languages and dialects of every sort mingled and how these people understood the sense of what was said in the foreign language with astonishing flair and picking up the meaning from subtle and weak similarities.

Heinz hesitated for a few minutes outside a compartment where Danish was being spoken. A young couple were trying to make themselves understood by some young people from the East, who were competing to figure out a halfway familiar crumb. The young woman was laughing, and those listening, glowing with effort as they hung on her every word, offered a charming picture.—In several compartments old Russian Jews were assisted to their seat by their young helpers. The students were putting away their luggage, while the old people observed with some mistrust and disapproval the fashionable clothing and especially the blue, white, and yellow fraternity banners.—Heinz skulked rapidly past the compartment where Chana and Yossel were sitting in hot debate with other young people. In the next compartment on the little drop-down window table a complete miniature portable household was being set up—out of a wooden box that stood open on one of the seats came table settings, cutlery, and napkins, and Heinz recalled having seen on his Russian journey how thoroughly the passengers were accustomed to equip themselves for the long stretches where no other provisions were available. Pillows and blankets were visible everywhere, and Heinz could see that people had made themselves quite at home. He was addressed several times as he made his way along, for some of the passengers going to Basel just could not wait to get to know their new like-minded colleagues from foreign lands. In particular, an older man with a full muttonchop beard wouldn't let him loose; with no introduction he began to tell how he had been on the train for twenty-eight days to travel to the congress.—Heinz hastily pressed onward, breathing a sigh of relief when he found his sleeping compartment.—

In the Zionist cars it was a long time before silence fell, and the few Aryans who happened to find themselves there would have certainly expressed their anger forcefully over the loud goings-on if one and all hadn't been so interested in and astonished by this unusual company. Jews who weren't trying to hide that they were Jewish but who talked gaily and in a carefree manner about Jewish matters—the Germans had never seen that in Germany before.—

Yossel and Chana sat with friends—with Hamburger, Kaiser, and other Berlin students.—

"Terribly nice of Klatzke to bring us such a large supply of cigarettes at the station," Hamburger said, pulling up the window. "He looks funny enough in his top hat. Do you want to have a Klatzéki, Kaiser?"

"Thanks. He is only getting us used to smoking so that later he will have customers.—He would have really liked to come along but said that first he has to be a rich man."

"That will be soon. His cigarette business is booming. The top hat is paying off."

"He lives on bread and cheese," Chana said. "But he dresses as elegantly as only he can. I'm happy he's now found a decent trade."

"He's so clever," Hamburger laughed, "that he knows that honesty is the best swindle. The Klatzéki is impeccable!—Any means of getting rich is fine with him, even the most decent and respectable."

"Basically, he's a decent man," Yossel said nervously. "He was trapped into this miserable letter-writing nonsense and didn't know how it happened. He left as soon as possible and started an honest business."

"So it goes with most Jews in the world," Chana exclaimed. "They are driven to things that don't suit them and aren't worthy of them, and they ardently yearn to escape."

"The whole movement of the Jewish renaissance comes from that," Kaiser interrupted.

"Klatzke at least becomes more decent and respectable the more he earns."

"Unfortunately, one sees just the opposite with so many people. Will Klatzke still count as a pillar of assimilated Judaism as well as a Berlin personage and pillar of Germanhood against the undesirable immigration of Russian Jews?"

"If he isn't deported first as a burdensome foreigner like us," Chana said with a smile. "For whom were we a burden? Who could be interested in preventing us from studying here?"

"It's not a real deportation," Hamburger said. "You just got a notice that you would be deported if you didn't leave voluntarily."

"That's a nice comfort!"

"We don't need comfort," Yossel said. "We can also study in Berne, or else we wouldn't have ever taken the opportunity to go to the congress and see for ourselves if a new Jewish way of life there can really become true. But that we are a burden to German Jews I know from my first day in Berlin, ever since my visit to Dr. Magnus. You were a witness, Kaiser, and if you hadn't been so nice to me, then I would've left with a very bitter taste in my mouth. You helped me a lot, and you were there at the right time."

"You helped me more than I helped you, and you were really there at the right time for me. I was in the middle of a crisis, and sadly I didn't find what I was seeking at the Rabbi's either. I was at least as disappointed as you were!—Then I learned gradually through you that Judaism is really based on something other than scholarly hypotheses, ingenious and opportunistic programs, or fossilized forms without living content. I can't say that this crisis is over. But I suspect that this trip to the congress will resolve things for me. I've gotten the courage to be Jewish again. People like Magnus can make you crazy."

"German Jews like Magnus are fighting the past as well as the future," Hamburger said. "The Russian Jew embodies his past, the baptized Jew his future. Without influx from the East there would be no more German Judaism, because so many leave. The transition happens in just a few generations; Eastern Jew, Orthodox, Conservative, Moderate, Liberal, Reform, baptized—these are the markers on the path. Some stations are skipped every time. It is like a large funnel, where so much is poured in that the level remains the same. Whether the process can be stopped strikes me as doubtful. The congress will perhaps help even someone like me make a decision.—I doubt if we German Jews will be called on to contribute there. I fear we are already too distant from natural feelings. We are no longer unbiased, which is the precondition of all creative activity."

"And I believe on the contrary that in Western Europe there are vast Jewish possibilities," Chana exclaimed. "It's all nothing more than a terrible misunderstanding. Jews don't know one another and don't know themselves. That was my first thought when I heard for the first time the strange German views that time on the Dragonerstrasse and at the same time about the schnorrer letter industry. The schnorrer doesn't represent the Eastern Jew, and Dr. Magnus doesn't represent the Western Jew. Above all, a new generation is growing up. Both sorts were just the necessary consequence of the odd position of Jews, exactly the same as the lives of Germersheim and Kluck.—But Dr. Herzl, who now is the one driving this new movement, is completely and totally a West European. He knew nothing of Jews until the suffering of his people screamed out to him. Only because he stood on the outside was he able to find the way to freedom. He himself wasn't involved in the turmoil that blocks the air and the view; but he found his way to his brothers."

"What about Moses or Nehemiah?" Yossel exclaimed, astonished. "Everything is repeated!"

"I think," Chana concluded, "that a great task has been given just to the German Jews!—"

"Excuse me," an older man who had been standing in the door of the compartment for a few minutes said. "You are going to the congress too!—I've been on the train for twenty-eight days now. I come from Manchuria."

And he told them how a year ago the news came for the first time with a notice in the newspaper in his country that a Viennese writer had undertaken to bring the Jews back to Palestine. So he asked around, wrote many letters, and finally heard of this congress. Now he had set out on this journey.—He was in Europe for the first time and completely dazed by the discovery that he met people everywhere who thought exactly as he did about so many things, above all, their hopes and wishes.

"Just think!" he said. "Twenty-eight days on the train! Jews everywhere who want to go to Zion. 'The exiles shall be gathered from all the nations of the world!' —Twenty-eight days!"

He was very proud of his long journey and went from compartment to compartment to harvest surprise and recognition.—Gradually even the cars filled with Zionists became hushed; people tried to sleep so they would arrive in Basel somewhat refreshed for the busy days ahead.—Only in one compartment, filled with cigarette smoke, where the Russian students sat, the heated debate did not die down for a long time. In the early morning twilight as they passed through the lovely Thuringia countryside, the last conversations fell silent without having resolved the question of how one would organize the educational system in a Jewish commonwealth.—

There were trains like this train traveling that night from every direction to the city where the congress was, which was gathering in from every country Jews who had set out filled with the same hopes and desires to see with their own eyes and to hear with their own ears if the call reaching them really was the call that generation after generation had been awaiting for two thousand years.

IV

In Frankfurt, Heinz had found a comfortable seat by the window because the second-class car was relatively empty compared with the third-class car, and he breakfasted by the half-open window to let the fresh morning air blow in. To avoid meeting Chana and Yossel he had tea brought to him in his compartment instead of going to the dining car. He had only one traveling companion, an elderly gentleman whose healthy, tanned face contrasted oddly with his completely white hair.—Both travelers were studying the Frankfurt morning papers; Heinz had also secured a few sports papers.

A gentleman went past in the corridor, started, came back, peered in, scuttled uncertainly back and forth, and then all of a sudden shot toward Heinz, shaking his hand with joy.

"Sorry. I didn't recognize you right away. How are you?"

Heinz searched his memory in vain. The other man laughed.

"You don't recognize me? Don't bother. You are often on the Auguststrasse— you know now—I recognized you right away! Good memory!"

"I believe we haven't introduced ourselves," Heinz said cautiously. He gradually began to remember.

"Introduced? Who's talking about introductions? There wasn't any opportunity at the time. I'm Pinkus—Doctor Pinkus—chemical laboratory.—You came just at the right time then. Do you remember? At that time I had—" He bent down close to Heinz and whispered in his ear, "Yahrzeit, and you were the minyan man."

"I remember," Heinz said coldly and reached for his newspaper.

"I'm delighted that I met you!" Pinkus exclaimed, then leaped up to close the door. "There's a terrible draft in here!" He looked anxiously at the open window and squinted at the elderly gentleman, who didn't move. Pinkus shrugged his shoulders and sat down again next to Heinz. "It is a pleasure to meet a civilized person. The passengers on the train—terrible. How can one relax? My assistant already annoys me enough—you saw him that time—he's been infected too. Totally meshuga!"

The last word he whispered again to Heinz, who shrank back into his corner, annoyed.—The elderly gentleman seemed to be amused by something in his newspaper.

"I'm traveling to Darmstadt—before I go to Switzerland—the League of Teetotalers—committee meeting—I'm on the committee! We have to fight this national vice. Whoever loves his people must help. It is the fight for the strength of the Germanic peoples—the future of the race depends on this."

Now he was speaking exceedingly loudly and looked defiantly at the stranger, who was smiling and apparently continuing to read on undisturbed.

"An anti-Semite!" he whispered to Heinz, who had to make an effort not to appear impolite.

"The health of our German folk is threatened!" Pinkus exclaimed angrily as if he had been contradicted, and he turned up his collar. "It's god-almighty drafty!—Alcohol destroys our nervous system, our inner strength.—It's first and foremost a patriotic duty to fight this!"

He took a breath. Then he bent down close to Heinz and whispered: "The whole train is full of Russian Jews!"

"You can go ahead and speak up. I too am a Jew!" the elderly gentleman said with a quiet smile.

Pinkus stared at him for a few seconds; then he jumped up to close the window with one movement.

"It's abominably drafty!—So—there!"

He fell back on the seat.

"So you're a Jew, too!—You say that yourself! Is that not a scandal?—One is embarrassed to walk through the train—nothing but Polacks! Everyone a Zionist! And they talk loudly about Jewish things! You don't need to go around advertising to the whole world you're a Jew!"

He looked around angrily. No one answered. So he continued by himself: "Take my assistant, for example. His name is Cohn." He looked around to see if the door was securely closed. "Cohn—Hans Cohn. Actually, I usually hire only Christian assistants, but I had to throw out my earlier assistants, and Cohn is a capable, first-rate man. But crazy! What does he think of? Suddenly he says his name is Hans Jacob Cohn! Jacob! As if Cohn weren't enough! Hans Jacob Cohn! Do you have to advertise it to the world?"

"Even without the ominous 'Jacob,' wouldn't someone not become suspicious about a pure Aryan hiding behind the Cohn?" the elderly gentleman asked politely.

"That's just what I'm saying!" Pinkus screeched. "So why? But it's just a disaster otherwise—my name is Pinkus, after all. This is the name I happen to have, and I use it, but if I'm not crazy, I don't flaunt it. My name is Isidor—my sign says J.—just J. Pinkus. It shows that I explicitly value that. People should notice that he's an Israelite, and that's what he wants to be, that he's still proud of that. If I sign my work with a modest J. Pinkus, and if the work is particularly good, then people will forgive my name in the end."

"Are you Pinkus the toxicologist?" the elderly gentleman said with interest and laid aside his newspaper.

"Yes—that's me. You've heard of me?" Pinkus said and looked suspiciously at the stranger.

"Of course. You've recently been mentioned frequently in the press. They wrote that you—"

"Complete slander! Vile, shameless lies!" Pinkus shrieked with a burst of fury, jumping up.

"Slander? Lies?" the elderly gentleman asked, completely baffled and amused. "We're probably talking of different things. I read the chemistry papers—I take interest in these sorts of things—your research has far-reaching significance. The author characterized your work as a shining testament to true German thoroughness and German diligence. He even went so far as to speak, if I recall correctly, of a new page of glory in the history of German science. If *you* call that slander, you are most demanding."

"That's something else, of course," Pinkus said, reassured, and he sat down as he stroked his beard, pleased with the flattery. "Yes—you see what I was saying before—if one accomplishes something, people look past your name: I was thinking of something else! That miserable rogue, Röder, my former assistant, whom I had to let go, has saddled me with a stupid lawsuit, and an anti-Semitic rag has seized on it—twisted and distorted everything and now berates me as a Jewish exploiter who squeezes innocent young German scholars with Jewish duplicity—it makes you sick!"

He punched the seat with fury.

"That's quite a splendid example," the elderly gentleman said with a chuckle, "of how the Jewish account is balanced by society. The positive things you accomplish are credited to the German-Germanic side of the ledger; if you should regrettably transgress, that is chalked up to the Jewish side. So it's certainly no wonder that the Jewish side closes out with a debit balance!"

"That may well be the case!" Pinkus murmured. "But there's just nothing to be done."

"Isn't that the fault of Jews who want to conceal their Jewishness as much as possible? Isn't it completely understandable that Jews are now trying to work even in their own companies and claim their share of cultural advancement?"

"What?—How?—That's quite—that's culturally hostile—that's reactionary—that's . . . Are we supposed to return to the ghetto?"

"On the contrary; we should first leave the ghetto! The ghetto is still everywhere. Only sometimes they close an eye if a Jew leaves it in the wrong dress, if he only pays enough in bribes, and then only as long as he excels at particularly good behavior and modest conduct. Otherwise his coat is ripped off, and he is chased away in disgrace and humiliated."

"Quite! Nicely said!—and what do you think about emancipation from the ghetto? Should we strike?"

Pinkus looked directly at the stranger with fury and scorn.

"A general strike by Jews, if it were possible, wouldn't be a bad idea—just a crime against culture. If all Jews suddenly wouldn't cooperate, people on the whole would perhaps see how great a factor Jews are culturally. But it's not intended that way. We should really begin to integrate. Very nice that you fight against the plague of alcohol and want to save threatened Germanhood. How would it be if we wanted to dedicate a part of our efforts to threatened Judaism? The Jewish people, I believe, still has something to say to humankind—every people has its mission, like every individual. If the Jews now, instead of always trying to deny and suppress what they are, were to open and develop their special values for all humankind—if Jews—"

"Pssst!" Pinkus hissed so sharply that the stranger broke off, surprised, and Heinz looked up, almost frightened. The waiter from the dining car entered to clear away the tea things. The elderly gentleman smiled and relit his cigar, which had gone out while he had been speaking.

"You were saying—?" Dr. Pinkus asked after the waiter had gone, closing the door behind him.

"Nothing!" the gentleman said, picking up his newspaper. "I was finished."

Pinkus looked at both gentlemen nervously.

"It's certainly not necessary that the waiter—" He attacked Heinz: "You aren't saying anything?—"

"I'm only a minyan man," Heinz said dismissively.

Pinkus looked at him suspiciously. Then he tugged out his watch and sprang up.

"Darmstadt next!—I have to get my things—. Good day!"

He turned once more in the corridor, came in again, closing the door behind him, and spoke venomously to the stranger, who barely looked up from his newspaper: "What you said there—I won't become upset—I'm traveling for plea-sure—but that is worse than Ahlwardt! You are a Jewish anti-Semite! Now you know!"

With that he finally disappeared.

V

The elderly gentleman looked up directly at Heinz. Then they both burst out laughing. Heinz was annoyed but couldn't help his laughter.

"You are right," the elderly gentleman said, folding his newspaper and becoming serious. "We really shouldn't laugh, but it is embarrassing. I wouldn't have allowed myself to be pulled into the conversation if it hadn't turned out that this gentleman is a scholar who really has accomplished something worthwhile in his field and if I hadn't been interested in his work for a long time. And such a man behaves in such a foolish fashion! Unfortunately, he's not the only one. One finds this mixture of tactless effrontery and cringing humility all too often. He screams into every ear that his mission is to be the savior of the Germanic cul-ture; but when he hears the word 'Jew' he trembles because a servant might over-hear!—and such a person wonders about anti-Semitism! Whoever denies and disparages who and what he is cannot expect that others will respect him. Ugh!!"

Heinz blushed and said, "It's not always very easy to judge these things im-partially!"

"You've hit the nail on the head, and everything follows from that!—Impar-tiality! That's just it! These people lack any impartiality! Jews who behave natu-rally and unforced are scarcely to be found in Germany. See, the Jews in Russia maybe—were you ever over there?"

Heinz cautiously said yes.

"Well, then, you will have noticed the difference yourself! The Jews in their prayer rooms and study houses and everywhere on the street and at home, they live their own lives like natural people. And here—divine service and school, salon furnishings and a plaque hung out for all to see bearing a business name, manner of speaking and clothing, everything indeed is done only with an eye to its effect on others.—Only in the East can one see unvarnished Judaism."

"That may be right," Heinz said. "But isn't that so because there the Jew is uni-laterally closed off from the surrounding world—or is shut off from it? That just cannot be ideal. If in this quiet world something really of value has come about—"

"If?—If?—Indeed, you don't know what is behind this Chinese wall, so to speak? A vast mass of culture and intellect, of energy and abundance of life! If the world only had the slightest notion of what hidden treasures lie there!"

"That's just what strikes me as so alarming! What kind of value for human-kind do hidden treasures have in the long run? Is it not more a crime than a virtue to maintain this isolation?"

"You're forgetting first of all that this isolation is not voluntary!"

"Admittedly! But that impartiality and genuineness of self that we discussed are, after all, so it seems, the downside of isolation—and perhaps paid for with too high a price. Doesn't everyone deserve recognition who makes his energies available to the world?"

"But not the way this Doctor Pinkus does it?—Of course, everybody has the obligation to put his capabilities at the service of the world, and it isn't only a crime, but, what is worse, it is Europe's stupidity to exclude the Jewish masses from working in society. But if someone, such as that splendid example of a chemist, conceals what he really is, he just cannot produce in accordance with his abilities and in the spirit of his best self."

"Do you really believe," Heinz said with a smile, "that his toxicological studies would have resulted in even more significant conclusions had he written his full name?"

Both men laughed heartily.

"I didn't mean it like that," the elderly man said lightly. "The buffoonery of playing hide-and-seek is another story. Pinkus accomplishes good things, and certainly what has been created by Western Jews as cultural values is phenomenal. But this intellectual influx amounts to nothing, because individual Jews try to disappear without a trace if possible into their surroundings. Only a few single drops escape the vast reservoir of Jewish vitality. The individual case has had a sensational effect now and then. That was the case with my friend Schapiro. At forty he emigrated from Russia to the West, Talmudically trained but illiterate, so to speak, in European knowledge. Everybody advised him against still studying at that age. Ten years later he was a professor of mathematics in Heidelberg!—These sorts of cases shine a spotlight! People note what is slumbering over there!"

"Yes, but isn't it the fault of the Jews that they preserve this hermetically sealed insularity?"

"Just wait!—Where the external ghetto walls have fallen, as in Germany, what happened was this: instead of using the freedom to now integrate their specifically Jewish culture into the greater intellectual assets of the community, the Jews practiced a centrifugal policy—trying to disrobe their essence and denying their uniqueness. So German Jews are slowly but surely assimilated, and worthy values disappear with them. The larger world just made a mistake back then by demanding this auctioning off of their selves as the price for certain rights granted on paper that were in fact very limited instead of getting for themselves massive cultural assistance that could ensure a Judaism that addressed their uniqueness. Only that influx seeping in from the East stems the collapse of everything Jewish. If the same process would someday start in the East, the concept of 'Jew' would soon disappear from the world—assuming that the Jews there, having learned from the events in the West, would expend enough energy to preserve their way of life."

"Then I come back again to my question: What is the purpose of this reservoir of vitality in the East? Is it not energy hoarded for naught?—and further: Didn't this life and hairsplitting behind walls necessarily lead to sterility? Have the Jews even developed since they began abiding in their ghetto?"

"One thing after the other! A development? In a certain sense, no. But as compensation their ability to develop has increased enormously.—You are amazed? Now pay attention!—History halted after the state collapsed. With the Jews scattered throughout the world, their fall as a nation would have been assured if they had not taken heroic measures, unheard of in world history. But it was foreseeable that the scattered parts would adapt everywhere to the history of their various homes and would disappear without a trace had they simply refused *any* history. They chose to remain at the stage where their natural national development was cut off through catastrophe."

"Meaning—?"

"—Meaning that they nullified the fact that their nation collapsed just as they survived everything else in the world's history. Ever since, they have lived a fiction, in a dream; they behave as if their nation still exists, and they are living in Palestine. They live their life according to the Palestinian calendar, and they now go to their harvest booths during Sukkos. because that was the law in their ancient land, no matter if it's raining or freezing there. In their schools and study houses they discuss questions that would only relate to living in Jordan—they hold fast to ancient customs no matter how pointless they are here today, and they lead exactly the same life in the most excruciatingly same way and for the same reasons as their parents and forebears back to the time of Titus!"

"And then there's really no fossilization?"

"Only where the Jews are torn from their Jewish world, where they are keeping the forms without historical understanding—without knowing that the forms are bridges from generation to generation! I concede that such externalizing can be found in Germany and is often strange and repugnant."

"But even in the East, it seems to me, there has to be as a matter of course something like intellectual incest."

"Don't you understand that engagement with spiritual problems of the same sort of intellectual nature over many generations has to promote the strengths in a particular way? The Jews have vast training behind them and are thereby capable, to an unbelievable degree, of the tasks that could be given to them as a people."

"I admit that such intellectual training—"

"Also training the body, you could say. The training includes eating and drinking."

"So, it could be that the special capabilities for development come from this. But do you believe that this development of strength that rests, as you yourself say, on a fiction can stand the test of reality? Can one still speak of the Jews today as a people, a community that has the capability to build a state?"

"But the Jews are—it sounds paradoxical, but it's not—the very people that has just brought the most unbelievable proof of its political gifts in this sense! In just these long centuries of diaspora!"

"I would indeed like to know!"

"You consider Germans, Englishmen, and Frenchmen to probably be politically talented because they have their national communities, territories, a constitution, laws and behind them a large force, a huge apparatus with barracks, prisons, state attorneys, and executioners to uphold them. That seems to me to prove little. But the Jews have preserved their law for centuries—and what a law, covering all circumstances in depth—without any force of compulsion, without an external power, only through moral suasion, through self-discipline, through the knowledge of the people!"

"Don't forget religion!"

"Call it what you will! The fact is that their instinct for national preservation, their sense of responsibility, their sense of community are amazingly developed and have been extensively and persuasively documented as with no other people in history. How many nations have collapsed, have disappeared without a trace when their states disintegrated? Even today Jews mourn on the day the Temple was destroyed, sitting on the floor, fasting, and lamenting just as in the days of Jeremiah. Three times a day they renew their hope for the resurrection of their national center in prayer and renew their vow to be faithful. They turn their faces toward Jerusalem when they pray and when they are buried.—Palestine and the Jewish state stand at the center of their thoughts, constitute the basis of all their intellectual efforts in school and in the house of prayer.—School! Right there you have another example! What an effort everywhere to introduce compulsory school attendance! There are no Jewish illiterates, and school is not compulsory. Every Jewish father sends his child to school, to cheder."

"Where he learns nothing but things he cannot use in life!"

"Not in this makeshift life, this as-if life—but probably in the true life after the return to the land of his forefathers. The people are schooled and prepared, at any moment, if they return to Palestine, to begin the development there where it was once broken off!—and then the nature of their schooling sharpens the intellect so that whoever has enjoyed such schooling can easily acquire the necessary tools at any time to fight for existence or to work in the open. You know yourself that Jews are fairly competent in dealing with what one calls life. For example, just take my friend the mathematician whom I mentioned to you earlier."

"Good! But why doesn't everyone follow such an example? Why not the people as a whole?"

"The people as a whole are only waiting for the moment when it can do just that! There's even a daily prayer: deliverance! When emancipation arrives someday—"

"Arrives?"

"I'm not talking about the so-called emancipation of the Jews—namely, of those Jews who have given up their Judaism—but of the emancipation of the Jewish people. If the Jewish people are considered the same as other people—"

"The Zionist dream!"

"The dream of the Jewish people for millennia, since the destruction of their nation! Sleeping Beauty's dream, if you like. When the exile is over, all life will begin exactly where it was broken off."

"So, yes, a state of sleeping—no life, no development!"

"But in this way you do comprehend that this is indeed the explanation of the miracle of the preservation of the Jewish people. Their national instinct has preserved the Jews even in the diaspora from developing in different directions from each other according to where they happen to be, losing their cohesion. The Jew from Łódz and the Jew from Chicago would intentionally let their life ossify in the old shared habits rather than become strangers to each other by assimilating into the current times or into their surroundings and take on a foreign life. Tomorrow—today they can take on the common task again."

"In this way the purpose of the peculiar ghetto culture would then be explained, but there's still no answer to my question: What use to humankind is there from this encapsulated and inaccessible culture as long as it continues to remain just as hermetically sealed?"

"Yes—that's just it! As long as it remains as is! That and that trickle through the locked keyhole, long since not so hermetically bolted shut, the culture of Europe has infinitely profited by much in the meantime—we are probably agreed on that. And through emancipation—the false one or the minor one, as I call it—that's been shown. But the advantage is in no proportion to the damage, because the danger is obvious that the great reservoir will become empty and the source of vitality will dry up. For that reason it's now the time that the great, true emancipation should arrive, that the Jewish people as such should have the opportunity to work just as all other people do."

"You believe in this opportunity?"

"I am sure of it coming to pass!—Then, when the curse of unemployment has been lifted from the Jewish people, when Jewish accomplishment is valued as Jewish accomplishment, when their original vitality is revealed—in other words, when a national Jewish homeland exists where the driving force of Jews can develop freely, then it will be seen that the quiet and tenacious work of centuries in the ghetto has not been in vain. Only then will the hidden treasures be recovered for humankind."

"So a Jewish state?"

"You can call it that, because the founder of the modern movement, Dr. Herzl, called it that. But the term 'state' is perhaps too ambiguous. It doesn't necessarily have to include isolation, envy of other people, militarism, and rape. Consider that in the ancient Jewish state the stranger was completely equal, that there was extensive social legislation, that in the Temple in Jerusalem sacrifices were made for all peoples. Rome destroyed Jerusalem, and the Roman spirit has ruled up until our day. I believe that the struggle was not completely decided at the time of Titus. The spirit of the ancient people of the Bible extends to our era!—"

He fell silent and stared out the window.

After a rather long silence, Heinz said, "It's odd! Now I am much younger than you are, and I cannot bring myself to believe in such a development.—Zionism might well be a lovely dream—I can see that—but can we ask of a people, can we demand of an individual that the agreeable present, the comfortable possibility of happiness, be sacrificed for a hope?"

"That the Jewish people has done that for so many generations is proof of its appeal!—and every weakness has been subject to temptation over the course of time. What has remained certain is that the strongest survived!"

Heinz was struck silent. The same idea that had occurred to him so often during the past year.

"Dr. Herzl didn't reveal anything new to me," the elderly gentleman said. "I come from a completely assimilated family. My father was one of the founders of the Berlin Reform Community at the beginning of the last century.—This sort of Judaism wasn't able to give me anything. I felt I was German, not only a German citizen but Germanic, I might say. I played a not insignificant role in politics. In the year '70 I enlisted as a volunteer; outside of Metz I discovered the Jew in me. That's a story in itself. Then came the anti-Semitism!—I withdrew from public life. I just couldn't sort out who I really was, what the word 'Jew' actually meant. I wasn't religious in the usual sense—I didn't even think in my dreams about anything like a Jewish nation. Well—I read a lot, traveled a lot, thought a lot—it didn't get me any further, but it didn't harm me either. Then I became acquainted with Professor Schapiro, whom I've mentioned, and then it came to me. I took a trip through Russia at his urging, stayed a long time in Vilnius and Kovno—I learned Yiddish and Hebrew. A new world opened up to me—I also now understand my old world for the first time. I noticed that there is indeed a spirit that floats above the utter chaos. And then came Herzl's Jewish state.—and then—"

He relit his cigar.

"I was in Palestine this past Easter."

He was silent for a while.

"You know," he continued, putting his fist on the little window table, "I am in my seventies and don't know how many years I have left. But I'm determined to emigrate to Palestine. I bought land—on the Sea of Galilee. I want to still see something of what it will grow to be.—Earlier I always wanted to be there when they dug out an ancient piece of art in Olympia or Herculaneum. But this is more!—What is shoveled from the debris of centuries is more! And now I'm traveling to Basel as I've traveled to every congress since the first one in '97. Even there what is old becomes alive again! Everything is still unfinished—lots of daydreaming and a lack of clarity—and only a few know what's needed. But it's a pleasure to see how this people scattered across the face of the earth is finding itself again and understands one another. It can even work with each other there—that is a pleasure! In my old age I once again feel totally full of life! I see a purpose for which I can work! That is happiness, young man! And I wish this happiness for all!—"

Again he was silent for a long time.

After a while the old man began again to speak of his trip to Palestine, of the modest settlements that enthusiastic Russian students had founded decades ago and now were beginning to bloom again after infinite effort and care after the first settlers had almost all collapsed—of the Pesach celebrations that he had participated in and that had been real folk festivals, but free of the nasty accompaniments that one usually associates with the word—of the hospitality of the Jewish farmers and of a thousand and one things associated with his journey.—The time passed quickly, and Heinz was sorry when the train pulled into Oos, where he had to transfer to the local to Baden-Baden.

"Perhaps I will see you in Basel," the elderly gentleman said. "The congress itself actually begins next week. This week it's only preliminary meetings!"

Heinz shook his head and said good-bye, thanking him cordially.—

He stood at a window shortly thereafter in the local train that would take him to Baden-Baden, looking over to the other track where the express train was just getting under way. The cars rolled by slowly, then faster, and from the third class a Hebrew song could be heard.—He watched the car where the yellow wrappers of *Die Welt* on the windows could still be recognized from afar.

To join in to build the land—to work with others in the future of the people and humankind—to have ideals—a life's purpose—to know where one belongs—to have a spiritual home, to be enthusiastic, young, like this elderly man who could still do that, who could participate in that!

What remained for him?—

He lowered himself into his corner. Mechanically, he reached for the newspaper lying next to him and read: "Will the Esterhazy stables be victorious this year, or shall we see the black-and-white colors of Graditz in front this time in Iffezheim? Will Ice Wind or will Faust reach the finish line as victors—that is the great question everyone is interested in. According to our information . . ."

NOTES AND GLOSSARY

Foreword by Joachim Schlör

p. xv *Yekke*: German Jews in Palestine in the 1930s were called Yekkes. Sammy Gronemann called his autobiography *The Memoirs of a Yekke* (1946). The word was a self-deprecating term among the Germans and a term of disdain among almost everyone else, most of whom were of Eastern European origin. The explanations given for the etymology of the word mirror the not-always-happy relationship between German Jews and Eastern European Jews. The word Yekke, according to one definition, refers to the German word for "jacket" (*Jacke*), which the German male insisted on wearing despite the heat and informality of dress in Palestine. According to another, less generous definition, Yekke is an acronym for the Hebrew phrase *Yehudi k'she Havan*, a slow-witted Jew. There are countless jokes about Yekkes as stubbornly holding on to their German *Bildungskultur* (the high culture of the bourgeoisie), which was seen as irrelevant to building a new Zionist homeland. An elderly German émigré in Israel offered a third, more poignant definition to the scholar Ruth Gray: "A Yekke is someone who lives in a past that never had a future." See "Danke Schön, Herr Doktor: German Jews in Palestine," *American Scholar* 58, no. 4 (Autumn 1989): 567–568, http://www.jstor.org/stable/41212384.

Chapter 1. Goethe in Borytshev

p. 1 Goethe in Borytshev: Sammy Gronemann expected his readers to be familiar with Karl Emil Franzos (1848–1904), whose popular short story "Schiller in Barnow" (1877) demonstrates the uplifting effect on an Ostjude from reading classics of German high culture (*Bildung*). Absorbing German culture was the escape route to modern civilization for many Jews from "Half-Asia," a term Franzos coined to describe Jews from Poland to the Black Sea. See Steven E. Aschheim, *Brothers and Strangers: The East European Jew in German and German Jewish Consciousness, 1800–1923* (Madison: University of Wisconsin Press, 1982).

p. 4   Poem by Goethe: A reference to Goethe's 1782 poem "Der Erlkönig," most famously set to music by Franz Schubert in 1815.

p. 8   Pasewalk: A town in Vorpommern (West Pomerania), a Baltic region, as well as a German administrative district.

p. 10   Jewish Missionary Society: The history of efforts to convert Jews to Christianity goes back centuries, but missionary societies with the sole purpose of converting Jews arose in Germany in the seventeenth century, fueled by the Pietism movement. What started out as a conversion success rate of about two conversions a year between 1600 and 1650 across all of Germany accelerated to more than two baptisms per year between 1700 and 1767 in Berlin alone. See Deborah Hertz, *How Jews Became Germans: The History of Conversion and Assimilation in Berlin* (New Haven, CT: Yale University Press, 2007). Missionary societies spread to England. In 1809 a baptized Jew named Joseph Frey, formerly Joseph Levi of Mayenstocheim, Germany, started the London Society for Promoting Christianity among the Jews. As exemplified in its holdings, the society took the tradition of Jewish thought seriously. The bookplate shown in figure 2 is in a copy of the first published Hasidic book, *Sefer Toldot Ya'akov* (The book of the generations of Jacob) by Ya'akov ben Eli'ezer ben Me'ir, a disciple of the founder of the Hasidic movement, the Baal Shem Tov (London: Be-vet Vilyam Tok, 530 [1769–1770]). In the same collection as in figure 2, the bookplate is also found in *Mashmi'a Yeshua* (Announcing salvation) on messianic prophecies by the Portuguese philosopher Isaac ben Judah Abravanel (1437–1508) (Ofibakh: Bi-defus Tsevi Hirsh Segal Shpits, 527 [1766 or 1767]); and in *Notitia Karaeorum* (Notes on the Karaites) by Mordecai ben Nisan (active seventeenth and eighteenth centuries) (Hamburg and Leipzig: Impensis Christiani Liebezeit, 1714). Frey set up industrial training and free schools for children of converts because he realized that Jews who accepted Jesus as the Messiah were cut off from their community. While the society reported with pride its successes to win Jews for Christianity in Great Britain, the society also reported that there were "difficulties and opposition" in Russian Poland, the area where the Lutheran pastor in the novel hopes to win Jewish souls; between 1859 and 1874, nearly fifty Jews, or about three per year, were baptized by a Lutheran pastor of the society in Kishinev, the site of a pogrom in 1903 that shocked Western observers. See *The History of the London Society for Promoting Christianity Amongst the Jews* by William Thomas Gidney (London: London Society for Promoting Christianity Amongst the Jews, 1908), 442.

p. 13–14   *Ceterum censeo*: "Further, I think." The full phrase, spoken by Cato the Elder in the Roman Senate to say that Carthage must be destroyed, is *Ceterum censeo Carthagenium esse delendam*. In the following paragraph, the Pastor changes the word for Carthage to the word for Jerusalem (*Hierosolymam*), teasing Dr. Strösser about his anti-Semitism by using a Latin phrase known to every German *Gymnasium* (high school) boy.

p. 16   Mrs. Heimberg or Mrs. Marlitt: Wilhelmine Heimberg (1848–1912, pseudonym of Bertha Behrens) and Eugenie Marlitt (1825–1887) wrote popular, best-selling novels.

Current critics consider the novels to be paradigmatic examples of *Trivialliteratur* (entertaining light fiction). After Marlitt died, Heimberg completed her unfinished work. See Katrin Kohl, "E. Marlitt's Bestselling Poetics," in *The German Bestseller in the Late Nineteenth Century*, edited by Charlotte Woodford and Benedict Schofeld (Rochester, NY: Camden House, 2012), 202.

p. 19   Petiscus: August Heinrich Petiscus (1780–1846) was the author of *Der Olymp oder Mythologie der Griechen und Römer* (Mount Olympus or myths of the Greeks and Romans). The book was intended for young adults and appeared in many editions from 1821 on. It was an esteemed school prize.

p. 20   Schnorrer: The verb *schnorren* is a German/Yiddish word meaning "to beg." In German, the word means to ask for small things without offering anything in return. In Yiddish, it means to ask with a sense of pride in one's profession as a beggar with real clients and regular rounds. The figure of the schnorrer is often a comic literary figure and a popular subject of jokes. Out of current fashion but once popular was the 1894 satirical novel, *The King of Schnorrers* by the British-born Israel Zangwill, set in late eighteenth-century London. Theodor Herzl referred to Ostjuden as an "army of schnorrers," reflecting Western Jewish discomfort at the stream of poverty-stricken Jewish immigrants to the West. Isaac Bashevis Singer referred to the word schnorrer in his banquet speech on the eve of winning the Nobel Prize for Literature in 1978 to illustrate the richness of Yiddish: in English the vocabulary to describe a poor man (*oreman*) is limited ("a poor man," "a pauper," "a beggar," "a panhandler"). "But in Yiddish," Singer continues, "you can say: 'an oreman,' 'an evyen' [an indigent person], 'a kapstn' [a pauper], 'a dalfn' [a poor man], 'a bettler' [a beggar], 'a shleper' [a tramp], 'a shnorer' [an extortionist]." See Singer's banquet speech, http://tinyurl.com/psm4bgn. To schnorr indicates that one has almost no status, but, as historian John Toland notes, one is more than a ditch digger. During Hitler's period of extreme poverty in Vienna, Hitler "tried his luck at begging. But he had neither the talent nor the gall for panhandling and became a client of a comrade at the Asyl [the Asylum for the Homeless] who made a living by selling addresses of those who were 'soft touches.' . . . [He] set off with not only the addresses but specific instructions for each customer." Hitler had bad luck with his prospects, not all of whom were Jewish, and soon drifted on to other things. See John Toland, *Adolf Hitler: A Definitive Biography* (New York: Random House, 1976), 41.

Chapter 2. A Literary Enterprise

p. 21   Dragonerstrasse: In response to the pogroms in Russia in the late nineteenth century, Ostjuden crowded into the Scheunenviertel (literally, the barn or warehouse quarter) and especially onto the Dragonerstrasse (Dragoon Street) and Grenadierstrasse. These names refer to long-gone military barracks. The quarter lay in what was East Berlin after the Second World War. The Dragonerstrasse, like many streets in Berlin, was renamed after the war; in 1951 it became the Max-Beer-Strasse in memory of Max Beer (1864–1943), the Austrian Jewish Marxist journalist.

Chapter 3. A Pious Fund

p. 36 Oertel: Georg Oertel (1856–1916) was a DKP (Deutschkonservative Partei, or German Conservative Party) member of the Reichstag (Parliament) from 1912 to 1916 and editor of the newspaper *Die deutsche Tageszeitung.*

p. 36 Theodor Wolff: Wolff was a journalist (1868–1943) and the editor of the *Berliner Tageblatt,* a liberal newspaper. His reporting on the Dreyfus affair made him well known in Germany. He fled Germany after the Reichstag fire in 1933 and found refuge in Nice, where he was arrested and handed over to the Gestapo. In his honor, the Federal Association of German Newspaper Publishers has awarded the Theodor Wolff Prize annually since 1962.

p. 36 Loeser & Wolff: Loeser & Wolf was a Berlin tobacco goods factory known especially for its cigars. It was founded by Jewish entrepreneurs in 1865 and "aryanized" in 1937.

p. 39 Gangster: The word Gronemann uses in the German original is *chavrusa,* which comes from the vocabulary of Talmudic study and means a "study companion." The *Gaunersprache* (thieves' slang) of Berlin was filled with repurposed Yiddishisms and Russian words brought by the huge influx of Ostjuden, and the word "chavrusa" probably came to mean a best friend in the bandits' world. Regional Court Director Lehnsen, a baptized Jew, who wants nothing to do with anything Jewish, is, ironically, making use of this vocabulary. Gronemann uses similar irony throughout to puncture the discreet, compartmentalized notions of self-identity of both his Jewish and non-Jewish German characters.

p. 39 Herr Professor Dr. Hirsch: Sammy Gronemann's character evokes the historical Rabbi Samuel Hirsch (1808–1888), the founder of Modern or Neo-Orthodoxy. Hirsch was concerned that Reform Judaism was jettisoning Jewish institutions, traditions, and Talmudic laws.

p. 49 Enrollment register: Regional Court Director Lehnsen is referring to the registers maintained by the government to record religious affiliation. From these registers and from baptismal records the Third Reich collated baptism records back to 1645 in a centralized *Judenkartei* (index of Jews). To establish the degree of Aryan purity, proof of an ancestor's baptism was evidence not only of being a Christian (a question of religious faith) but also, more importantly, of being an Aryan (a question of race and ethnicity). The *Judenkartei* was administered by the Reichssippenamt (Kinship Research Office), which coordinated the research into local archives and handled requests from those seeking certification of their Aryan status. See Deborah Hertz, *How Jews Became Germans: The History of Conversion and Assimilation in Berlin* (New Haven, CT: Yale University Press, 2007).

Chapter 4. Pastoral Care

p. 59   Well, fortunately [staying in Berlin is] not as easy as you think, my dear friend!: Dr. Magnus is an assimilated Jew, who, like many Reform Jews in Germany at the time, saw the huge influx of Ostjuden into the West as a danger to the precarious social status of German Jews. He is appalled at Yossel's presence in Berlin and only begrudgingly offers charity. The history of Berlin Jews is the story of fluctuating tolerance but never total acceptance. In 1573 the Jews were expelled from Brandenburg "for all eternity"; almost a century later, in 1671, two Jewish families received residency privileges in Berlin, and the continuous history of a Jewish community in Berlin began. Not until the unification of Germany under Prussian rule in 1871 were Jews assured of their legal status as German citizens. Only a few years later, beginning with the Russian pogroms of 1881, millions of Jews fled westward. Most went on to America, but many stayed in Berlin. By World War I, over two and a half million Jews had left Russia and Russian Poland. The German Jews were ready enough to give charity and aid but still saw the strange-looking Jews, with their caftans, odd hats, and long sidelocks, as provoking anti-Semitism.

p. 76   Prince of Homburg: *Prinz Friedrich von Homburg oder die Schlacht bei Fehrbellin* (Prince Friedrich von Homburg or the Battle of Fehrbellin; 1809) is a drama by Heinrich von Kleist (1777–1810). The battle (1675), in which Prussia defeated Sweden, the military power of the day, marked a turning point in Prussia's rise to a major European power. The historical prince, Frederick II of Hesse-Homburg (1633–1708), served at different times both Sweden and the elector of Brandenburg. His birthplace is now a popular spa town. When one of the novel's characters, Klatzke, mistakenly refers to the "Prince of Hamburg," he is revealing his lack of a refined education, having confused a small principality with the name of one of the largest cities in Germany, the old Hansa city of Hamburg.

Chapter 5. Paradise Apples

p. 104   Regional Court on the Grunerstrasse: The scene at court, the crowds of attorneys and plaintiffs playing chess or watching others play, the press of people chatting in the hallway awaiting their turn before the judge, the manufactured and real confusion due to baptized Jews adopting non-Jewish sounding German names, the real and pretended discomfort over a civil suit about a halachic (according to Jewish law) point of practice, even the case of the missing etrog stems, all of this was Gronemann's experience as an attorney. See Sammy Gronemann, *Erinnerungen an meine Jahre in Berlin* (Memoirs of my years in Berlin) (Berlin: Philo, 2004).

Chapter 6. The Sounds of Easter

p. 123   Körner: Carl Theodor Körner (1791–1813) wrote patriotic poetry and died a "hero's death" fighting to liberate Prussia from Napoleon, hence Frau Marie's admiration of him as "a real German poet." Gronemann had no way of knowing when he wrote *Utter Chaos* in 1920 that Körner would be idolized by the Nazis and that Heine, the baptized Jewish author of beloved German "folksongs" and tales as well as *The Rabbi of Bacharach,* would be censored as a Jew.

p. 129 Kishinev: The Bessarabian city, now the capital of Moldova, was the site of a three-day pogrom in April 1903 set off by charges of ritual murder or blood libel. The anti-Jewish riot began on Easter Sunday. The authorities made no attempt to intervene. Forty-nine Jews were killed, five hundred were injured, seven hundred houses were destroyed, and over two thousand Jews became homeless. The world press took note, and President Theodore Roosevelt tried to protest directly to the czar. The *Times* of London (December 7, 1903) objected to calling the pogroms massacres, explaining that "a mob assembled for purposes of devastation does not, however, constitute a pogrom unless it follows certain well-established and characteristic rules." It is "a national institution," the *Times* explained. Another pogrom in 1905 was met with Jewish self-defense units. After the pogroms, many Jews abandoned the city to emigrate to the United States and South America. For a study of thriving Jewish life in the Russian Pale of Settlement, destroyed by pogroms, war, and emigration, see Rebecca Kobrin, *Jewish Bialystok and Its Diaspora* (Bloomington: Indiana University Press, 2010). The belief that Jews murder children to use the blood to bake matzah lingers on in the twenty-first century in Europe and elsewhere. Joanna Tokarska-Bakir relates her interviews with townspeople of Sandomierz on the Vistula River who claimed their relatives had witnessed such murders. See the review of Joanna Tokarska-Bakir, *Anthropology of Prejudice: Blood Libel Myths,* Warsaw, W.A.B. Publishing House, 2008, http://www.booksandideas.net/spip .php?page=print&id_article=1054&lang=fr.

p. 131 Police Lieutenant or Pristav Kujaroff: Kujaroff is a Russian imperial official. A pristav represented and served the czar. The official supervised a small police and administrative force; his qualifications usually included having served in the military. See Richard A. Pierce, *Russian Central Asia, 1867–1917: A Study in Colonial Rule* (Berkeley: University of California Press, 1960), 337. "Pristav" was a police chief, captain, or officer. Gronemann uses "police lieutenant" and "pristav" interchangeably. Historically, a pristav has been translated as "conductor," "commissar," and even as "marshal."

p. 132 Marx and Lassalle were Jews: Karl Marx (1818–1883), whose writings on economics, philosophy, and history examined the relationship of capital and labor, was the descendant of rabbis and was baptized at the age of six. Ferdinand Lassalle (1825–1864) was a political philosopher and activist who was the first in Germany to organize a socialist party. He was born the son of Heymann Lassel and died a Jew with the name of Lasalle.

p. 133 Two witnesses are necessary: Sammy Gronemann wrote a treatise on criminal law in the Talmud titled "Abschnitte aus dem talmudischen Strafrecht" (Excerpts from the Talmud on criminal law) for the *Zeitschrift für vergleichende Strafrecht* (Journal for comparative criminal law), edited by Dr. J. Kohler et al., vol. 13, pp. 415ff. Gronemann wrote the essay in 1898 as a law student for a comparative legal studies seminar on the history of criminal law.

p. 138 Lessing's *Nathan*: The 1779 drama *Nathan der Weise* (Nathan the Wise) by Gottfried Ephraim Lessing (1729–1781) contains the famous ring parable, told by Nathan to answer Saladin's question: Which religion is the true religion? The ring made the wearer beloved of God and man. The ring passed to a father who could not choose an heir among his three sons, so he had replicas made. Upon the father's death, the sons asked a judge to determine which son had the true ring. The answer was the one whose behavior proved he had the true ring.

p. 140 Papiros: A Papiros is an unfiltered cigarette, originating in Russia. It is distinctive. To smoke a Papiros betrays the traveler as a Russian in the German borderlands in the tale "Who Is He?" by Theodor Hermann Pantenius in *Im Gottesländchen: Erzählungen aus dem Kurländischen Leben* (In God's little land: Tales from Courland life) (Mitau: E. Behre's Verlag, 1880). Michael Chabon uses "papiros" instead of "cigarette" to identify the shtetl origin of his Alaskan Jews in *The Yiddish Policeman's Union* (New York: HarperCollins, 2007). Gronemann has his upwardly mobile character, Klatzke, invent the French-sounding "Papyrosse," which appeals to his haute bourgeoisie clientele.

p. 140 Konitz affair: In March 1900 the discovery of the murdered body of Ernst Winter in the small West Prussian town of Konitz set off a charge of ritual murder. It was said that Jews had killed him to use the blood to bake the Passover matzah. Not one but two serious pogroms ensued. The affair was prominent in the press all over Germany; Kaiser Wilhelm himself took an interest and insisted on daily briefings. See *The Anti-Semitism of Ordinary People: Rumors and Riots in Prussian Konitz in 1900* by Eva Bischoff on H-Net, March 2004, http://www.h-net.org/reviews/showpdf.php?id=8969.

p. 141 Bismarck and Stöcker: Otto von Bismarck (1815–1898) opposed Jewish emancipation but advocated for personal liberties in his early years. After German unification in 1871, Bismarck did nothing to suppress anti-Semitic voices and politicians. Adolf Stöcker (1835–1909), the court chaplain, founded the anti-Semitic Christian Socialist Party in 1878. He saw the Jews as a threat to Germanic Christian culture and wrote about "Jewish conspiracies."

Chapter 7. The Trumpet Sounds

p. 145 The "Floor" and William Tell: Gronemann is comparing the *Trumpet*'s energetic refusal to use the French word for "floor" (*étage*) in accordance with the paper's nationalistic feelings about foreigners to the heroic refusal of the Swiss folk hero William Tell to obey the fourteenth-century Habsburg tyrant, Albrecht Gessler.

p. 146 Justus Brimann, Rohling, and Eisenmenger's *Entdecktes Judentum*: Aron Israel Brimann (pseudonym Dr. Justus) (1859–1934) was a baptized Romanian Jew. He wrote anti-

Semitic pamphlets, including the 1883 *Judenspiegel* (The Jew's mirror), which repeated known misquotations from the Talmud, including the call for ritual murder in the Kabbalah. August Rohling (1839–1931) was a Catholic theologian who based his writings on ritual murder on Brimann; his *Der Talmudjude* (The Talmud Jew, 1871) was influential in anti-Semitic circles and was a garbled extract of *Entdecktes Judenthum, oder Gründlicher und Wahrhaffter Bericht* (Judaism revealed, or thorough and true account), first published in 1700, by Johann Andreas Eisenmenger (1654–1704), a professor of Hebrew and Aramaic at the University of Heidelberg. So scurrilous was Eisenmenger's book that Emperor Leopold I of Austria banned it. The Jewish community offered Eisenmenger 12,000 florins (over $800,000 today) to suppress the work; Eisenmenger demanded 30,000 florins (over $2 million), which the community refused to pay. Such extortions were common, and the historical incident sheds light on the fictional regional court director's willingness to pay to suppress the *Trumpet*'s offensive story about his family.

p. 146 *The Maid of Orleans*: *Die Jungfrau von Orleans* (1801) is a drama by Friedrich Schiller (1759–1805). It was and still is a staple of the German high school curriculum.

p. 146 *Anabasis* by Xenophon: A drama about the Spartans' march to aid Cyrus by the Athenian soldier and poet Xenophon (ca. 430–354 BCE), once a standard high school text for students of Greek.

p. 150 *The Game of Klabrias* at Herrnfelds': The name of the play derives from a card game that is the basis of an enormously popular cabaret-style musical skit that spread from Budapest across Central and Eastern Europe. The plot was minimal, with gambling as the desperate antidote to poverty. It was crude and crass. The Herrnfeld brothers, Anton and Donat, were Ostjuden who set up their theater in the 1880s on the Alexanderplatz, near the Jewish quarter of Berlin. See Philip V. Bohlmann, *Jewish Music and Modernity* (Oxford: Oxford University Press, 2008).

Chapter 8. The Minyan Man

p. 171 His feet stepping backward: The custom is to take three steps backward at the Hebrew phrase "oisseh shalom" (He who brings peace) while saying the prayer known as the *Amidah*. The phrase, a Jewish Dutch émigré recalled, had entered Dutch slang but meant, as used by a Gentile driving instructor to his pupil, "reverse a little." See Bernhard Wasserstein, *On the Eve: The Jews of Europe Before the Second World War* (New York: Simon & Schuster, 2012), 239.

p. 176 Collection boxes: The students are collecting money for the Jewish National Fund, founded in 1901. The money is to buy land in Palestine. Charity boxes are a long-standing tradition for Jewish organizations and institutions. The idea for a blue-and-white box came from a Galician bank clerk, Haim Kleinman (1883[?]–unknown, died in the Holocaust), who wrote to *Die Welt*, the Zionist weekly newspaper, in 1902 to suggest placing a collection box in every Jewish home. The design has changed over the years, but the JNF collection boxes continue to be recognizable symbols of the Zionist idea (see figure 14).

p. 180   Ahlwardt: Hermann Ahlwardt (1846–1914) was an anti-Semitic journalist who cofounded the Antisemitische Volkspartei (Anti-Semitic People's Party). He is one of many examples of the increasingly virulent anti-Semitism in Wilhelmine Germany. Ahlwardt wrote a number of pamphlets and books vilifying Jews, such as *Der Verzweiflungskampf der arischen Völker mit den Juden* (The desperate struggle between Aryan and Jew) in 1890. As a member of the Reichstag, he called for closing German borders to Jews. The *New York Times* (December 6, 1895) reported Ahlwardt's arrival in the United States for a lecture tour with the headline "DR. AHLWARDT ARRIVES. He Was Met Only by a Delegation of Newspaper Men. EXPLAINS HIS ANTI-SEMITIC IDEAS. Says He Has Been Invited Here to Preach His Doctrine Against the Jews—He Gives No Names, However." In response to a reporter's question, Ahlwardt said, "I stand on the grounds of racial, not religious, anti-Semitism."

Chapter 9. The Firstborn

p. 193   Roswithania: Student associations at German universities took on a nationalistic and patriotic focus during and after the Wars of Liberation in 1813 and subsequently became increasingly strident in their German nationalism. Officially the Kösener Senioren-Convents-Verband (an umbrella organization for the fraternities, or "Student Corps") ruled out discrimination but in fact boasted in the 1850s that "we are . . . the strongest prophets of Germanic aspirations" and that "we mold our members' attitudes toward the highest questions of life." By the 1880s the fraternities excluded Jewish university students, seeing themselves engaged in a "struggle against Jewry [as their] national task"; in response, Jewish students founded their own Jewish fraternities. The Jewish fraternity members saw themselves as fighting anti-Semitism and showing that German Jews were a part of Germany, German history, and German culture. They imitated the established clubs, proudly wearing their fraternity's colors, often emphasizing German patriotism, drinking, and engaging in dueling rituals (the *Mensur,* in which the member's face was deliberately scarred). By the mid-1890s, however, the non-Jewish fraternities officially held accepting a dueling challenge from a Jewish fraternity member as beneath the dignity of a true German. The non-Jewish fraternities' notions about German Jews filtered into the mindset of many Germans and Austrians as the members took their place in adult society. Like their non-Jewish counterparts, the alumni of the Jewish fraternities reveled in their old-boy networks long after leaving university. See Konrad H. Jarausch, *Students, Society, and Politics in Imperial Germany: The Rise of Academic Illiberalism* (Princeton, NJ: Princeton University Press, 1982), 353–354.

Chapter 10. Resistance

p. 202   *Mishpocha:* The Yiddish word refers to the entire family, related by blood and marriage, the entire clan.

p. 206   Strack: Hermann Strack (1848–1922) was a German theologian and professor of Semitic languages at the University of Berlin. He denounced anti-Semitism (it caused Jews to lose confidence in Christianity) and anti-Semites such as Rohling; however, in 1883 he founded the Institutum Judaicum, whose purpose was to convert the Jews to Christianity.

p. 207 *Bis dat qui cito dat*: He who gives quickly gives twice. Here the phrase is used to indicate that the assessor would be doubling his "gift" if he confiscated the offending tabloid quickly.

Chapter 12. The Grand Festival Week

p. 236 Hapag: To meet the demand of emigrants fleeing the turbulence of mid-nineteenth-century revolutions and reaction, a new company, the Hamburg-Amerikanische Packettfahrt Actien-Gesellschaft (Hapag), began offering passage from Hamburg to New York on steamships, an exciting new technology. Wilhelm II, who was interested in all things seafaring, made ocean travel fashionable. Hapag not only provided shipping and travel but in 1881 also offered the first pleasure cruises, to predictions of financial disaster. Today, through expansion of its original business and mergers, Hapag-Lloyd is a major world transportation company.

p. 236 HMS *Hohenzollern*: Kaiser Wilhelm used the royal yacht to make state visits, including a visit in 1903 to the king of Denmark and then to Trondheim, located on the coast of Norway, as is Tromsø.

p. 237 Half-Asiatic cousin deported as the bacillus carrier: Assimilated German Jews, and here the character of Elsa Lehnsen, a baptized Jew, looked down on Ostjuden, especially those flooding into Germany, with its promise of economic opportunity. Karl Emil Franzos (1848–1904) spoke of Eastern European Jews in his book *Aus Halb-Asien* (1876). Whereas Heinz Lehnsen sees the Ostjude as the living embodiment of Jewish roots, Elsa rejects the "cult of the Ostjude." See Steven E. Aschheim, *Brothers and Strangers: The East European Jew in German and German Jewish Consciousness, 1800–1923* (Madison: University of Wisconsin Press, 1982).

p. 237 Aryan: Philologists used the word "Aryan" to indicate Indo-European languages, from which modern European languages derived. In the mid-nineteenth century, the writings of Arthur de Gobineau (1816–1882) adapted linguists' ideas about superiority and posited that human races were unequal. White, Nordic European "Aryans" were the "master race." Race theory was not limited to France or Germany; the British and Americans also contributed to the discussion. Writing in 1920, Gronemann uses "Aryans" to indicate the non-Jews who happen to be in the same railway car as the Zionists traveling to the Sixth Zionist Congress in Basel in 1903 without irony and without the knowledge of what came later.

p. 237 Hagenbeck: Carl Hagenbeck (1810–1887) was a Hamburg fishmonger and animal collector and trader. His son, also named Carl (1844–1913), was an inspired showman. He traveled the world to find exotics, both animals and humans, to display in his father's zoo.

His humans on display included Samoans, Nubians, Eskimos, and Volga Kalmyks. In 1907 the younger Hagenbeck opened a zoo with his patented concept of open enclosures for animals.

p. 238   A blue one: To risk a blue one is to bet a hundred-mark note.

p. 254   "I bought land": Following the wave of pogroms in Russia, Jews fled in large numbers to Germany, the United States, Argentina, and elsewhere, even to Palestine, then under Ottoman rule. On the whole, Jews settled mostly in cities there. The Jewish National Fund, established in 1901 at the Fifth Zionist Congress, collected money for the express purpose of buying land in Palestine, where Zionist ideals could be realized in agricultural settlements. The JNF as well as individuals bought land despite the fact that the Ottoman rulers restricted Jewish immigration and land purchases.

p. 254   Sea of Galilee: Gronemann uses the Hebrew name of Kinereth for this large inland sea.

p. 255   *Die Welt*: The weekly Zionist newspaper, the *World,* was founded by Theodor Herzl (1860–1904) in 1897. It ceased publication in 1914. For the Sixth Zionist Congress in Basel, August 23–28, 1903, a special edition of *Die Welt* was printed on yellow paper. It is this edition the novel's passengers going to the congress have pasted on the train windows. The entire front page of its August 27, 1903, edition was devoted to one story. Under the headline "Eine Erklärung der englischen Regierung" (A declaration of the English government), a letter from the British colonial secretary outlined the "Uganda proposal." The British government was offering a refuge in British East Africa for Jews fleeing Russian pogroms. The proposition nearly split the Zionist movement. The Seventh Zionist Congress in 1905 rejected any further consideration of the Uganda scheme.

SAMMY GRONEMANN (1875–1952) was the son of a Modern Orthodox rabbi. After a year of Talmud study in Halberstadt, he studied law in Berlin, where he encountered the new movement of Zionism. He had a flourishing law practice, founded the Association for the Protection of German Authors, and became an activist for Zionism. Drafted at the age of thirty-nine in 1914, he saw service on the Eastern Front, where he was exposed to both the extreme poverty of the shtetls and the vibrancy of Jewish centers of learning in Kovno, Vilna, and Bialystok. Rising anti-Semitism after the war meant his law practice had more and more cases from Jewish clients bringing libel suits. The 1920s saw the publication not only of *Utter Chaos* but also of sketches about Berlin and its Jews. Gronemann and his wife fled to Paris in 1933 and left for Palestine in 1936. On the day they arrived, his wife, Sonja, was killed in an accident. Gronemann never took the bar exam to practice law in Palestine but continued to consult on occasion. His writings, including his memoirs, are satirical but not cynical about both Germans and Jews. Gronemann was the quintessential German Jew of Berlin.

PENNY MILBOUER graduated from Bryn Mawr College and received her doctorate in German from McGill University. She taught at Boise State University and the University of Florida and has translated Michael Wieck's *A Childhood under Hitler and Stalin: Memoirs of a 'Certified' Jew* and Maria Roselli's *The Asbestos Lie: The Past and Present of an Industrial Catastrophe*. She lives in Houston with her husband.